ISBN 978-1-330-57233-7
PIBN 10080373

# 1 MONTH OF
# FREE
# READING

at

## www.ForgottenBooks.com

By purchasing this book you are eligible for one month membership to ForgottenBooks.com, giving you unlimited access to our entire collection of over 1,000,000 titles via our web site and mobile apps.

To claim your free month visit: www.forgottenbooks.com/free80373

English
Français
Deutsche
Italiano
Español
Português

# www.forgottenbooks.com

**Mythology** Photography **Fiction**
Fishing Christianity **Art** Cooking
Essays Buddhism Freemasonry
Medicine **Biology** Music **Ancient**
**Egypt** Evolution Carpentry Physics
Dance Geology **Mathematics** Fitness
Shakespeare **Folklore** Yoga Marketing
**Confidence** Immortality Biographies
Poetry **Psychology** Witchcraft
Electronics Chemistry History **Law**
Accounting **Philosophy** Anthropology
Alchemy Drama Quantum Mechanics
Atheism Sexual Health **Ancient History**
**Entrepreneurship** Languages Sport
Paleontology Needlework Islam
**Metaphysics** Investment Archaeology
Parenting Statistics Criminology
**Motivational**

# WAVERLEY NOVELS

*FORTY-EIGHT VOLUMES*

VOLUME XXXVI.

## BORDER EDITION

*The Introductory Essays and Notes by* ANDREW LANG *to this Edition of the Waverley Novels are Copyright*

Drawn and Etched by Frank Short.

# REDGAUNTLET

BY

SIR WALTER SCOTT, BART.

*WITH INTRODUCTORY ESSAY AND NOTES*

BY ANDREW LANG

TWELVE ETCHINGS

VOLUME II.

LONDON

JOHN C. NIMMO

14, KING WILLIAM STREET, STRAND

MDCCCXCIV

PRINTED BY BALLANTYNE, HANSON & CO.
*At the Ballantyne Press, Edinburgh*

# LIST OF ETCHINGS.

*PRINTED BY F. GOULDING, LONDON.*

## VOLUME THE SECOND.

# REDGAUNTLET.

## A TALE OF THE EIGHTEENTH CENTURY.

Master, go on ; and I will follow thee,
To the last gasp, with truth and loyalty.
*As You Like It.*

# REDGAUNTLET.

## CHAPTER I.

**Sheet 2.**

I HAVE rarely in my life, till the last alarming days, known what it was to sustain a moment's real sorrow. What I called such, was, I am now well convinced, only the weariness of mind, which, having nothing actually present to complain of, turns upon itself, and becomes anxious about the past and the future; those periods with which human life has so little connexion, that Scripture itself hath said, " Sufficient for the day is the evil thereof."

If, therefore, I have sometimes abused prosperity, by murmuring at my unknown birth and uncertain rank in society, I will make amends by bearing my present real adversity with patience and courage, and, if I can, even with gaiety. What can they — dare they, do to me ? — Foxley, I am persuaded, is a real Justice of Peace, and country gentleman of estate, though (wonderful to tell!) he is an ass notwithstanding ; and his functionary in the drab coat must have a shrewd guess at the consequences of being accessory to an act of murder or kidnapping. Men invite not such witnesses to deeds of darkness. I have also — Alan, I *have* hopes, arising out of the family of the oppressor himself. I am encouraged to believe that G. M. is likely again to enter on the field. More I dare not here say; nor must I drop a hint which another eye than thine might be able to construe. Enough, my feelings are lighter than they have been; and though fear and wonder are still around me, they are unable entirely to overcloud the horizon.

Even when I saw the spectral form of the old scarecrow of the Parliament House rush into the apartment where I had undergone so singular an examination, I thought of thy connexion with him, and could almost have parodied Lear —

> Death !—nothing could have thus subdued nature
> To such a lowness, but his "learned lawyers."

He was e'en as we have seen him of yore, Alan, when, rather to keep thee company than to follow my own bent, I formerly frequented the halls of justice. The only addition to his dress, in the capacity of a traveller, was a pair of boots, that seemed as if they might have seen the field of Sheriff-moor; so large and heavy, that, tied as they were to the creature's wearied hams with large bunches of worsted tape of various colours, they looked as if he had been dragging them along, either for a wager, or by way of penance.

Regardless of the surprised looks of the party on whom he thus intruded himself, Peter blundered into the middle of the apartment, with his head charged like a ram's in the act of butting, and saluted them thus : —

"Gude day to ye, gude day to your honours — Is't here they sell the fugie warrants ?"

I observed that, on his entrance, my friend — or enemy — drew himself back, and placed himself as if he would rather avoid attracting the observation of the new-comer. I did the same myself, as far as I was able ; for I thought it likely that Mr. Peebles might recognise me, as indeed I was too frequently among the group of young juridical aspirants who used to amuse themselves by putting cases for Peter's solution, and playing him worse tricks ; yet I was uncertain whether I had better avail myself of our acquaintance to have the advantage, such as it might be, of his evidence before the magistrate, or whether to make him, if possible, bearer of a letter which might procure me more effectual assistance. I resolved, therefore, to be guided by circumstances, and to watch carefully that nothing might escape me. I drew back as far as I could, and even reconnoitred the door and passage, to consider whether absolute escape might not be practicable. But there paraded Cristal Nixon, whose little black eyes, sharp as those of a basilisk, seemed, the instant when they encountered mine, to penetrate my purpose.

I sat down, as much out of sight of all parties as I could, and listened to the dialogue which followed — a dialogue how much more interesting to me than any I could have conceived, in which Peter Peebles was to be one of the *Dramatis Personæ!*

"Is it here where ye sell the warrants ? — the fugies, ye ken ?" said Peter.

"Hey — eh — what !" said Justice Foxley ; "what the devil does the fellow mean ? — What would you have a warrant for ?"

"It is to apprehend a young lawyer that is *in meditatione fugæ;* for he has ta'en my memorial and pleaded my cause, and a good fee I gave him, and as muckle brandy as he could drink that day at his father's house — he loes the brandy ower weel for sae youthful a creature."

"And what has this drunken young dog of a lawyer done to you, that you are come to me — eh — ha? Has he robbed you? Not unlikely, if he be a lawyer — eh — Nick — ha?" said Justice Foxley.

"He has robbed me of himself, sir," answered Peter; "of his help, comfort, aid, maintenance, and assistance, whilk, as a counsel to a client, he is bound to yield me *ratione officii* — that is it, ye see. He has pouched my fee, and drucken a mutchkin of brandy, and now he's ower the march, and left my cause, half won half lost — as dead a heat as e'er was run ower the back-sands. Now, I was advised by some cunning laddies that are used to crack a bit law wi' me in the House, that the best thing I could do was to take heart o' grace and set out after him; so I have taken post on my ain shanks, forby a cast in a cart, or the like. I got wind of him in Dumfries, and now I have run him ower to the English side, and I want a fugie warrant against him."

How did my heart throb at this information, dearest Alan! Thou art near me then, and I well know with what kind purpose; thou hast abandoned all to fly to my assistance; and no wonder that, knowing thy friendship and faith, thy sound sagacity and persevering disposition, "my bosom's lord should now sit lightly on his throne;" that gaiety should almost involuntarily hover on my pen; and that my heart should beat like that of a general, responsive to the drums of his advancing ally, without whose help the battle must have been lost.

I did not suffer myself to be startled by this joyous surprise, but continued to bend my strictest attention to what followed among this singular party. That Poor Peter Peebles had been put upon this wildgoose chase by some of his juvenile advisers in the Parliament House, he himself had intimated; but he spoke with much confidence, and the Justice, who seemed to have some secret apprehension of being put to trouble in the matter, and, as sometimes occurs on the English frontier, a jealousy lest the superior acuteness of their northern neighbours might overreach their own simplicity, turned to his clerk with a perplexed countenance.

"Eh — oh — Nick — d—n thee — Hast thou got nothing to say ? This is more Scots law, I take it, and more Scotsmen." (Here he cast a side-glance at the owner of the mansion, and winked to his clerk.) "I would Solway were as deep as it is wide, and we had then some chance of keeping of them out."

Nicholas conversed an instant aside with the supplicant, and then reported .—

"The man wants a border-warrant, I think; but they are only granted for debt — now he wants one to catch a lawyer."

"And what for no?" answered Peter Peebles, doggedly; "what for no, I would be glad to ken? If a day-labourer refuses to work, ye'll grant a warrant to gar him do out his daurg — if a wench quean rin away from her hairst, ye'll send her back to her heuck again — if sae mickle as a collier or a salter make a moonlight flitting, ye will cleek him by the back-spaul in a minute of time, — and yet the damage canna amount to mair than a creelfu' of coals, and a forpit or twa of saut; and here is a

chield taks leg from his engagement, and damages
me to the tune of sax thousand punds sterling;
that is, three thousand that I should win, and three
thousand mair that I am like to lose; and you that
ca' yoursell a justice canna help a poor man to catch
the rinaway? A bonny like justice I am like to
get amang ye!"

"The fellow must be drunk," said the clerk.

"Black-fasting from all but sin," replied the supplicant; "I havena had mair than a mouthful of
cauld water since I passed the Border, and deil a
ane of ye is like to say to me, 'Dog, will ye drink?'"

The Justice seemed moved by this appeal. "Hem
— tush, man," replied he; "thou speak'st to us as
if thou wert in presence of one of thine own beg-
garly justices — get down stairs — get something to
eat, man, (with permission of my friend to make so
free in his house,) and a mouthful to drink, and I
will warrant we get ye such justice as will please
ye."

"I winna refuse your neighbourly offer," said
Poor Peter Peebles, making his bow; "muckle
grace be wi' your honour, and wisdom to guide ye
in this extraordinary cause."

When I saw Peter Peebles about to retire from
the room, I could not forbear an effort to obtain
from him such evidence as might give me some
credit with the Justice. I stepped forward, therefore, and, saluting him, asked him if he remembered
me?

After a stare or two, and a long pinch of snuff,
recollection seemed suddenly to dawn on Peter
Peebles. "Recollect ye!" he said; "by my troth
do I. — Haud him a grip, gentlemen! — constables,
keep him fast! where that ill-deedy hempy is, ye

are sure that Alan Fairford is not far off. — Haud him fast, Master Constable; I charge ye wi' him, for I am mista'en if he is not at the bottom of this rinaway business. He was aye getting the silly callant Alan awa wi' gigs, and horse, and the like of that, to Roslin, and Prestonpans, and a' the idle gates he could think of. He's a rinaway apprentice, that ane."

"Mr. Peebles," I said, "do not do me wrong. I am sure you can say no harm of me justly, but can satisfy these gentlemen, if you will, that I am a student of law in Edinburgh — Darsie Latimer by name."

"Me satisfy! how can I satisfy the gentlemen," answered Peter, "that am sae far from being satisfied mysell? I ken naething about your name, and can only testify, *nihil novit in causa.*"

"A pretty witness you have brought forward in your favour," said Mr. Foxley. "But — ha — ay — I'll ask him a question or two. — Pray, friend, will you take your oath to this youth being a runaway apprentice?"

"Sir," said Peter, "I will make oath to ony thing in reason; when a case comes to my oath it's a won cause: But I am in some haste to prie your worship's good cheer;" for Peter had become much more respectful in his demeanour towards the Justice, since he had heard some intimation of dinner.

"You shall have — eh — hum — ay — a bellyful, if it be possible to fill it. First let me know if this young man be really what he pretends. — Nick, make his affidavit."

"Ou, he is just a wud harum-scarum creature, that wad never take to his studies; daft, sir, clean daft."

"Deft!" said the Justice; "what d'ye mean by deft — eh?"

"Just Fifish" (a),[1] replied Peter; "wowf — a wee bit by the East Nook or sae; it's a common case — the tae half of the warld thinks the tither daft. I have met with folk in my day that thought I was daft mysell; and, for my part, I think our Court of Session clean daft, that have had the great cause of Peebles against Plainstanes before them for this score of years, and have never been able to ding the bottom out of it yet."

"I cannot make out a word of his cursed brogue," said the Cumbrian justice; "can you, neighbour — eh? What can he mean by *deft?*"

"He means *mad,*" said the party appealed to, thrown off his guard by impatience of this protracted discussion.

"Ye have it — ye have it," said Peter; "that is, not clean skivie, but" ——

Here he stopped, and fixed his eye on the person he addressed with an air of joyful recognition. — "Ay, ay, Mr. Herries of Birrenswork, is this your ainsell in blood and bane? I thought ye had been hanged at Kennington Common, or Hairiebie, or some of these places, after the bonny ploy ye made in the forty-five."

"I believe you are mistaken, friend," said Herries, sternly, with whose name and designation I was thus made unexpectedly acquainted.

"The deil a bit," answered the undaunted Peter Peebles; "I mind ye weel, for ye lodged in my house the great year of forty-five, for a great year

----

[1] See Editor's Notes at the end of the Volume. Wherever a similar reference occurs, the reader will understand that the same direction applies.

it was; the Grand Rebellion broke out, and my cause — the great cause — Peebles against Plainstanes, *et per contra* — was called in the beginning of the winter Session, and would have been heard, but that there was a surcease of justice, with your plaids, and your piping, and your nonsense."

"I tell you, fellow," said Herries, yet more fiercely, "you have confused me with some of the other furniture of your crazy pate."

"Speak like a gentleman, sir," answered Peebles; "these are not legal phrases, Mr. Herries of Birrenswork. Speak in form of law, or I sall bid ye gude-day, sir. I have nae pleasure in speaking to proud folk, though I am willing to answer ony thing in a legal way; so if you are for a crack about auld langsyne, and the splores that you and Captain Redgimlet used to breed in my house, and the girded cask of brandy that ye drank and ne'er thought of paying for it, (not that I minded it muckle in thae days, though I have felt a lack of it sinsyne,) why, I will waste an hour on ye at ony time. — And where is Captain Redgimlet now? he was a wild chap, like yoursell, though they are nae sae keen after you poor bodies for these some years bygane; the heading and hanging is weel ower now — awful job — awful job — will ye try my sneeshing?"

He concluded his desultory speech by thrusting out his large bony paw, filled with a Scottish mull of huge dimensions, which Herries, who had been standing like one petrified by the assurance of this unexpected address, rejected with a contemptuous motion of his hand, which spilled some of the contents of the box.

"Aweel, aweel," said Peter Peebles, totally unabashed by the repulse, "e'en as ye like, a wilful man maun hae his way; but," he added, stooping down, and endeavouring to gather the spilt snuff from the polished floor, "I canna afford to lose my sneeshing for a' that ye are gumple-foisted wi' me."

My attention had been keenly awakened, during this extraordinary and unexpected scene. I watched, with as much attention as my own agitation permitted me to command, the effect produced on the parties concerned. It was evident that our friend, Peter Peebles, had unwarily let out something which altered the sentiments of Justice Foxley and his clerk towards Mr. Herries, with whom, until he was known and acknowledged under that name, they had appeared to be so intimate. They talked with each other aside, looked at a paper or two which the clerk selected from the contents of a huge black pocketbook, and seemed, under the influence of fear and uncertainty, totally at a loss what line of conduct to adopt.

Herries made a different and a far more interesting figure. However little Peter Peebles might resemble the angel Ithuriel, the appearance of Herries, his high and scornful demeanour, vexed at what seemed detection, yet fearless of the consequences, and regarding the whispering magistrate and his clerk with looks in which contempt predominated over anger or anxiety, bore, in my opinion, no slight resemblance to

> the regal port
> And faded splendour wan

with which the poet has invested the detected King of the Powers of the Air.

As he glanced round, with a look which he had endeavoured to compose to haughty indifference, his eye encountered mine, and, I thought, at the first glance sank beneath it. But he instantly rallied his natural spirit, and returned me one of those extraordinary looks, by which he could contort so strangely the wrinkles on his forehead. I started; but, angry at myself for my pusillanimity, I answered him by a look of the same kind, and, catching the reflection of my countenance in a large antique mirror which stood before me, I started again at the real or imaginary resemblance which my countenance, at that moment, bore to that of Herries. Surely my fate is somehow strangely interwoven with that of this mysterious individual. I had no time at present to speculate upon the subject, for the subsequent conversation demanded all my attention.

The Justice addressed Herries, after a pause of about five minutes, in which all parties seemed at some loss how to proceed. He spoke with embarrassment, and his faltering voice, and the long intervals which divided his sentences, seemed to indicate fear of him whom he addressed.

"Neighbour," he said, " I could not have thought this; or, if *I* — eh — *did* think — in a corner of my own mind as it were — that you, I say — that you might have unluckily engaged in — eh — the matter of the forty-five — there was still time to have forgot all that."

"And is it so singular that a man should have been out in the forty-five?" said Herries, with contemptuous composure; — "your father, I think, Mr. Foxley, was out with Derwentwater in the fifteen."

"And lost half of his estate," answered Foxley, with more rapidity than usual; "and was very near — hem — being hanged into the boot. But this is — another guess job — for — eh — fifteen is not forty-five; and my father had a remission, and you, I take it, have none."

"Perhaps I have," said Herries, indifferently; "or, if I have not, I am but in the case of half a dozen others whom government do not think worth looking after at this time of day, so they give no offence or disturbance."

"But you have given both, sir," said Nicholas Faggot, the clerk, who, having some petty provincial situation, as I have since understood, deemed himself bound to be zealous for government. "Mr. Justice Foxley cannot be answerable for letting you pass free, now your name and surname have been spoken plainly out. There are warrants out against you from the Secretary of State's office."

"A proper allegation, Mr. Attorney! that, at the distance of so many years, the Secretary of State should trouble himself about the unfortunate relics of a ruined cause!" answered Mr. Herries.

"But if it be so," said the clerk, who seemed to assume more confidence upon the composure of Herries's demeanour; "and if cause has been given by the conduct of a gentleman himself, who hath been, it is alleged, raking up old matters, and mixing them with new subjects of disaffection — I say, if it be so, I should advise the party, in his wisdom, to surrender himself quietly into the lawful custody of the next Justice of Peace — Mr. Foxley, suppose — where, and by whom, the matter should be regularly enquired into. I am only putting a case," he added, watching with apprehension the effect which his words were likely to produce upon the party to whom they were addressed.

"And were I to receive such advice," said Herries, with the same composure as before — " putting the case, as you say, Mr. Faggot — I should request to see the warrant which countenanced such a scandalous proceeding."

Mr. Nicholas, by way of answer, placed in his hand a paper, and seemed anxiously to expect the consequences which were to ensue. Mr. Herries looked it over with the same equanimity as before, and then continued, "And were such a scrawl as this presented to me in my own house, I would throw it into the chimney, and Mr. Faggot upon the top of it."

Accordingly, seconding the word with the action, he flung the warrant into the fire with one hand, and fixed the other, with a stern and irresistible gripe, on the breast of the attorney, who, totally unable to contend with him, in either personal strength or mental energy, trembled like a chicken in the raven's clutch. He got off, however, for the fright; for Herries, having probably made him fully sensible of the strength of his grasp, released him, with a scornful laugh.

"Deforcement — spulzie — stouthrief — masterful rescue!" exclaimed Peter Peebles, scandalized at the resistance offered to the law in the person of Nicholas Faggot. But his shrill exclamations were drowned in the thundering voice of Herries, who, calling upon Cristal Nixon, ordered him to take the bawling fool down stairs, fill his belly, and then give him a guinea, and thrust him out of doors. Under such injunctions, Peter easily suffered himself to be withdrawn from the scene.

Herries then turned to the Justice, whose visage, wholly abandoned by the rubicund hue which so lately beamed upon it, hung out the same pale livery as that of his dismayed clerk. " Old friend and acquaintance," he said, " you came here at my request, on a friendly errand, to convince this silly young man of the right which I have over his person for the present. I trust you do not intend to make your visit the pretext of disquieting me about other matters? All the world knows that I have been living at large, in these northern counties, for some months, not to say years, and might have been apprehended at any time, had the necessities of the state required, or my own behaviour deserved it. But no English magistrate has been ungenerous enough to trouble a gentleman under misfortune, on account of political opinions and disputes, which have been long ended by the success of the reigning powers. I trust, my good friend, you will not endanger yourself, by taking any other view of the subject than you have done ever, since we were acquainted?"

The Justice answered with more readiness, as well as more spirit than usual, " Neighbour Ingoldsby — what you say — is — eh — in some sort true; and when you were coming and going at markets, horse-races, and cock-fights, fairs, hunts, and such like — it was — eh — neither my business nor my wish to dispel — I say — to enquire into and dispel the mysteries which hung about you; for while you were a good companion in the field, and over a bottle now and then — I did not — eh — think it necessary to ask — into your private affairs. And if I thought you were — ahem — somewhat unfortunate in former undertakings, and enterprises, and connexions, which might cause you to live unsettledly and more private, I could have — eh — very little pleasure — to aggravate your case by interfering, or requiring explanations, which are often more easily asked than given. But when there are warrants and witnesses to names — and those names, christian and surname, belong to — eh — an attainted person — charged — I trust falsely — with — ahem — taking advantage of modern broils and heart-burnings to renew our civil disturbances, the case is altered; and I must — ahem — do my duty."

The Justice got on his feet as he concluded this speech, and looked as bold as he could. I drew close beside him and his clerk, Mr. Faggot, thinking the moment favourable for my own liberation, and intimated to Mr. Foxley my determination to stand by him. But Mr. Herries only laughed at the menacing posture which we assumed. "My good neighbour," said he, "you talk of a witness — Is yon crazy beggar a fit witness in an affair of this nature?"

"But you do not deny that you are Mr. Herries of Birrenswork, mentioned in the Secretary of State's warrant?" said Mr. Foxley.

"How can I deny or own any thing about it?" said Herries, with a sneer. "There is no such warrant in existence now; its ashes, like the poor traitor whose doom it threatened, have been dispersed to the four winds of heaven. There is now no warrant in the world."

" But you will not deny," said the Justice, "that you were the person named in it; and that — eh — your own act destroyed it?"

"I will neither deny my name nor my actions,

Justice," replied Mr. Herries, " when called upon
by competent authority to avow or defend them.
But I will resist all impertinent attempts either to
intrude into my private motives, or to control my
person. I am quite well prepared to do so; and I
trust that you, my good neighbour and brother
sportsman, in your expostulation, and my friend
Mr. Nicholas Faggot here, in his humble advice
and petition that I should surrender myself, will
consider yourselves as having amply discharged
your duty to King George and Government."

The cold and ironical tone in which he made
this declaration; the look and attitude, so nobly
expressive of absolute confidence in his own superior strength and energy, seemed to complete the
indecision which had already shown itself on the
side of those whom he addressed.

The Justice looked to the Clerk — the Clerk to
the Justice; the former *ha'd*, *eh'd*, without bringing
forth an articulate syllable; the latter only said,
" As the warrant is destroyed, Mr. Justice, I presume you do not mean to proceed with the
arrest ? "

" Hum — ay — why no — Nicholas — it would not
be quite advisable — and as the Forty-five was an
old affair — and — hem — as my friend here will, I
hope, see his error — that is, if he has not seen it
already — and renounce the Pope, the Devil, and
the Pretender — I mean no harm, neighbour — I
think we — as we have no *posse*, or constables, or
the like — should order our horses — and, in one
word, look the matter over."

" Judiciously resolved," said the person whom this
decision affected; " but before you go, I trust you
will drink and be friends ? "

"Why," said the Justice, rubbing his brow, " our busmess has been — hem — rather a thirsty one."

"Cristal Nixon," said Mr. Herries, "let us have a cool tankard instantly, large enough to quench the thirst of the whole commission."

While Cristal was absent on this genial errand, there was a pause, of which I endeavoured to avail myself, by bringing back the discourse to my own concerns. "Sir," I said to Justice Foxley, "I have no direct business with your late discussion with Mr. Herries, only just thus far — You leave me, a loyal subject of King George, an unwilling prisoner in the hands of a person whom you have reason to believe unfriendly to the King's cause. I humbly submit that this is contrary to your duty as a magistrate, and that you ought to make Mr. Herries aware of the illegality of his proceedings, and take steps for my rescue, either upon the spot, or, at least, as soon as possible after you have left this case " ——

"Young man," said Mr. Justice Foxley, "I would have you remember you are under the power, the lawful power — ahem — of your guardian."

"He calls himself so, indeed," I replied; "but he has shown no evidence to establish so absurd a claim; and if he had, his circumstances, as an attainted traitor excepted from pardon, would void such a right, if it existed. I do therefore desire you, Mr. Justice, and you, his clerk, to consider my situation, and afford me relief at your peril."

"Here is a young fellow now," said the Justice, with much embarrassed looks, "thinks that I carry the whole statute law of England in my head, and a *posse comitatus* to execute them in my pocket! Why, what good would my interference do ? — but

— hum — eh — I will speak to your guardian in your favour."

He took Mr. Herries aside, and seemed indeed to urge something upon him with much earnestness; and perhaps such a species of intercession was all which, in the circumstances, I was entitled to expect from him.

They often looked at me as they spoke together; and as Cristal Nixon entered with a huge four-pottle tankard, filled with the beverage his master had demanded, Herries turned away from Mr. Foxley somewhat impatiently, saying with emphasis, " I give you my word of honour, that you have not the slightest reason to apprehend any thing on his account." He then took up the tankard, and saying aloud in Gaelic, " *Slaint an Rey*," [1] just tasted the liquor, and handed the tankard to Justice Foxley, who, to avoid the dilemma of pledging him to what might be the Pretender's health, drank to Mr. Herries's own, with much pointed solemnity, but in a draught far less moderate.

The clerk imitated the example of his principal, and I was fain to follow their example, for anxiety and fear are at least as thirsty as sorrow is said to be. In a word, we exhausted the composition of ale, sherry, lemon-juice, nutmeg, and other good things, stranded upon the silver bottom of the tankard, the huge toast, as well as the roasted orange, which had whilome floated jollily upon the brim, and rendered legible Dr. Byrom's celebrated lines engraved thereon —

God bless the King ! — God bless the Faith's defender !
God bless — No harm in blessing — the Pretender.
Who that Pretender is, and who that King, —
God bless us all ! — is quite another thing.

---

[1] The King's health.

I had time enough to study this **effusion** of the Jacobite muse, while the Justice was engaged in the somewhat tedious ceremony of taking leave. That of Mr. Faggot was less ceremonious; but I suspect something besides empty compliment passed betwixt him and Mr. Herries; for I remarked that the latter slipped a piece of paper into the hand of the former, which might perhaps be a little atonement for the rashness with which he had burnt the warrant, and imposed no gentle hand on the respectable minion of the law by whom it was exhibited; and I observed that he made this propitiation in such a manner as to be secret from the worthy clerk's principal.

When this was arranged, the party took leave of each other, with much formality on the part of Squire Foxley, amongst whose adieus the following phrase was chiefly remarkable: — "I presume you do not intend to stay long in these parts?"

"Not for the present, Justice, you may be sure; there are good reasons to the contrary. But I have no doubt of arranging my affairs, so that we shall speedily have sport together again."

He went to wait upon the Justice to the courtyard; and, as he did so, commanded Cristal Nixon to see that I returned into my apartment. Knowing it would be to no purpose to resist or tamper with that stubborn functionary, I obeyed in silence, and was once more a prisoner in my former quarters.

# CHAPTER II.

I SPENT more than an hour, after returning to the apartment which I may call my prison, in reducing to writing the singular circumstances which I had just witnessed. Methought I could now form some guess at the character of Mr. Herries, upon whose name and situation the late scene had thrown considerable light; — one of those fanatical Jacobites, doubtless, whose arms, not twenty years since, had shaken the British throne, and some of whom, though their party daily diminished in numbers, energy, and power, retained still an inclination to renew the attempt they had found so desperate. He was indeed perfectly different from the sort of zealous Jacobites whom it had been my luck hitherto to meet with. Old ladies of family over their hyson, and grey-haired lairds over their punch, I had often heard utter a little harmless treason; while the former remembered having led down a dance with the Chevalier, and the latter recounted the feats they had performed at Preston, Clifton, and Falkirk.

The disaffection of such persons was too unimportant to excite the attention of government. I had heard, however, that there still existed partisans of the Stuart family of a more daring and dangerous description; men who, furnished with gold from Rome, moved, secretly and in disguise, through the various classes of society, and endeavoured to keep alive the expiring zeal of their party.

I had no difficulty in assigning an important post among this class of persons, whose agency and exertion are only doubted by those who look on the surface of things, to this Mr. Herries, whose mental energies, as well as his personal strength and activity, seemed to qualify him well to act so dangerous a part; and I knew that, all along the Western Border, both in England and Scotland, there are so many Nonjurors, that such a person may reside there with absolute safety, unless it becomes, in a very especial degree, the object of the government to secure his person; and which purpose, even then, might be disappointed by early intelligence, or, as in the case of Mr. Foxley, by the unwillingness of provincial magistrates to interfere in what is now considered an invidious pursuit of the unfortunate.

There have, however, been rumours lately, as if the present state of the nation, or at least of some discontented provinces, agitated by a variety of causes, but particularly by the unpopularity of the present administration, may seem to this species of agitators a favourable period for recommencing their intrigues; while, on the other hand, government may not, at such a crisis, be inclined to look upon them with the contempt which a few years ago would have been their most appropriate punishment.

That men should be found rash enough to throw away their services and lives in a desperate cause, is nothing new in history, which abounds with instances of similar devotion — that Mr. Herries is such an enthusiast. is no less evident; but all this explains not his conduct towards *me*. Had he sought to make me a proselyte to his ruined cause, violence

and compulsion were arguments very unlikely to
prevail with any generous spirit. But even if such
were his object, of what use to him could be the
acquisition of a single reluctant partisan, who could
bring only his own person to support any quarrel
which he might adopt? He had claimed over me
the rights of a guardian ; he had more than hinted
that I was in a state of mind which could not dispense with the authority of such a person. Was
this man, so sternly desperate in his purpose, — he
who seemed willing to take on his own shoulders
the entire support of a cause which had been ruinous to thousands, — was he the person that had the
power of deciding on my fate? Was it from him
those dangers flowed to secure me against which
I had been educated under such circumstances of
secrecy and precaution?

And if this was so, of what nature was the claim
which he asserted? — Was it that of propinquity?
— And did I share the blood, perhaps the features,
of this singular being? — Strange as it may seem, a
thrill of awe, which shot across my mind at that
instant, was not unmingled with a wild and myste-
rions feeling of wonder, almost amounting to pleasure.
I remembered the reflection of my own face in the
mirror, at one striking moment during the singular
interview of the day, and I hastened to the outward
apartment to consult a glass which hung there,
whether it were possible for my countenance to be
again contorted into the peculiar frown which so
much resembled the terrific look of Herries. But I
folded my brows in vain into a thousand complicated
wrinkles, and I was obliged to conclude, either that
the supposed mark on my brow was altogether
imaginary, or that it could not be called forth by

voluntary effort; or, in fine, what seemed most likely, that it was such a resemblance as the imagination traces in the embers of a wood fire, or among the varied veins of marble, distinct at one time, and obscure or invisible at another, according as the combination of lines strikes the eye or impresses the fancy.

While I was moulding my visage like a mad player, the door suddenly opened, and the girl of the house entered. Angry and ashamed at being detected in my singular occupation, I turned round sharply, and, I suppose, chance produced the change on my features which I had been in vain labouring to call forth.

The girl started back with her "Don't ye look so now — don't ye, for love's sake — you be as like the ould Squoire as — But here a comes," said she, huddling away out of the room; "and if you want a third, there is none but ould Harry, as I know of, that can match ye for a brent broo!"

As the girl muttered this exclamation, and hastened out of the room, Herries entered. He stopped on observing that I had looked again to the mirror, anxious to trace the look by which the wench had undoubtedly been terrified. He seemed to guess what was passing in my mind, for, as I turned towards him, he observed, "Doubt not that it is stamped on your forehead — the fatal mark of our race; though it is not now so apparent as it will become when age and sorrow, and the traces of stormy passions, and of bitter penitence, shall have drawn their furrows on your brow."

"Mysterious man," I replied, "I know not of what you speak; your language is as dark as your purposes."

" Sit down, then," he said, " and listen ; thus far,
at least, must the veil of which you complain be
raised. When withdrawn, it will only display guilt
and sorrow — guilt, followed by strange penalty, and
sorrow, which Providence has entailed upon the
posterity of the mourners."

He paused a moment, and commenced his narrative, which he told with the air of one who, remote
as the events were which he recited, took still the
deepest interest in them. The tone of his voice,
which I have already described as rich and powerful,
aided by its inflections the effects of his story, which
I will endeavour to write down, as nearly as possible,
in the very words which he used.

" It was not of late years that the English nation
learned that their best chance of conquering their
independent neighbours must be by introducing
amongst them division and civil war. You need
not be reminded of the state of thraldom to which
Scotland was reduced by the unhappy wars betwixt
the domestic factions of Bruce and Baliol ; nor how,
after Scotland had been emancipated from a foreign
yoke, by the conduct and valour of the immortal
Bruce, the whole fruits of the triumphs of Bannockburn were lost in the dreadful defeats of Dupplin
and Halidon ; and Edward Baliol, the minion and
feudatory of his namesake of England, seemed, for
a brief season, in safe and uncontested possession of
the throne so lately occupied by the greatest general and wisest prince in Europe. But the experience
of Bruce had not died with him. There were
many who had shared his martial labours, and all
remembered the successful efforts by which, under
circumstances as disadvantageous as those of his
son, he had achieved the liberation of Scotland.

"The usurper, Edward Baliol, was feasting with a few of his favourite retainers in the Castle of Annan, when he was suddenly surprised by a chosen band of insurgent patriots. Their chiefs were, Douglas, Randolph, the young Earl of Moray, and Sir Simon Fraser; and their success was so complete, that Baliol was obliged to fly for his life, scarcely clothed, and on a horse which there was no leisure to saddle. It was of importance to seize his person, if possible, and his flight was closely pursued by a valiant knight of Norman descent, whose family had been long settled in the marshes of Dumfriesshire. Their Norman appellation was Fitz-Aldin, but this knight, from the great slaughter which he had made of the Southron, and the reluctance which he had shown to admit them to quarter during the former wars of that bloody period, had acquired the name of Redgauntlet, which he transmitted to his posterity '——'

"Redgauntlet!" I involuntarily repeated.

"Yes, Redgauntlet," said my alleged guardian, looking at me keenly; "does that name recall any associations to your mind?"

"No," I replied, "except that I lately heard it given to the hero of a supernatural legend."

"There are many such current concerning the family," he answered; and then proceeded in his narrative.

"Alberick Redgauntlet, the first of his house so termed, was, as may be supposed from his name, of a stern and implacable disposition, which had been rendered more so by family discord. An only son, now a youth of eighteen, shared so much the haughty spirit of his father, that he became impatient of domestic control, resisted paternal authority, and

finally fled from his father's house, renounced his
political opinions, and awakened his mortal displeasure by joining the adherents of Baliol. It was said
that his father cursed in his wrath his degenerate
offspring, and swore that, if they met, he should
perish by his hand. Meantime, circumstances
seemed to promise atonement for this great deprivation. The lady of Alberick Redgauntlet was
again, after many years, in a situation which
afforded her husband the hope of a more dutiful
heir.

" But the delicacy and deep interest of his wife's
condition did not prevent Alberick from engaging
in the undertaking of Douglas and Moray. He
had been the most forward in the attack of the
castle, and was now foremost in the pursuit of
Baliol, eagerly engaged in dispersing or cutting
down the few daring followers who endeavoured
to protect the usurper in his flight.

"As these were successfully routed or slain, the
formidable Redgauntlet, the mortal enemy of the
House of Baliol, was within two lances' length of
the fugitive Edward Baliol, in a narrow pass, when
a youth, one of the last who attended the usurper
in his flight, threw himself between them, received
the shock of the pursuer, and was unhorsed and
overthrown. The helmet rolled from his head, and
the beams of the sun, then rising over the Solway,
showed Redgauntlet the features of his disobedient
son, in the livery, and wearing the cognizance, of
the usurper.

"Redgauntlet beheld his son lying before his
horse's feet; but he also saw Baliol, the usurper of
the Scottish crown, still, as it seemed, within his
grasp, and separated from him only by the prostrate

body of his overthrown adherent. Without pausing to enquire whether young Edward was wounded, he dashed his spurs into his horse, meaning to leap over him, but was unhappily frustrated in his purpose. The steed made indeed a bound forward, but was unable to clear the body of the youth, and with its hind foot struck him in the forehead, as he was in the act of rising. The blow was mortal. It is needless to add that the pursuit was checked, and Baliol escaped.

" Redgauntlet, ferocious as he is described, was yet overwhelmed with the thoughts of the crime he had committed. When he returned to his castle, it was to encounter new domestic sorrows. His wife had been prematurely seized with the pangs of labour, upon hearing the dreadful catastrophe which had taken place. The birth of an infant boy cost her her life. Redgauntlet sat by her corpse for more than twenty-four hours without changing either feature or posture, so far as his terrified domestics could observe. The Abbot of Dundrennan preached consolation to him in vain. Douglas, who came to visit in his affliction a patriot of such distinguished zeal, was more successful in rousing his attention. He caused the trumpets to sound an English point of war in the court-yard, and Redgauntlet at once sprang to his arms, and seemed restored to the recollection which had been lost in the extent of his misery.

" From that moment, whatever he might feel inwardly, he gave way to no outward emotion. Douglas caused his infant to be brought; but even the iron-hearted soldiers were struck with horror to observe that, by the mysterious law of nature, the cause of his mother's death, and the evidence of his father's guilt, was stamped on the innocent face of the babe, whose brow was distinctly marked by the miniature resemblance of a horseshoe. Redgauntlet himself pointed it out to Douglas, saying, with a ghastly smile, ' It should have been bloody.'

"Moved, as he was, to compassion for his brother-in-arms, and steeled against all softer feelings by the habits of civil war, Douglas shuddered at this sight, and displayed a desire to leave the house which was doomed to be the scene of such horrors. As his parting advice, he exhorted Alberick Redgauntlet to make a pilgrimage to Saint Ninian's of Whiteherne, then esteemed a shrine of great sanctity; and departed with a precipitation which might have aggravated, had that been possible, the forlorn state of his unhappy friend. But that seems to have been incapable of admitting any addition. Sir Alberick caused the bodies of his slaughtered son and the mother to be laid side by side in the ancient chapel of his house, after he had used the skill of a celebrated surgeon of that time to embalm them; and it was said that for many weeks he spent some hours nightly in the vault where they reposed.

"At length he undertook the proposed pilgrimage to Whiteherne, where he confessed himself for the first time since his misfortune, and was shrived by an aged monk, who afterwards died in the odour of sanctity. It is said that it was then foretold to the Redgauntlet, that on account of his unshaken patriotism, his family should continue to be powerful amid the changes of future times; but that, in detestation of his unrelenting cruelty to his own issue, Heaven had decreed that the valour of his race should always be fruitless, and that the cause which they espoused should never prosper.

"Submitting to such penance as was there imposed, Sir Alberick went, it is thought, on a pilgrimage either to Rome or to the Holy Sepulchre itself. He was universally considered as dead; and it was not till thirteen years afterwards, that, in the great battle of Durham, fought between David Bruce and Queen Philippa of England, a knight, bearing a horseshoe for his crest, appeared in the van of the Scottish army, distinguishing himself by his reckless and desperate valour; who, being at length overpowered and slain, was finally discovered to be the brave and unhappy Sir Alberick Redgauntlet."

"And has the fatal sign," said I, when Herries had ended his narrative, "descended on all the posterity of this unhappy house?"

"It has been so handed down from antiquity, and is still believed," said Herries. "But perhaps there is, in the popular evidence, something of that fancy which creates what it sees. Certainly, as other families have peculiarities by which they are distinguished, this of Redgauntlet is marked in most individuals by a singular indenture of the forehead, supposed to be derived from the son of Alberick, their ancestor, and brother to the unfortunate Edward who had perished in so piteous a manner. It is certain there seems to have been a fate upon the House of Redgauntlet, which has been on the losing side in almost all the civil broils which have divided the kingdom of Scotland, from David Bruce's days, till the late valiant and unsuccessful attempt of the Chevalier Charles Edward."

He concluded with a deep sigh, as one whom the subject had involved in a train of painful reflections,

"And am I then," I exclaimed, "descended from this unhappy race?—Do you too belong to it?—And if so, why do I sustain restraint and hard usage at the hands of a relation?"

"Enquire no farther for the present," he said. "The line of conduct which I am pursuing towards you is dictated not by choice but by necessity. You were withdrawn from the bosom of your family, and the care of your legal guardian, by the timidity and ignorance of a doting mother, who was incapable of estimating the arguments or feelings of those who prefer honour and principle to fortune, and even to life. The young hawk, accustomed only to the fostering care of its dam, must be tamed by darkness and sleeplessness, ere it is trusted on the wing for the purposes of the falconer."

I was appalled at this declaration, which seemed to threaten a long continuance, and a dangerous termination, of my captivity. I deemed it best, however, to show some spirit, and at the same time to mingle a tone of conciliation. "Mr. Herries," I said, " (if I call you rightly by that name,) let us speak upon this matter without the tone of mystery and fear in which you seem inclined to envelope it. I have been long, alas! deprived of the care of that affectionate mother to whom you allude — long under the charge of strangers — and compelled to form my own resolutions upon the reasoning of my own mind. Misfortune — early deprivation — has given me the privilege of acting for myself; and constraint shall not deprive me of an Englishman's best privilege."

"The true cant of the day," said Herries, in a tone of scorn. "The privilege of free action belongs to no mortal — we are tied down by the fetters of duty — our moral path is limited by the regulations of honour — our most indifferent actions are but meshes of the web of destiny by which we are all surrounded."

He paced the room rapidly, and proceeded in a tone of enthusiasm which, joined to some other parts of his conduct, seems to intimate an over-excited imagination, were it not contradicted by the general tenor of his speech and conduct.

"Nothing," he said, in an earnest yet melancholy voice — "nothing is the work of chance — nothing is the consequence of free-will — the liberty of which the Englishman boasts gives as little real freedom to its owner as the despotism of an Eastern Sultan permits to his slave. The usurper, William of Nassau, went forth to hunt, and thought, doubtless, that it was by an act of his own royal pleasure that the horse of his murdered victim was prepared for his kingly sport. But Heaven had other views; and before the sun was high, a stumble of that very animal over an obstacle so inconsiderable as a mole-hillock cost the haughty rider his life and his usurped crown. Do you think an inclination of the rein could have avoided that trifling impediment? — I tell you, it crossed his way as inevitably as all the long chain of Caucasus could have done. Yes, young man, in doing and suffering, we play but the part allotted by Destiny, the manager of this strange drama, stand bound to act no more than is prescribed, to say no more than is set down for us; and yet we month about free-will, and freedom of thought and action, as if Richard must not die, or Richmond conquer, exactly where the Author has decreed it shall be so!"

He continued to pace the room after this speech,

with folded arms and downcast looks; and the sound
of his steps and tone of his voice brought to my
remembrance that I had heard this singular person,
when I met him on a former occasion, uttering such
soliloquies in his solitary chamber. I observed that,
like other Jacobites, in his inveteracy against the
memory of King William, he had adopted the party
opinion, that the monarch, on the day he had his
fatal accident, rode upon a horse once the property
of the unfortunate Sir John Friend (*b*), executed for
High Treason in 1696.

It was not my business to aggravate, but, if possible, rather to soothe him in whose power I was
so singularly placed. When I conceived that the
keenness of his feelings had in some degree subsided,
I answered him as follows : — "I will not — indeed
I feel myself incompetent to argue a question of
such metaphysical subtlety, as that which involves
the limits betwixt free-will and predestination. Let
us hope we may live honestly and die hopefully,
without being obliged to form a decided opinion
upon a point so far beyond our comprehension."

"Wisely resolved," he interrupted, with a sneer
— "there came a note from some Geneva sermon."

"But," I proceeded, "I call your attention to
the fact that I, as well as you, am acted upon by
impulses, the result either of my own free-will, or
the consequences of the part which is assigned to
me by destiny. These may be — nay, at present
they are — in direct contradiction to those by which
you are actuated; and how shall we decide which
shall have precedence ? — *You* perhaps feel yourself destined to act as my jailer. I feel myself,
on the contrary, destined to attempt and effect
my escape. One of us must be wrong, but who

can say which errs till the event has decided betwixt
us ? "

"I shall feel myself destined to have recourse
to severe modes of restraint," said he, in the same
tone of half jest, half earnest which I had used.

"In that case," I answered, "it will be my destiny
to attempt every thing for my freedom."

"And it may be mine, young man," he replied,
in a deep and stern tone, "to take care that you
should rather die than attain your purpose."

This was speaking out indeed, and I did not
allow him to go unanswered. "You threaten me
in vain," said I; "the laws of my country will protect me; or whom they cannot protect, they will
avenge."

I spoke this firmly, and he seemed for a moment
silenced; and the scorn with which he at last
answered me had something of affectation in it.

"The laws!" he said; "and what, stripling, do
you know of the laws of your country ? — Could
you learn jurisprudence under a base-born blotter
of parchment, such as Saunders Fairford; or from
the empty pedantic coxcomb, his son, who now,
forsooth, writes himself advocate ? — When Scotland was herself, and had her own King and Legis-
lature, such plebeian cubs, instead of being called
to the bar of her Supreme Courts, would scarce
have been admitted to the honour of bearing a
sheepskin process-bag."

Alan, I could not bear this, but answered indignantly, that he knew not the worth and honour
from which he was detracting.

"I know as much of these Fairfords as I do of
you," he replied.

"As much," said I, "and as little; for you can

neither estimate their real worth nor mine.  I know
you saw them when last in Edinburgh."

"Ha!" he exclaimed, and turned on me an
inquisitive look.

"It is true," said I; "you cannot deny it; and
having thus shown you that I know something of
your motions, let me warn you I have modes of
communication with which you are not acquainted.
Oblige me not to use them to your prejudice."

"Prejudice *me!*" he replied.  "Young man, I
smile at and forgive your folly.  Nay, I will tell
you that of which you are not aware, namely, that
it was from letters received from these Fairfords
that I first suspected, what the result of my visit
to them confirmed, that you were the person whom
I had sought for years."

"If you learned this," said I, "from the papers
which were about my person on the night when I
was under the necessity of becoming your guest at
Brokenburn, I do not envy your indifference to the
means of acquiring information.  It was dishonour-
able to " ——

"Peace, young man," said Herries, more calmly
than I might have expected; "the word dishonour must not be mentioned as in conjunction with
my name.  Your pocketbook was in the pocket
of your coat, and did not escape the curiosity of
another, though it would have been sacred from
mine.  My servant, Cristal Nixon, brought me the
intelligence after you were gone.  I was displeased
with the manner in which he had acquired his
information; but it was not the less my duty to
ascertain its truth, and for that purpose I went to
Edinburgh.  I was in hopes to persuade Mr. Fairford to have entered into my views; but I found

him too much prejudiced to permit me to trust him. He is a wretched, yet a timid slave of the present government, under which our unhappy country is dishonourably enthralled; and it would have been altogether unfit and unsafe to have intrusted him with the secret either of the right which I possess to direct your actions, or of the manner in which I purpose to exercise it."

I was determined to take advantage of his communicative humour, and obtain, if possible, more light upon his purpose. He seemed most accessible to being piqued on the point of honour, and I resolved to avail myself, but with caution, of his sensibility upon that topic. "You say," I replied, "that you are not friendly to indirect practices, and disapprove of the means by which your domestic obtained information of my name and quality — Is it honourable to avail yourself of that knowledge which is dishonourably obtained?"

"It is boldly asked," he replied; "but, within certain necessary limits, I dislike not boldness of expostulation. You have, in this short conference, displayed more character and energy than I was prepared to expect. You will, I trust, resemble a forest plant, which has indeed, by some accident, been brought up in the greenhouse, and thus rendered delicate and effeminate, but which regains its native firmness and tenacity when exposed for a season to the winter air. I will answer your question plainly. In business, as in war, spies and informers are necessary evils, which all good men detest; but which yet all prudent men must use, unless they mean to fight and act blindfold. But nothing can justify the use of falsehood and treachery in our own person."

"You said to the elder Mr. Fairford," continued I, with the same boldness, which I began to find was my best game, "that I was the son of Ralph Latimer of Langcote Hall? — How do you reconcile this with your late assertion that my name is not Latimer?"

He coloured as he replied, "The doting old fool lied; or perhaps mistook my meaning. I said, that gentleman *might* be your father. To say truth, I wished you to visit England, your native country; because, when you might do so, my rights over you would revive."

This speech fully led me to understand a caution which had been often impressed upon me, that if I regarded my safety I should not cross the southern Border; and I cursed my own folly, which kept me fluttering like a moth around the candle, until I was betrayed into the calamity with which I had dallied. "What are those rights," I said, "which you claim over me? — To what end do you propose to turn them?"

"To a weighty one, you may be certain," answered Mr. Herries; "but I do not, at present, mean to communicate to you either its nature or extent. You may judge of its importance, when, in order entirely to possess myself of your person, I condescended to mix myself with the fellows who destroyed the fishing station of yon wretched Quaker. That I held him in contempt, and was displeased at the greedy devices with which he ruined a manly sport, is true enough; but, unless as it favoured my designs on you, he might have, for me, maintained his stake-nets till Solway should cease to ebb and flow."

"Alas!" I said, "it doubles my regret to have

been the unwilling cause of misfortune to an honest
and friendly man."

"Do not grieve for that," said Herries ; "honest
Joshua is one of those who, by dint of long prayers,
can possess themselves of widows' houses — he will
quickly repair his losses.   When he sustains any
mishap, he and the other canters set it down as a
debt against Heaven, and, by way of set-off, prac-
tise rogueries without compunction, till they make
the balance even, or incline it to the winning side.
Enough of this for the present. — I must immediately shift my quarters ; for although I do not
fear the over-zeal of Mr. Justice Foxley or his clerk
will lead them to any extreme measure, yet that
mad scoundrel's unhappy recognition of me may
make it more serious for them to connive at me,
and I must not put their patience to an over severe
trial.   You must prepare to attend me, either as a
captive or a companion ; if as the latter, you must
give your parole of honour to attempt no escape.
Should you be so ill advised as to break your word
once pledged, be assured that I will blow your
brains out without a moment's scruple."

"I am ignorant of your plans and purposes,"
I replied, "and cannot but hold them dangerous.
I do not mean to aggravate my present situation
by any unavailing resistance to the superior force
which detains me ; but I will not renounce the
right of asserting my natural freedom should a
favourable opportunity occur.   I will, therefore,
rather be your prisoner than your confederate."

"That is spoken fairly," he said ; "and yet not
without the canny caution of one brought up in
the Gude Town of Edinburgh.   On my part, I will
impose no unnecessary hardship upon you ; but, on

the contrary, your journey shall be made as easy as
is consistent with your being kept safely. Do you
feel strong enough to ride on horseback as yet, or
would you prefer a carriage ? The former mode of
travelling is best adapted to the country through
which we are to travel, but you are at liberty to
choose between them."

I said I felt my strength gradually returning,
and that I should much prefer travelling on horseback. "A carriage," I added, "is so close"——

"And so easily guarded," replied Herries, with
a look as if he would have penetrated my very
thoughts, — "that, doubtless, you think horseback
better calculated for an escape."

"My thoughts are my own," I answered; "and
though you keep my person prisoner, these are
beyond your control."

"O, I can read the book," he said, "without
opening the leaves. But I would recommend to you
to make no rash attempt, and it will be my care to
see that you have no power to make any that is
likely to be effectual. Linen, and all other necessaries for one in your circumstances, are amply
provided. Cristal Nixon will act as your valet,— I
should rather, perhaps, say, your *femme de chambre.*
Your travelling dress you may perhaps consider as
singular ; but it is such as the circumstances require ;
and, if you object to use the articles prepared for
your use, your mode of journeying will be as personally unpleasant as that which conducted you
hither.— Adieu — We now know each other better
than we did — it will not be my fault if the consequences of farther intimacy be not a more favourable
mutual opinion."

He then left me, with a civil good-night, to my

own reflections, and only turned back to say that we should proceed on our journey at daybreak next morning, at farthest; perhaps earlier, he said; but complimented me by supposing that, as I was a sportsman, I must always be ready for a sudden start.

We are then at issue, this singular man and myself. His personal views are to a certain point explained. He has chosen an antiquated and desperate line of politics, and he claims, from some pretended tie of guardianship, or relationship, which he does not deign to explain, but which he seems to have been able to pass current on a silly country Justice and his knavish clerk, a right to direct and to control my motions. The danger which awaited me in England, and which I might have escaped had I remained in Scotland, was doubtless occasioned by the authority of this man. But what my poor mother might fear for me as a child — what my English friend, Samuel Griffiths, endeavoured to guard against during my youth and nonage, is now, it seems, come upon me; and, under a legal pretext, I am detained in what must be a most illegal manner, by a person, too, whose own political immunities have been forfeited by his conduct. It matters not — my mind is made up — neither persuasion nor threats shall force me into the desperate designs which this man meditates. Whether I am of the trifling consequence which my life hitherto seems to intimate, or whether I have (as would appear from my adversary's conduct) such importance, by birth or fortune, as may make me a desirable acquisition to a political faction, my resolution is taken in either case. Those who read this Journal, if it shall be perused by impartial eyes, shall judge of me truly ; and if they consider me as a fool in encountering danger unnecessarily, they shall have no reason to believe me a coward or a turncoat, when I find myself engaged in it. I have been bred in sentiments of attachment to the family on the throne, and in these sentiments I will live and die. I have, indeed, some idea that Mr. Herries has already discovered that I am made of different and more unmalleable metal than he had at first believed. There were letters from my dear Alan Fairford, giving a ludicrous account of my instability of temper, in the same pocketbook, which, according to the admission of my pretended guardian, fell under the investigation of his domestic, during the night I passed at Brokenburn, where, as I now recollect, my wet clothes, with the contents of my pockets, were, with the thoughtlessness of a young traveller, committed too rashly to the care of a strange servant. And my kind friend and hospitable landlord, Mr. Alexander Fairford, may also, and with justice, have spoken of my levities to this man. But he shall find he has made a false estimate upon these plausible grounds, since ——

But I must break off for the present.

# CHAPTER III.

THERE is at length a halt — at length I have gained so much privacy as to enable me to continue my Journal. It has become a sort of task of duty to me, without the discharge of which I do not feel that the business of the day is performed. True, no friendly eye may ever look upon these labours, which have amused the solitary hours of an unhappy prisoner. Yet, in the meanwhile, the exercise of the pen seems to act as a sedative upon my own agitated thoughts and tumultuous passions. I never lay it down but I rise stronger in resolution, more ardent in hope. A thousand vague fears, wild expectations, and indigested schemes, hurry through one's thoughts in seasons of doubt and of danger. But by arresting them as they flit across the mind, by throwing them on paper, and even by that mechanical act compelling ourselves to consider them with scrupulous and minute attention, we may perhaps escape becoming the dupes of our own excited imagination; just as a young horse is cured of the vice of starting, by being made to stand still and look for some time without any interruption at the cause of its terror.

There remains but one risk, which is that of discovery. But, besides the small characters in which my residence in Mr. Fairford's house enabled me to excel, for the purpose of transferring as many scroll sheets as possible to a huge sheet of stamped paper, I have, as I have elsewhere intimated, had hitherto the comfortable reflection, that if the record of my misfortunes should fall into the hands of him by whom they are caused, they would, without harming any one, show him the real character and disposition of the person who has become his prisoner — perhaps his victim. Now, however, that other names, and other characters, are to be mingled with the register of my own sentiments, I must take additional care of these papers, and keep them in such a.manner that, in case of the least hazard of detection, I may be able to destroy them at a moment's notice. I shall not soon or easily forget the lesson I have been taught, by the prying disposition which Cristal Nixon, this man's agent and confederate, manifested at Brokenburn, and which proved the original cause of my sufferings.

My laying aside the last sheet of my Journal hastily was occasioned by the unwonted sound of a violin, in the farm-yard beneath my windows. It will not appear surprising to those who have made music their study, that, after listening to a few notes, I became at once assured that the musician was no other than the itinerant, formerly mentioned as present at the destruction of Joshua Geddes's stake-nets, the superior delicacy and force of whose execution would enable me to swear to his bow amongst a whole orchestra. I had the less reason to doubt his identity, because he played twice over the beautiful Scottish air called Wandering Willie; and I could not help concluding that he did so for the purpose of intimating his own presence, since what the French call the *nom de guerre* of the performer was described by the tune.

Hope will catch at the most feeble twig for support in extremity. I knew this man, though deprived of sight, to be bold, ingenious, and perfectly capable of acting as a guide. I believed I had won his good-will, by having, in a frolic, assumed the character of his partner; and I remembered that, in a wild, wandering, and disorderly course of life, men, as they become loosened from the ordinary bonds of civil society, hold those of comradeship more closely sacred; so that honour is sometimes found among thieves, and faith and attachment in such as the law has termed vagrants. The history of Richard Cœur de Lion and his minstrel, Blondel, rushed, at the same time, on my mind, though I could not even then suppress a smile at the dignity of the example, when applied to a blind fiddler and myself. Still there was something in all this to awaken a hope that, if I could open a correspondence with this poor violer, he might be useful in extricating me from my present situation.

His profession furnished me with some hope that this desired communication might be attained; since it is well known that, in Scotland, where there is so much national music, the words and airs of which are generally known, there is a kind of freemasonry amongst performers, by which they can, by the mere choice of a tune, express a great deal to the hearers. Personal allusions are often made in this manner, with much point and pleasantry; and nothing is more usual at public festivals than that the air played to accompany a particular health or toast is made the vehicle of compliment, of wit, and sometimes of satire.[1]

[1] Every one must remember instances of this festive custom, in which the adaptation of the tune to the toast was remarkably

While these things passed through my mind rapidly, I heard my friend beneath recommence, for the third time, the air from which his own name had been probably adopted, when he was interrupted by his rustic auditors.

"If thou canst play no other spring but that, mon, ho hadst best put up ho's pipes and be jogging. Squoire will be back anon, or Master Nixon, and we'll see who will pay poiper then."

Oho, thought I, if I have no sharper ears than those of my friends Jan and Dorcas to encounter, I may venture an experiment upon them; and, as most expressive of my state of captivity, I sang two or three lines of the 137th Psalm —

> By Babel's streams we sat and wept.

The country people listened with attention, and when I ceased I heard them whisper together in tones of commiseration, "Lack-a-day, poor soul! so pretty a man to be beside his wits!"

"An he be that gate," said Wandering Willie, in a tone calculated to reach my ears, "I ken naething will raise his spirits like a spring." And he struck up, with great vigour and spirit, the lively Scottish air, the words of which instantly occurred to me,—

> O whistle and I'll come t'ye, my lad,
> O whistle and I'll come t'ye, my lad;
> Though father and mother and a' should gae mad,
> O whistle and I'll come t'ye, my lad.

I soon heard a clattering noise of feet in the court-yard, which I concluded to be Jan and Dorcas dancing a jig in their Cumberland wooden clogs.

felicitous. Old Neil Gow and his son Nathaniel were peculiarly happy on such occasions.

Under cover of this din, I endeavoured to answer
Willie's signal by whistling, as loud as I could,

> Come back again and loe me
> When a' the lave are gane.

He instantly threw the dancers out, by changing
his air to

> There's my thumb, I'll ne'er beguile thee.

I no longer doubted that a communication betwixt
us was happily established, and that, if I had an
opportunity of speaking to the poor musician, I
should find him willing to take my letter to the
post, to invoke the assistance of some active magistrate, or of the commanding-officer of Carlisle
Castle, or, in short, to do whatever else I could point
out, in the compass of his power, to contribute to
my liberation. But to obtain speech of him, I
must have run the risk of alarming the suspicions
of Dorcas, if not of her yet more stupid Corydon.
My ally's blindness prevented his receiving any
communication by signs from the window — even if
I could have ventured to make them, consistently
with prudence — so that, notwithstanding the mode
of intercourse we had adopted was both circuitous
and peculiarly liable to misapprehension, I saw
nothing I could do better than to continue it, trusting my own and my correspondent's acuteness in
applying to the airs the meaning they were intended
to convey. I thought of singing the words themselves of some significant song, but feared I might,
by doing so, attract suspicion. I endeavoured,
therefore, to intimate my speedy departure from
my present place of residence, by whistling the

well-known air with which festive parties in
Scotland usually conclude the dance—

> Good-night and joy be wi' ye a',
> For here nae langer maun I stay;
> There's neither friend nor foe of mine
> But wishes that I were away.

It appeared that Willie's powers of intelligence
were much more active than mine, and that, like
a deaf person accustomed to be spoken to by signs,
he comprehended, from the very first notes, the
whole meaning I intended to convey; and he
accompanied me in the air with his violin, in such a
manner as at once to show he understood my meaning, and to prevent my whistling from being attended
to.

His reply was almost immediate, and was conveyed in the old martial air of "Hey, Johnnie lad,
cock up your beaver." I ran over the words, and
fixed on the following stanza, as most applicable to
my circumstances :—

> Cock up your beaver, and cock it fu' sprush,
> We'll over the Border and give them a brush;
> There's somebody there we'll teach better behaviour—
> Hey, Johnnie lad, cock up your beaver.

If these sounds alluded, as I hope they do, to
any chance of assistance from my Scottish friends,
I may indeed consider that a door is open to hope
and freedom. I immediately replied with,

> My heart's in the Highlands, my heart is not here;
> My heart's in the Highlands, a-chasing the deer;
> A-chasing the wild deer, and following the roe;
> My heart's in the Highlands wherever I go.

> Farewell to the Highlands! farewell to the North!
> The birthplace of valour, the cradle of worth;
> Wherever I wander, wherever I rove,
> The hills of the Highlands for ever I love.

Willie instantly played, with a degree of spirit which might have awakened hope in Despair herself, if Despair could be supposed to understand Scotch music, the fine old Jacobite air,

> For a' that, and a' that,
> And twice as much as a' that.

I next endeavoured to intimate my wish to send notice of my condition to my friends; and, despairing to find an air sufficiently expressive of my purpose, I ventured to sing a verse which, in various forms, occurs so frequently in old ballads—

> Whaur will I get a bonny boy
> That will win hose and shoon;
> That will gae down to Durisdeer,
> And bid my merry men come?

He drowned the latter part of the verse by playing, with much emphasis,

> Kind Robin loes me.

Of this, though I ran over the verses of the song in my mind, I could make nothing; and before I could contrive any mode of intimating my uncertainty, a cry arose in the court-yard that Cristal Nixon was coming. My faithful Willie was obliged to retreat; but not before he had half played, half bummed, by way of farewell,

> Leave thee—leave thee, lad—
> I'll never leave thee;
> The stars shall gae withershins
> Ere I will leave thee.

I am thus, I think, secure of one trusty adherent in my misfortunes; and, however whimsical it may be to rely much on a man of his idle profession and deprived of sight withal, it is deeply impressed on my mind that his services may be both useful and necessary. There is another quarter from which I look for succour, and which I have indicated to thee, Alan, in more than one passage of my Journal. Twice, at the early hour of daybreak, I have seen the individual alluded to in the court of the farm, and twice she made signs of recognition in answer to the gestures by which I endeavoured to make her comprehend my situation; but on both occasions she pressed her finger on her lips, as expressive of silence and secrecy.

The manner in which G. M. entered upon the scene for the first time seems to assure me of her good-will, so far as her power may reach; and I have many reasons to believe it is considerable. Yet she seemed hurried and frightened during the very transitory moments of our interview, and I think was, upon the last occasion, startled by the entrance of some one into the farm-yard, just .as she was on the point of addressing me. You must not ask whether I am an early riser, since such objects are only to be seen at daybreak; and although I have never again seen her, yet I have reason to think she is not distant. It was but three nights ago, that, worn out by the uniformity of my confinement, I had manifested more symptoms of despondence than I had before exhibited, which I conceive may have attracted the attention of the domestics, through whom the circumstance might transpire. On the next morning, the following lines lay on my table; but how conveyed there I can-

not tell. The hand in which they are written is a
beautiful Italian manuscript —

As lords their labourers' hire delay,
    Fate quits our toil with hopes to come,
Which, if far short of present pay,
    Still owns a debt and names a sum.

Quit not the pledge, frail sufferer, then,
    Although a distant date be given ;
Despair is treason towards man,
    And blasphemy to Heaven.

That these lines are written with the friendly
purpose of inducing me to keep up my spirits, I
cannot doubt ; and I trust the manner in which I
shall conduct myself may show that the pledge is
accepted.

The dress is arrived in which it seems to be my
self-elected guardian's pleasure that I shall travel ;
and what does it prove to be ? — A skirt, or upper-
petticoat of camlet, like those worn by country
ladies of moderate rank when on horseback, with
such a riding-mask as they frequently use on journeys to preserve their eyes and complexion from
the sun and dust, and sometimes, it is suspected, to
enable them to play off a little coquetry. From
the gayer mode of employing the mask, however,
I suspect I shall be precluded ; for instead of being
only pasteboard, covered with black velvet, I
observe with anxiety that mine is thickened with a
plate of steel, which, like Quixote's visor, serves to
render it more strong and durable.

This apparatus, together with a steel clasp for
securing the mask behind me with a padlock, gave
me fearful recollections of the unfortunate being
who, never being permitted to lay aside such a visor,

acquired the well-known historical epithet of the Man in the Iron Mask. I hesitated a moment whether I should so far submit to the acts of oppression designed against me as to assume this disguise, which was, of course, contrived to aid their purposes. But then I remembered Mr. Herries's threat, that I should be kept close prisoner in a carriage, unless I assumed the dress which should be appointed for me ; and I considered the comparative degree of freedom which I might purchase by wearing the mask and female dress as easily and advantageously purchased. Here, therefore, I must pause for the present, and await what the morning may bring forth.

[To carry on the story from the documents before us, we think it proper here to drop the Jcurnal of the captive Darsie Latimer, and adopt, instead, a narrative of the proceedings of Alan Fairford in pursuit of his friend, which forms another series in this history.]

# CHAPTER IV.

## NARRATIVE OF ALAN FAIRFORD.

THE reader ought, by this time, to have formed some idea of the character of Alan Fairford. He had a warmth of heart which the study of the law and of the world could not chill, and talents which they had rendered unusually acute. Deprived of the personal patronage enjoyed by most of his contemporaries, who assumed the gown under the proteotion of their aristocratic alliances and descents, he early saw that he should have that to achieve for himself which fell to them as a right of birth. He laboured hard in silence and solitude, and his labours were crowned with success. But Alan doted on his friend Darsie, even more than he loved his profession, and, as we have seen, threw every thing aside when he thought Latimer in danger; forgetting fame and fortune, and hazarding even the serious displeasure of his father, to rescue him whom he loved with an elder brother's affection. Darsie, though his parts were more quick and brilliant than those of his friend, seemed always to the latter a being under his peculiar charge, whom he was called upon to cherish and protect, in cases where the youth's own experience was unequal to the exigency; and now, when the fate of Latimer seemed worse than doubtful, and Alan's whole prudence and energy were to be exerted in his behalf, an adventure which might have seemed perilous to

most youths of his age had no terrors for him. He
was well acquainted with the laws of his country,
and knew how to appeal to them; and, besides his
professional confidence, his natural disposition was
steady, sedate, persevering, and undaunted. With
these requisites he undertook a quest which, at that
time, was not unattended with actual danger, and
had much in it to appal a more timid disposition.

Fairford's first enquiry concerning his friend was
of the chief magistrate of Dumfries, Provost Crosbie,
who had sent the information of Darsie's disappear-
ance. On his first application, he thought he
discerned in the honest dignitary a desire to get rid
of the subject. The Provost spoke of the riot at
the fishing station as an "outbreak among those
lawless loons the fishermen, which concerned the
Sheriff," he said, "more than us poor Town-Council
bodies, that have enough to do to keep peace within
burgh, amongst such a set of commoners as the town
is plagued with."

"But this is not all, Provost Crosbie," said Mr.
Alan Fairford; "a young gentleman of rank and
fortune has disappeared amongst their hands — you
know him. My father gave him a letter to you —
Mr. Darsie Latimer."

"Lack-a-day, yes! lack-a-day, yes!" said the
Provost; "Mr. Darsie Latimer — he dined at my
house — I hope he is well?"

"I hope so too," said Alan, rather indignantly;
"but I desire more certainty on that point. You
yourself wrote my father that he had disappeared."

"Troth, yes, and that is true," said the Provost.
"But did he not go back to his friends in Scotland?
it was not natural to think he would stay here."

"Not unless he is under restraint," said Fairford,

surprised at the coolness with which the Provost
seemed to take up the matter.

"Rely on it, sir," said Mr. Crosbie, "that if he
has not returned to his friends in Scotland, he must
have gone to his friends in England."

"I will rely on no such thing," said Alan; "if
there is law or justice in Scotland, I will have the
thing cleared to the very bottom."

"Reasonable, reasonable," said the Provost, "so
far as is possible; but you know I have no power
beyond the ports of the burgh."

"But you are in the commission besides, Mr.
Crosbie; a Justice of Peace for the county."

"True, very true — that is," said the cautious magistrate, "I will not say but my name may stand on the list,
but I cannot remember that I have ever qualified."[1]

"Why, in that case," said young Fairford, "there
are ill-natured people might doubt your attachment
to the Protestant line, Mr. Crosbie."

"God forbid, Mr. Fairford! I who have done and
suffered in the Forty-five! I reckon the Highlandmen did me damage to the amount of L.100 Scots,
forby all they ate and drank — no, no, sir, I stand
beyond challenge: but as for plaguing myself with
county business, let them that aught the mare shoe
the mare. The Commissioners of Supply would see
my back broken before they would help me in the
burgh's work, and all the world kens the difference
of the weight between public business in burgh and
landward. What are their riots to me? have we not
riots enough of our own? — But I must be getting
ready, for the council meets this forenoon. I am
blithe to see your father's son on the causeway of
our ancient burgh, Mr. Alan Fairford. Were you

[1] By taking the oaths to Government.

a twelvemonth aulder, we would make a burgess
of you, man. I hope you will come and dine with
me before you go away. What think you of to-day
at two o'clock — just a roasted chucky and a drappit egg ?"

Alan Fairford resolved that his friend's hospitality should not, as it seemed the inviter intended,
put a stop to his queries. "I must delay you for
a moment," he said, " Mr. Crosbie; this is a serious
affair; a young gentleman of high hopes, my own
dearest friend, is missing — you cannot think it will
be passed over slightly, if a man of your high character and known zeal for the government do not
make some active enquiry. Mr. Crosbie, you are my
father's friend, and I respect you as such — but to
others it will have a bad appearance."

The withers of the Provost were not unwrung;
he paced the room in much tribulation, repeating,
" But what can I do, Mr. Fairford ? I warrant your
friend casts up again — he will come back again,
like the ill shilling — he is not the sort of gear that
tynes — a hellicat boy, running through the country
with a blind fiddler, and playing the fiddle to a parcel of blackguards, who can tell where the like of
him may have scampered to ? "

" There are persons apprehended, and in the jail
of the town, as I understand from the Sheriff-Sub-
stitute," said Mr. Fairford; " you must call them
before you, and enquire what they know of this
young gentleman."

" Ay, ay — the Sheriff-Depute did commit some
poor creatures, I believe — wretched, ignorant fishermen bodies, that had been quarrelling with Quaker
Geddes and his stake-nets, whilk, under favour of
your gown be it spoken, Mr. Fairford, are not over

and above lawful, and the Town-Clerk thinks they may be lawfully removed *via facti* — but that is by the by. But, sir, the creatures were a' dismissed for want of evidence ; the Quaker would not swear to them, and what could the Sheriff and me do but just let them .loose ? Come awa, cheer up, Master Alan, and take a walk till dinner-time — I must really go to the council."

"Stop a moment, Provost," said Alan ; "I lodge a complaint before you, as a magistrate, and you will find it serious to slight it over. You must have these men apprehended again."

" Ay, ay — easy said ; but catch them that can," answered the Provost; "they are ower the March by this time, or by the point of Cairn.— Lord help ye ! they are a kind of amphibious deevils, neither land nor water beasts — neither English nor Scots — neither county nor stewartry, as we say — they are dispersed like so much quicksilver. You may as well try to whistle a sealgh out of the Solway, as to get hold of one of them till all the fray is over."

" Mr. Crosbie, this will not do," answered the young counsellor ; "there is a person of more impor- tance than such wretches as you describe concerned in this unhappy business — I must name to you a certain Mr. Herries."

He kept his eye on the Provost as he uttered the name, which he did rather at a venture, and from the connexion which that gentleman, and his real or supposed niece, seemed to have with the fate of Darsie Latimer, than from any distinct cause of suspicion which he entertained. He thought the Provost seemed embarrassed, though he showed much desire to assume an appearance of indifference, in which he partly succeeded.

"Herries!" he said — "What Herries?—There are many of that name — not so many as formerly, for the old stocks are wearing out; but. there is Herries of Heathgill, and Herries of Auchintulloch, and Herries " ——

"To save you farther trouble, this person's designation is Herries of Birrenswork."

"Of Birrenswork?" said Mr. Crosbie; "I have you now, Mr. Alan. Could you not as well have said, the Laird of Redgauntlet?"

Fairford was too wary to testify any surprise at this identification of names, however unexpected. "I thought," said he, "he was more generally known by the name of Herries. I have seen and been in company with him under that name, I am sure."

"O ay; in Edinburgh, belike. You know Redgauntlet was unfortunate a great while ago, and though he was maybe not deeper in the mire than other folk, yet, for some reason or other, he did not get so easily out."

"He was attainted, I understand; and has no remission," said Fairford.

The cautious Provost only nodded, and said, "You may guess, therefore, why it is so convenient he should hold his mother's name, which is also partly his own, when he is about Edinburgh. To bear his proper name might be accounted a kind of flying in the face of government, ye understand. But he has been long connived at — the story is an old story — and the gentleman has many excellent qualities, and is of a very ancient and honourable house — has cousins among the great folk — counts kin with the Advocate and with the Sheriff — hawks, you know, Mr. Alan, will not pike out hawks' een — he is widely connected — *my* wife is à fourth cousin of Redgauntlet's."

*Hinc illæ lachrymæ!* thought Alan Fairford to himself; but the hint presently determined him to proceed by soft means, and with caution. "I beg you to understand," said Fairford, "that in the investigation which I am about to make, I design no harm to Mr. Herries, or Redgauntlet — call him what you will. All I wish is, to ascertain the safety of my friend. I know that he was rather foolish in once going upon a mere frolic, in disguise, to the neighbourhood of this same gentleman's house. In his circumstances, Mr. Redgauntlet may have misinterpreted the motives, and considered Darsie Latimer as a spy. His influence, I believe, is great, among the disorderly people you spoke of but now?"

The Provost answered with another sagacious shake of his head, that would have done honour to Lord Burleigh in the Critic.

"Well, then," continued Fairford, "is it not possible that, in the mistaken belief that Mr. Latimer was a spy, he may, upon such suspicion, have caused him to be carried off and confined somewhere? — Such things are done at elections, and on occasions less pressing than when men think their lives are in danger from an informer."

"Mr. Fairford," said the Provost, very earnestly, "I scarce think such a mistake possible; or if, by any extraordinary chance, it should have taken place, Redgauntlet, whom I cannot but know well, being, as I have said, my wife's first cousin, (fourth cousin, I should say,) is altogether incapable of doing any thing harsh to the young gentleman — he might send him ower to Ailsay for a night or two, or maybe land him on the north coast of Ireland, or in Islay, or some of the Hebrides; but depend upon it, he is incapable of harming a hair of his head."

"I am determined not to trust to that, Provost," answered Fairford, firmly; "and I am a good deal surprised at your way of talking so lightly of such an aggression on the liberty of the subject. You are to consider, and Mr. Herries or Mr. Redgauntlet's friends would do very well also to consider, how it will sound in the ears of an English Secretary of State, that an attainted traitor (for such is this gentleman) has not only ventured to take up his abode in this realm — against the King of which he has been in arms — but is suspected of having proceeded, by open force and violence, against the person of one of the lieges, a young man, who is neither without friends nor property to secure his being righted."

The Provost looked at the young counsellor with a face in which distrust, alarm, and vexation seemed mingled. "A fashious job," he said at last, "a fashious job; and it will be dangerous meddling with it. I should like ill to see your father's son turn informer against an unfortunate gentleman."

"Neither do I mean it," answered Alan, "provided that unfortunate gentleman and his friends give me a quiet opportunity of securing *my* friend's safety. If I could speak with Mr. Redgauntlet, and hear his own explanation, I should probably be satisfied. If I am forced to denounce him to government, it will be in his new capacity of a kidnapper. I may not be able, nor is it my business, to prevent his being recognised in his former character of an attainted person, excepted from the general pardon."

"Master Fairford," said the Provost, "would ye ruin the poor innocent gentleman on an idle suspicion?"

"Say no more of it, Mr. Crosbie; my line of conduct is determined — unless that suspicion is removed."

"Weel, sir," said the Provost, "since so it be, and since you say that you do not seek to harm Redgauntlet personally, I'll ask a man to dine with us to-day that kens as much about his matters as most folk. You must think, Mr. Alan Fairford, though Redgauntlet be my wife's near relative, and though, doubtless, I wish him weel, yet I am not the person who is like to be intrusted with his incomings and outgoings. I am not a man for that — I keep the kirk, and I abhor Popery — I have stood up for the House of Hanover, and for liberty and property — I carried arms, sir, against the Pretender, when three of the Highlandmen's baggage-carts were stopped at Ecclefechan ; and I had an especial loss of a hundred pounds " ——

"Scots," interrupted Fairford. " You forget you told me all this before."

' Scots or English, it was too much for me to lose," said the Provost; "so you see I am not a person to pack or peel with Jacobites, and such unfreemen as poor Redgauntlet."

"Granted, granted, Mr. Crosbie ; and what then ? " said Alan Fairford.

" Why, then, it follows, that if I am to help you at this pinch, it cannot be by and through my ain personal knowledge, but through some fitting agent or third person."

" Granted again," said Fairford. " And pray who may this third person be ? "

" Wha but Pate Maxwell of Summertrees — him they call Pate-in-Peril."

" An old forty-five man, of course ? " said Fairford.

"Ye may swear that," replied the Provost — "as black a Jacobite as the auld leaven can make him; but a sonsy, merry companion, that none of us think it worth while to break wi' for all his brags and his clavers. You would have thought, if he had had but his own way at Derby, he would have marched Charlie Stuart through between Wade and the Duke, as a thread goes through the needle's ee, and seated him in Saint James's before you could have said haud your hand. But though he is a windy body when he gets on his auld-warld stories, he has mair gumption in him than most people — knows business, Mr. Alan, being bred to the law; but never took the gown, because of the oaths, which kept more folk out then than they do now — the more's the pity."

"What! are you sorry, Provost, that Jacobitism is upon the decline?" said Fairford.

"No, no," answered the Provost — "I am only sorry for folks losing the tenderness of conscience which they used to have. I have a son breeding to the bar, Mr. Fairford; and, no doubt, considering my services and sufferings, I might have looked for some bit postie to him; but if the muckle tikes come in — I mean a' these Maxwells, and Johnstones, and great lairds, that the oaths used to keep out lang syne — the bits o' messan dogies, like my son, and maybe like your father's son, Mr. Alan, will be sair put to the wall."

"But to return to the subject, Mr. Crosbie," said Fairford, "do you really think it likely that this Mr. Maxwell will be of service in this matter?"

"It's very like he may be, for he is the tongue of the trump to the whole squad of them," said the Provost; "and Redgauntlet, though he will not stick at times to call him a fool, takes more of his counsel than any man's else that I am aware of. If Pate can bring him to a communing, the business is done. He's a sharp chield, Pate-in-Peril."

"Pate-in-Peril!" repeated Alan; "a very singular name."

"Ay, and it was in as queer a way he got it; but I'll say naething about that," said the Provost, "for fear of forestalling his market; for ye are sure to hear it once at least, however oftener, before the punch-bowl gives place to the tea-pot. — And now, fare ye weel; for there is the council-bell clinking in earnest; and if I am not there before it jows in, Bailie Laurie will be trying some of his manœuvres."

The Provost, repeating his expectation of seeing Mr. Fairford at two o'clock, at length effected his escape from the young counsellor, and left him at a considerable loss how to proceed. The Sheriff, it seems, had returned to Edinburgh, and he feared to find the visible repugnance of the Provost to interfere with this Laird of Birrenswork, or Redgauntlet, much stronger amongst the country gentlemen, many of whom were Catholics as well as Jacobites, and most others unwilling to quarrel with kinsmen and friends, by prosecuting with severity political offences which had almost run a prescription.

To collect all the information in his power, and not to have recourse to the higher authorities until he could give all the light of which the case was capable, seemed the wiser proceeding in a choice of difficulties. He had some conversation with the Procurator-Fiscal, who, as well as the Provost, was an old correspondent of his father. Alan expressed

to that officer a purpose of visiting Brokenburn,
but was assured by him that it would be a step
attended with much danger to his own person, and
altogether fruitless; that the individuals who had
been ringleaders in the riot were long since safely
sheltered in their various lurking-holes in the Isle
of Man, Cumberland, and elsewhere; and that
those who might remain would undoubtedly commit violence on any who visited their settlement
with the purpose of enquiring into the late
disturbances.

There were not the same objections to his hastening to Mount Sharon, where he expected to find the
latest news of his friend; and there was time enough
to do so, before the hour appointed for the Provost's
dinner.  Upon the road, he congratulated himself
on having obtained one point of almost certain
information.  The person who had in a manner
forced himself upon his father's hospitality, and had
appeared desirous to induce Darsie Latimer to visit
England, against whom, too, a sort of warning had
been received from an individual connected with
and residing in his own family, proved to be a
promoter of the disturbance in which Darsie had
disappeared.

What could be the cause of such an attempt on
the liberty of an inoffensive and amiable man?  It
was impossible it could be merely owing to Redgauntlet's mistaking Darsie for a spy; for though
that was the solution which Fairford had offered to
the Provost, he well knew that, in point of fact, he
himself had been warned by his singular visitor of
some danger to which his friend was exposed, before
such suspicion could have been entertained; and
the injunctions received by Latimer from his guar-

dian, or him who acted as such, Mr. Griffiths of London, pointed to the same thing. He was rather glad, however, that he had not let Provost Crosbie into his secret farther than was absolutely necessary ; since it was plain that the connexion of his wife with the suspected party was likely to affect his impartiality as a magistrate.

When Alan Fairford arrived at Mount Sharon, Rachel Geddes hastened to meet him, almost before the servant could open the door. She drew back in disappointment when she beheld a stranger, and said, to excuse her precipitation, that "she had thought it was her brother Joshua returned from Cumberland."

"Mr. Geddes is, then, absent from home?" said Fairford, much disappointed in his turn.

"He hath been gone since yesterday, friend," answered Rachel, once more composed to the quietude which characterises her sect, but her pale cheek and red eye giving contradiction to her assumed equanimity.

"I am," said Fairford, hastily, "the particular friend of a young man not unknown to you, Miss Geddes — the friend of Darsie Latimer — and am come hither in the utmost anxiety, having understood from Provost Crosbie that he had disappeared in the night when a destructive attack was made upon the fishing-station of Mr. Geddes."

"Thou dost afflict me, friend, by thy enquiries," said Rachel, more affected than before ; " for although the youth was like those of the worldly generation, wise in his own conceit, and lightly to be moved by the breath of vanity, yet Joshua loved him, and his heart clave to him as if he had been his own son. And when he himself escaped

from the sons of Belial, which was not until they
had tired themselves with reviling, and with idle
reproach, and the jests of the scoffer, Joshua, my
brother, returned to them once and again, to give
ransom for the youth called Darsie Latimer, with
offers of money and with promise of remission, but
they would not hearken to him. Also, he went
before the Head Judge, whom men call the Sheriff,
and would have told him of the youth's peril; but
he would in no way hearken to him unless he
would swear unto the truth of his words, which
thing he might not do without sin, seeing it is
written, Swear not at all — also, that our conversation shall be yea or nay. Therefore, Joshua
returned to me disconsolate, and said, 'Sister
Rachel, this youth hath run into peril for my
sake; assuredly I shall not be guiltless if a hair
of his head be harmed, seeing I have sinned in
permitting him to go with me to the fishing-station
when such evil was to be feared. Therefore, I will
take my horse, even Solomon, and ride swiftly into
Cumberland, and I will make myself friends with
Mammon of Unrighteousness, among the magistrates of the Gentiles, and among their mighty
men; and it shall come to pass that Darsie
Latimer shall be delivered, even if it were at the
expense of half my substance.' And I said, 'Nay,
my brother, go not, for they will but scoff at and
revile thee; but hire with thy silver one of the
scribes, who are eager as hunters in pursuing their
prey, and he shall free Darsie Latimer from the
men of violence by his cunning, and thy soul shall
be guiltless of evil towards the lad.' But he
answered and said, 'I will not be controlled in
this matter.' And he is gone forth, and hath

not returned, and I fear me that he may never
return; for though he be peaceful, as becometh
one who holds all violence as offence against his
own soul, yet neither the floods of water, nor the
fear of the snare, nor the drawn sword of the
adversary brandished in the path, will overcome
his purpose. Wherefore the Solway may swallow
him up, or the sword of the enemy may devour
him — nevertheless, my hope is better in Him
who directeth all things, and ruleth over the
waves of the sea, and overruleth the devices of
the wicked, and who can redeem us even as a
bird from the fowler's net."

This was all that Fairford could learn from Miss
Geddes; but he heard with pleasure that the good
Quaker, her brother, had many friends among those
of his own profession in Cumberland, and without
exposing himself to so much danger as his sister
seemed to apprehend, he trusted he might be able
to discover some traces of Darsie Latimer. He
himself rode back to Dumfries, having left with
Miss Geddes his direction in that place, and an
earnest request that she would forward thither
whatever information she might obtain from her
brother.

On Fairford's return to Dumfries, he employed
the brief interval which remained before dinner-
time in writing an account of what had befallen
Latimer, and of the present uncertainty of his condition, to Mr. Samuel Griffiths, through whose hands
the remittances for his friend's service had been
regularly made, desiring he would instantly acquaint
him with such parts of his history as might direct
him in the search which he was about to institute
through the border counties, and which he pledged

himself not to give up until he had obtained news of his friend, alive or dead. The young lawyer's mind felt easier when he had dispatched this letter. He could not conceive any reason why his friend's life should be aimed at; he knew Darsie had done nothing by which his liberty could be legally affected; and although, even of late years, there had been singular histories of men, and women also, who had been trepanned, and concealed in solitudes and distant islands, in order to serve some temporary purpose, such violences had been chiefly practised by the rich on the poor, and by the strong on the feeble; whereas, in the present case, this Mr. Herries, or Redgauntlet, being amenable, for more reasons than one, to the censure of the law, must be the weakest in any struggle in which it could be appealed to. It is true that his friendly anxiety whispered that the very cause which rendered this oppressor less formidable might make him more desperate. Still, recalling his language, so strikingly that of the gentleman, and even of the man of honour, Alan Fairford concluded that though, in his feudal pride, Redgauntlet might venture on the deeds of violence exercised by the aristocracy in other times, he could not be capable of any action of deliberate atrocity. And in these convictions he went to dine with Provost Crosbie, with a heart more at ease than might have been expected.[1]

[1] Note I.

# CHAPTER V.

FIVE minutes had elapsed after the town-clock struck two before Alan Fairford, who had made a small detour to put his letter into the post-house, reached the mansion of Mr. Provost Crosbie, and was at once greeted by the voice of that civic dignitary, and the rural dignitary his visitor, as by the voices of men impatient for their dinner.

"Come away, Mr. Fairford — the Edinburgh time is later than ours," said the Provost.

And, "Come away, young gentleman," said the Laird; "I remember your father weel, at the Cross, thirty years ago — I reckon you are as late in Edinburgh as at London, four o'clock hours — eh?"

"Not quite so degenerate," replied Fairford; "but certainly many Edinburgh people are so ill-advised as to postpone their dinner till three, that they may have full time to answer their London correspondents."

"London correspondents!" said Mr. Maxwell; "and pray, what the devil have the people of Auld Reekie to do with London correspondents?"[1]

---

[1] Not much in those days, for within my recollection the London post was brought north in a small mail-cart; and men are yet alive who recollect when it came down with only one single letter for Edinburgh, addressed to the manager of the British Linen Company.

"The tradesmen must have their goods," said Fairford.

"Can they not buy our own Scottish manufactures, and pick their customers' pockets in a more patriotic manner?"

"Then the ladies must have fashions," said Fairford.

"Can they not busk the plaid over their heads, as their mothers did? A tartan screen, and once a year a new cockernony from Paris, should serve a Countess. But ye have not many of them left, I think — Mareschal, Airley, Winton, Wemyss, Balmerino, all passed and gone — ay, ay, the countesses and ladies of quality will scarce take up too much of your ball-room floor with their quality hoops now-a-days."

"There is no want of crowding, however, sir," said Fairford; "they begin to talk of a new Assembly Room."

"A new Assembly Room!" said the old Jacobite Laird — "Umph — I mind quartering three hundred men in the old Assembly Room[1] — But come, come — I'll ask no more questions — the answers all smell of new lords new lands, and do but spoil my appetite, which were a pity, since here comes Mrs. Crosbie to say our mutton's ready."

It was even so. Mrs. Crosbie had been absent, like Eve, "on hospitable cares intent," a duty which she did not conceive herself exempted from, either by the dignity of her husband's rank in the municipality, or the splendour of her Brussels silk gown, or even by the more highly prized lustre of her

---

[1] I remember hearing this identical answer given by an old Highland gentleman of the Forty-Five, when he heard of the opening of the New Assembly Rooms in George Street.

birth ; for she was born a Maxwell, and allied, as her husband often informed his friends, to several of the first families in the county. She had been handsome, and was still a portly good-looking woman of her years ; and though her peep into the kitchen had somewhat heightened her complexion, it was no more than a modest touch of rouge might have done.

The Provost was certainly proud of his lady, nay, some said he was afraid of her; for of the females of the Redgauntlet family there went a rumour that, ally where they would, there was a grey mare as surely in the stables of their husbands, as there is a white horse in Wouvermans' pictures. The good dame, too, was supposed to have brought a spice of politics into Mr. Crosbie's household along with her ; and the Provost's enemies at the Council-table of the burgh used to observe that he uttered there many a bold harangue against the Pretender, and in favour of King George and government, of which he dared not have pronounced a syllable in his own bedchamber; and that, in fact, his wife's predominating influence had now and then occasioned his acting, or forbearing to act, in a manner very different from his general professions of zeal for Revolution principles. If this was in any respect true, it was certain, on the other hand, that Mrs. Crosbie, in all external points, seemed to acknowledge the "lawful sway and right supremacy" of the head of the house, and if she did not in truth reverence her husband, she at least seemed to do so.

This stately dame received Mr. Maxwell (a cousin of course) with cordiality, and Fairford with civility ; answering, at the same time, with respect, to the magisterial complaints of the Provost, that dinner was just coming up. "But since you changed poor Peter MacAlpin, that used to take care of the town-clock, my dear, it has never gone well a single day."

"Peter MacAlpin, my dear," said the Provost, "made himself too busy for a person in office, and drunk healths and so forth, which it became no man to drink or to pledge, far less one that is in point of office a servant of the public. I understand that he lost the music-bells in Edinburgh, for playing 'Ower the water to Charlie' upon the tenth of June. He is a black sheep, and deserves no encouragement."

"Not a bad tune, though, after all," said Summertrees ; and, turning to the window, he half hummed, half whistled the air in question, then sang the last verse aloud:

"Oh, I loe weel my Charlie's name,'
　Though some there be that abhor him;
But oh to see the deil gang hame
　Wi' a' the Whigs before him !
Over the water, and over the sea,
　And over the water to Charlie ;
Come weal, come woe, we'll gather and go,
　And live or die with Charlie."

Mrs. Crosbie smiled furtively on the Laird, wearing an aspect at the same time of deep submission ; while the Provost, not choosing to hear his visitor's ditty, took a turn through the room, in unquestioned dignity and independence of authority.

"Aweel, aweel, my dear," said the lady, with a quiet smile of submission, "ye ken these matters best, and you will do your pleasure — they are far

above my hand — only, I doubt if ever the town-
clock will go right, or your meals be got up so
regular as I should wish, till Peter MacAlpin gets
his office back again. The body's auld, and can
neither work nor want, but he is the only hand to
set a clock."

It may be noticed in passing, that, notwithstanding this prediction, which, probably, the fair
Cassandra had the full means of accomplishing, it
was not till the second council-day thereafter that
the misdemeanours of the Jacobite clock-keeper
were passed over, and he was once more restored to
his occupation of fixing the town's time, and the
Provost's dinner-hour.

Upon the present occasion the dinner passed
pleasantly away. Summertrees talked and jested
with the easy indifference of a man who holds himself superior to his company. He was indeed an
important person, as was testified by his portly
appearance; his hat laced with *point d'Espagne;*
his coat and waistcoat once richly embroidered,
though now almost threadbare; the splendour of
his solitaire and laced ruffles, though the first was
sorely creased, and the other sullied; not to forget
the length of his silver-hilted rapier. His wit,
or rather humour, bordered on the sarcastic, and
intimated a discontented man; and although he
showed no displeasure when the Provost attempted
a repartee, yet it seemed that he permitted it upon
mere sufferance, as a fencing-master, engaged with
a pupil, will sometimes permit the tyro to hit
him, solely by way of encouragement. The Laird's
own jests, in the meanwhile, were eminently successful, not only with the Provost and his lady, but
with the red-cheeked and red-ribboned servant-maid

who waited at table, and who could scarce perform
her duty with propriety, so effectual were the
explosions of Summertrees. Alan Fairford alone
was unmoved among all this mirth; which was the
less wonderful, that, besides the important subject
which occupied his thoughts, most of the Laird's
good things consisted in sly allusions to little
parochial or family incidents, with which the Edinburgh visitor was totally unacquainted; so that the
laughter of the party sounded in his ear like the idle
crackling of thorns under the pot, with this difference, that they did not accompany or second any
such useful operation as the boiling thereof.

Fairford was glad when the cloth was withdrawn;
and when Provost Crosbie (not without some points
of advice from his lady, touching the precise mixture of the ingredients) had accomplished the com-
pounding of a noble bowl of punch, at which the
old Jacobite's eyes seemed to glisten, the glasses
were pushed round it, filled, and withdrawn each
by its owner, when the Provost emphatically named
the toast, "The King," with an important look to
Fairford, which seemed to say, You can have no
doubt whom I mean, and therefore there is no
occasion to particularize the individual.

Summertrees repeated the toast with a sly wink
to the lady, while Fairford drank his glass in
silence.

"Well, young advocate," said the landed proprietor, "I am glad to see there is some shame, if
there is little honesty, left in the Faculty. Some
of your black-gowns, now-a-days, have as little of
the one as of the other."

"At least, sir," replied Mr. Fairford, "I am so
much of a lawyer as not willingly to enter into

disputes which I am not retained to support — it would be but throwing away both time and argument."

"Come, come," said the lady, "we will have no argument in this house about Whig or Tory — the Provost kens what he maun *say*, and I ken what he should *think*; and for a' that has come and gane yet, there may be a time coming when honest men may say what they think, whether they be Provosts or not."

"D'ye hear that, Provost?" said Summertrees; " your wife's a witch, man ; you should nail a horseshoe on your chamber-door — Ha, ha, ha !"

This sally did not take quite so well as former efforts of the Laird's wit. The lady drew up, and the Provost said, half aside, "The sooth bourd is nae bourd.[1] You will find the horseshoe hissing hot, Summertrees."

"You can speak from experience, doubtless, Provost," answered the Laird ; "but I crave pardon — I need not tell Mrs. Crosbie that I have all respect for the auld and honourable House of Redgauntlet."

"And good reason ye have, that are sae sib to them," quoth the lady, "and kend weel baith them that are here, and them that are gane."

" In troth, and ye may say sae, madam," answered the Laird ; "for poor Harry Redgauntlet, that suffered at Carlisle, was hand and glove with me ; and yet we parted on short leave-taking."

"Ay, Summertrees," said the Provost ; "that was when you played Cheat-the-woodie, and gat the by-name of Pate-in-Peril. I wish you would tell

---

[1] The true joke is no joke.

the story to my young friend here. He likes weel
to hear of a sharp trick, as most lawyers do."

"I wonder at your want of circumspection, Provost," said the Laird, — much after the manner of
a singer when declining to sing the song that is
quivering upon his tongue's very end. "Ye should
mind there are some auld stories that cannot be
ripped up again with entire safety to all concerned.
*Tace* is Latin for a candle."

"I hope," said the lady, "you are not afraid of
any thing being said out of this house to your prejudice, Summertrees? I have heard the story
before; but the oftener I hear it, the more wonderful I think it."

"Yes, madam; but it has been now a wonder
of more than nine days, and it is time it should be
ended," answered Maxwell.

Fairford now thought it civil to say, "that he
had often heard of Mr. Maxwell's wonderful escape,
and that nothing could be more agreeable to him
than to hear the right version of it."

But Summertrees was obdurate, and refused to
take up the time of the company with such "auld-
warld nonsense."

"Weel, weel," said the Provost, "a wilful man
maun hae his way. — What do your folk in the
county think about the disturbances that are beginning to spunk out in the colonies?"

"Excellent, sir, excellent. When things come
to the worst they will mend; and to the worst
they are coming. — But as to that nonsense ploy
of mine, if ye insist on hearing the particulars," —
said the Laird, who began to be sensible that the
period of telling his story gracefully was gliding
fast away.

"Nay," said the Provost, "it was not for myself, but this young gentleman."

"Aweel, what for should I not pleasure the young gentleman?—I'll just drink the honest folk at hame and abroad, and deil ane else. And then— but you have heard it before, Mrs. Crosbie?"

"Not so often as to think it tiresome, I assure ye," said the lady; and without further preliminaries, the Laird addressed Alan Fairford.

"Ye have heard of a year they call the *forty-five*, young gentleman; when the Southrons' heads made their last acquaintance with Scottish claymores? There was a set of rampauging chields in the country then that they called rebels—I never could find out what for—Some men should have been wi' them that never came, Provost—Skye and the Bush aboon Traquair (c) for that, ye ken— Weel, the job was settled at last. Cloured crowns were plenty, and raxed necks came into fashion. I dinna mind very weel what I was doing, swaggering about the country with dirk and pistol at my belt for five or six months, or thereaway; but I had a weary waking out of a wild dream. Then did I find myself on foot in a misty morning, with my hand, just for fear of going astray, linked into a handcuff, as they call it, with poor Harry Redgauntlet's fastened into the other; and there we were, trudging along, with about a score more that had thrust their horns ower deep in the bog, just like ourselves, and a sergeant's guard of redcoats, with twa file of dragoons, to keep all quiet, and give us heart to the road. Now, if this mode of travelling was not very pleasant, the object did not partienlarly recommend it; for you understand, young man, that they did not trust these poor rebel bodies

to be tried by juries of their ain kindly countrymen,
though ane would have thought they would have
found Whigs enough in Scotland to hang us all;
but they behoved to trounce us away to be tried at
Carlisle, where the folk had been so frightened, that
had you brought a whole Highland clan at once
into the court, they would have put their hands
upon their een, and cried, 'hang them a',' just to be
quit of them."

"Ay, ay," said the Provost, "that was a snell
law, I grant ye."

"Snell!" said his wife, "snell! I wish they
that passed it had the jury I would recommend
them to!"

"I suppose the young lawyer thinks it all very
right," said Summertrees, looking at Fairford —
"an *old* lawyer might have thought otherwise.
However, the cudgel was to be found to beat the
dog, and they chose a heavy one. Well, I kept my
spirits better than my companion, poor fellow; for
I had the luck to have neither wife nor child to
think about, and Harry Redgauntlet had both one
and t'other. — You have seen Harry, Mrs. Crosbie?"

"In troth have I," said she, with the sigh which
we give to early recollections, of which the object
is no more. "He was not so tall as his brother,
and a gentler lad every way. After he married the
great English fortune, folk called him less of a
Scotchman than Edward."

"Folk lee'd, then," said Summertrees; "poor
Harry was none of your bold-speaking, ranting
reivers, that talk about what they did yesterday,
or what they will do to-morrow: it was when something was to do at the moment that you should have
looked at Harry Redgauntlet. I saw him at Cul-

loden, when all was lost, doing more than twenty
of these bleezing braggarts, till the very soldiers
that took him cried not to hurt him — for all some-
body's orders, Provost — for he was the bravest
fellow of them all. Weel, as I went by the side of
Harry, and felt him raise my hand up in the mist
of the morning, as if he wished to wipe his eye —
for he had not that freedom without my leave —
my very heart was like to break for him, poor
fellow. In the meanwhile, I had been trying and
trying to make my hand as fine as a lady's, to see if
I could slip it out of my iron wristband. You may
think," he said, laying his broad bony hand on the
table, " I had work enough with such a shoulder-of-
mutton fist ; but if you observe, the shakle-bones
are of the largest, and so they were obliged to keep
the handcuff wide ; at length I got my hand slipped
out, and slipped in again : and poor Harry was sae
deep in his ain thoughts, I could not make him sensible what I was doing."

" Why not ? " said Alan Fairford, for whom the
tale began to have some interest.

" Because there was an unchancy beast of a
dragoon riding close beside us on the other side ;
and if I had let him into my confidence as well as
Harry, it would not have been long before a pistol-
ball slapped through my bonnet. — Well, I had
little for it but to do the best I could for myself ;
and, by my conscience, it was time, when the gallows was staring me in the face. We were to halt
for breakfast at Moffat. Well did I know the moors
we were marching over, having hunted and hawked
on every acre of ground in very different times.
So I waited, you see, till I was on the edge of
Errickstane-brae — Ye ken the place they call the

Marquis's Beef-stand, because the Annandale loons
used to put their stolen cattle in there ? "

Fairford intimated his ignorance.

"Ye must have seen it as ye cam this way; it
looks as if four hills were laying their heads
together, to shut out daylight from the dark hollow
space between them. A d—d deep, black, black-
guard-looking abyss of a hole it is, and goes straight
down from the road-side, as perpendicular as it can
do, to be a heathery brae. At the bottom there is
a small bit of a brook, that you would think could
hardly find its way out from the hills that are so
closely jammed round it."

" A bad pass indeed," said Alan.

"You may say that," continued the Laird.
"Bad as it was, sir, it was my only chance; and
though my very flesh creeped when I thought what
a rumble I was going to get, yet I kept my heart
up all the same. And so just when we came on the
edge of this Beef-stand of the Johnstones, I slipped
out my hand from the handcuff, cried to Harry
Gauntlet, 'Follow me!' — whisked under the belly
of the dragoon horse—flung my plaid round me
with the speed of lightning — threw myself on my
side, for there was no keeping my feet, and down
the brae hurled I, over heather and fern, and
blackberries, like a barrel down Chalmers's Close,
in Auld Reekie. G—, sir, I never could help
laughing when I think how the scoundrel redcoats
must have been bumbazed; for the mist being, as
I said, thick, they had little notion, I take it, that
they were on the verge of such a dilemma. I was
half way down — for rowing is faster wark than
rinning — ere they could get at their arms; and
then it was flash, flash, flash — rap, rap, rap —from

the edge of the road; but my head was too jumbled
to think any thing either of that or the hard knocks
I got among the stones. I kept my senses thegither,
whilk has been thought wonderful by all that ever
saw the place; and I helped myself with my hands
as gallantly as I could, and to the bottom I came.
There I lay for half a moment; but the thoughts
of a gallows is worth all the salts and scent-bottles
in the world for bringing a man to himself. Up
I sprung, like a four-year-auld colt. All the hills
were spinning round with me, like so many great
big humming-tops. But there was nae time to
think of that neither; more especially as the mist
had risen a little with the firing. I could see the
villains, like sae mony craws on the edge of the
brae; and I reckon that they saw me; for some of
the loons were beginning to crawl down the hill,
but liker auld wives in their red cloaks coming frae
a field-preaching than such a souple lad as I was.
Accordingly, they soon began to stop and load their
pieces. Good-e'en to you, gentlemen, thought I, if
that is to be the gate of it. If you have any
further word with me, you maun come as far as
Carriefraw-gauns. And so off I set, and never buck
went faster ower the braes than I did; and I never
stopped till I had put three waters, reasonably
deep, as the season was rainy, half a dozen moun-
tains, and a few thousand acres of the worst moss
and ling in Scotland, betwixt me and my friends
the redcoats."

"It was that job which got you the name of
Pate-in-Peril," said the Provost, filling the glasses,
and exclaiming with great emphasis, while his
guest, much animated with the recollections which
the exploit excited, looked round with an air of

triumph for sympathy and applause, — "Here is to your good health; and may you never put your neck in such a venture again."[1]

"Humph!—I do not know," answered Summertrees. "I am not like to be tempted with another opportunity[2]— Yet who knows?" And then he made a deep pause.

"May I ask what became of your friend, sir?" said Alan Fairford.

"Ah, poor Harry!" said Summertrees. "I'll tell you what, sir, it takes time to make up one's mind to such a venture, as my friend the Provost calls it; and I was told by Neil Maclean,— who was next file to us, but had the luck to escape the gallows by some slight-of-hand trick or other, — that, upon my breaking off, poor Harry stood like one motionless, although all our brethren in captivity made as much tumult as they could, to distract the attention of the soldiers. And run he did at last; but he did not know the ground, and either from confusion, or because he judged the descent altogether perpendicular, he fled up the hill to the left, instead of going down at once, and so was easily pursued and taken. If he had followed my example, he would have found enough among the shepherds to hide him, and feed him, as they

---

[1] Note II. — Escape of Pate-in-Peril.

[2] An old gentleman of the author's name was engaged in the affair of 1715, and with some difficulty was saved from the gallows, by the intercession of the Duchess of Buccleuch and Monmouth. Her Grace, who maintained a good deal of authority over her clan, sent for the object of her intercession, and warning him of the risk which he had run, and the trouble she had taken on his account, wound up her lecture by intimating that in case of such disloyalty again he was not to expect her interest in his favour. "An it please your Grace," said the stout old Tory, "I fear I am too old to see another opportunity."

did me, on bearmeal scones and braxy mutton,[1] till
better days came round again."

"He suffered, then, for his share in the insurrection ?" said Alan.

"You may swear that," said Summertrees. "His
blood was too red to be spared when that sort of
paint was in request. He suffered, sir, as you call
it — that is, he was murdered in cold blood, with
many a pretty fellow besides. — Well, we may have
our day next — what is fristed is not forgiven —
they think us all dead and buried — but " ——
Here he filled his glass, and muttering some indis-
tinct denunciations, drank it off, and assumed his
usual manner, which had been a little disturbed
towards the end of the narrative.

"What became of Mr. Redgauntlet's child ?" said
Fairford.

"*Mister* Redgauntlet ! — He was Sir Henry Redgauntlet, as his son, if the child now lives, will be
Sir Arthur — I called him Harry from intimacy,
and Redgauntlet, as the chief of his name — His
proper style was Sir Henry Redgauntlet."

"His son, therefore, is dead ?" said Alan Fairford.
"It is a pity so brave a line should draw to a close."

"He has left a brother," said Summertrees,
"Edward Hugh Redgauntlet, who has now the
representation of the family. And well it is; for
though he be unfortunate in many respects, he will
keep up the honour of the house better than a boy
bred up amongst these bitter Whigs, the relations
of his elder brother Sir Henry's lady. Then they
are on no good terms with the Redgauntlet line —

---

[1] BRAXY MUTTON. — The flesh of sheep that has died of dis-
ease, not by the hand of the butcher. In pastoral countries it is
used as food with little scruple.

bitter Whigs they are, in every sense. It was a runaway match betwixt Sir Henry and his lady. . Poor thing, they would not allow her to see him when in confinement — they had even the meanness to leave him without pecuniary assistance; and as all his own property was seized upon and plundered, he would have wanted common necessaries, but for the attachment of a fellow who was a famous fiddler — a blind man — I have seen him with Sir Henry myself, both before the affair broke out and while it was going on. I have heard that he fiddled in the streets of Carlisle, and carried what money he got to his master, while he was confined in the castle."

"I do not believe a word of it," said Mrs. Crosbie, kindling with indignation. "A Redgauntlet would have died twenty times before he had touched a fiddler's wages."

" Hout fye — hout fye — all nonsense and pride," said the Laird of Summertrees. "Scornful dogs will eat dirty puddings, cousin Crosbie — ye little ken what some of your friends were obliged to do yon time for a sowp of brose, or a bit of bannock. — G—d, I carried a cutler's wheel for several weeks, partly for need, and partly for disguise — there I went bizz — bizz — whizz — zizz, at every auld wife's door; and if ever you want your shears sharpened, Mrs. Crosbie, I am the lad to do it for you, if my wheel was but in order."

" You must ask my leave first," said the Provost; " for I have been told you had some queer fashions of taking a kiss instead of a penny, if you liked your customer."

" Come, come, Provost," said the lady, rising, " if the maut gets abune the meal with you, it is time for me to take myself away — And you will come to my room, gentlemen, when you want a cup of tea."

Alan Fairford was not sorry for the lady's departure. She seemed too much alive to the honour of the house of Redgauntlet, though only a fourth cousin, not to be alarmed by the enquiries which he proposed to make after the whereabout of its present head. Strange confused suspicions arose in his mind, from his imperfect recollection of the tale of Wandering Willie, and the idea forced itself upon him that his friend Darsie Latimer might be the son of the unfortunate Sir Henry. But before indulging in such speculations, the point was, to discover what had actually become of him. If he were in the hands of his uncle, might there not exist some rivalry in fortune, or rank, which might induce so stern a man as Redgauntlet to use unfair measures towards a youth whom he would find himself unable to mould to his purpose? He considered these points in silence, during several revolutions of the glasses as they wheeled in galaxy round the bowl, waiting until the Provost, agreeably to his own proposal, should mention the subject, for which he had expressly introduced him to Mr. Maxwell of Summertrees.

Apparently the Provost had forgot his promise, or at least was in no great haste to fulfil it. He debated with great earnestness upon the Stamp Act, which was then impending over the American colonies, and upon other political subjects of the day, but said not a word of Redgauntlet. Alan soon saw that the investigation he meditated must advance, if at all, on his own special motion, and determined to proceed accordingly.

Acting upon this resolution, he took the first opportunity afforded by a pause in the discussion of colonial politics to say, " I must remind you, Provost Crosbie, of your kind promise to procure some intelligence upon the subject I am so anxious about."

" Gadso ! " said the Provost, after a moment's hesitation, " it is very true.— Mr. Maxwell, we wish to consult you on a piece of important business. You must know — indeed I think you must have heard, that the fishermen at Brokenburn, and higher up the Solway, have made a raid upon Quaker Geddes's stake-nets, and levelled all with the sands."

" In troth I heard it, Provost, and I was glad to hear the scoundrels had so much pluck left as to right themselves against a fashion which would make the upper heritors a sort of clocking-hens, to hatch the fish that folk below them were to catch and eat."

" Well, sir," said Alan, " that is not the present point. But a young friend of mine was with Mr. Geddes at the time this violent procedure took place. and he has not since been heard of. Now, our friend, the Provost, thinks that you may be able to advise "——

Here he was interrupted by the Provost and Summertrees speaking out both at once, the first endeavouring to disclaim all interest in the question, and the last to evade giving an answer.

" Me think ! " said the Provost ; " I never thought twice about it, Mr. Fairford ; it was neither fish, nor flesh, nor salt herring of mine."

" And I able to advise ! " said Mr. Maxwell of Summertrees ; " what the devil can I advise you to do, excepting to send the bellman through the town to cry your lost sheep, as they do spaniel dogs or stray ponies ? "

"With your pardon," said Alan, calmly, but resolutely, " I must ask a more serious answer."

"Why, Mr. Advocate," answered Summertrees, " I thought it was your business to give advice to the lieges, and not to take it from poor stupid country gentlemen."

"If not exactly advice, it is sometimes our duty to ask questions, Mr. Maxwell."

" Ay, sir, when you have your bag-wig and your gown on, we must allow you the usual privilege of both gown and petticoat, to ask what questions you please. But when you are out of your canonicals the case is altered. How come you, sir, to suppose that I have any business with this riotous proceeding, or should know more than you do what happened there ? The question proceeds on an uncivil supposition."

"I will explain," said Alan, determined to give Mr. Maxwell no opportunity of breaking off the conversation. "You are an intimate of Mr. Redgauntlet — he is accused of having been engaged in this affray, and of having placed under forcible restraint the person of my friend, Darsie Latimer, a young man of property and consequence, whose fate I am here for the express purpose of investigating. This is the plain state of the case ; and all parties concerned, — your friend, in particular, — will have reason to be thankful for the temperate manner in which it is my purpose to conduct the matter, if I am treated with proportionate frankness."

"You have misunderstood me," said Maxwell, with a tone changed to more composure ; " I told you I was the friend of the late Sir Henry Redgauntlet, who was executed, in 1745, at Hairibie, near Carlisle, but I know no one who at present bears the name of Redgauntlet."

"You know Mr. Herries of Birrenswork," said Alan, smiling, "to whom the name of Redgauntlet belongs?"

Maxwell darted a keen reproachful look towards the Provost, but instantly smoothed his brow, and changed his tone to that of confidence and candour.

"You must not be angry, Mr. Fairford, that the poor persecuted nonjurors are a little upon the *qui vive* when such clever young men as you are making enquiries after us. I myself now, though I am quite out of the scrape, and may cock my hat at the Cross as I best like, sunshine or moonshine, have been yet so much accustomed to walk with the lap of my cloak cast over my face, that, faith, if a redcoat walk suddenly up to me, I wish for my wheel and whetstone again for a moment. Now Redgauntlet, poor fellow, is far worse off — he is, you may have heard, still under the lash of the law, — the mark of the beast is still on his forehead, poor gentleman, — and that makes us cautious — very cautious — which I am sure there is no occasion to be towards you, as no one of your appearance and manners would wish to trepan a gentleman under misfortune."

"On the contrary, sir," said Fairford, "I wish to afford Mr. Redgauntlet's friends an opportunity to get him out of the scrape, by procuring the instant liberation of my friend Darsie Latimer. I will engage that, if he has sustained no greater bodily harm than a short confinement, the matter may be passed over quietly, without enquiry; but to attain this end, so desirable for the man who

has committed a great and recent infraction of the
laws, which he had before grievously offended, very
speedy reparation of the wrong must be rendered."

Maxwell seemed lost in reflection, and exchanged
a glance or two, not of the most comfortable or
congratulatory kind, with his host the Provost.
Fairford rose and walked about the room, to allow
them an opportunity of conversing together; for he
was in hopes that the impression he had visibly made
upon Summertrees was likely to ripen into something favourable to his purpose. They took the
opportunity, and engaged in whispers to each other,
eagerly and reproachfully on the part of the Laird,
while the Provost answered in an embarrassed and
apologetical tone. Some broken words of the conversation reached Fairford, whose presence they
seemed to forget, as he stood at the bottom of the
room, apparently intent upon examining the figures
upon a fine Indian screen, a present to the Provost
from his brother, captain of a vessel in the Company's service. What he overheard made it evident
that his errand, and the obstinacy with which
he pursued it, occasioned altercation between the
whisperers.

Maxwell at length let out the words, "A good
fright; and so send him home with his tail scalded,
like a dog that has come a-privateering on strange
premises."

The Provost's negative was strongly interposed
— "Not to be thought of" — "making bad worse"
— "my situation" — "my utility" — "you cannot
conceive how obstinate — just like his father."

They then whispered more closely, and at length
the Provost raised his drooping crest, and spoke in
a cheerful tone. "Come, sit down to your glass,

Mr. Fairford; we have laid our heads thegither, and you shall see it will not be our fault if you are not quite pleased, and Mr. Darsie Latimer let loose to take his fiddle under his neck again. But Summertrees thinks it will require you to put yourself into some bodily risk, which maybe you may not be so keen of."

"Gentlemen," said Fairford, " I will not certainly shun any risk by which my object may be accomplished; but I bind it on your consciences — on yours, Mr. Maxwell, as a man of honour and a gentleman; and on yours, Provost, as a magistrate and a loyal subject, that you do not mislead me in this matter."

"Nay, as for me," said Summertrees, "I will tell you the truth at once, and fairly own that I can certainly find you the means of seeing Redgauntlet, poor man; and that I will do, if you require it, and conjure him also to treat you as your errand requires; but poor Redgauntlet is much changed — indeed, to say truth, his temper never was the best in the world; however, I will warrant you from any very great danger."

"I will warrant myself from such," said Fairford, "by carrying a proper force with me."

"Indeed," said Summertrees, "you will do no such thing; for, in the first place, do you think that we will deliver up the poor fellow into the hands of the Philistines, when, on the contrary, my only reason for furnishing you with the clew I am to put into your hands is to settle the matter amicably on all sides? And secondly, his intelligence is so good, that were you coming near him with soldiers, or constables, or the like, I shall answer for it, you will never lay salt on his tail."

Fairford mused for a moment. He considered, that to gain sight of this man, and knowledge of his friend's condition, were advantages to be purchased at every personal risk; and he saw plainly, that were he to take the course most safe for himself, and call in the assistance of the law, it was clear he would either be deprived of the intelligence necessary to guide him, or that Redgauntlet would be apprized of his danger, and might probably leave the country, carrying his captive along with him. He therefore repeated, "I put myself on your honour, Mr. Maxwell; and I will go alone to visit your friend. I have little doubt I shall find him amenable to reason; and that I shall receive from him a satisfactory account of Mr. Latimer."

"I have little doubt that you will," said Mr. Maxwell of Summertrees; "but still I think it will be only in the long run, and after having sustained some delay and inconvenience. My warrandice goes no farther."

"I will take it as it is given," said Alan Fairford. "But let me ask, would it not be better, since you value your friend's safety so highly, and surely would not willingly compromise mine, that the Provost or you should go with me to this man, if he is within any reasonable distance, and try to make him hear reason?"

"Me!—I will not go my foot's length," said the Provost; "and that, Mr. Alan, you may be well assured of. Mr. Redgauntlet is my wife's fourth cousin, that is undeniable; but were he the last of her kin and mine both, it would ill befit my office to be communing with rebels."

"Ay, or drinking with nonjurors," said Maxwell, filling his glass. "I would as soon expect to have met Claverhouse at a field-preaching. And as for myself, Mr. Fairford, I cannot go, for just the opposite reason. It would be *infra dig.* in the Provost of this most flourishing and loyal town to associate with Redgauntlet; and for me, it would be *noscitur a socio.* There would be post to London, with the tidings that two such Jacobites as Redgauntlet and I had met on a braeside — the Habeas Corpus would be suspended — fame would sound a charge from Carlisle to the Land's End — and who knows but the very wind of the rumour might blow my estate from between my fingers, and my body over Errickstane-brae again? No, no; bide a gliff — I will go into the Provost's closet, and write a letter to Redgauntlet, and direct you how to deliver it."

"There is pen and ink in the office," said the Provost, pointing to the door of an inner apartment, in which he had his walnut-tree desk and east-country cabinet.

"A pen that can write, I hope?" said the old Laird.

"It can write and spell baith, — in right hands," answered the Provost, as the Laird retired and shut the door behind him.

# CHAPTER VI.

THE room was no sooner deprived of Mr. Maxwell of Summertrees's presence, than the Provost looked very warily above, beneath, and around the apartment, hitched his chair towards that of his remaining guest, and began to speak in a whisper which could not have startled "the smallest mouse that creeps on floor."

"Mr. Fairford," said he, "you are a good lad; and, what is more, you are my auld friend your father's son. Your father has been agent for this burgh for years, and has a good deal to say with the council; so there have been a sort of obligations between him and me; it may have been now on this side and now on that; but obligations there have been. I am but a plain man, Mr. Fairford; but I hope you understand me?"

"I believe you mean me well, Provost; and I am sure," replied Fairford, "you can never better show your kindness than on this occasion."

"That's it — that's the very point I would be at, Mr. Alan," replied the Provost; "besides, I am, as becomes well my situation, a stanch friend to Kirk and King, meaning this present establishment in Church and State; and so, as I was saying, you may command my best—advice."

"I hope for your assistance and co-operation also," said the youth.

"Certainly, certainly," said the wary magistrate.
"Well, now, you see one may love the Kirk, and
yet not ride on the rigging of it; and one may
love the King, and yet not be cramming him
eternally down the throat of the unhappy folk
that may chance to like another King better. I
have friends and connexions among them, Mr.
Fairford, as your father may have clients — they
are flesh and blood like ourselves, these poor
Jacobite bodies — sons of Adam and Eve, after
all; and therefore — I hope you understand me? —
I am a plain-spoken man."

"I am afraid I do *not* quite understand you,"
said Fairford; "and if you have any thing to say
to me in private, my dear Provost, you had better
come quickly out with it, for the Laird of Summertrees must finish his letter in a minute or two."

"Not a bit, man — Pate is a lang-headed fellow,
but his pen does not clear the paper as his grey-
hound does the Tinwald-furs. I gave him a wipe
about that, if you noticed; I can say any thing
to Pate-in-Peril — indeed, he is my wife's near
kinsman."

"But your advice, Provost," said Alan, who
perceived that, like a shy horse, the worthy magistrate always started off from his own purpose just
when he seemed approaching to it.

"Weel, you shall have it in plain terms, for I
am a plain man. — Ye see, we will suppose that any
friend like yourself were in the deepest hole of the
Nith, and making a sprattle for your life. Now,
you see, such being the case, I have little chance
of helping you, being a fat, short-armed man, and
no swimmer, and what would be the use of my
jumping in after you?"

" I understand you, I think," said Alan Fairford.
" You think that Darsie Latimer is in danger of
his life."

" Me ! — I think nothing about it, Mr. Alan ; but
if he were, as I trust he is not, he is nae drap's
blood akin to you, Mr. Alan."

" But here your friend, Summertrees," said the
young lawyer, " offers me a letter to this Redgauntlet of yours — What say you to that ? "

" Me ! " ejaculated the Provost, " me, Mr. Alan ? I
say neither buff nor stye to it — But ye dinna ken
what it is to look a Redgauntlet in the face ; —
better try my wife, who is but a fourth cousin,
before ye venture on the Laird himself — just say
something about the Revolution, and see what a
look she can gie you."

" I shall leave you to stand all the shots from
that battery, Provost," replied Fairford. " But
speak out like a man — Do you think Summertrees
means fairly by me ? "

" Fairly — he is just coming — fairly ? I am a
plain man, Mr. Fairford — but ye said *Fairly ?* "

" I do so," replied Alan, " and it is of importance
to me to know, and to you to tell me, if such is the
case ; for if you do not, you may be an accomplice to
murder before the fact, and that under circumstances
which may bring it near to murder under trust."

" Murder ! — who spoke of murder ? " said the
Provost ; " no danger of that, Mr. Alan — only, if
I were you — to speak my plain mind " — Here he
approached his mouth to the ear of the young
lawyer, and, after another acute pang of travail,
was safely delivered of his advice in the following
abrupt words : — " Take a keek into Pate's letter
before ye deliver it."

Fairford started, looked the Provost hard in the face, and was silent; while Mr. Crosbie, with the self-approbation of one who has at length brought himself to the discharge of a great duty, at the expense of a considerable sacrifice, nodded and winked to Alan, as if enforcing his advice; and then swallowing a large glass of punch, concluded, with the sigh of a man released from a heavy burden, "I am a plain man, Mr. Fairford."

"A plain man?" said Maxwell, who entered the room at that moment, with the letter in his hand, — "Provost, I never heard you make use of the word but when you had some sly turn of your own to work out."

The Provost looked silly enough, and the Laird of Summertrees directed a keen and suspicious glance upon Alan Fairford, who sustained it with professional intrepidity. — There was a moment's pause.

"I was trying," said the Provost, "to dissuade our young friend from his wildgoose expedition."

"And I," said Fairford, "am determined to go through with it. Trusting myself to you, Mr. Maxwell, I conceive that I rely, as I before said, on the word of a gentleman."

"I will warrant you," said Maxwell, "from all serious consequences — some inconveniences you must look to suffer."

"To these I shall be resigned," said Fairford, "and stand prepared to run my risk."

"Well, then," said Summertrees, "you must go" ——

"I will leave you to yourselves, gentlemen," said the Provost, rising; "when you have done with your crack, you will find me at my wife's tea-table."

"And a more accomplished old woman never drank cat-lap," said Maxwell, as he shut the door; "the last word has him, speak it who will — and yet because he is a whilly-whaw body, and has a plausible tongue of his own, and is well enough connected, and especially because nobody could ever find out whether he is Whig or Tory, this is the third time they have made him Provost! — But to the matter in hand. This letter, Mr. Fairford," putting a sealed one into his hand, "is addressed, you observe, to Mr. H—— of B——, and contains your credentials for that gentleman, who is also known by his family name of Redgauntlet, but less frequently addressed by it, because it is mentioned something invidiously in a certain Act of Parliament. I have little doubt he will assure you of your friend's safety, and in a short time place him at freedom — that is, supposing him under present restraint. But the point is, to discover where he is — and, before you are made acquainted with this necessary part of the business, you must give me your assurance of honour that you will acquaint no one, either by word or letter, with the expedition which you now propose to yourself."

"How, sir?" answered Alan; "can you expect that I will not take the precaution of informing some person of the route I am about to take, that in case of accident it may be known where I am, and with what purpose I have gone thither?"

"And can you expect," answered Maxwell, in the same tone, "that I am to place my friend's safety, not merely in your hands, but in those of any person you may choose to confide in, and who may use the knowledge to his destruction? — Na — na — I have pledged my word for your safety, and you must give me yours to be private in the matter—giff-gaff, you know."

Alan Fairford could not help thinking that this obligation to secrecy gave a new and suspicious colouring to the whole transaction; but, considering that his friend's release might depend upon his accepting the condition, he gave it in the terms proposed, and with the resolution of abiding by it.

"And now, sir," he said, "whither am I to proceed with this letter? Is Mr. Herries at Brokenburn?"

"He is not: I do not think he will come thither again, until the business of the stake-nets be hushed up, nor would I advise him to do so — the Quakers, with all their demureness, can bear malice as long as other folk; and though I have not the prudence of Mr. Provost, who refuses to ken where his friends are concealed during adversity, lest, perchance, he should be asked to contribute to their relief, yet I do not think it necessary or prudent to enquire into Redgauntlet's wanderings, poor man, but wish to remain at perfect freedom to answer, if asked at, that I ken nothing of the matter. You must, then, go to old Tom Trumbull's, at Annan — Tam Turnpenny, as they call him, — and he is sure either to know where Redgauntlet is himself, or to find some one who can give a shrewd guess. But you must attend that old Turnpenny will answer no question on such a subject without you give him the password, which at present you must do, by asking him the age of the moon; if he answers, 'Not light enough to land a cargo,' you are to answer, 'Then plague on Aberdeen Almanacks,' and upon that he will hold free intercourse with you. — And now, I would advise you to lose no time, for the parole is often changed — and take care of yourself among these moonlight lads, for laws and lawyers do not stand very high in their favour."

"I will set out this instant," said the young barrister; "I will but bid the Provost and Mrs. Crosbie farewell, and then get on horseback so soon as the hostler of the George Inn can saddle him; — as for the smugglers, I am neither gauger nor supervisor, and, like the man who met the devil, if they have nothing to say to me, I have nothing to say to them."

" You are a mettled young man," said Summertrees, evidently with increasing good-will, on observing an alertness and contempt .of danger, which perhaps he did not expect from Alan's appearance and profession, — " a very mettled young fellow indeed! and it is almost a pity " —— Here he stopped short.

" What is a pity ? " said Fairford.

" It is almost a pity that I cannot go with you myself, or at least send a trusty guide."

They walked together to the bedchamber of Mrs. Crosbie, for it was in that asylum that the ladies of the period dispensed their tea, when the parlour was occupied by the punch-bowl.

" You have been good bairns to-night, gentlemen," said Mrs. Crosbie: " I am afraid, Summertrees, that the Provost has given you a bad browst; you are not used to quit the lee-side of the punch-bowl in such a hurry. I say nothing to you, Mr. Fairford, for you are too young a man yet for stoup and bicker; but I hope you will not tell the Edinburgh fine folk that the Provost has scrimped you of your cogie, as the sang says ? "

" I am much obliged for the Provost's kindness,

and yours, madam," replied Alan; "but the truth
is, I have still a long ride before me this evening,
and the sooner I am on horseback the better."

"This evening?" said the Provost, anxiously;
"had you not better take daylight with you to-
morrow morning?"

"Mr. Fairford will ride as well in the cool of the
evening," said Summertrees, taking the word out
of Alan's mouth.

The Provost said no more, nor did his wife ask
any questions, nor testify any surprise at the sud-
denness of their guest's departure.

Having drunk tea, Alan Fairford took leave
with the usual ceremony. The Laird of Summertrees seemed studious to prevent any further
communication between him and the Provost, and
remained lounging on the landing-place of the stair
while they made their adieus — heard the Provost
ask if Alan proposed a speedy return, and the latter
reply that his stay was uncertain, and witnessed
the parting shake of the hand, which, with a pressure more warm than usual, and a tremulous, "God
bless and prosper you!" Mr. Crosbie bestowed on
his young friend. Maxwell even strolled with
Fairford as far as the George, although resisting all
his attempts at further enquiry into the affairs of
Redgauntlet, and referring him to Tom Trumbull,
alias Turnpenny, for the particulars which he might
find it necessary to enquire into.

At length Alan's hack was produced; an animal
long in neck, and high in bone, accoutred with a
pair of saddle-bags containing the rider's travelling
wardrobe. Proudly surmounting his small stock
of necessaries, and no way ashamed of a mode of
travelling which a modern Mr. Silvertongue would

consider as the last of degradations, Alan Fairford
took leave of the old Jacobite, Pate-in-Peril, and
set forward on the road to the royal burgh of Annan.
His reflections during his ride were none of the
most pleasant. He could not disguise from himself that he was venturing rather too rashly into
the power of outlawed and desperate persons; for
with such only, a man in the situation of Redgauntlet could be supposed to associate. There were
other grounds for apprehension. Several marks of
intelligence betwixt Mrs. Crosbie and the Laird of
Summertrees had not escaped Alan's acute observation; and it was plain that the Provost's inclinations
towards him, which he believed to be sincere and
good, were not firm enough to withstand the
influence of this league between his wife and friend.
The Provost's adieus, like Macbeth's amen, had stuck
in his throat, and seemed to intimate that he apprehended more than he dared give utterance to.

Laying all these matters together, Alan thought,
with no little anxiety, on the celebrated lines of
Shakspeare,

A drop,<br>
That in the ocean seeks another drop, &c.

But pertinacity was a strong feature in the young
lawyer's character. He was, and always had been,
totally unlike the "horse hot at hand," who tires
before noon through his own over eager exertions
in the beginning of the day. On the contrary, his
first efforts seemed frequently inadequate to accomplishing his purpose, whatever that for the time
might be; and it was only as the difficulties of the
task increased, that his mind seemed to acquire the
energy necessary to combat and subdue them. If,
therefore, he went anxiously forward upon his

uncertain and perilous expedition, the reader must acquit him of all idea, even in a passing thought, of the possibility of abandoning his search, and resigning Darsie Latimer to his destiny.

A couple of hours' riding brought him to the little town of Annan, situated on the shores of the Solway, between eight and nine o'clock. The sun had set, but the day was not yet ended; and when he had alighted and seen his horse properly cared for at the principal inn of the place, he was readily directed to Mr. Maxwell's friend, old Tom Trumbull, with whom every body seemed well acquainted. He endeavoured to fish out from the lad that acted as a guide something of this man's situation and profession; but the general expressions of "a very decent man" — "a very honest body" — "weel to pass in the world," and such like, were all that could be extracted from him; and while Fairford was following up the investigation with closer interrogatories, the lad put an end to them by knocking at the door of Mr. Trumbull, whose decent dwelling was a little distance from the town, and considerably nearer to the sea. It was one of a little row of houses running down to the waterside, and having gardens and other accommodations behind. There was heard within the uplifting of a Scottish psalm; and the boy saying, "They are at exercise, sir," gave intimation they might not be admitted till prayers were over.

When, however, Fairford repeated the summons with the end of his whip, the singing ceased, and Mr. Trumbull himself, with his psalm-book in his hand, kept open by the insertion of his forefinger between the leaves, came to demand the meaning of this unseasonable interruption.

Nothing could be more different than his whole appearance seemed to be from the confidant of a desperate man, and the associate of outlaws in their unlawful enterprises. He was a tall, thin, bony figure, with white hair combed straight down on each side of his face, and an iron-grey hue of complexion; where the lines, or rather, as Quin said of Macklin, the cordage, of his countenance were so sternly adapted to a devotional and even ascetic expression, that they left no room for any indication of reckless daring or sly dissimulation. In short, Trumbull appeared a perfect specimen of the rigid old Covenanter, who said only what he thought right, acted on no other principle but that of duty, and, if he committed errors, did so under the full impression that he was serving God rather than man.

"Do you want me, sir?" he said to Fairford, whose guide had slunk to the rear, as if to escape the rebuke of the severe old man.—"We were engaged, and it is the Saturday night."

Alan Fairford's preconceptions were so much deranged by this man's appearance and manner, that he stood for a moment bewildered, and would as soon have thought of giving a cant pass-word to a clergyman descending from the pulpit, as to the respectable father of a family just interrupted in his prayers for and with the objects of his care. Hastily concluding Mr. Maxwell had passed some idle jest on him, or rather that he had mistaken the person to whom he was directed, he asked if he spoke to Mr. Trumbull.

"To Thomas Trumbull," answered the old man —"What may be your business, sir?" And he glanced his eye to the book he held in his hand,

with a sigh like that of a saint desirous of
dissolution.

"Do you know Mr. Maxwell of Summertrees?"
said Fairford.

"I have heard of such a gentleman in the country-side, but have no acquaintance with him,"
answered Mr. Trumbull; "he is, as I have heard, a
Papist; for the whore that sitteth on the seven
hills ceaseth not yet to pour forth the cup of her
abomination on these parts."

"Yet he directed me hither, my good friend,"
said Alan. "Is there another of your name in
this town of Annan?"

"None," replied Mr. Trumbull, "since my worthy
father was removed; he was indeed a shining light.
— I wish you good-even, sir."

"Stay one single instant," said Fairford; "this
is a matter of life and death."

"Not more than the casting the burden of our
sins where they should be laid," said Thomas Trumbull, about to shut the door in the enquirer's face.

"Do you know," said Alan Fairford, "the Laird
of Redgauntlet?"

"Now Heaven defend me from treason and rebellion!" exclaimed Trumbull. "Young gentleman,
you are importunate. I live here among my own
people, and do not consort with Jacobites and
mass-mongers."

He seemed about to shut the door, but did *not*
shut it, a circumstance which did not escape Alan's
notice.

"Mr. Redgauntlet is sometimes," he said, "called
Herries of Birrenswork; perhaps you may know
him under that name."

"Friend, you are uncivil," answered Mr. Trumbull; "honest men have enough to do to keep one name undefiled. I ken nothing about those who have two. Good-even to you, friend."

He was now about to slam the door in his visitor's face without further ceremony, when Alan, who had observed symptoms that the name of Redgauntlet did not seem altogether so indifferent to him as he pretended, arrested his purpose by saying, in a low voice, "At least you can tell me what age the moon is?"

The old man started, as if from a trance, and, before answering, surveyed the querist with a keen penetrating glance, which seemed to say, "Are you really in possession of this key to my confidence, or do you speak from mere accident?"

To this keen look of scrutiny, Fairford replied by a smile of intelligence.

The iron muscles of the old man's face did not, however, relax, as he dropped, in a careless manner, the countersign, "Not light enough to land a cargo."

"Then plague of all Aberdeen Almanacks!"

"And plague of all fools that waste time," said Thomas Trumbull. "Could you not have said as much at first? — And standing wasting time, and encouraging lookers-on, in the open street too? Come in by — in by."

He drew his visitor into the dark entrance of the house, and shut the door carefully; then putting his head into an apartment which the murmurs within announced to be filled with the family, he said aloud, "A work of necessity and mercy — Malachi, take the book — you will sing six double verses of the hundred and nineteen — and you may lecture out of the Lamentations. And, Malachi,"

— this he said in an under tone, — " see you give them a screed of doctrine that will last them till I come back ; or else these inconsiderate lads will be out of the house, and away to the publics, wasting their precious time, and, it may be, putting themselves in the way of missing the morning tide."

An inarticulate answer from within intimated Malachi's acquiescence in the commands imposed; and Mr. Trumbull, shutting the door, muttered something about fast bind, fast find, turned the key, and put it into his pocket; and then bidding his visitor have a care of his steps, and make no noise, he led him through the house, and out at a back-door, into a little garden. Here a plaited alley conducted them, without the possibility of their being seen by any neighbour, to a door in the garden-wall, which being opened proved to be a private entrance into a three-stalled stable; in one of which was a horse, that whinnied on their entrance. "Hush, hush!" cried the old man, and presently seconded his exhortations to silence by throwing a handful of corn into the manger, and the horse soon converted his acknowledgment of their presence into the usual sound of munching and grinding his provender.

As the light was now failing fast, the old man, with much more alertness than might have been expected from the rigidity of his figure, closed the window-shutters in an instant, produced phosphorus and matches, and lighted a stable-lantern, which he placed on the corn bin, and then addressed Fairford. "We are private here, young man ; and as some time has been wasted already, you will be so kind as to tell me what is your errand. Is it about the way of business, or the other job?"

" My business with you, Mr. Trumbull, is to request you will find me the means of delivering this letter from Mr. Maxwell of Summertrees to the Laird of Redgauntlet."

"Humph — fashious job ! — Pate Maxwell will still be the auld man — always Pate-in-Peril — Craig-in-Peril, for what I know. Let me see the letter from him."

He examined it with much care, turning it up and down, and looking at the seal very attentively. " All's right, I see; it has the private mark for haste and speed. I bless my Maker that I am no great man, or great man's fellow; and so I think no more of these passages than just to help them forward in the way of business. You are an utter stranger in these parts, I warrant ? "

Fairford answered in the affirmative.

" Ay — I never saw them make a wiser choice — I must call some one to direct you what to do — Stay, we must go to him, I believe. You are well recommended to me, friend, and doubtless trusty; otherwise you may see more than I would like to show, or am in the use of showing in the common line of business."

Saying this, he placed his lantern on the ground, beside the post of one of the empty stalls, drew up a small spring-bolt which secured it to the floor, and then forcing the post to one side, discovered a small trap-door. " Follow me," he said, and dived into the subterranean descent to which this secret aperture gave access.

Fairford plunged after him, not without apprehensions of more kinds than one, but still resolved to prosecute the adventure.

The descent, which was not above six feet, led

to a very narrow passage, which seemed to have
been constructed for the precise purpose of exclud-
ing every one who chanced to be an inch more
in girth than was his conductor. A small vaulted
room, of about eight feet square, received them at
the end of this lane. Here Mr. Trumbull left
Fairford alone, and returned for an instant, as he
said, to shut his concealed trapdoor.

Fairford liked not his departure, as it left him
in utter darkness; besides that his breathing was
much affected by a strong and stifling smell of
spirits, and other articles of a savour more powerful than agreeable to the lungs. He was very glad,
therefore, when he heard the returning steps of
Mr. Trumbull, who, when once more by his side,
opened a strong though narrow door in the wall,
and conveyed Fairford into an immense magazine
of spirit-casks, and other articles of contraband trade.

There was a small light at the end of this range
of well-stocked subterranean vaults, which, upon a
low whistle, began to flicker and move towards
them. An undefined figure, holding a dark lantern,
with the light averted, approached them, whom
Mr. Trumbull thus addressed: — "Why were you
not at worship, Job; and this Saturday at e'en?"

"Swanston was loading the Jenny, sir; and I
stayed to serve out the article."

"True — a work of necessity, and in the way of
business. Does the Jumping Jenny sail this tide?"

"Ay, ay, sir; she sails for " ——

"I did not ask you *where* she sailed for, Job,"
said the old gentleman, interrupting him. "I
thank my Maker, I know nothing of their incomings or outgoings. I sell my article fairly and in
the ordinary way of business; and I wash my

hands of every thing else. But what I wished to know is, whether the gentleman called the Laird of the Solway Lakes is on the other side of the Border even now ? ”

“ Ay, ay,” said Job, “ the Laird is something in my own line, you know — a little contraband or so. There is a statute for him — But no matter ; he took the sands after the splore at the Quaker’s fish-traps yonder ; for he has a leal heart, the Laird, and is always true to the country-side. But avast — is all snug here ? ”

So saying, he suddenly turned on Alan Fairford the light side of the lantern he carried, who, by the transient gleam which it threw in passing on the man who bore it, saw a huge figure, upwards of six feet high, with a rough hairy cap on his head, and a set of features corresponding to his bulky frame. He thought also he observed pistols at his belt.

“ I will answer for this gentleman,” said Mr. Trumbull ; “ he must be brought to speech of the Laird.”

“ That will be kittle steering,” said the subordinate personage ; “ for I understood that the Laird and his folk were no sooner on the other side than the land-sharks were on them, and some mounted lobsters from Carlisle ; and so they were obliged to split and squander. There are new brooms out to sweep the country of them, they say ; for the brush was a hard one ; and they say there was a lad drowned ; — he was not one of the Laird’s gang, so there was the less matter.”

“ Peace ! prithee, peace, Job Rutledge,” said honest, pacific Mr. Trumbull. “ I wish thou couldst remember, man, that I desire to know nothing of your roars and splores, your brooms and brushes.

I dwell here among my own people; and I sell my commodity to him who comes in the way of business; and so wash my hands of all consequences, as becomes a quiet subject and an honest man. I never take payment, save in ready money."

"Ay, ay," muttered he with the lantern, "your worship, Mr. Trumbull, understands that in the way of business."

"Well, I hope you will one day know, Job," answered Mr. Trumbull, —"the comfort of a conscience void of offence, and that fears neither gauger nor collector, neither excise nor customs. The business is to pass this gentleman to Cumberland upon earnest business, and to procure him speech with the Laird of the Solway Lakes — I suppose that can be done? Now I think Nanty Ewart, if he sails with the brig this morning tide, is the man to set him forward."

"Ay, ay, truly is he," said Job; "never man knew the Border, dale and fell, pasture and ploughland, better than Nauty; and he can always bring him to the Laird, too, if you are sure the gentleman's right. But indeed that's his own look-out; for were he the best man in Scotland, and the chairman of the d—d Board to boot, and had fifty men at his back, he were as well not visit the Laird for any thing but good. As for Nanty, he is word and blow, a d—d deal fiercer than Cristie Nixon that they keep such a din about. I have seen them both tried, by ——."

Fairford now found himself called upon to say something; yet his feelings, upon finding himself thus completely in the power of a canting hypocrite, and of his retainer, who had so much the air of a determined ruffian, joined to the strong and

abominable fume which they snuffed up with indifference, while it almost deprived him of respiration,
combined to render utterance difficult. He stated,
however, that he had no evil intentions towards the
Laird, as they called him, but was only the bearer
of a letter to him on particular business, from Mr.
Maxwell of Summertrees.

"Ay, ay," said Job, " that may be well enough ;
and if Mr. Trumbull is satisfied that the scrive is
right, why, we will give you a cast in the Jumping
Jenny this tide, and Nanty Ewart will put you on
a way of finding the Laird, I warrant you."

" I may for the present return, I presume, to the
inn where I have left my horse ? " said Fairford.

"With pardon," replied Mr. Trumbull, "you
have been ower far ben with us for that; but Job
will take you to a place where you may sleep rough
till he calls you. I will bring you what little baggage you can need — for those who go on such
errands must not be dainty. I will myself see
after your horse, for a merciful man is merciful to
his beast — a matter too often forgotten in our way
of business."

" Why, Master Trumbull," replied Job, "you
know that when we are chased, it's no time to
shorten sail, and so the boys do ride whip and
spur " —— He stopped in his speech, observing the
old man had vanished through the door by which
he had entered — " That's always the way with old
Turnpenny," he said to Fairford; "he cares for
nothing of the trade but the profit — now, d— me,
if I don't think the fun of it is better worth while.
But come along, my fine chap; I must stow you
away in safety until it is time to go aboard."

# CHAPTER VII.

FAIRFORD followed his gruff guide among a labyrinth of barrels and puncheons, on which he had more than once like to have broken his nose, and from thence into what, by the glimpse of the passing lantern upon a desk and writing materials, seemed to be a small offioe for the dispatch of business. Here there appeared no exit; but the smuggler, or smuggler's ally, availing himself of a ladder, seven feet from the ground, and Fairford, still following Job, was involved in another tortuous and dark passage, which involuntarily reminded him of Peter Peebles's lawsuit. At the end of this labyrinth, when he had little guess where he had been conducted, and was, according to the French phrase, totally *désorienté*, Job suddenly set down the lantern, and availing himself of the flame to light two candles which stood on the table, asked if Alan would choose any thing to eat, recommending, at all events, a slug of brandy to keep out the night air. Fairford declined both, but enquired after his baggage.

"The old master will take care of that himself," said Job Rutledge; and drawing back in the direction in which he had entered, he vanished from the further end of the apartment, by a mode which the candles, still shedding an imperfect light, gave Alan no means of ascertaining. Thus the adventurous young lawyer was left alone in the apartment to

which he had been conducted by so singular a
passage.

In this condition, it was Alan's **first** employment
to survey, with some accuracy, the place where he
was ; and accordingly, having trimmed the lights,
he walked slowly round the apartment, examining
its appearance and dimensions.   It seemed to be such
a small dining-parlour as is usually found in the
house of the better class of artisans, shopkeepers,
and such persons, having a recess at the upper end,
and the usual furniture of an ordinary description.
He found a door, which he endeavoured to open, but
it was locked on the outside.   A corresponding door
on the same side of the apartment admitted **him** into
a closet, upon the front shelves of which were punch-
bowls, glasses, tea-cups, and the like, while on one
side was hung a horseman's great-coat of the coarsest
materials, with two great horse-pistols peeping out
of the pocket, and on the floor stood a pair of well-
spattered jack-boots, the usual equipment of the
time, at least for long journeys.

Not greatly liking the contents of the closet, Alan
Fairford shut the door, and resumed his scrutiny
round the walls of the apartment, in order to discover
the mode of Job Rutledge's retreat.   The secret
passage was, however, too artificially concealed, and
the young lawyer had nothing better to do than to
meditate on the singularity of his present situation.
He had long known that the excise laws had occasioned an active contraband trade betwixt Scotland
and England, which then, as now, existed, and will
continue to exist, until the utter abolition of the
wretched system which establishes an inequality of
duties betwixt the different parts of the same kingdom; a system, be it said in passing, mightily

resembling the conduct of a pugilist, who should tie up one arm that he might fight the better with the other. But Fairford was unprepared for the expensive and regular establishments by which the illicit traffic was carried on, and could not have conceived that the capital employed in it should have been adequate to the erection of these extensive buildings, with all their contrivances for secrecy of communication. He was musing on these circumstances, not without some anxiety for the progress of his own journey, when suddenly, as he lifted his eyes, he discovered old Mr. Trumbull at the upper end of the apartment, bearing in one hand a small bundle, in the other his dark lantern, the light of which, as he advanced, he directed full upon Fairford's countenance.

Though such an apparition was exactly what he expected, yet he did not see the grim, stern old man present himself thus suddenly without emotion; especially when he recollected, what to a youth of his pious education was peculiarly shocking, that the grizzled hypocrite was probably that instant arisen from his knees to Heaven, for the purpose of engaging in the mysterious transactions of a desperate and illegal trade.

The old man, accustomed to judge with ready sharpness of the physiognomy of those with whom he had business, did not fail to remark something like agitation in Fairford's demeanour. "Have ye taken the rue?" said he. "Will ye take the sheaf from the mare, and give up the venture?"

"Never!" said Fairford, firmly, stimulated at once by his natural spirit, and the recollection of his friend; "never, while I have life and strength to follow it out!"

"I have brought you," said Trumbull, "a clean shirt and some stockings, which is all the baggage you can conveniently carry, and I will cause one of the lads lend you a horseman's coat, for it is ill sailing or riding without one; and, touching your valise, it will be as safe in my poor house, were it full of the gold of Ophir, as if it were in the depth of the mine."

"I have no doubt of it," said Fairford.

"And now," said Trumbull, again, "I pray you to tell me by what name I am to name you to Nanty [which is Antony] Ewart?"

"By the name of Alan Fairford," answered the young lawyer.

"But that," said Mr. Trumbull, in reply, "is your own proper name and surname."

"And what other should I give?" said the young man; "do you think I have any occasion for an alias? And besides, Mr. Trumbull," added Alan, thinking a little raillery might intimate confidence of spirit, "you blessed yourself, but a little while since, that you had no acquaintance with those who defiled their names so far as to be obliged to change them."

"True, very true," said Mr. Trumbull; "nevertheless, young man, my grey hairs stand unreproved in this matter; for, in my line of business, when I sit under my vine and my fig-tree, exchanging the strong waters of the north for the gold which is the price thereof, I have, I thank Heaven, no disguises to keep with any man, and wear my own name of Thomas Trumbull, without any chance that the same may be polluted. Whereas, thou, who art to journey in miry ways, and amongst a strange people, mayst do well to have two names, as thou hast two shirts, the one to keep the other clean."

Here he emitted a chuckling grunt, which lasted for two vibrations of the pendulum exactly, and was the only approach towards laughter in which old **Turnpenny**, as he was nicknamed, was ever known to indulge.

"You are witty, Mr. Trumbull," said Fairford; "but jests are no arguments — I shall keep my own name."

"At your own pleasure," said the merchant; "there is but one name which," &c. &c. &c.

We will not follow the hypocrite through the impious cant which he added, in order to close the subject.

Alan followed him, in silent abhorrence, to the recess in which the beaufet was placed, and which was so artificially made as to conceal another of those traps with which the whole building abounded. This concealment admitted them to the same winding passage by which the young lawyer had been brought thither. The path which they now took amid these mazes differed from the direction in which he had been guided by Rutledge. It led upwards, and terminated beneath a garret window. Trumbull opened it, and, with more agility than his age promised, clambered out upon the leads. If Fairford's journey had been hitherto in a stifled and subterranean atmosphere, it was now open, lofty, and airy enough; for he had to follow his guide over leads and slates, which the old smuggler traversed with the dexterity of a cat. It is true his course was facilitated by knowing exactly where certain stepping-places and holdfasts were placed, of which Fairford could not so readily avail himself; but, after a difficult and somewhat perilous progress along the roofs of two or three houses, they at length descended by a skylight into a garret room, and from thence by the stairs into a public-house; for such it appeared by the ringing of bells, whistling for waiters and attendance, bawling of "House, house, here!" chorus of sea songs, and the like noises.

Having descended to the second story, and entered a room there, in which there was a light, old Mr. Trumbull rung the bell of the apartment thrice, with an interval betwixt each, during which he told deliberately the number twenty. Immediately after the third ringing the landlord appeared, with stealthy step, and an appearance of mystery on his buxom visage. He greeted Mr. Trumbull, who was his landlord as it proved, with great respect, and expressed some surprise at seeing him so late, as he termed it, " on Saturday at e'en."

"And I, Robin Hastie," said the landlord to the tenant, "am more surprised than pleased to hear sae muckle din in your house, Robie, so near the honourable Sabbath; and I must mind you that it is contravening the terms of your tack, whilk stipulate that you should shut your public on Saturday at nine o'clock, at latest."

"Yes, sir," said Robin Hastie, no way alarmed at the gravity of the rebuke, "but you must take tent that I have admitted naebody but you, Mr. Trumbull, (who, by the way, admitted yoursell,) since nine o'clock; for the most of the folk have been here for several hours about the lading, and so on, of the brig. It is not full tide yet, and I cannot put the men out into the street. If I did, they would go to some other public, and their souls

would be nane the better, and my purse muckle the
waur; for how am I to pay the rent, if I do not sell
the liquor?"

"Nay, then," said Thomas Trumbull, "if it is
a work of necessity, and in the honest independent
way of business, no doubt there is balm in Gilead.
But prithee, Robin, wilt thou see if Nanty Ewart
be, as is most likely, amongst these unhappy topers;
and if so, let him step this way cannily, and speak
to me and this young gentleman. And it's dry
talking, Robin — you must minister to us a bowl of
punch — ye ken my gage."

"From a mutchkin to a gallon, I ken your honour's taste, Mr. Thomas Trumbull," said mine host;
"and ye shall hang me over the sign-post if there
be a drap mair lemon or a curn less sugar than
just suits you. There are three of you — you will
be for the auld Scots peremptory pint-stoup [1] for
the success of the voyage?"

"Better pray for it than drink for it, Robin,"
said Mr. Trumbull. "Yours is a dangerous trade,
Robin; it hurts mony a ane — baith host and guest.
But ye will get the blue bowl, Robin — the blue
bowl — that will sloken all their drouth, and prevent
the sinful repetition of whipping for an eke of a
Saturday at e'en. Ay, Robin, it is a pity of Nanty
Ewart — Nanty likes the turning up of his little
finger unco weel, and we maunna stint him, Robin,
so as we leave him sense to steer by."

"Nanty Ewart could steer through the Pentland

---

[1] The Scottish pint of liquid measure comprehends four English
measures of the same denomination. The jest is well known of
my poor countryman, who, driven to extremity by the raillery
of the Southern, on the small denomination of the Scottish coin,
at length answered, "Ay, ay! But the deil tak them that has the
*least pint-stoup.*"

Frith though he were as drunk as the Baltic Ocean," said Robin Hastie; and instantly tripping down stairs, he speedily returned with the materials for what he called his *browst*, which consisted of two English quarts of spirits, in a huge blue bowl, with all the ingredients for punch in the same formidable proportion. At the same time he introduced Mr. Antony or Nanty Ewart, whose person, although he was a good deal flustered with liquor, was different from what Fairford expected. His dress was what is emphatically termed the shabby genteel — a frock with tarnished lace — a small cocked-hat, ornamented in a similar way — a scarlet waistcoat, with faded embroidery, breeches of the same, with silver knee-bands, and he wore a smart hanger and a pair of pistols in a sullied sword-belt.

"Here I come, patron," he said, shaking hands with Mr. Trumbull. "Well, I see you have got some grog aboard."

"It is not my custom, Mr. Ewart," said the old gentleman, "as you well know, to become a chamberer or carouser thus late on Saturday at e'en; but I wanted to recommend to your attention a young friend of ours, that is going upon a something particular journey, with a letter to our friend the Laird, from Pate-in-Peril, as they call him."

"Ay — indeed? — he must be in high trust for so young a gentleman. — I wish you joy, sir," bowing to Fairford. "By'r lady, as Shakspeare says, you are bringing up a neck to a fair end. — Come, patron, we will drink to Mr. What-shall-call-um — What is his name? — Did you tell me? — And have I forgot it already?"

" Mr. Alan Fairford," said Trumbull.

" Ay, Mr. Alan Fairford — a good name for a fair
trader — Mr. Alan Fairford; and may he be long
withheld from the topmost round of ambition, which
I take to be the highest round of a certain ladder."

While he spoke, he seized the punch ladle, and
began to fill the glasses. But Mr. Trumbull
arrested his hand, until he had, as he expressed
himself, sanctified the liquor by a long grace;
during the pronunciation of which he shut indeed
his eyes, but his nostrils became dilated, as if he
were snuffing up the fragrant beverage with peculiar
complacency.

When the grace was at length over, the three
friends sat down to their beverage, and invited
Alan Fairford to partake. Anxious about his
situation, and disgusted as he was with his company, he craved, and with difficulty obtained
permission, under the allegation of being fatigued,
heated, and the like, to stretch himself on a couch
which was in the apartment, and attempted at least
to procure some rest before high water, when the
vessel was to sail.

He was at length permitted to use his freedom,
and stretched himself on the couch, having his
eyes for some time fixed on the jovial party he
had left, and straining his ears to catch if possible
a little of their conversation. This he soon found
was to no purpose; for what did actually reach
his ears was disguised so completely by the use of
cant words, and the thieves-Latin called slang,
that even when he caught the words he found
himself as far as ever from the sense of their
conversation. At length he fell asleep.

It was after Alan had slumbered for three or

rwn by Sir James D.Linton, P.R.I. Etched by C.E.Deblois

NANTY EWART.

four hours that he was wakened by voices bidding him rise up and prepare to be jogging. He started up accordingly, and found himself in presence of the same party of boon companions, who had just dispatched their huge bowl of punch. To Alan's surprise, the liquor had made but little innovation on the brains of men who were accustomed to drink at all hours, and in the most inordinate quantities. The landlord indeed spoke a little thick, and the texts of Mr. Thomas Trumbull stumbled on his tongue; but Nanty was one of those topers who, becoming early what *bon vivants* term flustered, remain whole nights and days at the same point of intoxication; and, in fact, as they are seldom entirely sober, can be as rarely seen absolutely drunk. Indeed, Fairford, had he not known how Ewart had been engaged whilst he himself was asleep, would almost have sworn when he awoke that the man was more sober than when he first entered the room.

He was confirmed in this opinion when they descended below, where two or three sailors and ruffian-looking fellows awaited their commands. Ewart took the whole direction upon himself, gave his orders with briefness and precision, and looked to their being executed with the silence and celerity which that peculiar crisis required. All were now dismissed for the brig, which lay, as Fairford was given to understand, a little farther down the river, which is navigable for vessels of light burden till almost within a mile of the town.

When they issued from the inn, the landlord bid them good-by. Old Trumbull walked a little way with them, but the air had probably considerable effect on the state of his brain; for, after reminding

Alan Fairford that the next day was the honourable Sabbath, he became extremely excursive in an
attempt to exhort him to keep it holy. At length,
being perhaps sensible that he was becoming unin-
telligible, he thrust a volume into Fairford's hand
— hiccupping at the same time — "Good book —
good book — fine hymn-book — fit for the honourable Sabbath, whilk awaits us to-morrow morning."
— Here the iron tongue of time told five from the
town steeple of Annan, to the further confusion of
Mr. Trumbull's already disordered ideas. "Ay?
is Sunday come and gone already? — Heaven be
praised! Only it is a marvel the afternoon is sae
dark for the time of the year — Sabbath has slipped
ower quietly, but we have reason to bless oursells
it has not been altogether misemployed. I heard
little of the preaching — a cauld moralist, I doubt,
served that out — but, eh — the prayer — I mind it as
if I had said the words mysell." — Here he repeated
one or two petitions, which were probably a part of
his family devotions, before he was summoned forth
to what he called the way of business. "I never
remember a Sabbath pass so cannily off in my life."
— Then he recollected himself a little, and said to
Alan, "You may read that book, Mr. Fairford,
to-morrow, all the same, though it be Monday; for
you see, it was Saturday when we were thegither,
and now it's Sunday, and it's dark night — so the
Sabbath has slipped clean away through our fingers,
like water through a sieve, which abideth not; and
we have to begin again to-morrow morning, in the
weariful, base, mean, earthly employments, whilk are
unworthy of an immortal spirit — always excepting
the way of business."

Three of the fellows were now returning to the

town, and, at Ewart's command, they cut short
the patriarch's exhortation, by leading him back
to his own residence. The rest of the party then
proceeded to the brig, which only waited their
arrival to get under weigh and drop down the
river. Nanty Ewart betook himself to steering the
brig, and the very touch of the helm seemed to
dispel the remaining influence of the liquor which
he had drunk, since, through a troublesome and
intricate channel, he was able to direct the course
of his little vessel with the most perfect accuracy
and safety.

Alan Fairford, for some time, availed himself
of the clearness of the summer morning to gaze on
the dimly seen shores betwixt which they glided,
becoming less and less distinct as they receded from
each other, until at length, having adjusted his
little bundle by way of pillow, and wrapt around
him the great-coat with which old Trumbull had
equipped him, he stretched himself on the deck,
to try to recover the slumber out of which he had
been awakened. Sleep had scarce begun to settle
on his eyes, ere he found something stirring about
his person. With ready presence of mind he
recollected his situation, and resolved to show no
alarm until the purpose of this became obvious ; but
he was soon relieved from his anxiety, by finding
it was only the result of Nanty's attention to his
comfort, who was wrapping around him, as softly as
he could, a great boat-cloak, in order to defend him
from the morning air.

"Thou art but a cockerel," he muttered, " but
'twere pity thou wert knocked off the perch before
seeing a little more of the sweet and sour of this
world — though, faith, if thou hast the usual luck of

it, the best way were to leave thee to the chance
of a seasoning fever."

These words, and the awkward courtesy with
which the skipper of the little brig tucked the sea-
coat round Fairford, gave him a confidence of
safety which he had not yet thoroughly possessed.
He stretched himself in more security on the hard
planks, and was speedily asleep, though his slumbers
were feverish and unrefreshing.

It has been elsewhere intimated that Alan Fairford
inherited from his mother a delicate constitution,
with a tendency to consumption; and, being an
only child, with such a cause for apprehension, care,
to the verge of effeminacy, was taken to preserve
him from damp beds, wet feet, and those various
emergencies to which the Caledonian boys of much
higher birth, but more active habits, are generally
accustomed. In man, the spirit sustains the consti-
tutional weakness, as in the winged tribes the
feathers bear aloft the body. But there is a bound
to these supporting qualities; and as the pinions of
the bird must at length grow weary, so the *vis
animi* of the human struggler becomes broken down
by continued fatigue.

When the voyager was awakened by the light
of the sun now riding high in heaven, he found
himself under the influence of an almost intolerable
headache, with heat, thirst, shootings across the back
and loins, and other symptoms intimating violent
cold, accompanied with fever. The manner in
which he had passed the preceding day and night,
though perhaps it might have been of little consequence to most young men, was to him, delicate in
constitution and nurture, attended with bad and
even perilous consequences. He felt this was the

case, yet would fain have combated the symptoms of indisposition, which, indeed, he imputed chiefly to sea-sickness. He sat up on deck, and looked on the scene around, as the little vessel, having borne down the Solway Firth, was beginning, with a favourable northerly breeze, to bear away to the southward, crossing the entrance of the Wampool river, and preparing to double the most northerly point of Cumberland.

But Fairford felt annoyed with deadly sickness, as well as by pain of a distressing and oppressive character; and neither Criffel, rising in majesty on the one hand, nor the distant yet more picturesque outline of Skiddaw and Glaramara upon the other, could attract his attention in the manner in which it was usually fixed by beautiful scenery, and especially that which had in it something new as well as striking. Yet it was not in Alan Fairford's nature to give way to despondence, even when seconded by pain. He had recourse, in the first place, to his pocket; but instead of the little Sallust he had brought with him, that the perusal of a favourite classical author might help to pass away a heavy hour, he pulled out the supposed hymn-book with which he had been presented a few hours before, by that temperate and scrupulous person, Mr. Thomas Trumbull, alias Turnpenny. The volume was bound in sable, and its exterior might have become a psalter. But what was Alan's astonishment to read on the titlepage the following words:— "Merry Thoughts for Merry Men; or, Mother Midnight's Miscellany for the small Hours;" and, turning over the leaves, he was disgusted with profligate tales, and more profligate songs, ornamented with figures corresponding in infamy with the letterpress.

"Good God!" he thought, "and did this hoary reprobate summon his family together, and, with such a disgraceful pledge of infamy in his bosom, venture to approach the throne of his Creator? -It must be so; the book is bound after the manner of those dedicated to devotional subjects, and doubtless the wretch, in his intoxication, confounded the books he carried with him, as he did the days of the week." — Seized with the disgust with which the young and generous usually regard the vices of advanced life, Alan, having turned the leaves of the book over in hasty disdain, flung it from him, as far as he could, into the sea. He then had recourse to the Sallust, which he had at first sought for in vain. As he opened the book, Nanty Ewart, who had been looking over his shoulder, made his own opinion heard.

"I think now, brother, if you are so much scandalized at a little piece of sculduddery, which, after all, does nobody any harm, you had better have given it to me than have flung it into the Solway."

"I hope, sir," answered Fairford, civilly, "you are in the habit of reading better books."

"Faith," answered Nanty, "with help of a little Geneva text, I could read my Sallust as well as you can;" and snatching the book from Alan's hand, he began to read, in the Scottish accent: —"'*Igitur ex divitiis juventutem luxuria atque avaritia cum superbiâ invasêre: rapere, consumere; sua parvi pendere, aliena cupere; pudorem, amicitiam, pudicitiam, divina atque humana promiscua, nihil pensi neque moderati habere.*' [1] — There is a slap in the face

[1] The translation of the passage is thus given by Sir Henry Steuart of Allanton. — "The youth, taught to look up to riches as the sovereign good, became apt pupils in the school of Luxury.

now, for an honest fellow that has been buccaniering! Never could keep a groat of what he got, or hold his fingers from what belonged to another, said you? Fie, fie, friend Crispus, thy morals are as crabbed and austere as thy style — the one has as little mercy as the other has grace. By my soul, it is unhandsome to make personal reflections on an old acquaintance, who seeks a little civil intercourse with you after nigh twenty years' separation. On my soul, Master Sallust deserves to float on the Solway better than Mother Midnight herself."

"Perhaps, in some respects, he may merit better usage at our hands," said Alan; "for if he has described vice plainly, it seems to have been for the purpose of rendering it generally abhorred."

"Well," said the seaman, "I have heard of the Sortes Virgilianæ, and I dare say the Sortes Sallustianæ are as true every tittle. I have consulted honest Crispus on my own account, and have had a cuff for my pains. But now see, I open the book on your behalf, and behold what occurs first to my eye! — Lo you there — ' *Catilina . . . omnium flagitiosorum atque facinorosorum circum se habebat.*' And then again —' *Etiam si quis a culpâ vacuus in amicitiam ejus inciderat, quotidiano usu par similisque cæteris efficiebatur.*' [1] That is what I call plain speaking on the part of the old Roman, Mr. Fairford. By the way, that is a capital name for a lawyer."

Rapacity and profusion went hand in hand. Careless of their own fortunes, and eager to possess those of others, shame and remorse, modesty and moderation, every principle gave way." — *Works of Sallust, with Original Essays*, vol. ii. p. 17.

[1] After enumerating the evil qualities of Catiline's associates, the author adds, "If it happened that any as yet uncontaminated by vice were fatally drawn into his friendship, the effects of intercourse and snares artfully spread subdued every scruple, and early assimilated them to their conductors." — *Ibidem*, p. 19.

"Lawyer as I am," said Fairford, "I do not understand your innuendo."

"Nay, then," said Ewart, "I can try it another way, as well as the hypocritical old rascal Turnpenny himself could do. I would have you to know that I am well acquainted with my Bible-book, as well as with my friend Sallust." He then, in a snuffling and canting tone, began to repeat the Scripture text — "'*David therefore departed thence, and went to the cave of Adullam. And every one that was in distress, and every one that was in debt, and every one that was discontented, gathered themselves together unto him, and he became a captain over them.*' What think you of that?" he said, suddenly changing his manner. "Have I touched you now, sir?"

"You are as far off as ever," replied Fairford.

"What the devil! and you a repeating frigate between Summertrees and the Laird! Tell that to the marines — the sailors won't believe it. But you are right to be cautious, since you can't say who are right, who not.— But you look ill; it's but the cold morning air — Will you have a can of flip, or a jorum of hot rumbo? — or will you splice the main-brace" — (showing a spirit-flask) — "Will you have a quid — or a pipe — or a cigar? — a pinch of snuff, at least, to clear your brains and sharpen your apprehension?"

Fairford rejected all these friendly propositions.

"Why, then," continued Ewart, "if you will do nothing for the free trade, I must patronise it myself."

So saying, he took a large glass of brandy.

" A hair of the dog that bit me," he continued, — " of the dog that will worry me one day soon ; and

yet, and be d—d to me for an idiot, I must always have him at my throat.   But, says the old catch"—
Here he sung, and sung well—

"Let's drink—let's drink—while life we have;
We'll find but cold drinking, cold drinking in the grave.

All this," he continued, "is no charm against the headache.   I wish I had any thing that could do you good. — Faith, and we have tea and coffee aboard!   I'll open a chest or a bag, and let you have some in an instant.   You are at the age to like such catlap better than better stuff."

Fairford thanked him, and accepted his offer of tea.

Nanty Ewart was soon heard calling about, " Break open yon chest — take out your capful, you bastard of a powder-monkey; we may want it again. — No sugar ? — all used up for grog, say you ? — knock another loaf to pieces, can't ye ? — and get the kettle boiling, ye hell's baby, in no time at all ! "

By dint of these energetic proceedings, he was in a short time able to return to the place where his passenger lay sick and exhausted, with a cup, or rather a canful, of tea; for every thing was on a large scale on board of the Jumping Jenny.   Alan drank it eagerly, and with so much appearance of being refreshed, that Nanty Ewart swore he would have some too, and only laced it, as his phrase went, with a single glass of brandy.[1]

1 Note III. — Concealments for Theft and Smuggling.

# CHAPTER VIII.

WE left Alan Fairford on the deck of the little smuggling brig, in that disconsolate situation, when sickness and nausea attacked a heated and fevered frame, and an anxious mind. His share of sea-sickness, however, was not so great as to engross his sensations entirely, or altogether to divert his attention from what was passing around. If he could not delight in the swiftness and agility with which the "little frigate" walked the waves, or amuse himself by noticing the beauty of the sea-views around him, where the distant Skiddaw raised his brow, as if in defiance of the clouded eminence of Criffel, which lorded it over the Scottish side of the estuary, he had spirits and composure enough to pay particular attention to the master of the vessel, on whose character his own safety in all probability was dependent.

Nanty Ewart had now given the helm to one of his people, a bald-pated, grizzled old fellow, whose whole life had been spent in evading the revenue laws, with now and then the relaxation of a few months' imprisonment, for deforcing officers, resisting seizures, and the like offences.

Nanty himself sat down by Fairford, helped him to his tea, with such other refreshments as he could think of, and seemed in his way sincerely desirous to make **his** situation as comfortable as things admitted. Fairford had thus an opportunity to study his countenance and manners more closely.

It was plain, Ewart, though a good seaman, had not been bred upon that element. He was a reasonably good scholar, and seemed fond of showing it, by recurring to the subject of Sallust and Juvenal; while, on the other hand, sea-phrases seldom chequered his conversation. He had been in person what is called a smart little man; but the tropical sun had burnt his originally fair complexion to a dusty red; and the bile which was diffused through his system had stained it with a yellowish black — what ought to have been the white part of his eyes, in particular, had a hue as deep as the topaz. He was very thin, or rather emaciated, and his countenance, though still indicating alertness and activity, showed a constitution exhausted with excessive use of his favourite stimulus.

"I see you look at me hard," said he to Fairford. "Had you been an officer of the d—d customs, my terriers' backs would have been up." He opened his breast, and showed Alan a pair of pistols disposed between his waistcoat and jacket, placing his finger at the same time upon the cock of one of them. "But come, you are an honest fellow, though you're a close one. I dare say you think me a queer customer; but I can tell you, they that see the ship leave harbour know little of the seas she is to sail through. My father, honest old gentleman, never would have thought to see me master of the Jumping Jenny."

Fairford said, it seemed very clear indeed that Mr. Ewart's education was far superior to the line he at present occupied.

"O, Criffel to Solway Moss!" said the other. "Why, man, I should have been an expounder of the word, with a wig like a snow-wreath, and a stipend like — like — like a hundred pounds a-year, I suppose. I can spend thrice as much as that, though, being such as I am." Here he sang a scrap of an old Northumbrian ditty, mimicking the burr of the natives of that county —:

"Willy Foster's gone to sea,
Siller buckles at his knee,
He'll come back and marry me —
Canny Willy Foster."

"I have no doubt," said Fairford, "your present occupation is more lucrative; but I should have thought the Church might have been more"——

He stopped, recollecting that it was not his business to say any thing disagreeable.

"More respectable, you mean, I suppose?" said Ewart, with a sneer, and squirting the tobacco-juice through his front teeth; then was silent for a moment, and proceeded in a tone of candour which some internal touch of conscience dictated. "And so it would, Mr. Fairford — and happier, too, by a thousand degrees — though I have had my pleasures too. But there was my father, (God bless the old man!) a true chip of the old Presbyterian block, walked his parish like a captain on the quarter-deck, and was always ready to do good to rich and poor — Off went the laird's hat to the minister, as fast as the poor man's bonnet. When the eye saw him — Pshaw! what have I to do with that now? — Yes, he was, as Virgil hath it, ' *Vir sapientia et pietate gravis.*' But he might have been the wiser man had he kept me at home, when he sent me at

nineteen to study Divinity at the head of the highest
stair in the Covenant Close. It was a cursed mistake in the old gentleman. What though Mrs.
Cantrips of Kittlebasket (for she wrote herself no
less) was our cousin five times removed, and took
me on that account to board and lodging at six
shillings instead of seven shillings a-week? it was
a d—d bad saving, as the case proved. Yet her
very dignity might have kept me in order; for she
never read a chapter excepting out of a Cambridge
Bible, printed by Daniel, and bound in embroidered
velvet. I think I see it at this moment! And on
Sundays, when we had a quart of twopenny ale,
instead of buttermilk, to our porridge, it was always
served up in a silver posset-dish. Also she used
silver-mounted spectacles, whereas even my father's
were cased in mere horn. These things had their
impression at first, but we get used to grandeur by
degrees. Well, sir! — Gad, I can scarce get on with
my story — it sticks in my throat — must take a trifle
to wash it down. — Well, this dame had a daughter
— Jess Cantrips, a black-eyed, bouncing wench —
and, as the devil would have it, there was the d—d
five-story stair — her foot was never from it, whether
I went out or came home from the Divinity Hall.
I would have eschewed her, sir — I would, on my
soul; for I was as innocent a lad as ever came from
Lammermuir; but there was no possibility of
escape, retreat, or flight, unless I could have got a
pair of wings, or made use of a ladder seven stories
high, to scale the window of my attic. It signifies
little talking — you may suppose how all this was to
end — I would have married the girl, and taken my
chance — I would, by Heaven! for she was a pretty
girl, and a good girl, till she and I met; but you

know the old song, 'Kirk would not let us be.' A
gentleman, in my case, would have settled the matter with the Kirk-treasurer for a small sum of
money ; but the poor stibbler, the penniless dominie,
having married his cousin of Kittlebasket, must
next have proclaimed her frailty to the whole parish,
by mounting the throne of Presbyterian penance,
and proving, as Othello says, 'his love a whore,' in
face of the whole congregation.

"In this extremity I dared not stay where I was,
and so thought to go home to my father. But first
I got Jack Hadaway, a lad from the same parish,
and who lived in the same infernal stair, to make
some enquiries how the old gentleman had taken
the matter. I soon, by way of answer, learned, to
the great increase of my comfortable reflections, that
the good old man made as much clamour as if such
a thing as a man's eating his wedding dinner without saying grace had never happened since Adam's
time. He did nothing for six days but cry out,
'Ichabod, Ichabod, the glory is departed from my
house!' and on the seventh he preached a sermon,
in which he enlarged on this incident as illustrative
of one of the great occasions for humiliation, and
causes of national defection. I hope the course
he took comforted himself — I am sure it made me
ashamed to show my nose at home. So I went
down to Leith, and, exchanging my hoddin grey
coat of my mother's spinning for such a jacket as
this, I entered my name at the rendezvous as an
able-bodied landsman, and sailed with the tender
round to Plymouth, where they were fitting out a
squadron for the West Indies. There I was put
aboard the Fearnought, Captain Daredevil — among
whose crew I soon learned to fear Satan, (the ter-

ror of my early youth,) as little as the toughest
Jack on board. I had some qualms at first, but I
took the remedy" (tapping the case-bottle) "which
I recommended to you, being as good for sickness of
the soul as for sickness of the stomach — What, you
won't? — very well, I must, then — here is to ye."

" You would, I am afraid, find your education of
little use in your new condition?" said Fairford.

"Pardon me, sir," resumed the Captain of the
Jumping Jenny; " my handful of Latin, and small
pinch of Greek, were as useless as old junk, to be
sure; but my reading, writing, and accompting,
stood me in good stead, and brought me forward.
I might have been schoolmaster — ay, and master,
in time; but that valiant liquor, rum, made a con-
quest of me rather too often, and so, make what
sail I could, I always went to leeward. We were
four years broiling in that blasted climate, and I
came back at last with a little prize-money. — I
always had thoughts of putting things to rights in
the Covenant Close, and reconciling myself to my
father. I found out Jack Hadaway, who was *Tuptowing* away with a dozen of wretched boys, and a
fine string of stories he had ready to regale my ears
withal. My father had lectured on what he called
'my falling away' for seven Sabbaths, when, just
as his parishioners began to hope that the course
was at an end, he was found dead in his bed on the
eighth Sunday morning. Jack Hadaway assured
me, that if I wished to atone for my errors, by
undergoing the fate of the first martyr, I had only
to go to my native village, where the very stones of
the street would rise up against me as my father's
murderer. Here was a pretty item — well, my
tongue clove to my mouth for an hour, and was

only able at last to utter the name of Mrs. Cantrips.
O, this was a new theme for my Job's comforter.
My sudden departure — my father's no less sudden
death — had prevented the payment of the arrears
of my board and lodging — the landlord was a
haberdasher, with a heart as rotten as the muslin
wares he dealt in. Without respect to her age or
gentle kin, my Lady Kittlebasket was ejected from
her airy habitation — her porridge-pot, silver posset-dish, silver-mounted spectacles, and Daniel's
Cambridge Bible, sold, at the Cross of Edinburgh,
to the cadie who would bid highest for them, and
she herself driven to the workhouse, where she got
in with difficulty, but was easily enough lifted out, at
the end of the month, as dead as her friends could
desire. Merry tidings this to me, who had been
the d—d" (he paused a moment) "*origo mali* —
Gad, I think my confession would sound better in
Latin than in English!

"But the best jest was behind — I had just
power to stammer out something about Jess — by
my faith he *had* an answer! I had taught Jess
one trade, and, like a prudent girl, she had found
out another for herself; unluckily, they were both
contraband, and Jess Cantrips, daughter of the
Lady Kittlebasket, had the honour to be trans-
ported to the plantations, for street-walking and
pocket-picking, about six months before I touched
shore."

He changed the bitter tone of affected pleasantry
into an attempt to laugh; then drew his swarthy
hand across his swarthy eyes, and said in a more
natural accent, "Poor Jess!"

There was a pause — until Fairford, pitying the
poor man's state of mind, and believing he saw

something in him that, but for early error and subsequent profligacy, might have been excellent and
noble, helped on the conversation by asking, in a
tone of commiseration, how he had been able to
endure such a load of calamity.

" Why, very well," answered the seaman; "exceed-
ingly well — like a tight ship in a brisk gale. —
Let me recollect. — I remember thanking Jack,
very composedly, for the interesting and agreeable
communication; I then pulled out my canvas
pouch, with my hoard of moidores, and, taking out
two pieces, I bid Jack keep the rest till I came back,
as I was for a cruise about Auld Reekie. The poor
devil looked anxiously, but I shook him by the
hand and ran down stairs, in such confusion of
mind, that, notwithstanding what I had heard, I
expected to meet Jess at every turning.

"It was market-day, and the usual number of
rogues and fools were assembled at the Cross. I
observed every body looked strange on me, and I
thought some laughed. I fancy I had been making
queer faces enough, and perhaps talking to myself.
When I saw myself used in this manner, I held
out my clenched fists straight before me, stooped
my head, and, like a ram when he makes his race,
darted off right down the street, scattering groups
of weatherbeaten lairds and periwigged burgesses,
and bearing down all before me. I heard the cry of
' Seize the madman !' echoed, in Celtic sounds, from
the City Guard, with ' Ceaze ta matman !' — but pursuit and opposition were in vain. I pursued my
career; the smell of the sea, I suppose, led me to
Leith, where, soon after, I found myself walking
very quietly, on the shore, admiring the tough
round and sound cordage of the vessels, and think-

ing how a loop, with a man at the end of one of
them, would look, by way of tassel.

"I was opposite to the rendezvous, formerly my
place of refuge — in I bolted — found one or two old
acquaintances, made half-a-dozen new ones — drank
for two days — was put aboard the tender — off to
Portsmouth — then landed at the Haslar hospital
in a fine hissing-hot fever.   Never mind — I got
better — nothing can kill me — the West Indies
were my lot again, for since I did not go where I
deserved in the next world, I had something as like
such quarters as can be had in this — black devils
for inhabitants — flames and earthquakes, and so
forth, for your element.   Well, brother, something
or other I did or said — I can't tell what — How
the devil should I when I was as drunk as David's
sow, you know ? — But I was punished, my lad —
made to kiss the wench that never speaks but
when she scolds, and that's the gunner's daughter,
comrade.   Yes, the minister's son of — no matter
where — has the cat's scratch on his back !   This
roused me — and when we were ashore with the
boat, I gave three inches of the dirk, after a stout
tussle, to the fellow I blamed most, and so took the
bush for it.   There were plenty of wild lads then
along shore — and, I don't care who knows — I
went on the account, look you — sailed under the
black flag and marrow-bones — was a good friend
to the sea, and an enemy to all that sailed on it."

Fairford, though uneasy in his mind at finding
himself, a lawyer, so close to a character so lawless,
thought it best, nevertheless, to put a good face on
the matter, and asked Mr. Ewart, with as much
unconcern as he could assume, " whether he was
fortunate as a rover ? "

" No, no — d—n it, no," replied Nanty ; " the devil
a crumb of butter was ever churned that would
stick upon my bread.  There was no order among
us — he that was captain to-day was swabber
to-morrow ; and as for plunder — they say old Avery,
and one or two close hunks, made money ; but in
my time, all went as it came : and reason good, for
if a fellow had saved five dollars, his throat would
have been cut in his hammock — And then it was
a cruel, bloody work — Pah — we'll say no more
about it.  I broke with them at last, for what they
did on board of a bit of a snow — no matter what it
was — bad enough, since it frightened me — I took
French leave, and came in upon the proclamation,
so I am free of all that business.  And here I sit,
the skipper of the Jumping Jenny — a nutshell of
a thing, but goes through the water like a dolphin.
If it were not for yon hypocritical scoundrel at
Annan, who has the best end of the profit, and takes
none of the risk, I should be well enough — as well
as I want to be.  Here is no lack of my best friend,"
— touching his case-bottle ; — " but, to tell you a
secret, he and I have got so used to each other, I
begin to think he is like a professed joker, that
makes your sides sore with laughing, if you see him
but now and then ; but if you take up house with
him, he can only make your head stupid.  But I
warrant the old fellow is doing the best he can for
me, after all."

" And what may that be ? " said Fairford.

 . " He is KILLING me," replied Nanty Ewart ; " and
I am only sorry he is so long about it."

So saying he jumped on his feet, and tripping up
and down the deck, gave his orders with his usual
clearness and decision, notwithstanding the .consi-

derable quantity of spirits which he had contrived to
swallow while recounting his history.

Although far from feeling well, Fairford endeavoured to rouse himself and walk to the head of
the brig, to enjoy the beautiful prospect, as well as
to take some note of the course which the vessel
held. To his great surprise, instead of standing
across to the opposite shore from which she had
departed, the brig was going down the Firth, and
apparently steering into the Irish Sea. He called
to Nanty Ewart, and expressed his surprise at the
course they were pursuing, and asked why they did
not stand straight across the Firth for some port in
Cumberland.

"Why, this is what I call a reasonable question, now," answered Nanty; "as if a ship could
go as straight to its port as a horse to the
stable, or a free-trader could sail the Solway as
securely as a King's cutter! Why, I'll tell ye,
brother — if I do not see a smoke on Bowness,
that is the village upon the headland yonder, I
must stand out to sea for twenty-four hours at
least, for we must keep the weathergage if there
are hawks abroad."

"And if you do see the signal of safety, Master
Ewart, what is to be done then?"

"Why then, and in that case, I must keep off
till night, and then run you, with the kegs and the
rest of the lumber, ashore at Skinburness."

"And then I am to meet with this same Laird
whom I have the letter for?" continued Fairford.

"That," said Ewart, "is thereafter as it may
be: the ship has its course — the fair-trader has his
port — but it is not so easy to say where the Laird
may be found. But he will be within twenty miles

of us, off or on — and it will be my business to guide
you to him."

Fairford could not withstand the passing impulse
of terror which crossed him, when thus reminded
that he was so absolutely in the power of a man,
who, by his own account, had been a pirate, and
who was at present, in all probability, an outlaw
as well as a contraband trader. Nanty Ewart
guessed the cause of his involuntary shuddering.

"What the devil should I gain," he said, "by
passing so poor a card as you are? — Have I not
had ace of trumps in my hand, and did I not play
it fairly? — Ay, I say the Jumping Jenny can run
in other ware as well as kegs. Put *sigma* and *tau*
to *Ewart*, and see how that will spell — D'ye take
me now?"

"No indeed," said Fairford; "I am utterly
ignorant of what you allude to."

"Now, by Jove!" said Nanty Ewart, "thou art
either the deepest or the shallowest fellow I ever
met with — or you are not right after all. I wonder where Summertrees could pick up such a tender
along-shore. Will you let me see his letter?"

Fairford did not hesitate to gratify his wish,
which, he was aware, he could not easily resist.
The master of the Jumping Jenny looked at the
direction very attentively, then turned the letter to
and fro, and examined each flourish of the pen, as
if he were judging of a piece of ornamented manuscript; then handed it back to Fairford, without a
single word of remark.

"Am I right now?" said the young lawyer.

"Why, for that matter," answered Nanty, "the
letter is right, sure enough; but whether *you* are
right or not is your own business, rather than

mine." — And, striking upon a flint with the back of a knife, he kindled a cigar as thick as his finger, and began to smoke away with great perseverance.

Alan Fairford continued to regard him with a melancholy feeling, divided betwixt the interest he took in the unhappy man and a not unnatural apprehension for the issue of his own adventure.

Ewart, notwithstanding the stupifying nature of his pastime, seemed to guess what was working in his passenger's mind; for, after they had remained some time engaged in silently observing each other, he suddenly dashed his cigar on the deck, and said to him, "Well, then, if you are sorry for me, I am sorry for you. D—n me, if I have cared a button for man or mother's son, since two years since, when I had another peep of Jack Hadaway. The fellow was got as fat as a Norway whale — married to a great Dutch-built quean that had brought him six children. I believe he did not know me, and thought I was come to rob his house; however, I made up a poor face, and told him who I was. Poor Jack would have given me shelter and clothes, and began to tell me of the moidores that were in bank, when I wanted them. Egad, he changed his note when I told him what my life had been, and only wanted to pay me my cash and get rid of me. I never saw so terrified a visage. I burst out a-laughing in his face, told him it was all a humbug, and that the moidores were all his own, henceforth and for ever, and so ran off. I caused one of our people send him a bag of tea and a keg of brandy before I left — poor Jack! I think you are the second person these ten years that has cared a tobacco-stopper for Nanty Ewart."

"Perhaps, Mr. Ewart," said Fairford, " you live

chiefly with men too deeply interested for their own immediate safety to think much upon the distress of others ? "

" And with whom do you yourself consort, I pray ?" replied Nanty, smartly. " Why, with plotters, that can make no plot to better purpose than their own hanging; and incendiaries, that are snapping the flint upon wet tinder. You'll as soon raise the dead as raise the Highlands — you'll as soon get a grunt from a dead sow as any comfort from Wales or Cheshire. You think because the pot is boiling, that no scum but yours can come uppermost — I know better, by ——. All these rackets and riots that you think are trending your way have no relation at all to your interest; and the best way to make the whole kingdom friends again at once would be the alarm of such an undertaking as these mad old fellows are trying to launch into."

" I really am not in such secrets as you seem to allude to," said Fairford ; and, determined at the same time to avail himself as far as possible of Nanty's communicative disposition, he added, with a smile, " And if I were, I should not hold it prudent to make them much the subject of conversation. But I am sure, so sensible a man as Summertrees and the Laird may correspond together without offence to the State.

" I take you, friend — I take you," said Nanty Ewart, upon whom, at length, the liquor and tobacco-smoke began to make considerable innovation. " As to what gentlemen may or may not correspond about, why we may pretermit the question, as the old Professor used to say at the Hall; and as to Summertrees, I will say nothing, knowing

him to be an old fox. But I say that this fellow
the Laird is a firebrand in the country; that he is
stirring up all the honest fellows who should be
drinking their brandy quietly, by telling them
stories about their ancestors and the Forty-five; and
that he is trying to turn all waters into his own
mill-dam, and to set his sails to all winds. And
because the London people are roaring about for
some pinches of their own, he thinks to win them
to his turn with a wet finger. And he gets encouragement from some, because they want a spell of
money from him; and from others, because they
fought for the cause once, and are ashamed to go
back; and others, because they have nothing to
lose; and others, because they are discontented
fools. But if he has brought you, or any one, I
say not whom, into this scrape, with the hope of
doing any good, he's a d—d decoy-duck, and that's
all I can say for him; and you are geese, which is
worse than being decoy-ducks, or lame-ducks either.
And so here is to the prosperity of King George
the Third, and the true Presbyterian religion, and
confusion to the Pope, the Devil, and the Pretender! — I'll tell you what, Mr. Fairbairn, I am
but tenth owner of this bit of a craft, the Jumping
Jenny — but tenth owner — and must sail her by
my owners' directions. But if I were whole owner, I
would not have the brig be made a ferry-boat for
your jacobitical, old-fashioned Popish riff-raff, Mr.
Fairport — I would not, by my soul; they should
walk the plank, by the gods, as I have seen better
men do when I sailed under the What-d'ye-callum
colours. But being contraband goods, and on board
my vessel, and I with my sailing orders in my
hand, why, I am to forward them as directed — I

say, John Roberts, keep her up a bit with the helm. — And so, Mr. Fairweather, what I do is — as the d—d villain Turnpenny says — all in the way of business."

He had been speaking with difficulty for the last five minutes, and now at length dropped on the deck, fairly silenced by the quantity of spirits which he had swallowed, but without having shown any glimpse of the gaiety, or even of the extravagance, of intoxication.

The old sailor stepped forward and flung a sea-cloak over the slumberer's shoulders, and added, looking at Fairford, "Pity of him he should have this fault; for, without it, he would have been as clever a fellow as ever trode a plank with ox leather."

"And what are we to do now?" said Fairford.

"Stand off and on, to be sure, till we see the signal, and then obey orders."

So saying, the old man turned to his duty, and left the passenger to amuse himself with his own meditations. Presently afterward a light column of smoke was seen rising from the little headland.

"I can tell you what we are to do now, master," said the sailor. "We'll stand out to sea, and then run in again with the evening tide, and make Skinburness; or, if there's not light, we can run into the Wampool river. and put you ashore about Kirkbride or Leaths, with the long-boat."

Fairford, unwell before, felt this destination condemned him to an agony of many hours, which his disordered stomach and aching head were ill able to endure. There was no remedy, however, but patience, and the recollection that he was suffering in the cause of friendship. As the sun

rose high, he became worse; his sense of smell
appeared to acquire a morbid degree of acuteness,
for the mere purpose of inhaling and distinguishing all the various odours with which he was
surrounded, from that of pitch to all the complicated smells of the hold. His heart, too, throbbed
under the heat, and he felt as if in full progress
towards a high fever.

The seamen, who were civil and attentive,
considering their calling, observed his distress,
and one contrived to make an awning out of an
old sail, while another compounded some lemonade,
the only liquor which their passenger could be
prevailed upon to touch. After drinking it off, he
obtained, but could not be said to enjoy, a few hours
of troubled slumber.

# CHAPTER IX.

ALAN FAIRFORD'S spirit was more ready to encounter labour than his frame was adequate to support it. In spite of his exertions, when he awoke, after five or six hours' slumber, he found that he was so much disabled by dizziness in his head, and pains in his limbs, that he could not raise himself without assistance. He heard with some pleasure that they were now running right for the Wampool river, and that he would be put on shore in a very short time. The vessel accordingly lay to, and presently showed a weft in her ensign, which was hastily answered by signals from on shore. Men and horses were seen to come down the broken path which leads to the shore; the latter all properly tackled for carrying their loading. Twenty fishing barks were pushed afloat at once, and crowded round the brig with much clamour, laughter, cursing, and jesting. Amidst all this apparent confusion there was the essential regularity. Nanty Ewart again walked his quarterdeck as if he had never tasted spirits in his life, issued the necessary orders with precision, and saw them executed with punctuality. In half an hour the loading of the brig was in a great measure disposed in the boats; in a quarter of an hour more, it was landed on the beach, and another interval of about the same duration was sufficient to distribute it on the various strings of packhorses which waited for that purpose, and which instantly dispersed, each on its own proper adventure. More mystery was observed in loading the ship's boat with a quantity of small barrels, which seemed to contain ammunition. This was not done until the commercial customers had been dismissed; and it was not until this was performed that Ewart proposed to Alan, as he lay stunned with pain and noise, to accompany him ashore.

It was with difficulty that Fairford could get over the side of the vessel, and he could not seat himself on the stern of the boat without assistance from the captain and his people. Nauty Ewart, who saw nothing in this worse than an ordinary fit of sea-sickness, applied the usual topics of consolation. He assured his passenger that he would be quite well by and by, when he had been half an hour on terra firma, and that he hoped to drink a can and smoke a pipe with him at Father Crackenthorp's, for all that he felt a little out of the way for riding the wooden horse.

"Who is Father Crackenthorp?" said Fairford, though scarcely able to articulate the question.

"As honest a fellow as is of a thousand," answered Nanty. "Ah, how much good brandy he and I have made little of in our day! By my soul, Mr. Fairbird, he is the prince of skinkers, and the father of the free trade — not a stingy hypocritical devil like old Turnpenny Skinflint, that drinks drunk on other folk's cost, and thinks it sin when he has to pay for it — but a real hearty old cock; — the sharks have been at and about him this many a day, but Father Crackenthorp knows how to trim

his sails — never a warrant but he hears of it before
the ink's dry. He is *bonus socius* with headborough
and constable. The King's Exchequer could not
bribe a man to inform against him. If any such
rascal were to cast up, why, he would miss his ears
next morning, or be sent to seek them in the Solway. He is a statesman,[1] though he keeps a public;
but, indeed, that is only for convenience, and to
excuse his having cellarage and folk about him;
his wife's a canny woman — and his daughter Doll
too. Gad, you'll be in port there till you get round
again; and I'll keep my word with you, and bring
you to speech of the Laird. Gad, the only trouble
I shall have is to get you out of the house; for
Doll is a rare wench, and my dame a funny old one,
and Father Crackenthorp the rarest companion!
He'll drink you a bottle of rum or brandy without
starting, but never wet his lips with that nasty
Scottish stuff that the canting old scoundrel Turnpenny has brought into fashion. He is a gentleman,
every inch of him, old Crackenthorp; in his own
way, that is; and besides, he has a share in the
Jumping Jenny, and many a moonlight outfit
besides. He can give Doll a pretty penny, if he
likes the tight fellow that would turn in with her
for life."

In the midst of this prolonged panegyric on
Father Crackenthorp, the boat touched the beach,
the rowers backed their oars to keep her afloat,
whilst the other fellows jumped into the surf, and,
with the most rapid dexterity, began to hand the
barrels ashore.

" Up with them higher on the beach, my hearties,"
exclaimed Nanty Ewart — " High and dry — high

---

[1] A small landed proprietor.

and dry — this gear will not stand wetting. Now,
out with our spare hand here — high and dry with
him too. What's that? — the galloping of horse!
Oh, I hear the jingle of the packsaddles — they are
our own folk."

By this time all the boat's load was ashore, consisting of the little barrels; and the boat's crew,
standing to their arms, ranged themselves in front,
waiting the advance of the horses which came clattering along the beach. A man, overgrown with
corpulence, who might be distinguished in the
moonlight, panting with his own exertions, appeared
at the head of the cavalcade, which consisted of
horses linked together, and accommodated with
packsaddles, and chains for securing the kegs,
which made a dreadful clattering.

"How now, Father Crackenthorp?" said Ewart
— "Why this hurry with your horses? — We mean
to stay a night with you, and taste your old brandy,
and my dame's home-brewed. The signal is up,
man, and all is right."

"All is wrong, Captain Nanty," cried the man
to whom he spoke; "and you are the lad that is
like to find it so, unless you bundle off — there are
new brooms bought at Carlisle yesterday to sweep
the country of you and the like of you — so you
were better be jogging inland."

"How many rogues are the officers? — If not
more than ten, I will make fight."

"The devil you will!" answered Crackenthorp,
"You were better not, for they have the bloody-
backed dragoons from Carlisle with them."

"Nay, then," said Nanty, "we must make sail.
— Come, Master Fairlord, you must mount and ride.
— He does not hear me — he has fainted, I believe

— What the devil shall I do? — Father Crackenthorp, I must leave this young fellow with you till
the gale blows out — hark ye — goes between the
Laird and the t'other old one; he can neither ride
nor walk — I must send him up to you."

"Send him up to the gallows!" said Crackenthorp; "there is Quartermaster Thwacker, with
twenty men, up yonder; an he had not some kindness for Doll, I had never got hither for a start —
but you must get off, or they will be here to seek
us, for his orders are woundy particular; and these
kegs contain worse than whisky — a hanging
matter, I take it."

"I wish they were at the bottom of Wampool
river, with them they belong to," said Nanty Ewart.
"But they are part of cargo; and what to do with
the poor young fellow " ——

"Why, many a better fellow has roughed it on
the grass, with a cloak o'er him," said Crackenthorp.
"If he hath a fever, nothing is so cooling as the
night air."

"Yes, he would be cold enough in the morning,
no doubt; but it's a kind heart, and shall not cool
so soon, if I can help it," answered the Captain of
the Jumping Jenny.

"Well, Captain, an ye will risk your own neck
for another man's, why not take him to the old
girls at Fairladies?"

"What, the Miss Arthurets! — The Papist jades!
But never mind; it will do — I have known them
take in a whole sloop's crew that were stranded on
the sands."

"You may run some risk, though, by turning
up to Fairladies; for I tell you they are all up
through the country."

" Never mind — I may chance to put some of them down again," said Nanty, cheerfully. — " Come, lads, bustle to your tackle. Are you all loaded ? "

" Ay, ay, Captain ; we will be ready in a jiffy," answered the gang.

" D—n your captains ! — Have you a mind to have me hanged if I am taken ? — All's hail-fellow, here."

" A sup at parting," said Father Crackenthorp, extending a flask to Nanty Ewart.

" Not the twentieth part of a drop," said Nanty. " No Dutch courage for me — my heart is always high enough when there's a chance of fighting ; besides, if I live drunk, I should like to die sober. — Here, old Jephson — you are the best-natured brute amongst them — get the lad between us on a quiet horse, and we will keep him upright, I warrant."

As they raised Fairford from the ground, he groaned heavily, and asked faintly where they were taking him to.

" To a place where you will be as snug and quiet as a mouse in his hole," said Nanty, " if so be that we can get you there safely. — Good-bye, Father Crackenthorp — poison the quartermaster, if you can."

The loaded horses then sprang forward at a hard trot, following each other in a line, and every second horse being mounted by a stout fellow in a smock-frock, which served to conceal the arms with which most of these desperate men were provided. Ewart followed in the rear of the line, and, with the occasional assistance of old Jephson, kept his young charge erect in the saddle. He groaned heavily from time to time ; and Ewart, more moved

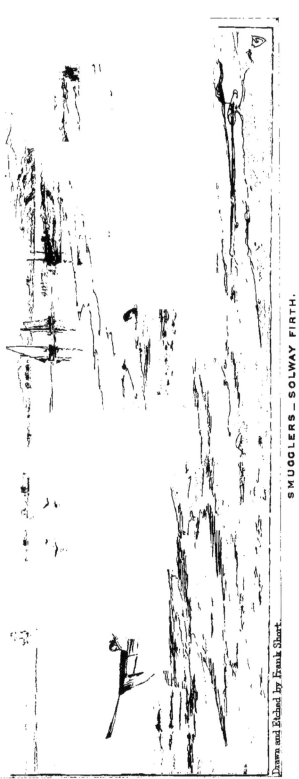

SMUGGLERS — SOLWAY FIRTH.

Drawn and Etched by Frank Short.

with compassion for his situation than might have
been expected from his own habits, endeavoured
to amuse him and comfort him, by some account of
the place to which they were conveying him — his
words of consolation being, however, frequently
interrupted by the necessity of calling to his people,
and many of them being lost amongst the rattling
of the barrels, and clinking of the tackle and small
chains by which they are secured on such occasions.

"And you see, brother, you will be in safe quarters at Fairladies — good old scrambling house —
good old maids enough, if they were not Papists. —
Hollo, you Jack Lowther ; keep the line, can't ye,
and shut your rattle-trap, you broth of a —— !
And so, being of a good family, and having enough,
the old lasses have turned a kind of saints, and
nuns, and so forth. The place they live in was
some sort of nun-shop long ago, as they have them
still in Flanders ;. so folk call them the Vestals of
Fairladies — that may be or may not be ; and I
care not whether it be or no. — Blinkinsop, hold
your tongue, and bè d—d ! — And so, betwixt great
alms and good dinners, they are well thought of
by rich and poor, and their trucking with Papists is
looked over. There are plenty of priests, and stout
young scholars, and such like, about the house —
it's a hive of them — More shame that government
send dragoons out after a few honest fellows that
bring the old women of England a drop of brandy,
and let these ragamuffins smuggle in as much
papistry and — Hark ! — was that a whistle ? — No,
it's only a plover. You, Jem Collier, keep a look-
out a-head — we'll meet them at the High Whins,
or Brotthole bottom, or nowhere. Go a furlong
a-head, I say, and 'look sharp. —These Miss

Arthurets feed the hungry, and clothe the naked,
and such like acts — which my poor father used to
say were filthy rags, but he dressed himself out with
as many of them as most folk. — D—n that stumbling horse! Father Crackenthorp should be d—d
himself for putting an honest fellow's neck in such
jeopardy."

Thus, and with much more to the same purpose,
Nanty ran on, increasing, by his well-intended
annoyance, the agony of Alan Fairford, who, tor-
mented by racking pain along the back and loins,
which made the rough trot of the horse torture to
him, had his aching head still further rended and
split by the hoarse voice of the sailor, close to his
ear. Perfectly passive, however, he did not even
essay to give any answer; and indeed his own
bodily distress was now so great and engrossing,
that to think of his situation was impossible, even
if he could have mended it by doing so.

Their course was inland; but in what direction,
Alan had no means of ascertaining. They passed
at first over heaths and sandy downs; they crossed
more than one brook, or *beck*, as they are called in
that country — some of them of considerable depth
— and at length reached a cultivated country,
divided, according to the English fashion of agri-
culture, into very small fields or closes, by high
banks, overgrown with underwood, and surmounted
by hedge-row trees, amongst which winded a number of impracticable and complicated lanes, where
the boughs projecting from the embankments on
each side intercepted the light of the moon, and
endangered the safety of the horsemen. But
through this labyrinth the experience of the guides
conducted them without a blunder, and without

even the slackening of their pace. In many places, however, it was impossible for three men to ride abreast; and therefore the burden of supporting Alan Fairford fell alternately to old Jephson and to Nanty; and it was with much difficulty that they could keep him upright in his saddle.

At length, when his powers of sufferance were quite worn out, and he was about to implore them to leave him to his fate in the first cottage or shed — or under a haystack or a hedge — or anywhere, so he was left at ease, Collier, who rode a-head, passed back the word that they were at the avenue to Fairladies — " Was he to turn up ? "

Committing the charge of Fairford to Jephson, Nanty dashed up to the head of the troop, and gave his orders. — " Who knows the house best ? "

" Sam Skelton's a Catholic," said Lowther.

" A d—d bad religion," said Nanty, of whose Presbyterian education a hatred of Popery seemed to be the only remnant. " But I am glad there is one amongst us, any how. — You, Sam, being a Papist, know Fairladies, and the old maidens, I dare say ; so do you fall out of the line, and wait here with me ; and do you, Collier, carry on to Walinford bottom, then turn down the beck till you come to the old mill, and Goodman Grist the Miller, or old Peel-the-Causeway, will tell you where to stow ; but I will be up with you before that."

The string of loaded horses then struck forward at their former pace, while Nanty, with Sam Skel-, waited by the road-side till the rear came up, when Jephson and Fairford joined them, and, to great relief of the latter, they began to proceed at an easier pace than formerly, suffering the gang to precede them, till the clatter and clang attending their progress began to die away in the distance. They had not proceeded a pistol-shot from the place where they parted, when a short turning brought them in front of an old mouldering gateway, whose heavy pinnacles were decorated in the style of the seventeenth century, with clumsy architectural ornaments; several of which had fallen down from decay, and lay scattered about, no further care having been taken than just to remove them out of the direct approach to the avenue. The great stone pillars, glimmering white in the moonlight, had some fanciful resemblance to supernatural apparitions, and the air of neglect all around gave an uncomfortable idea of the habitation to those who passed its avenue.

"There used to be no gate here," said Skelton, finding their way unexpectedly stopped.

"But there is a gate now, and a porter too," said a rough voice from within. "Who be you, and what do you want at this time of night?"

"We want to come to speech of the ladies — of the Miss Arthurets," said Nanty; "and to ask lodging for a sick man."

"There is no speech to be had of the Miss Arthurets at this time of night, and you may carry your sick màn to the doctor," answered the fellow from within, gruffly; "for as sure as there is savour in salt, and scent in rosemary, you will get no entrance — put your pipes up and be jogging on."

"Why, Dick Gardener," said Skelton, "be thou then turned porter?"

"What, do you know who I am?" said the domestic sharply.

"I know you, by your by-word," answered the

other. "What, have you forgot little Sam Skelton, and the brock in the barrel?"

"No, I have not forgotten you," answered the acquaintance of Sam Skelton; "but my orders are peremptory to let no one up the avenue this night, and therefore"——

"But we are armed, and will not be kept back," said Nanty. "Hark ye, fellow, were it not better for you to take a guinea and let us in, than to have us break the door first, and thy pate afterwards? for I won't see my comrade die at your door — be assured of that."

"Why, I dunna know," said the fellow; "but what cattle were those that rode by in such hurry?"

"Why, some of our folk from Bowness, Stonie-cultrum, and thereby," answered Skelton; "Jack Lowther, and old Jephson, and broad Will Lam-plugh, and such like."

"Well," said Dick Gardener, "as sure as there is savour in salt, and scent in rosemary, I thought it had been the troopers from Carlisle and Wigton, and the sound brought my heart to my mouth."

"Had thought thou wouldst have known the clatter of a cask from the clash of a broadsword, as well as e'er a quaffer in Cumberland," answered Skelton.

"Come, brother, less of your jaw, and more of your legs, if you please," said Nanty; "every moment we stay is a moment lost. Go to the ladies, and tell them that Nanty Ewart, of the Jumping Jenny, has brought a young gentleman, charged with letters from Scotland, to a certain gentleman of consequence in Cumberland — that the soldiers are out, and the gentleman is very ill, and if he is not received at Fairladies he must be left either to

die at the gate, or to be taken, with all his papers
about him, by the redcoats."

Away ran Dick Gardener with this message;
and in a few minutes lights were seen to flit about,
which convinced Fairford, who was now, in
consequence of the halt, a little restored to self-
possession, that they were traversing the front of a
tolerably large mansion-house.

"What if thy friend, Dick Gardener, comes not
back again?" said Jephson to Skelton.

"Why, then," said the person addressed, "I
shall owe him just such a licking as thou, old Jephson, hadst from Dan Cooke, and will pay as duly
and truly as he did."

The old man was about to make an angry reply,
when his doubts were silenced by the return of
Dick Gardener, who announced that Miss Arthuret
was coming herself as far as the gateway to speak
with them.

Nanty Ewart cursed, in a low tone, the suspicion
of old maids and the churlish scruples of Catholics,
that made so many obstacles to helping a fellow-
creature, and wished Miss Arthuret a hearty
rheumatism or toothache as the reward of her excursion; but the lady presently appeared, to cut short
farther grumbling. She was attended by a waiting-
maid with a lantern, by means of which she
examined the party on the outside, as closely as the
imperfect light, and the spars of the newly-erected
gate, would permit.

"I am sorry we have disturbed you so late, Madam
Arthuret," said Nanty; "but the case is this"——

"Holy Virgin," said she, "why do you speak
so loud? Pray, are you not the Captain of the
Sainte Genevieve?"

"Why, ay, ma'am," answered Ewart, "they call the brig so at Dunkirk, sure enough ; but along shore here, they call her the Jumping Jenny."

"You brought over the holy Father Buonaventure, did you not?"

"Ay, ay, madam, I have brought over enough of them black cattle," answered Nanty.

"Fie! fie! friend," said Miss Arthuret; "it is a pity that the saints should commit these good men to a heretic's care."

"Why, no more they would, ma'am," answered Nanty, "could they find a Papish lubber that knew the coast as I do; then I am trusty as steel to own-ers, and always look after cargo — live lumber, or dead flesh, or spirits, all is one to me; and your Catholics have such d—d large hoods, with pardon, ma'am, that they can sometimes hide two faces under them. But here is a gentleman dying, with letters about him from the Laird of Summertrees to the Laird of the Lochs, as they call him, along Solway, and every minute he lies here is a nail in his coffin."

"Saint Mary! what shall we do?" said Miss Arthuret; "we must admit him, I think, at all risks. — You, Richard Gardener, help one of these men to carry the gentleman up to the Place; and you, Selby, see him lodged at the end of the long gallery. — You are a heretic, Captain, but I think you are trusty, and I know you have been trusted — but if you are imposing on me"——

"Not I, madam — never attempt to impose on ladies of your experience — my practice that way has been all among the young ones. — Come, cheerly, Mr. Fairford — you will be taken good care of — try to walk."

Alan did so; and, refreshed by his halt, declared himself able to walk to the house with the sole assistance of the gardener.

"Why, that's hearty. Thank thee, Dick, for lending him thine arm,"—and Nanty slipped into his hand the guinea he had promised.—"Farewell then, Mr. Fairford, and farewell, Madam Arthuret, for I have been too long here."

So saying, he and his two companions threw themselves on horseback, and went off at a gallop. Yet even above the clatter of their hoofs did the incorrigible Nanty holloa out the old ballad—

> "A lovely lass to a friar came,
>    To confession a-morning early;—
> 'In what, my dear, are you to blame?
>    Come tell me most sincerely.'
> 'Alas! my fault I dare not name—
>    But my lad he loved me dearly.'"

"Holy Virgin!" exclaimed Miss Seraphina, as the unhallowed sounds reached her ears; "what profane heathens be these men, and what frights and pinches we be put to among them! The saints be good to us, what a night has this been!—the like never seen at Fairladies.—Help me to make fast the gate, Richard, and thou shalt come down again to wait on it, lest there come more unwelcome visitors—Not that you are unwelcome, young gentleman, for it is sufficient that you need such assistance as we can give you, to make you welcome to Fairladies—only, another time would have done as well—but, hem! I dare say it is all for the best. The avenue is none of the smoothest, sir, look to your feet. Richard Gardener should have had it mown and levelled, but he was obliged to go on a

pilgrimage to Saint Winifred's Well, in Wales."—
(Here Dick gave a short dry cough, which, as if he
had found it betrayed some internal feeling a little
at variance with what the lady said, he converted
into a muttered *Sancta Winifreda, ora pro nobis.*
Miss Arthuret, meantime, proceeded)—"We never
interfere with our servants' vows or penances, Master Fairford—I know a very worthy father of your
name, perhaps a relation—I say, we never interfere
with our servants' vows. Our Lady forbid they
should not know some difference between our service
and a heretic's.—Take care, sir, you will fall if you
have not a care. Alas! by night and day there are
many stumbling-blocks in our paths!"

With more talk to the same purpose, all of which
tended to show a charitable and somewhat silly
woman, with a strong inclination to her superstitious devotion, Miss Arthuret entertained her new
guest, as, stumbling at every obstacle which the
devotion of his guide, Richard, had left in the path,
he at last, by ascending some stone steps decorated
on the side with griffins, or some such heraldic
anomalies, attained a terrace extending in front of
the Place of Fairladies; an old-fashioned gentleman's house of some consequence, with its range of
notched gable-ends and narrow windows, relieved
by here and there an old turret about the size of a
pepper-box. The door was locked during the brief
absence of the mistress; a dim light glimmered
through the sashed door of the hall, which opened
beneath a huge stone porch, loaded with jessamine
and other creepers. All the windows were dark as
pitch.

Miss Arthuret tapped at the door. "Sister, Sister
Angelica!"

"Who is there?" was answered from within; "is it you, Sister Seraphina?"

"Yes, yes, undo the door; do you not know my voice?"

"No doubt, sister," said Angelica, undoing bolt and bar; "but you know our charge, and the enemy is watchful to surprise us — *incedit sicut leo vorans*, saith the breviary. — Whom have you brought here? Oh, sister, what have you done?"

"It is a young man," said Seraphina, hastening to interrupt her sister's remonstrance, "a relation, I believe, of our worthy Father Fairford; left at the gate by the captain of that blessed vessel the Sainte Genevieve — almost dead — and charged with dispatches to "——

She lowered her voice as she mumbled over the last words.

"Nay, then, there is no help," said Angelica; "but it is unlucky."

During this dialogue between the vestals of Fairladies, Dick Gardener deposited his burden in a chair, where the young lady, after a moment of hesitation, expressing a becoming reluctance to touch the hand of a stranger, put her finger and thumb upon Fairford's wrist, and counted his pulse.

"There is fever here, sister," she said; "Richard must call Ambrose, and we must send some of the febrifuge."

Ambrose arrived presently, a plausible and respectable-looking old servant, bred in the family, and who had risen from rank to rank in the Arthuret service, till he was become half-physician, half-almoner, half-butler, and entire governor; that is, when the Father Confessor, who frequently eased him of the toils of government, chanced to be abroad.

Under the direction, and with the assistance, of this venerable personage, the unlucky Alan Fairford was conveyed to a decent apartment at the end of a long gallery, and, to his inexpressible relief, consigned to a comfortable bed. He did not attempt to resist the prescription of Mr. Ambrose, who not only presented him with the proposed draught, but proceeded so far as to take a considerable quantity of blood from him, by which last operation he probably did his patient much service.

# CHAPTER X

ON the next morning, when Fairford awoke, after
no very refreshing slumbers, in which were mingled
many wild dreams of his father and of Darsie
Latimer, — of the damsel in the green mantle,
and the vestals of Fairladies, — of drinking small
beer with Nanty Ewart and being immersed in the
Solway with the Jumping Jenny, — he found himself in no condition to dispute the order of Mr.
Ambrose, that he should keep his bed, from which,
indeed, he could not have raised himself without
assistance. He became sensible that his anxiety,
and his constant efforts for some days past, had been
too much for his health, and that, whatever might
be his impatience, he could not proceed in his
undertaking until his strength was re-established.

In the meanwhile, no better quarters could have
been found for an invalid. The attendants spoke
under their breath, and moved only on tiptoe —
nothing was done unless *par ordonnance du médecin*
— Esculapius reigned paramount in the premises
at Fairladies. Once a day, the ladies came in great
state to wait upon him, and enquire after his health,
and it was then that Alan's natural civility, and
the thankfulness which he expressed for their timely
and charitable assistance, raised him considerably
in their esteem. He was on the third day removed
to a better apartment than that in which he had

been at first accommodated. When he was permitted to drink a glass of wine, it was of the first quality; one of those curious old-fashioned cobwebbed bottles being produced on the occasion which are only to be found in the crypts of old country seats, where they may have lurked undisturbed for more than half a century.

But however delightful a residence for an invalid, Fairladies, as its present inmate became soon aware, was not so agreeable to a convalescent. When he dragged himself to the window so soon as he could crawl from bed, behold it was closely grated, and commanded no view except of a little paved court. This was nothing remarkable, most old Border houses having their windows so secured; but then Fairford observed, that whoever entered or left the room always looked the door with great care and circumspection; and some proposals which he made to take a walk in the gallery, or even in the garden, were so coldly received, both by the ladies and their prime minister, Mr. Ambrose, that he saw plainly such an extension of his privileges as a guest would not be permitted.

Anxious to ascertain whether this excessive hospitality would permit him his proper privilege of free agency, he announced to this important functionary, with grateful thanks for the care with which he had been attended, his purpose to leave Fairladies next morning, requesting only, as a continuance of the favours with which he had been loaded, the loan of a horse to the next town; and, assuring Mr. Ambrose that his gratitude would not be limited by such a trifle, he slipped three guineas into his hand, by way of seconding his proposal. The fingers of that worthy domestic closed as naturally upon the *honorarium* as if a degree in the learned faculty had given him a right to clutch it; but his answer concerning Alan's proposed departure was at first evasive, and, when he was pushed, it amounted to a peremptory assurance that he could not be permitted to depart to-morrow; it was as much as his life was worth, and his ladies would not authorize it.

"I know best what my own life is worth," said Alan; "and I do not value it in comparison to the business which requires my instant attention."

Receiving still no satisfactory answer from Mr. Ambrose, Fairford thought it best to state his resolution to the ladies themselves, in the most measured, respectful, and grateful terms; but still such as expressed a firm determination to depart on the morrow, or next day at farthest. After some attempts to induce him to stay, on the alleged score of health, which were so expressed that he was convinced they were only used to delay his departure, Fairford plainly told them that he was intrusted with dispatches of consequence to the gentleman known by the name of Herries, Redgauntlet, and the Laird of the Lochs; and that it was matter of life and death to deliver them early.

"I dare say, Sister Angelica," said the elder Miss Arthuret, "that the gentleman is honest; and if he is really a relation of Father Fairford, we can run no risk."

"Jesu Maria!" exclaimed the younger. "Oh fie, Sister Seraphina! Fie, fie! — *Vade retro* — get thee behind me!"

"Well, well; but, sister — Sister Angelica — let me speak with you in the gallery."

So out the ladies rustled in their silks and

tissues, and it was a good half-hour ere they rustled in again, with importance and awe on their countenances.

"To tell you the truth, Mr. Fairford, the cause of our desire to delay you is — there is a religious gentleman in this house at present"——

"A most excellent person indeed," said the sister Angelica.

"An anointed of his Master!" echoed Seraphina, — "and we should be glad that, for conscience' sake, you would hold some discourse with him before your departure."

"Oho!" thought Fairford, "the murder is out — here is a design of conversion! — I must not affront the good old ladies, but I shall soon send off the priest, I think." — He then answered aloud, "that he should be happy to converse with any friend of theirs — that in religious matters he had the greatest respect for every modification of Christianity, though, he must say, his belief was made up to that in which he had been educated; nevertheless, if his seeing the religious person they recommended could in the least show his respect " ——

"It is not quite that," said Sister Seraphina, "although I am sure the day is too short to hear him — Father Buonaventure, I mean — speak upon the concerns of our souls; but "——

"Come, come, Sister Seraphina," said the younger, "it is needless to talk so much about it. His — his Eminence — I mean Father Buonaventure — will himself explain what he wants this gentleman to know.".

"His Eminence," said Fairford, surprised — "Is this gentleman so high in the Catholic Church? — The title is given only to Cardinals, I think."

"He is not a Cardinal as yet," answered Seraphina; "but I assure you, Mr. Fairford, he is as high in rank as he is eminently endowed with good gifts, and " ——

"Come away," said Sister Angelica. "Holy Virgin, how you do talk! — What has Mr. Fairford to do with Father Buonaventure's rank? — Only, sir, you will remember that the Father has been always accustomed to be treated with the most profound deference; — indeed " ——

"Come away, sister," said Sister Seraphina, in her turn; "who talks now, I pray you? Mr. Fairford will know how to comport himself."

"And we had best both leave the room," said the younger lady, "for here his Eminence comes."

She lowered her voice to a whisper as she pronounced the last words; and as Fairford was about to reply, by assuring her that any friend of hers should be treated by him with all the ceremony he could expect, she imposed silence on him, by holding up her finger.

A solemn and stately step was now heard in the gallery; it might have proclaimed the approach not merely of a bishop or cardinal, but of the Sovereign Pontiff himself. Nor could the sound have been more respectfully listened to by the two ladies, had it announced that the Head of the Church was approaching in person. They drew themselves, like sentinels on duty, one on each side of the door by which the long gallery communicated with Fairford's apartment, and stood there immovable, and with countenances expressive of the deepest reverence.

The approach of Father Buonaventure was so slow, that Fairford had time to notice all this, and to marvel in his mind what wily and ambitious priest could have contrived to subject his worthy but simple-minded hostesses to such superstitious trammels. Father Buonaventure's entrance and appearance in some degree accounted for the whole.

He was a man of middle life, about forty or upwards ; but either care, or fatigue, or indulgence, had brought on the appearance of premature old age, and given to his fine features a cast of seriousness or even sadness. A noble countenance, however, still remained; and though his complexion was altered, and wrinkles stamped upon his brow in many a melancholy fold, still the lofty forehead, the full and well-opened eye, and the well-formed nose, showed how handsome in better days he must have been. He was tall, but lost the advantage of his height by stooping ; and the cane which he wore always in his hand, and occasionally used, as well as his slow though majestic gait, seemed to intimate that his form and limbs felt already some touch of infirmity. The colour of his hair could not be discovered, as, according to the fashion, he wore a periwig. He was handsomely though gravely dressed in a secular habit, and had a cockade in his hat ; circumstances which did not surprise Fairford, who knew that a military disguise was very often assumed by the seminary priests, whose visits to England, or residence there, subjected them to legal penalties.

As this stately person entered the apartment, the two ladies facing inward, like soldiers on their post when about to salute a superior officer, dropped on either hand of the Father a courtesy so profound, that the hoop petticoats which performed

the feat seemed to sink down to the very floor,
nay, through it, as if a trapdoor had opened for
the descent of the dames who performed this act
of reverence.

The Father seemed accustomed to such homage,
profound as it was ; he turned his person a little
way first towards one sister, and then towards the
other, while, with a gracious inclination of his person, which certainly did not amount to a bow, he
acknowledged their courtesy. But he passed forward without addressing them, and seemed by
doing so to intimate that their presence in the
apartment was unnecessary.

They accordingly glided out of the room, retreating backwards, with hands clasped and eyes cast
upwards, as if imploring blessings on the religious
man whom they venerated so highly. The door of
the apartment was shut after them, but not before
Fairford had perceived that there were one or two
men in the gallery, and that, contrary to what he
had before observed, the door, though shut, was not
locked on the outside.

"Can the good souls apprehend danger from me
to this god of their idolatry?" thought Fairford.
But he had no time to make farther observations,
for the stranger had already reached the middle of
the apartment.

Fairford rose to receive him respectfully, but as
he fixed his eyes on the visitor he thought that
the Father avoided his looks. His reasons for
remaining incognito were cogent enough to account
for this, and Fairford hastened to relieve him, by
looking downwards in his turn ; but when again
he raised his face, he found the broad light eye of
the stranger so fixed on him, that he was almost

put out of countenance by the steadiness of his gaze. During this time they remained standing.

"Take your seat, sir," said the Father; "you have been an invalid."

He spoke with the tone of one who desires an inferior to be seated in his presence, and his voice was full and melodious.

Fairford, somewhat surprised to find himself overawed by the airs of superiority which could be only properly exercised towards one over whom religion gave the speaker influence, sat down at his bidding, as if moved by springs, and was at a loss how to assert the footing of equality on which he felt that they ought to stand. The stranger kept the advantage which he had obtained.

"Your name, sir, I am informed, is Fairford?" said the Father.

Alan answered by a bow.

"Called to the Scottish bar," continued his visitor. "There is, I believe, in the West, a family of birth and rank called Fairford of Fairford."

Alan thought this a strange observation from a foreign ecclesiastic, as his name intimated Father Buonaventure to be; but only answered, he believed there was such a family.

"Do you count kindred with them, Mr. Fairford?" continued the enquirer.

"I have not the honour to lay such a claim," said Fairford. "My father's industry has raised his family from a low and obscure situation — I have no hereditary claim to distinction of any kind. — May I ask the cause of these enquiries?"

"You will learn it presently," said Father Buonaventure, who had given a dry and dissatisfied *hem* at the young man's acknowledging a plebeian descent.

He then motioned to him to be silent, and proceeded with his queries.

"Although not of condition, you are, doubtless, by sentiments and education, a man of honour and a gentleman?"

"I hope so, sir," said Alan, colouring with displeasure. "I have not been accustomed to have it questioned."

"Patience, young man," said the unperturbed querist — "we are on serious business, and no idle etiquette must prevent its being discussed seriously. —You are probably aware that you speak to a person proscribed by the severe and unjust laws of the present government?"

"I am aware of the statute 1700, chapter 3," said Alan, "banishing from the realm Priests and trafficking Papists, and punishing by death, on summary conviction, any such person who being so banished may return. The English law, I believe, is equally severe. But I have no means of knowing you, sir, to be one of those persons; and I think your prudence may recommend to you to keep your own counsel."

"It is sufficient, sir; and I have no apprehensions of disagreeable consequences from your having seen me in this house," said the Priest.

"Assuredly no," said Alan. "I consider myself as indebted for my life to the Mistresses of Fairladies; and it would be a vile requital on my part to pry into or make known what I may have seen or heard under this hospitable roof. If I were to meet the Pretender himself in such a situation, he should, even at the risk of a little stretch to my loyalty, be free from any danger from my indiscretion."

"The Pretender!" said the Priest, with some angry emphasis; but immediately softened his tone and added, "No doubt, however, that person *is* a pretender; and some people think his pretensions are not ill founded. But, before running into politics, give me leave to say that I am surprised to find a gentleman of your opinions in habits of intimacy with Mr. Maxwell of Summertrees and Mr. Redgauntlet, and the medium of conducting the intercourse betwixt them."

"Pardon me, sir," replied Alan Fairford; "I do not aspire to the honour of being reputed their confidant or go-between. My concern with those gentlemen is limited to one matter of business, dearly interesting to me, because it concerns the safety — perhaps the life — of my dearest friend."

"Would you have any objections to intrust me with the cause of your journey?" said Father Buona-venture. "My advice may be of service to you, and my influence with one or both these gentlemen is considerable."

Fairford hesitated a moment, and, hastily revolving all circumstances, concluded that he might perhaps receive some advantage from propitiating this personage; while, on the other hand, he endangered nothing by communicating to him the occasion of his journey. He, therefore, after stating shortly that he hoped Mr. Buonaventure would render him the same confidence which he required on his part, gave a short account of Darsie Latimer — of the mystery which hung over his family — and of the disaster which had befallen him. Finally, of his own resolution to seek for his friend, and to deliver him, at the peril of his own life.

The Catholic Priest, whose manner it seemed

to be to avoid all conversation which did not arise
from his own express motion, made no remarks
upon what he had heard, but only asked one or two
abrupt questions, where Alan's narrative appeared
less clear to him; then rising from his seat, he took
two turns through the apartment, muttering between
his teeth, with emphasis, the word "Madman!"
But apparently he was in the habit of keeping all
violent emotions under restraint; for he presently addressed Fairford with the most perfect
indifference.

"If," said he, "you thought you could do so
without breach of confidence, I wish you would
have the goodness to show me the letter of Mr.
Maxwell of Summertrees. I desire to look particularly at the address."

Seeing no cause to decline this extension of his
confidence, Alan, without hesitation, put the letter
into his hand. Having turned it round as old
Trumbull and Nauty Ewart had formerly done,
and, like them, having examined the address with
much minuteness, he asked whether he had observed
these words, pointing to a pencil-writing upon the
under side of the letter. Fairford answered in the
negative, and, looking at the letter, read with surprise, " *Cave ne literas Bellerophontis (d) adferres ;* "
a caution which coincided so exactly with the
Provost's admonition, that he would do well to
inspect the letter of which he was bearer, that he
was about to spring up and attempt an escape, he
knew not wherefore or from whom.

"Sit still, young man," said the Father, with
the same tone of authority which reigned in his
whole manner, although mingled with stately courtesy. "You are in no danger — my character shall

be a pledge for your safety. — By whom do you suppose these words have been written?"

Fairford could have answered, "by Nanty Ewart," for he remembered seeing that person scribble something with a pencil, although he was not well enough to observe with accuracy where, or upon what. But not knowing what suspicions, or what worse consequences, the seaman's interest in his affairs might draw upon him, he judged it best to answer that he knew not the hand.

Father Buonaventure was again silent for a moment or two, which he employed in surveying the letter with the strictest attention; then stepped to the window, as if to examine the address and writing of the envelope with the assistance of a stronger light, and Alan Fairford beheld him, with no less amazement than high displeasure, coolly and deliberately break the seal, open the letter, and peruse the contents.

"Stop, sir, hold!" he exclaimed, so soon as his astonishment permitted him to express his resentment in words: "by what right do you dare" ——

"Peace, young gentleman," said the Father, repelling him with a wave of his hand; "be assured I do not act without warrant — nothing can pass betwixt Mr. Maxwell and Mr. Redgauntlet that I am not fully entitled to know."

"It may be so," said Alan, extremely angry; "but though you may be these gentlemen's father confessor, you are not mine; and in breaking the seal of a letter intrusted to my care, you have done me " ——

"No injury, I assure you," answered the unperturbed priest; "on the contrary, it may be a service."

"I desire no advantage at such a rate, or to be obtained in such a manner," answered Fairford; "restore me the letter instantly, or "——

"As you regard your own safety," said the priest, " forbear all injurious expressions, and all menacing gestures. I am not one who can be threatened or insulted with impunity; and there are enough within hearing to chastise any injury or affront offered to me, in case I may think it unbecoming to protect or avenge myself with my own hand."

In saying this, the Father assumed an air of such fearlessness and calm authority, that the young lawyer, surprised and overawed, forbore, as he had intended, to snatch the letter from his hand, and confined himself to bitter complaints of the impropriety of his conduct, and of the light in which he himself must be placed to Redgauntlet, should he present him a letter with a broken seal.

"That," said Father Buonaventure, "shall be fully cared for. I will myself write to Redgauntlet, and enclose Maxwell's letter, provided always you continue to desire to deliver it, after perusing the contents."

He then restored the letter to Fairford, and, observing that he hesitated to peruse it, said emphatically, "Read it, for it concerns you."

This recommendation, joined to what Provost Crosbie had formerly recommended, and to the warning which he doubted not that Nanty intended to convey by his classical allusion, decided Fairford's resolution. "If these correspondents," he thought, "are conspiring against my person, I have a right to counterplot them; self-preservation, as well as my friend's safety, require that I should not be too scrupulous."

So thinking, he read the letter, which was in the following words : —

" DEAR RUGGED AND DANGEROUS, — Will you never cease meriting your old nickname ? You have springed your dottrel, I find, and what is the consequence ? — why, that there will be hue and cry after you presently. The bearer is a pert young lawyer, who has brought a formal complaint against you, which, luckily, he has preferred in a friendly court. Yet, favourable as the judge was disposed to be, it was with the utmost difficulty that Cousin Jenny and I could keep him to his tackle. He begins to be timid, suspicious, and intractable, and I fear Jenny will soon bend her brows on him in vain. I know not what to advise — the lad who carries this is a good lad — active for his friend — and I have pledged my honour he shall have no personal ill-usage — Pledged my honour, remark these words, and remember I can be rugged and dangerous as well as my neighbours. But I have not ensured him against a short captivity, and as he is a stirring active fellow, I see no remedy but keeping him out of the way till this business of the good Father B—— is safely blown over, which God send it were ! — Always thine, even should I be once more

.                    " CRAIG-IN-PERIL."

" What think you, young man, of the danger you have been about to encounter so willingly ? "

" As strangely," replied Alan Fairford, " as of the extraordinary means which you have been at present pleased to use for the discovery of Mr. Maxwell's purpose."

" Trouble not yourself to account for my conduct," said the Father ; " I have a warrant for what I do, and fear no responsibility. But tell me what is your present purpose."

"I should not perhaps name it to you, whose own safety may be implicated."

"I understand you," answered the Father; "you would appeal to the existing government?—That can at no rate be permitted—we will rather detain you at Fairladies by compulsion."

"You will probably," said Fairford, "first weigh the risk of such a proceeding in a free country."

"I have incurred more formidable hazard," said the priest, smiling; "yet I am willing to find a milder expedient. Come; let us bring the matter to a compromise."—And he assumed a conciliating graciousness of manner, which struck Fairford as being rather too condescending for the occasion; "I presume you will be satisfied to remain here in seclusion for a day or two longer, provided I pass my solemn word to you that you shall meet with the person whom you seek after—meet with him in perfect safety, and, I trust, in good health, and be afterwards both at liberty to return to Scotland, or dispose of yourselves as each of you may be minded?"

"I respect the *verbum sacerdotis* as much as can reasonably be expected from a Protestant," answered Fairford; "but, methinks, you can scarce expect me to repose so much confidence in the word of an unknown person, as is implied in the guarantee which you offer me."

"I am not accustomed, sir," said the Father, in a very haughty tone, "to have my word disputed. But," he added, while the angry hue passed from his cheek, after a moment's reflection, "you know me not, and ought to be excused. I will repose more confidence in your honour than you seem willing to rest upon mine; and since we are so situated

that one must rely upon the other's faith, I will
cause you to be set presently at liberty, and furnished with the means of delivering your letter as
addressed, provided that now, knowing the contents, you think it safe for yourself to execute the
commission."

Alan Fairford paused. "I cannot see," he at
length replied, "how I can proceed with respect to
the accomplishment of my sole purpose, which is
the liberation of my friend, without appealing to the
law, and obtaining the assistance of a magistrate. If I present this singular letter of Mr. Maxwell, with the contents of which I have become
so unexpectedly acquainted, I shall only share his
captivity."

"And if you apply to a magistrate, young man,
you will bring ruin on these hospitable ladies, to
whom, in all human probability, you owe your life.
You cannot obtain a warrant for your purpose,
without giving a clear detail of all the late scenes
through which you have passed. A magistrate
would oblige you to give a complete account of
yourself, before arming you with his authority
against a third party; and in giving such an account,
the safety of these ladies will necessarily be com-
promised. A hundred spies have had, and still
have, their eyes upon this mansion; but God will
protect his own." — He crossed himself devoutly,
and then proceeded. — "You can take an hour to
think of your best plan, and I will pledge myself to
forward it thus far, provided it be not asking you
to rely more on my word than your prudence can
warrant. You shall go to Redgauntlet, — I name
him plainly, to show my confidence in you, — and
you shall deliver him this letter of Mr. Maxwell's,

with one from me, in which I will enjoin him to set your friend at liberty, or at least to make no attempts upon your own person, either by detention or otherwise. If you can trust me thus far," he said, with a proud emphasis on the words, " I will on my side see you depart from this place with the most perfect confidence that you will not return armed with powers to drag its inmates to destruction. You are young and inexperienced — bred to a profession also which sharpens suspicion, and gives false views of human nature. I have seen much of the world, and have known better than most men how far mutual confidence is requisite in managing affairs of consequence."

He spoke with an air of superiority, even of authority, by which Fairford, notwithstanding his own internal struggles, was silenced and overawed so much, that it was not till the Father had turned to leave the apartment that he found words to ask him what the consequences would be, should he decline to depart on the terms proposed.

" You must then, for the safety of all parties, remain for some days an inhabitant of Fairladies, where we have the means of detaining you, which self-preservation will in that case compel us to make use of. Your captivity will be short; for matters cannot long remain as they are — The cloud must soon rise, or it must sink upon us for ever. — *Benedicite !* "

With these words he left the apartment.

Fairford, upon his departure, felt himself much at a loss what course to pursue. His line of education, as well as his father's tenets in matters of Church and State, had taught him a holy horror for Papists, and a devout belief in whatever had been

said of the Punic faith of Jesuits, and of the expe-
dients of mental reservation by which the Catholic
priests in general were supposed to evade keeping
faith with heretics. Yet there was something of
majesty, depressed indeed and overclouded, but
still grand and imposing, in the manner and words
of Father Buonaventure, which it was difficult to
reconcile with those preconceived opinions which
imputed subtlety and fraud to his sect and order.
Above all, Alan was aware that, if he accepted
not his freedom upon the terms offered him, he
was likely to be detained by force; so that, in
every point of view, he was a gainer by adopting
them.

A qualm, indeed, came across him, when he considered, as a lawyer, that this Father was probably,
in the eye of law, a traitor; and that there was an
ugly crime on the Statute Book called Misprision
of Treason. On the other hand, whatever he might
think or suspect, he could not take upon him to
say that the man was a priest whom he had never
seen in the dress of his order, or in the act of cele-
brating mass; so that he felt himself at liberty to
doubt of that respecting which he possessed no legal
proof. He therefore arrived at the conclusion that
he would do well to accept his liberty, and proceed to Redgauntlet under the guarantee of Father
Buonaventure, which he scarce doubted would be
sufficient to save him from personal inconvenience.
Should he once obtain speech of that gentleman, he
felt the same confidence as formerly that he might
be able to convince him of the rashness of his conduct, should he not consent to liberate Darsie
Latimer. At all events, he should learn where his
friend was, and how circumstanced.

Having thus made up his mind, Alan waited anxiously for the expiration of the hour which had been allowed him for deliberation. He was not kept on the tenter-hooks of impatience an instant longer than the appointed moment arrived, for, even as the clock struck, Ambrose appeared at the door of the gallery, and made a sign that Alan should follow him. He did so, and after passing through some of the intricate avenues common in old houses, was ushered into a small apartment, commodiously fitted up; in which he found Father Buonaventure reclining on a couch, in the attitude of a man exhausted by fatigue or indisposition. On a small table beside him, a silver embossed salver sustained a Catholic book of prayer, a small flask of medicine, a cordial, and a little tea-cup of old china. Ambrose did not enter the room — he only bowed profoundly, and closed the door with the least possible noise, so soon as Fairford had entered.

"Sit down, young man," said the Father, with the same air of condescension which had before surprised and rather offended Fairford. "You have been ill, and I know too well by my own case, that indisposition requires indulgence. — Have you," he continued, so soon as he saw him seated, "resolved to remain, or to depart?"

"To depart," said Alan, "under the agreement that you will guarantee my safety with the extraordinary person who has conducted himself in such a lawless manner towards my friend, Darsie Latimer."

"Do not judge hastily, young man," replied the Father. "Redgauntlet has the claims of a guardian over his ward, in respect to the young gentleman, and a right to dictate his place of residence, although he may have been injudicious in selecting the means by which he thinks to enforce his authority."

"His situation as an attainted person abrogates such rights," said Fairford, hastily.

"Surely," replied the priest, smiling at the young lawyer's readiness, "in the eye of those who acknowledge the justice of the attainder — but that do not I. However, sir, here is the guarantee — look at its contents, and do not again carry the letters of Uriah."

Fairford read these words : —

"Good Friend, — We send you hither a young man desirous to know the situation of your ward, since he came under your paternal authority, and hopeful of dealing with you for having your relative put at large. This we recommend to your prudence, highly disapproving, at the same time, of any force or coercion, when such can be avoided, and wishing, therefore, that the bearer's negotiation may be successful. At all rates, however, the bearer hath our pledged word for his safety and freedom, which, therefore, you are to see strictly observed, as you value our honour and your own. We farther wish to converse with you, with as small loss of time as may be, having matters of the utmost confidence to impart. For this purpose we desire you to repair hither with all haste, and thereupon we bid you heartily farewell.

"P. B."

"You will understand, sir," said the Father, when he saw that Alan had perused his letter, "that, by accepting charge of this missive, you bind yourself to try the effect of it before having recourse to any legal means, as you term them, for your friend's release."

"There are a few ciphers added to this letter," said Fairford, when he had perused the paper attentively, — "may I enquire what their import is ? "

"They respect my own affairs," answered the Father, briefly ; "and have no concern whatever with yours."

"It seems to me, however," replied Alan, "natural to suppose "——

"Nothing must be supposed incompatible with my honour," replied the priest, interrupting him ; "when such as I am confer favours, we expect that they shall be accepted with gratitude, or declined with thankful respect — not questioned or discussed."

"I will accept your letter, then," said Fairford, after a minute's consideration, " and the thanks you expect shall be most liberally paid, if the result answer what you teach me to expect."

"God only commands the issue," said Father Buonaventure. "Man uses means. — You understand that, by accepting this commission, you engage yourself in honour to try the effect of my letter upon Mr. Redgauntlet, before you have recourse to informations or legal warrants ? "

"I hold myself bound, as a man of good faith and honour, to do so," said Fairford.

"Well, I trust you," said the Father. "I will now tell you, that an express, dispatched by me last night, has, I hope, brought Redgauntlet to a spot many miles nearer this place, where he will not find it safe to attempt any violence on your friend, should he be rash enough to follow the advice of Mr. Maxwell of Summertrees rather than my commands. We now understand each other."

Drawn and Etched by W. Boucher

AT FAIRLADIES.

He extended his hand towards Alan, who was about to pledge his faith in the usual form by grasping it with his own, when the Father drew back hastily. Ere Alan had time to comment upon this repulse, a small side-door, covered with tapestry, was opened; the hangings were drawn aside, and a lady, as if by sudden apparition, glided into the apartment. It was neither of the Miss Arthurets, but a woman in the prime of life, and in the full-blown expansion of female beauty, tall, fair, and commanding in her aspect. Her locks, of paly gold, were taught to fall over a brow which, with the stately glance of the large open blue eyes, might have become Juno herself; her neck and bosom were admirably formed, and of a dazzling whiteness. She was rather inclined to *embonpoint*, but not more than became her age, of apparently thirty years. Her step was that of a queen, but it was of Queen Vashti, not Queen Esther — the bold and commanding, not the retiring beauty.

Father Buonaventure raised himself on the couch, angrily, as if displeased by this intrusion. "How now, madam," he said, with some sternness; "why have we the honour of your company?"

"Because it is my pleasure," answered the lady, composedly.

"Your pleasure, madam!" he repeated in the same angry tone.

"My pleasure, sir," she continued, "which always keeps exact pace with my duty. I had heard you were unwell — let me hope it is only business which produces this seclusion."

"I am well," he replied; "perfectly well, and I thank you for your care — but we are not alone, and this young man" ——

"That young man?" she said, bending her large and serious eye on Alan Fairford, as if she had been for the first time aware of his presence — "may I ask who he is?"

"Another time, madam; you shall learn his history after he is gone. His presence renders it impossible for me to explain farther."

"After he is gone may be too late," said the lady; "and what is his presence to me, when your safety is at stake? He is the heretic lawyer whom those silly fools, the Arthurets, admitted into this house, at a time when they should have let their own father knock at the door in vain, though the night had been a wild one. You will not surely dismiss him?"

"Your own impatience can alone make that step perilous," said the Father; "I have resolved to take it — do not let your indiscreet zeal, however excellent its motive, add any unnecessary risk to the transaction."

"Even so?" said the lady, in a tone of reproach, yet mingled with respect and apprehension. "And thus you will still go forward, like a stag upon the hunter's snares, with undoubting confidence, after all that has happened?"

"Peace, madam," said Father Buonaventure, rising up; "be silent, or quit the apartment; my designs do not admit of female criticism."

To this peremptory command the lady seemed about to make a sharp reply; but she checked herself, and pressing her lips strongly together, as if to secure the words from bursting from them which were already formed upon her tongue, she made a deep reverence, partly as it seemed in reproach, partly in respect, and left the room as suddenly as she had entered it.

The Father looked disturbed at this incident, which he seemed sensible could not but fill Fairford's imagination with an additional throng of bewildering suspicions ; he bit his lip, and muttered something to himself as he walked through the apartment ; then suddenly turned to his visitor with a smile of much sweetness, and a countenance in which every rougher expression was exchanged for those of courtesy and kindness.

" The visit we have been just honoured with, my young friend, has given you," he said, " more secrets to keep than I would have wished you burdened with. The lady is a person of condition — of rank and fortune — but nevertheless is so circumstanced that the mere fact of her being known to be in this country would occasion many evils. I should wish you to observe secrecy on this subject, even to Redgauntlet or Maxwell, however much I trust them in all that concerns my own affairs."

" I can have no occasion," replied Fairford, " for holding any discussion with these gentlemen, or with any others, on the circumstance which I have just witnessed — it could only have become the subject of my conversation by mere accident, and I will now take care to avoid the subject entirely."

" You will do well, sir, and I thank you," said the Father, throwing much dignity into the expression of obligation which he meant to convey. " The time may perhaps come when you will learn what it is to have obliged one of my condition. As to the lady,.she has the highest merit, and nothing can be said of her justly which would not 'redound to her praise. Nevertheless — in short, sir, we wan-

der at present as in a morning mist — the sun will,
I trust, soon rise and dispel it, when all that now
seems mysterious will be fully revealed — or it will
sink into rain," he added, in a solemn tone, " and
then explanation will be of little consequence. —
Adieu, sir; I wish you well."

He made a graceful obeisance, and vanished
through the same side-door by which the lady had
entered; and Alan thought he heard their voices
high in dispute in the adjoining apartment.

Presently afterwards, Ambrose entered, and told
him that a horse and guide waited him beneath the
terrace.

"The good Father Buonaventure," added the
butler, "has been graciously pleased to consider
your situation, and desired me to enquire whether
you have any occasion for a supply of money ?"

"Make my respects to his reverence," answered
Fairford, " and assure him I am provided in that
particular. I beg you also to make my acknowledgments to the Miss Arthurets, and assure them
that their kind hospitality, to which I probably
owe my life, shall be remembered with gratitude as
long as that life lasts. You yourself, Mr. Ambrose,
must accept of my kindest thanks for your skill and
attention."

Mid these acknowledgments they left the house,
descended the terrace, and reached the spot where
the gardener, Fairford's old acquaintance, waited
for him, mounted upon one horse, and leading
another.

Bidding adieu to Ambrose, our young lawyer
mounted, and rode down the avenue, often looking
back to the melancholy and neglected dwelling in
which he had witnessed such strange scenes, and

musing upon the character of its mysterious inmates; especially the noble and almost regal-seeming priest, and the beautiful but capricious dame, who, if she was really Father Buonaventure's penitent, seemed less docile to the authority of the Church than, as Alan conceived, the Catholic discipline permitted. He could not indeed help being sensible that the whole deportment of these persons differed much from his preconceived notions of a priest and devotee. Father Buonaventure, in particular, had more natural dignity and less art and affectation in his manner, than accorded with the idea which Calvinists were taught to entertain of that wily and formidable person, a Jesuitical missionary.

While reflecting on these things, he looked back so frequently at the house, that Dick Gardener, a forward, talkative fellow, who began to tire of silence, at length said to him, "I think you will know Fairladies when you see it again, sir?"

"I dare say I shall, Richard," answered Fairford, good-humouredly. "I wish I knew as well where I am to go next. But you can tell me, perhaps?"

"Your worship should know better than I," said Dick Gardener; "nevertheless, I have a notion you are going where all you Scotsmen should be sent, whether you will or no."

"Not to the devil, I hope, good Dick?" said Fairford.

"Why, no. That is a road which you may travel as heretics; but as Scotsmen, I would only send you three-fourths of the way — and that is back to Scotland again — always craving your honour's pardon."

"Does our journey lie that way?" said Fairford.

"As far as the water side," said Richard. "I

am to carry you to old Father Crackenthorp's, and
then you are within a spit and a stride of Scotland,
as the saying is.   But mayhap you may think twice
of going thither, for all that; for Old England is
fat feeding-ground for north-country cattle."

# CHAPTER XI.

OUR history must now, as the old romancers were wont to say, "leave to tell" of the quest of Alan Fairford, and instruct our readers of the adventures which befell Darsie Latimer, left as he was in the precarious custody of his self-named tutor, the Laird of the Lochs of Solway, to whose arbitrary pleasure he found it necessary for the present to conform himself.

In consequence of this prudent resolution, and although he did not assume such a disguise without some sensations of shame and degradation, Darsie permitted Cristal Nixon to place over his face, and secure by a string, one of those silk masks which ladies frequently wore to preserve their complexions, when exposed to the air during long journeys on horseback. He remonstrated somewhat more vehemently against the long riding-skirt, which converted his person from the waist into the female guise, but was obliged to concede this point also.

The metamorphosis was then complete; for the fair reader must be informed that in those rude times the ladies, when they honoured the masculine dress by assuming any part of it, wore just such hats, coats, and waistcoats as the male animals themselves made use of, and had no notion of the elegant compromise betwixt male and female attire which has now acquired, *par excellence*, the name of a *habit*. Trolloping things our mothers must have looked, with long square-cut coats, lacking collars, and with waistcoats plentifully supplied with a length of pocket, which hung far downwards from the middle. But then they had some advantage from the splendid colours, lace, and gay embroidery, which masculine attire then exhibited; and, as happens in many similar instances, the finery of the materials made amends for the want of symmetry and grace of form in the garments themselves. But this is a digression.

In the court of the old mansion, half manor-place, half farm-house, or rather a decayed manor-house, converted into an abode for a Cumberland tenant, stood several saddled horses. Four or five of them were mounted by servants or inferior retainers, all of whom were well armed with sword, pistol, and carabine. But two had riding furniture for the use of females — the one being accoutred with a side-saddle, the other with a pillion attached to the saddle.

Darsie's heart beat quicker within him; he easily comprehended that one of these was intended for his own use; and his hopes suggested that the other was designed for that of the fair Green Mantle, whom, according to his established practice, he had adopted for the queen of his affections, although his opportunities of holding communication with her had not exceeded the length of a silent supper on one occasion, and the going down a country-dance on another. This, however, was no unwonted mood of passion with Darsie Latimer, upon whom Cupid was used to triumph only in the degree of a Mahratta conqueror, who overruns a province with the rapidity of lightning, but finds it impossible to retain it beyond a very brief space. Yet this new love was rather more serious than the scarce skinned-up wounds which his friend Fairford used to ridicule. The damsel had shown a sincere interest in his behalf; and the air of mystery with which that interest was veiled, gave her, to his lively imagination, the character of a benevolent and protecting spirit, as much as that of a beautiful female.

At former times, the romance attending his short-lived attachments had been of his own creating, and had disappeared soon as ever he approached more closely to the object with which he had invested it. On the present occasion, it really flowed from external circumstances, which might have interested less susceptible feelings, and an imagination less lively than that of Darsie Latimer, young, inexperienced, and enthusiastic as he was.

He watched, therefore, anxiously to whose service the palfrey bearing the lady's saddle was destined. But ere any female appeared to occupy it, he was himself summoned to take his seat on the pillion behind Cristal Nixon, amid the grins of his old acquaintance Jan, who helped him to horse, and the unrestrained laughter of Cicely, who displayed on the occasion a case of teeth which might have rivalled ivory.

Latimer was at an age when being an object of general ridicule even to clowns and milkmaids was not a matter of indifference, and he longed heartily to have laid his horsewhip across Jan's shoulders. That, however, was a solacement of his feelings which was not at the moment to be thought of; and Cristal Nixon presently put an end to his unplea-

sant situation by ordering the riders to go on. He
himself kept the centre of the troop, two men riding
before and two behind him, always, as it seemed to
Darsie, having their eye upon him, to prevent any
attempt to escape. He could see from time to time,
when the straight line of the road or the advantage
of an ascent permitted him, that another troop of
three or four riders followed them at about a quarter
of a mile's distance, amongst whom he could discover the tall form of Redgauntlet, and the powerful
action of his gallant black horse. He had little
doubt that Green Mantle made one of the party,
though he was unable to distinguish her from the
others.

In this manner they travelled from six in the
morning until nearly ten of the clock, without
Darsie's exchanging a word with any one; for he
loathed the very idea of entering into conversation
with Cristal Nixon, against whom he seemed to
feel an instinctive aversion; nor was that domestic's
saturnine and sullen disposition such as to have
encouraged advances, had he thought of making
them.

At length the party halted for the purpose of
refreshment; but as they had hitherto avoided all
villages and inhabited places upon their route, so
they now stopped at one of those large ruinous
Dutch barns, which are sometimes found in the
fields, at a distance from the farm-houses to which
they belong. Yet in this desolate place some preparations had been made for their reception. There
were in the end of the barn racks filled with provender for the horses, and plenty of provisions for
the party were drawn from the trusses of straw,
under which the baskets that contained them had

been deposited. The choicest of these were selected and arranged apart by Cristal Nixon, while the men of the party threw themselves upon the rest, which he abandoned to their discretion. In a few minutes afterwards the rearward party arrived and dismounted, and Redgauntlet himself entered the barn with the green-mantled maiden by his side. He presented her to Darsie with these words : —

"It is time you two should know each other better. I promised you my confidence, Darsie, and the time is come for reposing it. But first we will have our breakfast ; and then, when once more in the saddle, I will tell you that which it is necessary that you should know. Salute Lilias, Darsie."

The command was sudden, and surprised Latimer, whose confusion was increased by the perfect ease and frankness with which Lilias offered at once her cheek and her hand, and pressing his, as she rather took it than gave her own, said very frankly, "Dearest Darsie, how rejoiced I am that our uncle has at last permitted us to become acquainted ! "

Darsie's head turned round ; and it was perhaps well that Redgauntlet called on him to sit down, as even that movement served to hide his confusion. There is an old song which says —

> when ladies are willing,
> A man can but look like a fool;

and on the same principle Darsie Latimer's looks at this unexpected frankness of reception would have formed an admirable vignette for illustrating the passage. "Dearest Darsie," and such a ready, nay, eager salute of lip and hand ! — It was all very gracious, no doubt — and ought to have been received with much gratitude ; but, constituted as our friend's temper was, nothing could be more inconsistent with his tone of feeling. If a hermit had proposed to him to club for a pot of beer, the illusion of his reverend sanctity could not have been dispelled more effectually than the divine qualities of Green Mantle faded upon the ill-imagined frank-heartedness of poor Lilias. Vexed with her forwardness, and affronted at having once more cheated himself, Darsie could hardly help muttering two lines of the song we have already quoted:

> The fruit that must fall without shaking
> Is rather too mellow for me.

And yet it was pity for her too—she was a very pretty young woman — his fancy had scarce overrated her in that respect — and the slight derangement of the beautiful brown locks which escaped in natural ringlets from under her riding-hat, with the bloom which exercise had brought into her cheek, made her even more than usually fascinating. Redgauntlet modified the sternness of his look when it was turned towards her, and, in addressing her, used a softer tone than his usual deep bass. Even the grim features of Cristal Nixon relaxed when he attended on her, and it was then, if ever, that his misanthropical visage expressed some sympathy with the rest of humanity.

"How can she," thought Latimer, "look so like an angel, yet be so mere a mortal after all? — How could so much seeming modesty have so much forwardness of manner, when she ought to have been most reserved? How can her conduct be reconciled to the grace and ease of her general deportment?"

The confusion of thoughts which occupied Darsie's imagination gave to his looks a disordered appearance, and his inattention to the food which was placed before him, together with his silence and absence of mind, induced Lilias solicitously to enquire whether he did not feel some return of the disorder under which he had suffered so lately. This led Mr. Redgauntlet, who seemed also lost in his own contemplations, to raise his eyes, and join in the same enquiry with some appearance of interest. Latimer explained to both that he was perfectly well.

"It is well it is so," answered Redgauntlet; "for we have that before us which will brook no delay from indisposition — we have not, as Hotspur says, leisure to be sick."

Lilias, on her part, endeavoured to prevail upon Darsie to partake of the food which she offered him, with a kindly and affectionate courtesy, corresponding to the warmth of the interest she had displayed at their meeting; but so very natural, innocent, and pure in its character, that it would have been impossible for the vainest coxcomb to have mistaken it for coquetry, or a desire of captivating a prize so valuable as his affections. Darsie, with no more than the reasonable share of self-opinion common to most youths when they approach twenty-one, knew not how to explain her conduct.

Sometimes he was tempted to think that his own merits had, even during the short intervals when they had seen each other, secured such a hold of the affections of a young person who had probably been bred up in ignorance of the world and its forms that she was unable to conceal her partiality. Sometimes he suspected that she acted by her guardian's order, who, aware that he, Darsie, was

entitled to a considerable fortune, might have taken
this bold stroke to bring about a marriage betwixt
him and so near a relative.

But neither of these suppositions was applicable
to the character of the parties. Miss Lilias's manners, however soft and natural, displayed in their
ease and versatility considerable acquaintance with
the habits of the world, and in the few words she
said during the morning repast there were mingled
a shrewdness and good sense which could scarce
belong to a Miss capable of playing the silly part
of a love-smitten maiden so broadly. As for Redgauntlet, with his stately bearing, his fatal frown,
his eye of threat and of command, it was impossible, Darsie thought, to suspect him of a scheme
having private advantage for its object; — he could
as soon have imagined Cassius picking Cæsar's
pocket, instead of drawing his poniard on the
Dictator.

While he thus mused, unable either to eat, drink,
or answer to the courtesy of Lilias, she soon ceased
to speak to him, and sat silent as himself.

They had remained nearly an hour in their halt-
ing-place, when Redgauntlet said aloud, "Look
out, Cristal Nixon. If we hear nothing from Fairladies, we must continue our journey."

Cristal went to the door, and presently returned
and said to his master, in a voice as harsh as his
features, "Gilbert Gregson is coming, his horse as
white with foam as if a fiend had ridden him."

Redgauntlet threw from him the plate on which
he had been eating, and hastened towards the door
of the barn, which the courier at that moment
entered; a smart jockey, with a black velvet hunt-
ing-cap, and a broad belt drawn tight round his

waist, to which was secured his express-bag. The variety of mud with which he was splashed from cap to spur showed he had had a rough and rapid ride. He delivered a letter to Mr. Redgauntlet, with an obeisance, and then retired to the end of the barn, where the other attendants were sitting or lying upon the straw, in order to get some refreshment.

Redgauntlet broke the letter open with haste, and read it with anxious and discomposed looks. On a second perusal, his displeasure seemed to increase, his brow darkened, and was distinctly marked with the fatal sign peculiar to his family and house. Darsie had never before observed his frown bear such a close resemblance to the shape which tradition assigned it.

Redgauntlet held out the open letter with one hand, and struck it with the forefinger of the other, as, in a suppressed and displeased tone, he said to Cristal Nixon, "Countermanded — ordered northward once more ! — Northward, when all our hopes lie to the south — a second Derby direction, when we turned our back on glory, and marched in quest of ruin !"

Cristal Nixon took the letter and ran it over, then returned it to his master with the cold observation, "A female influence predominates."

"But it shall predominate no longer," said Redgauntlet; "it shall wane as ours rises in the horizon. Meanwhile, I will on before — and you, Cristal, will bring the party to the place assigned in the letter. You may now permit the young persons to have unreserved communication together; only mark that you watch the young man closely enough to prevent his escape, if he should

be idiot enough to attempt it, but not approaching
so close as to watch their free conversation."

"I care nought about their conversation," said
Nixon, surlily.

"You hear my commands, Lilias," said the
Laird, turning to the young lady. "You may use
my permission and authority to explain so much
of our family matters as you yourself know. At
our next meeting I will complete the task of
disclosure, and I trust I shall restore one Redgauntlet more to the bosom of our ancient family.
Let Latimer, as he calls himself, have a horse to
himself; he must for some time retain his disguise.
— My horse — my horse!"

In two minutes they heard him ride off from the
door of the barn, followed at speed by two of the
armed men of his party.

The commands of Cristal Nixon, in the meanwhile, put all the remainder of the party in motion,
but the Laird himself was long out of sight ere
they were in readiness to resume their journey.
When at length they set out, Darsie was aecom-
modated with a horse and side-saddle, instead of
being obliged to resume his place on the pillion
behind the detestable Nixon. He was obliged,
however, to retain his riding-skirt, and to reassume
his mask. Yet, notwithstanding this disagreeable
circumstance, and although he observed that they
gave him the heaviest and slowest horse of the party,
and that, as a farther precaution against escape, he
was closely watched on every side, the riding in
company with the pretty Lilias was an advantage
which overbalanced these inconveniences.

It is true that this society, to which that very
morning he would have looked forward as a glimpse

of heaven, had, now that it was thus unexpectedly indulged, something much less rapturous than he had expected.

It was in vain that, in order to avail himself of a situation so favourable for indulging his romantic disposition, he endeavoured to coax back, if I may so express myself, that delightful dream of ardent and tender passion; he felt only such a confusion of ideas at the difference between the being whom he had imagined, and her with whom he was now in contact, that it seemed to him like the effect of witchcraft. What most surprised him was, that this sudden flame should have died away so rapidly, notwithstanding that the maiden's personal beauty was even greater than he had expected — her demeanour, unless it should be deemed over kind towards himself, as graceful and becoming as he could have fancied it, even in his gayest dreams. It were judging hardly of him to suppose that the mere belief of his having attracted her affections more easily than he expected was the cause of his ungratefully undervaluing a prize too lightly won, or that his transient passion played around his heart with the flitting radiance of a wintry sunbeam flashing against an icicle, which may brighten it for a moment, but cannot melt it. Neither of these was precisely the case, though such fickleness of disposition might also have some influence in the change.

The truth is, perhaps, that the lover's pleasure, like that of the hunter, is in the chase; and that the brightest beauty loses half its merit, as the fairest flower its perfume, when the willing hand can reach it too easily. There must be doubt — there must be danger — there must be difficulty;

and if, as the poet says, the course of ardent affec-tion never does run smooth, it is perhaps because, without some intervening obstacle, that which is called the romantic passion of love, in its high poetical character and colouring, can hardly have an existence; — any more than there can be a current in a river without the stream being narrowed by steep banks, or checked by opposing rocks.

Let not those, however, who enter into a union for life without those embarrassments which delight a Darsie Latimer or a Lydia Languish, and which are perhaps necessary to excite an enthusiastic passion in breasts more firm than theirs, augur worse of their future happiness, because their own alliance is formed under calmer auspices. Mutual esteem, an intimate knowledge of each other's character, seen, as in their case, undisguised by the mists of too partial passion — a suitable proportion of parties in rank and fortune, in taste and pursuits — are more frequently found in a marriage of reason than in a union of romantic attachment; where the imagination, which probably created the virtues and accomplishments with which it invested the beloved object, is frequently afterwards employed in magnifying the mortifying consequences of its own delusion, and exasperating all the stings of disappointment. Those who follow the banners of Reason are like the well-disciplined battalion which, wearing a more sober uniform, and making a less dazzling show, than the light troops commanded by Imagination, enjoy more safety, and even more honour, in the conflicts of human life. All this, however, is foreign to our present purpose.

Uncertain in what manner to address her whom he had been lately so anxious to meet with, and embarrassed by a *tête-à-tête* to which his own timid inexperience gave some awkwardness, the party had proceeded more than a hundred yards before Darsie assumed courage to accost, or even to look at, his companion. Sensible, however, of the impropriety of his silence, he turned to speak to her; and observing that, although she wore her mask, there was something like disappointment and dejection in her manner, he was moved by self-reproach for his own coldness, and hastened to address her in the kindest tone he could assume.

"You must think me cruelly deficient in gratitude, Miss Lilias, that I have been thus long in your company, without thanking you for the interest which you have deigned to take in my unfortunate affairs?"

"I am glad you have at length spoken," she said, "though I own it is more coldly than I expected. — *Miss* Lilias! *Deign* to take interest — In whom, dear Darsie, *can* I take interest but in you? and why do you put this barrier of ceremony betwixt us, whom adverse circumstances have already separated for such a length of time?"

Darsie was again confounded at the extra candour, if we may use the term, of this frank avowal — "One must love partridge very well," thought he, "to accept it when thrown in one's face — if this is not plain speaking, there is no such place as downright Dunstable in being!"

Embarrassed with these reflections, and himself of a nature fancifully, almost fastidiously, delicate, he could only in reply stammer forth an acknowledgment of his companion's goodness, and his own gratitude. She answered in a tone partly sorrowful and partly impatient, repeating, with displeased emphasis, the only distinct words he had been able to bring forth — "Goodness — gratitude! — O Darsie, should these be the phrases between you and me? — Alas! I am too sure you are displeased with me, though I cannot even guess on what account. Perhaps you think I have been too free in venturing upon my visit to your friend. But then remember it was in your behalf, and that I knew no better way to put you on your guard against the misfortunes and restraint which you have been subjected to, and are still enduring."

"Dear lady" — said Darsie, rallying his recollection, and suspicious of some error in apprehension, — a suspicion which his mode of address seemed at once to communicate to Lilias, for she interrupted him, —

"*Lady!* dear *lady!* — For whom, or for what, in Heaven's name, do you take me, that you address me so formally?"

Had the question been asked in that enchanted hall in Fairy-land, where all interrogations must be answered with absolute sincerity, Darsie had certainly replied that he took her for the most frank-hearted and ultra-liberal lass that had ever lived since Mother Eve ate the pippin without paring. But as he was still on middle-earth, and free to avail himself of a little polite deceit, he barely answered that he believed he had the honour of speaking to the niece of Mr. Redgauntlet.

"Surely," she replied; "but were it not as easy for you to have said, to your own only sister?"

Darsie started in his saddle, as if he had received a pistol-shot.

"My sister!" he exclaimed.

"And you did *not* know it, then?" said she.
"I thought your reception of me was cold and
indifferent!"

A kind and cordial embrace took place betwixt
the relatives; and so light was Darsie's spirit, that
he really felt himself more relieved, by getting quit
of the embarrassments of the last half-hour, during
which he conceived himself in danger of being per-
scouted by the attachment of a forward girl, than
disappointed by the vanishing of so many day-
dreams as he had been in the habit of encouraging
during the time when the green-mantled maiden
was goddess of his idolatry. He had been already
flung from his romantic Pegasus, and was too happy
at length to find himself with bones unbroken,
though with his back on the ground. He was,
besides, with all his whims and follies, a generous,
kind-hearted youth, and was delighted to acknowledge so beautiful and amiable a relative, and to
assure her in the warmest terms of his immediate
affection and future protection, so soon as they
should be extricated from their present situation.
Smiles and tears mingled on Lilias's cheeks, like
showers and sunshine in April weather.

"Out on me," she said, "that I should be so
childish as to cry at what makes me so sincerely
happy! since, God knows, family love is what my
heart has most longed after, and to which it has
been most a stranger. My uncle says that you
and I, Darsie, are but half Redgauntlets, and that
the metal of which our father's family was made
has been softened to effeminacy in our mother's
offspring."

"Alas!" said Darsie, "I know so little of our
family story, that I almost doubted that I belonged

to the House of Redgauntlet, although the chief of
the family himself intimated so much to me."

"The Chief of the family!" said Lilias. "You
must know little of your own descent indeed, if
you mean my uncle by that expression. You
yourself, my dear Darsie, are the heir and representative of our ancient House, for our father was the
elder brother — that brave and unhappy Sir Henry
Darsie Redgauntlet who suffered at Carlisle in the
year 1746. He took the name of Darsie, in conjunction with his own, from our mother, heiress to
a Cumberland family of great wealth and antiquity,
of whose large estates you are the undeniable heir,
although those of your father have been involved
in the general doom of forfeiture. But all this
must be necessarily unknown to you."

"Indeed I hear it for the first time in my life,"
answered Darsie.

"And you knew not that I was your sister?"
said Lilias. "No wonder you received me so coldly.
What a strange, wild, forward young person you
must have thought me — mixing myself in the
fortunes of a stranger whom I had only once
spoken to — corresponding with him by signs —
Good Heaven! what can you have supposed me?"

"And how should I have come to the knowledge
of our connexion?" said Darsie. "You are aware
I was not acquainted with it when we danced
together at Brokenburn."

"I saw that with concern, and fain I would have
warned you," answered Lilias; "but I was closely
watched, and before I could find or make an opportunity of coming to a full explanation with you on
a subject so agitating, I was forced to leave the
room. What I did say was, you may remember,

a caution to leave the southern border, for I foresaw what has since happened. But since my uncle has had you in his power, I never doubted he had communicated to you our whole family history."

"He has left me to learn it from you, Lilias; and assure yourself that I will hear it with more pleasure from your lips than from his. I have no reason to be pleased with his conduct towards me."

"Of that," said Lilias, "you will judge better when you have heard what I have to tell you;" and she began her communication in the following manner.

# CHAPTER XII.

"The House of Redgauntlet," said the young lady, "has for centuries been supposed to lie under a doom, which has rendered vain their courage, their talents, their ambition, and their wisdom. Often making a figure in history, they have been ever in the situation of men striving against both wind and tide, who distinguish themselves by their desperate exertions of strength and their persevering endurance of toil, but without being able to advance themselves upon their course, by either vigour or resolution. They pretend to trace this fatality to a legendary history, which I may tell you at a less busy moment."

Darsie intimated that he had already heard the tragic story of Sir Alberick Redgauntlet.

"I need only say, then," proceeded Lilias, "that our father and uncle felt the family doom in its full extent. They were both possessed of considerable property, which was largely increased by our father's marriage, and were both devoted to the service of the unhappy House of Stuart; but (as our mother at least supposed) family considerations might have withheld her husband from joining openly in the affair of 1745, had not the high influence which the younger brother possessed over the elder, from his more decided energy of character, hurried him along with himself into that undertaking.

"When, therefore, the enterprise came to the fatal conclusion which bereaved our father of his life and consigned his brother to exile, Lady Redgauntlet fled from the north of England, determined to break off all communication with her late husband's family, particularly his brother, whom she regarded as having, by their insane political enthusiasm, been the means of his untimely death; and determined that you, my brother, an infant, and that I, to whom she had just given birth, should be brought up as adherents of the present dynasty. Perhaps she was too hasty in this determination — too timidly anxious to exclude, if possible, from the knowledge of the very spot where we existed, a relation so nearly connected with us as our father's only brother. But you must make allowance for what she had suffered. See, brother," she said, pulling her glove off, "these five blood-specks on my arm are a mark by which mysterious Nature has impressed, on an unborn infant, a record of its father's violent death and its mother's miseries." [1]

"You were not, then, born when my father suffered?" said Darsie.

"Alas, no!" she replied; "nor were you a twelvemonth old. It was no wonder that my mother, after going through such scenes of agony, became irresistibly anxious for the sake of her

[1] Several persons have brought down to these days the impressions which Nature had thus recorded, when they were yet babes unborn. One lady of quality, whose father was long under sentence of death, previous to the rebellion, was marked on the back of the neck by the sign of a broad axe. Another, whose kinsmen had been slain in battle and died on the scaffold to the number of seven, bore a child spattered on the right shoulder and down the arm with scarlet drops, as if of blood. Many other instances might be quoted.

children — of her son in particular; the more especially as the late Sir Henry, her husband, had, by a settlement of his affairs, confided the custody of the persons of her children, as well as the estates which descended to them, independently of those which fell under his forfeiture, to his brother Hugh, in whom he placed unlimited confidence.''

"But my mother had no reason to fear the operation of such a deed, conceived in favour of an attainted man," said Darsie.

"True," replied Lilias; "but our uncle's attainder might have been reversed, like that of so many other persons, and our mother, who both feared and hated him, lived in continual terror that this would be the case, and that she should see the author, as she thought him, of her husband's death, come armed with legal powers, and in a capacity to use them, for the purpose of tearing her children from her protection. Besides, she feared, even in his incapacitated condition, the adventurous and pertinacious spirit of her brother-in-law, Hugh Redgauntlet, and felt assured that he would make some attempt to possess himself of the persons of the children. On the other hand, our uncle, whose proud disposition might, perhaps, have been soothed by the offer of her confidence, revolted against the distrustful and suspicious manner in which Lady Darsie Redgauntlet acted towards him. She basely abused, he said, the unhappy circumstances in which he was placed, in order to deprive him of his natural privilege of protecting and educating the infants, whom nature and law, and the will of their father, had committed to his charge, and he swore solemnly he would not submit to such an injury. Report of his threats was made to Lady Redgauntlet, and tended to increase those fears which proved but too well founded. While you and I, children at that time of two or three years old, were playing together in a walled orchard, adjacent to our mother's residence, which she had fixed somewhere in Devonshire, my uncle suddenly scaled the wall with several men, and I was snatched up and carried off to a boat which waited for them. My mother, however, flew to your rescue, and as she seized on and held you fast, my uncle could not, as he has since told me, possess himself of your person, without using unmanly violence to his brother's widow. Of this he was incapable; and, as people began to assemble upon, my mother's screaming, he withdrew, after darting upon you and her one of those fearful looks, which, it is said, remain with our family, as a fatal bequest of Sir Alberick, our ancestor."

"I have some recollection of the scuffle which you mention," said Darsie; "and I think it was my uncle himself (since my uncle he is) who recalled the circumstance to my mind on a late occasion. I can now account for the guarded seclusion under which my poor mother lived — for her frequent tears, her starts of hysterical alarm, and her constant and deep melancholy. Poor lady! what a lot was hers, and what must have been her feelings when it approached to a close!"

"It was then that she adopted," said Lilias, "every precaution her ingenuity could suggest, to keep your very existence concealed from the person whom she feared — nay, from yourself; for she dreaded, as she is said often to have expressed herself, that the wildfire blood of Redgauntlet would

urge you to unite your fortunes to those of your
uncle, who was well known still to carry on political
intrigues which most other persons had considered
as desperate. It was also possible that he, as well
as others, might get his pardon, as government
showed every year more lenity towards the remnant
of the Jacobites, and then he might claim the custody of your person, as your legal guardian. Either
of these events she considered as the direct road to
your destruction."

"I wonder she had not claimed the protection of
Chancery for me," said Darsie; "or confided me to
the care of some powerful friend."

"She was on indifferent terms with her relations, on account of her marriage with our father,"
said Lilias, "and trusted more to secreting you
from your uncle's attempts than to any protection
which law might afford against them. Perhaps she
judged unwisely, but surely not unnaturally, for
one rendered irritable by so many misfortunes and
so many alarms. Samuel Griffiths, an eminent
banker, and a worthy clergyman now dead, were,
I believe, the only persons whom she intrusted
with the execution of her last will; and my uncle
believes that she made them both swear to observe
profound secrecy concerning your birth and pretensions, until you should come to the age of majority,
and, in the meantime, to breed you up in the most
private way possible, and that which was most
likely to withdraw you from my uncle's observation."

"And I have no doubt," said Darsie, "that,
betwixt change of name and habitation, they might
have succeeded perfectly, but for the accident —
lucky or unlucky, I know not which to term it —
which brought me to Brokenburn, and into contact

with Mr. Redgauntlet. I see also why I was warned against England, for in England " ——

"In England alone, if I understand rightly," said Miss Redgauntlet, "the claims of your uncle to the custody of your person could have been enforced, in case of his being replaced in the ordinary rights of citizenship, either by the lenity of the government or by some change in it. In Scotland, where you possess no property, I understand his authority might have been resisted, and measures taken to put you under the protection of the law. But, pray, think it not unlucky that you have taken the step of visiting Brokenburn — I feel confident that the consequences must be ultimately fortunate, for have they not already brought us into contact with each other ? "

So saying, she held out her hand to her brother, who grasped it with a fondness of pressure very different from the manner in which they first clasped hands that morning. There was a moment's pause, while the hearts of both were overflowing with a feeling of natural affection, to which circumstances had hitherto rendered them strangers.

At length Darsie broke silence : " I am ashamed," he said, " my dearest Lilias, that I have suffered you to talk so long about matters concerning myself only, while I remain ignorant of your story, and your present situation."

" The former is none of the most interesting, nor the latter the most safe or agreeable," answered Lilias ; " but now, my dearest brother, I shall have the inestimable support of your countenance and affection ; and were I but sure that we could weather the formidable crisis which I find so close at hand, I should have little apprehensions for the future."

"Let me know," said Darsie, "what our present situation is; and rely upon my utmost exertions both in your defence and my own. For what reason can my uncle desire to detain me a prisoner? —If in mere opposition to the will of my mother, she has long been no more; and I see not why he should wish, at so much trouble and risk, to interfere with the free will of one to whom a few months will give a privilege of acting for himself, with which he will have no longer any pretence to interfere."

"My dearest Arthur," answered Lilias — " for that name, as well as Darsie, properly belongs to you — it is the leading feature in my uncle's character that he has applied every energy of his powerful mind to the service of the exiled family of Stuart. The death of his brother, the dilapidation of his own fortunes, have only added to his hereditary zeal for the House of Stuart a deep and almost personal hatred against the present reigning family. He is, in short, a political enthusiast of the most dangerous character, and proceeds in his agency with as much confidence as if he felt himself the very Atlas who is alone capable of supporting a sinking cause."

"And where or how did you, my Lilias, educated, doubtless, under his auspices, learn to have a different view of such subjects?"

"By a singular chance," replied Lilias, " in the nunnery where my uncle placed me. Although the Abbess was a person exactly after his own heart, my education as a pensioner devolved much on an excellent old mother who had adopted the tenets of the Jansenists, with perhaps a still further tendency towards the reformed doctrines than those of Porte-Royale. The mysterious secrecy with which she inculcated these tenets gave them charms to my young mind, and I embraced them the rather that they were in direct opposition to the doctrines of the Abbess, whom I hated so much for her severity that I felt a childish delight in setting her control at defiance, and contradicting in my secret soul all that I was openly obliged to listen to with reverence. Freedom of religious opinion brings on, I suppose, freedom of political creed; for I had no sooner renounced the Pope's infallibility, than I began to question the doctrine of hereditary and indefeasible right. In short, strange as it may seem, I came out of a Parisian convent, not indeed an instructed Whig and Protestant, but with as much inclination to be so as if I had been bred up, like you, within the Presbyterian sound of St. Giles's chimes."

"More so, perhaps," replied Darsie; "for the nearer the church —— the proverb is somewhat musty. But how did these liberal opinions of yours agree with the very opposite prejudices of my uncle?"

"They would have agreed like fire and water," answered Lilias, "had I suffered mine to become visible; but as that would have subjected me to constant reproach and upbraiding, or worse, I took great care to keep my own secret; so that occasioual censures for coldness, and lack of zeal for the good cause, were the worst I had to undergo; and these were bad enough."

"I applaud your caution," said Darsie.

"You have reason," replied his sister; "but I got so terrible a specimen of my uncle's determination of character before I had been acquainted

with him for much more than a week, that it taught
me at what risk I should contradict his humour. I
will tell you the circumstances; for it will better
teach you to appreciate the romantic and resolved
nature of his character, than any thing which I
could state of his rashness and enthusiasm.

" After I had been many a long year at the convent, I was removed from thence, and placed with a
meagre old Scottish lady of high rank, the daughter
of an unfortunate person whose head had in the
year 1715 been placed on Temple Bar. She sub-
sisted on a small pension from the French Court,
aided by an occasional gratuity from the Stuarts,
to which the annuity paid for my board formed a
desirable addition. She was not ill-tempered, nor
very covetous — neither beat me nor starved me —
but she was so completely trammelled by rank and
prejudices, so awfully profound in genealogy, and
so bitterly keen, poor lady, in British politics, that
I sometimes thought it pity that the Hanoverians,
who murdered, as she used to tell me, her poor
dear father, had left his dear daughter in the land
of the living. Delighted, therefore, was I, when
my uncle made his appearance, and abruptly
announced his purpose of conveying me to England.
My extravagant joy at the idea of leaving Lady
Rachel Rougedragon was somewhat qualified by
observing the melancholy look, lofty demeanour,
and commanding tone of my near relative. He
held more communication with me on the journey,
however, than consisted with his taciturn demeanour in general, and seemed anxious to ascertain my
tone of character, and particularly in point of courage. Now, though I am a tamed Redgauntlet,
yet I have still so much of our family spirit as

enables me to be as composed in danger as most of my sex; and upon two occasions in the course of our journey — a threatened attack by banditti, and the overturn of our carriage — I had the fortune so to conduct myself as to convey to my uncle a very favourable idea of my intrepidity. Probably this encouraged him to put in execution the singular scheme which he had in agitation.

"Ere we reached London we changed our means of conveyance, and altered the route by which we approached the city, more than once; then, like a hare which doubles repeatedly at some distance from the seat she means to occupy, and at last leaps into her form from a distance as great as she can clear by a spring, we made a forced march, and landed in private and obscure lodgings in a little old street in Westminster, not far distant from the Cloisters.

"On the morning of the day on which we arrived my uncle went abroad, and did not return for some hours. Meantime I had no other amusement than to listen to the tumult of noises which succeeded each other, or reigned in confusion together, during the whole morning. Paris I had thought the most noisy capital in the world, but Paris seemed midnight silence compared to London. Cannon thundered near and at a distance — drums, trumpets, and military music of every kind rolled, flourished, and pierced the clouds, almost without intermission. To fill up the concert, bells pealed incessantly from a hundred steeples. The acclamations of an immense multitude were heard from time to time, like the roaring of a mighty ocean, and all this without my being able to glean the least idea of what was going on, for the windows of our apartment looked upon a waste back-yard, which seemed totally deserted.

My curiosity became extreme, for I was satisfied, at length, that it must be some festival of the highest order which called forth these incessant sounds.

"My uncle at length returned, and with him a man of an exterior singularly unprepossessing. I need not describe him to you, for — do not look round — he rides behind us at this moment."

"That respectable person, Mr. Cristal Nixon, I suppose ?" said Darsie.

"The same," answered Lilias ; "make no gesture that may intimate we are speaking of him."

Darsie signified that he understood her, and she pursued her relation.

"They were both in full dress, and my uncle, taking a bundle from Nixon, said to me, ' Lilias, I am come to carry you to see a grand ceremony — put on as hastily as you can the dress you will find in that parcel, and prepare to attend me.' I found a female dress, splendid and elegant, but somewhat bordering upon the antique fashion. It might be that of England, I thought, and I went to my apartment full of curiosity, and dressed myself with all speed.

" My uncle surveyed me with attention — ' She may pass for one of the flower-girls,' he said to Nixon, who only answered with a nod.

" We left the house together, and such was their knowledge of the lanes, courts, and bypaths, that though there was the roar of a multitude in the broad streets, those which we traversed were silent and deserted ; and the strollers whom we met, tired of gazing upon gayer figures, scarcely honoured us with a passing look, although, at any other time, we should, among these vulgar suburbs, have attracted a troublesome share of observation. We crossed at length a broad street, where many soldiers were on guard, while others, exhausted with previous duty, were eating, drinking, smoking, and sleeping beside their piled arms.

"'One day, Nixon,' whispered my uncle, 'we will make these redcoated gentry stand to their muskets more watchfully.'

"'Or it will be the worse for them,' answered his attendant, in a voice as unpleasant as his physiognomy.

"Unquestioned and unchallenged by any one, we crossed among the guards, and Nixon tapped thrice at a small postern door in a huge ancient building which was straight before us. It opened, and we entered without my perceiving by whom we were admitted. A few dark and narrow passages at length conveyed us into an immense Gothic hall, the magnificence of which baffles my powers of description.

"It was illuminated by ten thousand wax lights, whose splendour at first dazzled my eyes, coming as we did from these dark and secret avenues. But when my sight began to become steady, how shall I describe what I beheld! Beneath were huge ranges of tables, occupied by princes and nobles in their robes of state — high officers of the crown, wearing their dresses and badges of authority — reverend prelates and judges, the sages of the Church and law, in their more sombre, yet not less awful robes — with others whose antique and striking costume announced their importance, though I could not even guess who they might be. But at length the truth burst on me at once — it was, and the murmurs around confirmed it, the Coronation Feast. At a table above the rest, and extending across the

upper end of the hall, sat enthroned the youthful
Sovereign himself, surrounded by the princes of the
blood and other dignitaries, and receiving the suit
and homage of his subjects. Heralds and pursui-
vants, blazing in their fantastic yet splendid armorial
habits, and pages of honour, gorgeously arrayed
in the garb of other days, waited upon the princely
banqueters. In the galleries with which this
spacious hall was surrounded shone all, and more
than all, that my poor imagination could conceive,
of what was brilliant in riches or captivating in
beauty. Countless rows of ladies, whose diamonds,
jewels, and splendid attire were their least powerful
charms, looked down from their lofty seats on the rich
scene beneath, themselves forming a show as dazzling and as beautiful as that of which they were
spectators. Under these galleries, and behind the
banqueting tables, were a multitude of gentlemen,
dressed as if to attend a court, but whose garb,
although rich enough to have adorned a royal drawingroom, could not distinguish them in such a
high scene as this. Amongst these we wandered
for a few minutes, undistinguished and unregarded.
I saw several young persons dressed as I was, so
was under no embarrassment from the singularity of
my habit, and only rejoiced, as I hung on my uncle's
arm, at the magical splendour of such a scene, and
at his goodness for procuring me the pleasure of
beholding it.

"By and by, I perceived that my uncle had
acquaintances among those who were under the galleries, and seemed, like ourselves, to be mere
spectators of the solemnity. They recognised each
other with a single word, sometimes only with a
gripe of the hand — exchanged some private signs,

doubtless — and gradually formed a little group, in the centre of which we were placed.

"'Is it not a grand sight, Lilias?' said my uncle. 'All the noble, and all the wise, and all the wealthy of Britain are there assembled.'

"'It is indeed,' said I, 'all that my mind could have fancied of regal power and splendour.'

"'Girl,' he whispered, — and my uncle can make his whispers as terribly emphatic as his thundering voice or his blighting look, — 'all that is noble and worthy in this fair land are there assembled — but it is to bend like slaves and sycophants before the throne of a new usurper.'

"I looked at him, and the dark hereditary frown of our unhappy ancestor was black upon his brow.

"'For God's sake,' I whispered, 'consider where we are.'

"'Fear nothing,' he said; 'we are surrounded by friends.' — As he proceeded, his strong and muscular frame shook with suppressed agitation. — 'See,' he said, 'yonder bends Norfolk, renegade to his Catholic faith; there stoops the Bishop of ——, traitor to the Church of England; and, — shame of shames! yonder the gigantic form of Errol bows his head before the grandson of his father's murderer! But a sign shall be seen this night amongst them — *Mene, Mene, Tekel, Upharsin* shall be read on these walls, as distinctly as the spectral handwriting made them visible on those of Belshazzar!'

"'For God's sake,' said I, dreadfully alarmed, 'it is impossible you can meditate violence in such a presence!'

"'None is intended, fool,' he answered, 'nor

can the slightest mischance happen, provided you
will rally your boasted courage, and obey my directions.   But do it coolly and quickly, for there are
an hundred lives at stake.'

" 'Alas! what can I do?' I asked in the utmost
terror.

" 'Only be prompt to execute my bidding,' said
he; 'it is but to lift a glove — Here, hold this in
your hand — throw the train of your dress over it,
be firm, composed, and ready — or, at all events, I
step forward myself.'

" 'If there is no violence designed,' I said, taking, mechanically, the iron glove he put into my
hand.

" I could not conceive his meaning; but, in the
excited state of mind in which I beheld him, I was
convinced that disobedience on my part would lead
to some wild explosion.   I felt, from the emergency
of the occasion, a sudden presence of mind, and
resolved to do any thing that might avert violence
and bloodshed.   I was not long held in suspense.
A loud flourish of trumpets and the voice of heralds
were mixed with the clatter of horses' hoofs, while
a champion armed at all points, like those I had
read of in romances, attended by squires, pages,
and the whole retinue of chivalry, pranced forward,
mounted upon a barbed steed.   His challenge, in
defiance of all who dared impeach the title of the
new sovereign, was recited aloud — once and again.

" 'Rush in at the third sounding,' said my uncle
to me; 'bring me the parader's gage, and leave
mine in lieu of it.'

" I could not see how this was to be done, as we
were surrounded by people on all sides.   But, at the
third sounding of the trumpets, a lane opened as if

by word of command, betwixt me and the champion, and my uncle's voice said, 'Now, Lilias, NOW!'

"With a swift and yet steady step, and with a presence of mind for which I have never since been able to account, I discharged the perilous commission. I was hardly seen, I believe, as I exchanged the pledges of battle, and in an instant retired. 'Nobly done, my girl!' said my uncle, at whose side I found myself, shrouded as I was before by the interposition of the bystanders. 'Cover our retreat, gentlemen,' he whispered to those around him.

"Room was made for us to approach the wall, which seemed to open, and we were again involved in the dark passages through which we had formerly passed. In a small anteroom my uncle stopped, and hastily muffling me in a mantle which was lying there, we passed the guards — threaded the labyrinth of empty streets and courts, and reached our retired lodgings without attracting the least attention."

"I have often heard," said Darsie, "that a female, supposed to be a man in disguise, — and yet, Lilias, you do not look very masculine, — had taken up the champion's gauntlet (e) at the present King's Coronation, and left in its place a gage of battle, with a paper, offering to accept the combat, provided a fair field should be allowed for it. I have hitherto considered it as an idle tale. I little thought how nearly I was interested in the actors of a scene so daring — How could you have courage to go through with it?" [1]

"Had I had leisure for reflection," answered his sister, "I should have refused, from a mixture of principle and of fear. But, like many people who

[1] Note IV. — Coronation of George III.

do daring actions, I went on because I had not time to think of retreating. The matter was little known, and it is said the King had commanded that it should not be farther enquired into; — from prudence, as I suppose, and lenity, though my uncle chooses to ascribe the forbearance of the Elector. of Hanover, as he calls him, sometimes to pusillanimity, and sometimes to a presumptuous scorn of the faction who opposes his title."

" And have your subsequent agencies under this frantic enthusiast," said Darsie, "equalled this in danger?"

" No — nor in importance," replied Lilias; "though I have witnessed much of the strange and desperate machinations by which, in spite of every obstacle, and in contempt of every danger, he endeavours to awaken the courage of a broken party. I have traversed, in his company, all England and Scotland, and have visited the most extraordinary and contrasted scenes; now lodging at the castles of the proud gentry of Cheshire and Wales, where the retired aristocrats, with opinions as antiquated as their dwellings and their manners, still continue to nourish jacobitical principles; and the next week, perhaps, spent among outlawed smugglers or Highland banditti. I have known my uncle often act the part of a hero, and sometimes that of a mere vulgar conspirator, and turn himself, with the most surprising flexibility, into all sorts of shapes to attract proselytes to his cause."

" Which, in the present day," said Darsie, " he finds, I presume, no easy task."

" So difficult," said Lilias, " that I believe he has, at different times, disgusted with the total falling away of some friends, and the coldness of others, been almost on the point of resigning his undertaking. How often have I known him affect an open brow and a jovial manner, joining in the games of the gentry, and even in the sports of the common people, in order to invest himself with a temporary degree of popularity; while, in fact, his heart was bursting to witness what he called the degeneracy of the times, the decay of activity among the aged, and the want of zeal in the rising generation. After the day has been passed in the hardest exercise, he has spent the night in pacing his solitary chamber, bewailing the downfall of the cause, and wishing for the bullet of Dundee or the axe of Balmerino."

'A strange delusion," said Darsie; "and it is wonderful that it does not yield to the force of reality."

'Ah, but," replied Lilias, "realities of late have seemed to flatter his hopes. The general dissatisfaction with the peace — the unpopularity of the minister, which has extended itself even to the person of his master — the various uproars which have disturbed the quiet of the metropolis, and a general state of disgust and dissatisfaction, which seems to affect the body of the nation, have given unwonted encouragement to the expiring hopes of the Jacobites, and induced many, both at the Court of Rome and, if it can be called so, of the Pretender, to lend a more favourable ear than they had hitherto done to the insinuations of those who, like my uncle, hope, when hope is lost to all but themselves. Nay, I really believe that at this moment they meditate some desperate effort. My uncle has been doing all in his power, of late, to conciliate the affections of those wild communities that dwell on the Solway, over whom our family possessed a seigniorial interest before the forfeiture, and amongst whom, on the occasion of 1745, our unhappy father's interest, with his own, raised a considerable body of men. But they are no longer willing to obey his summons; and, as one apology among others, they allege your absence as their natural head and leader. This has increased his desire to obtain possession of your person, and, if he possibly can, to influence your mind, so as to obtain your authority to his proceedings."

"That he shall never obtain," answered Darsie; "my principles and my prudence alike forbid such a step. Besides, it would be totally unavailing to his purpose. Whatever these people may pretend, to evade your uncle's importunities, they cannot, at this time of day, think of subjecting their necks again to the feudal yoke, which was effectually broken by the Act of 1748, abolishing vassalage and hereditary jurisdictions."

"Ay, but that my uncle considers as the act of a usurping government," said Lilias.

"Like enough *he* may think so," answered her brother, "for he is a superior, and loses his authority by the enactment. But the question is, what the vassals will think of it who have gained their freedom from feudal slavery, and have now enjoyed that freedom for many years? However, to cut the matter short, if five hundred men would rise at the wagging of my finger, that finger should not be raised in a cause which I disapprove of, and upon that my uncle may reckon."

"But you may temporize," said Lilias, upon whom the idea of her uncle's displeasure made evidently a strong impression, — "you may temporize, as most of the gentry in this country do, and let the bubble burst of itself; for it is singular how few of them venture to oppose my uncle directly. I entreat you to avoid direct collision with him. To hear you, the head of the House of Redgauntlet, declare against the family of Stuart would either break his heart or drive him to some act of desperation.

"Yes, but, Lilias, you forget that the consequences of such an act of complaisance might be, that the House of Redgauntlet and I might lose both our heads at one blow."

"Alas!" said she, "I had forgotten that danger. I have grown familiar with perilous intrigues, as the nurses in a pest-house are said to become accustomed to the air around them, till they forget even that it is noisome."

"And yet," said Darsie, "if I could free myself from him without coming to an open rupture — Tell me, Lilias, do you think it possible that he can have any immediate attempt in view?"

"To confess the truth," answered Lilias, "I cannot doubt that he has. There has been an unusual bustle among the Jacobites of late. They have hopes, as I told you, from circumstances unconnected with their own strength. Just before you came to the country, my uncle's desire to find you out became, if possible, more eager than ever — he talked of men to be presently brought together, and of your name and influence for raising them. At this very time, your first visit to Brokenburn took place. A suspicion arose in my uncle's mind that you might be the youth he sought, and it was strengthened by papers and letters which the rascal Nixon did not hesitate to take from your pocket.

Yet a mistake might have occasioned a fatal explosion; and my uncle therefore posted to Edinburgh to follow out the clew he had obtained, and fished enough of information from old Mr. Fairford to make him certain that you were the person he sought. Meanwhile, and at the expense of some personal, and perhaps too bold exertion, I endeavoured, through your friend young Fairford, to put you on your guard."

"Without success," said Darsie, blushing under his mask, when he recollected how he had mistaken his sister's meaning.

"I do not wonder that my warning was fruitless," said she; "the thing was doomed to be. Besides, your escape would have been difficult. You were dogged the whole time you were at the Shepherd's Bush and at Mount Sharon by a spy who scarcely ever left you."

"The wretch little Benjie!" exclaimed Darsie. "I will wring the monkey's neck round the first time we meet."

"It was he indeed who gave constant information of your motions to Cristal Nixon," said Lilias.

"And Cristal Nixon — I owe him, too, a day's work in harvest," said Darsie; "for I am mistaken if he is not the person that struck me down when I was made prisoner among the rioters."

"Like enough; for he has a head and hand for any villainy. My uncle was very angry about it; for though the riot was made to have an opportunity of carrying you off in the confusion, as well as to put the fishermen at variance with the public law, it would have been his last thought to have injured a hair of your head. But Nixon has insinuated himself into all my uncle's secrets, and some of these are so dark and dangerous that, though there are few things he would *not* dare, I doubt if he dare quarrel with him. — And yet I know that of Cristal would move my uncle to pass his sword through his body."

"What is it, for Heaven's sake?" said Darsie. "I have a particular desire for wishing to know."

"The old brutal desperado, whose face and mind are a libel upon human nature, has had the insolence to speak to his master's niece as one whom he was at liberty to admire; and when I turned on him with the anger and contempt he merited, the wretch grumbled out something as if he held the destiny of our family in his hand."

"I thank you, Lilias," said Darsie, eagerly, — "I thank you with all my heart for this communication. I have blamed myself as a Christian man for the indescribable longing I felt from the first moment I saw that rascal to send a bullet through his head; and now you have perfectly accounted for and justified this very laudable wish. I wonder my uncle, with the powerful sense you describe him to be possessed of, does not see through such a villain."

"I believe he knows him to be capable of much evil," answered Lilias — "selfish, obdurate, brutal, and a man-hater. But then he conceives him to possess the qualities most requisite for a conspirator — undaunted courage, imperturbable coolness and address, and inviolable fidelity. In the last particular he may be mistaken. I have heard Nixon blamed for the manner in which our poor father was taken after Culloden."

"Another reason for my innate aversion," said Darsie; "but I will be on my guard with him."

" See, he observes us closely," said Lilias. " What a thing is conscience ! — He knows we are now speaking of him, though he cannot have heard a word that we have said."

It seemed as if she had guessed truly ; for Cristal Nixon at that moment rode up to them, and said, with an affectation of jocularity, which sat very ill upon his sullen features, " Come, young ladies, you have had time enough for your chat this morning, and your tongues, I think, must be tired. We are going to pass a village, and I must beg you to separate — you, Miss Lilias, to ride a little behind — and you, Mrs., or Miss, or Master, whichever you choose to be called, to be jogging a little bit before."

Lilias checked her horse without speaking, but not until she had given her brother an expressive look recommending caution ; to which he replied by a signal indicating that he understood and would comply with her request.

# CHAPTER XIII.

LEFT to his solitary meditations, Darsie (for we will still term Sir Arthur Darsie Redgauntlet of that Ilk by the name to which the reader is habituated) was surprised not only at the alteration of his own state and condition, but at the equanimity with which he felt himself disposed to view all these vicissitudes.

His fever-fit of love had departed like a morning's dream, and left nothing behind but a painful sense of shame, and a resolution to be more cautious ere he again indulged in such romantic visions. His station in society was changed from that of a wandering, unowned youth, in whom none appeared to take an interest, excepting the strangers by whom he had been educated, to the heir of a noble house, possessed of such influence and such property that it seemed as if the progress or arrest of important political events were likely to depend upon his resolution. Even this sudden elevation, the more than fulfilment of those wishes which had haunted him ever since he was able to form a wish on the subject, was contemplated by Darsie, volatile as his disposition was, without more than a few thrills of gratified vanity.

It is true, there were circumstances in his present situation to counterbalance such high advantages.

To be a prisoner in the hands of a man so determined as his uncle was no agreeable consideration, when he was calculating how he might best dispute his pleasure, and refuse to join him in the perilous enterprise which he seemed to meditate. Outlawed and desperate himself, Darsie could not doubt that his uncle was surrounded by men capable of any thing — that he was restrained by no personal considerations — and therefore what degree of compulsion he might apply to his brother's son, or in what manner he might feel at liberty to punish his contumacy, should he disavow the Jacobite cause, must depend entirely upon the limits of his own conscience; and who was to answer for the conscience of a heated enthusiast, who considers opposition to the party he has espoused as treason to the welfare of his country? After a short interval, Cristal Nixon was pleased to throw some light upon the subject which agitated him.

When that grim satellite rode up without ceremony close to Darsie's side, the latter felt his very flesh creep with abhorrence, so little was he able to endure his presence, since the story of Lilias had added to his instinctive hatred of the man. His voice, too, sounded like that of a screech-owl, as he said, "So, my young cock of the north, you now know it all, and no doubt are blessing your uncle for stirring you up to such an honourable action."

"I will acquaint my uncle with my sentiments on the subject before I make them known to any one else," said Darsie, scarcely prevailing on his tongue to utter even these few words in a civil manner.

"Umph," murmured Cristal between his teeth. "Close as wax, I see; and perhaps not quite so pliable. — But take care, my pretty youth," he added, scornfully; "Hugh Redgauntlet will prove a rough colt-breaker — he will neither spare whipcord nor spur-rowel, I promise you."

"I have already said, Mr. Nixon," answered Darsie, "that I will canvass those matters of which my sister has informed me with my uncle himself, and with no other person."

"Nay, but a word of friendly advice would do you no harm, young master," replied Nixon. "Old Redgauntlet is apter at a blow than a word — likely to bite before he barks — the true man for giving Scarborough warning, first knock you down, then bid you stand. — So, methinks, a little kind warning as to consequences were not amiss, lest they come upon you unawares."

"If the warning is really kind, Mr. Nixon," said the young man, "I will hear it thankfully; and indeed, if otherwise, I must listen to it whether I will or no, since I have at present no choice of company or of conversation."

"Nay, I have but little to say," said Nixon, affecting to give to his sullen and dogged manner the appearance of an honest bluntness; "I am as little apt to throw away words as any one. But here is the question — Will you join heart and hand with your uncle, or no?"

"What if I should say **Ay**?" said Darsie, determined, if possible, to conceal his resolution from this man.

"Why, then," said Nixon, somewhat surprised at the readiness of his answer, "all will go smooth, of course — you will take share in this noble undertaking, and, when it succeeds, you will exchange your open helmet for an Earl's coronet perhaps."

"And how if it fails?" said Darsie.

"Thereafter as it may be," said Nixon; "they who play at bowls must meet with rubbers."

"Well, but suppose, then, I have some foolish tenderness for my windpipe, and that, when my uncle proposes the adventure to me, I should say No — how then, Mr. Nixon?"

"Why, then, I would have you look to yourself, young master — There are sharp laws in France against refractory pupils — *lettres de cachet* are easily come by, when such men as we are concerned with interest themselves in the matter."

"But we are not in France," said poor Darsie, through whose blood ran a cold shivering at the idea of a French prison.

"A fast-sailing lugger will soon bring you there though, snug stowed under hatches, like a cask of moonlight."

"But the French are at peace with us," said Darsie, "and would not dare" ——

"Why, who would ever hear of you?" interrupted Nixon; "do you imagine that a foreign Court would call you up for judgment, and put the sentence of imprisonment in the *Courrier de l'Europe*, as they do at the Old Bailey? — No, no, young gentleman — the gates of the Bastile, and of Mont Saint Michel, and the Castle of Vincennes, move on d—d easy hinges when they let folk in—not the least jar is heard. There are cool cells there for hot heads — as calm, and quiet, and dark as you could wish in Bedlam — and the dismissal comes when the carpenter brings the prisoner's coffin, and not sooner."

"Well, Mr. Nixon," said Darsie, affecting a cheerfulness which he was far from feeling, "mine is a hard case — a sort of hanging choice, you will allow — since I must either offend our own government here, and run the risk of my life for doing so, or be doomed to the dungeons of another country, whose laws I have never offended, since I have never trod its soil — Tell me what you would do if you were in my place."

"I'll tell you that when I *am* there," said Nixon, and, checking his horse, fell back to the rear of the little party.

"It is evident," thought the young man, "that the villain believes me completely noosed, and perhaps has the ineffable impudence to suppose that my sister must eventually succeed to the possessions which have occasioned my loss of freedom, and that his own influence over the destinies of our unhappy family may secure him possession of the heiress; but he shall perish by my hand first! — I must now be on the alert to make my escape, if possible, before I am forced on shipboard — Blind Willie will not, I think, desert me without an effort on my behalf, especially if he has learned that I am the son of his late unhappy patron. — What a change is mine! Whilst I possessed neither rank nor fortune, I lived safely and unknown, under the protection of the kind and respectable friends whose hearts Heaven had moved towards me — Now that I am the head of an honourable house, and that enterprises of the most daring character wait my decision, and retainers and vassals seem ready to rise at my beck, my safety consists chiefly in the attachment of a blind stroller!"

While he was revolving these things in his mind, and preparing himself for the interview with his uncle, which could not but be a stormy one, he saw

Hugh Redgauntlet come riding slowly back to meet
them, without any attendants. Cristal Nixon rode
up as he approached, and, as they met, fixed on him
a look of enquiry.

"The fool, Crackenthorp," said Redgauntlet, "has
let strangers into his house. Some of his smuggling
comrades, I believe; we must ride slowly, to give
him time to send them packing."

"Did you see any of your friends?" said Cristal.

"Three, and have letters from many more. They
are unanimous on the subject you wot of — and the
point must be conceded to them, or, far as the
matter has gone, it will go no farther."

"You will hardly bring the Father to stoop to
his flock," said Cristal, with a sneer.

"He must, and shall!" answered Redgauntlet,
briefly. "Go to the front, Cristal — I would speak
with my nephew. — I trust, Sir Arthur Redgauntlet,
you are satisfied with the manner in which I have
discharged my duty to your sister?"

"There can be no fault found to her manners
or sentiments," answered Darsie; "I am happy in
knowing a relative so amiable."

"I am glad of it," answered Mr. Redgauntlet.
"I am no nice judge of women's qualifications, and
my life has been dedicated to one great object; so
that since she left France she has had but little
opportunity of improvement. I have subjected her,
however, as little as possible to the inconveniences
and privations of my wandering and dangerous life.
From time to time she has resided for weeks and
months with families of honour and respectabil-
ity, and I am glad that she has, in your opinion,
the manners and behaviour which become her
birth."

Darsie expressed himself perfectly satisfied, and there was a little pause, which Redgauntlet broke by solemnly addressing his nephew.

' For you, my nephew, I also hoped to have done much. The weakness and timidity of your mother sequestered you from my care, or it would have been my pride and happiness to have trained up the son of my unhappy brother in those paths of honour in which our ancestors have always trod."

" Now comes the storm," thought Darsie to himself, and began to collect his thoughts, as the cautious master of a vessel furls his sails and makes his ship snug when he discerns the approaching squall.

" My mother's conduct, in respect to me, might be misjudged," he said, " but it was founded on the most anxious affection."

" Assuredly," said his uncle, " and I have no wish to reflect on her memory, though her mistrust has donè so much injury, I will not say to me, but to the cause of my unhappy country. Her scheme was, I think, to have made you that wretched pettifogging being which they still continue to call in derision by the once respectable name of a Scottish Advocate ; one of those mongrel things that must creep to learn the ultimate decision of his causes to the bar of a foreign Court, instead of pleading before the independent and august Parliament of his own native kingdom."

" I did prosecute the study of law for a year or two," said Darsie, " but I found I had neither taste nor talents for the science."

" And left it with scorn, doubtless," said Mr. Redgauntlet. " Well, I now hold up to you, my dearest nephew, a more worthy object of ambition.

Look eastward — do you see a monument standing
on yonder plain, near a hamlet?"

Darsie replied that he did.

"The hamlet is called Burgh-upon-sands, and yonder monument is erected to the memory of the tyrant
Edward I. The just hand of Providence overtook
him on that spot, as he was leading his bands to
complete the subjugation of Scotland, whose civil
dissensions began under his accursed policy. The
glorious career of Bruce might have been stopped in
its outset; the field of Bannockburn might have
remained a bloodless turf, if God had not removed,
in the very crisis, the crafty and bold tyrant who
had so long been Scotland's scourge. Edward's grave
is the cradle of our national freedom. It is within
sight of that great landmark of our liberty that I
have to propose to you an undertaking, second in
honour and importance to none since the immortal
Bruce stabbed the Red Comyn, and grasped, with
his yet bloody hand, the independent crown of
Scotland."

He paused for an answer; but Darsie, overawed
by the energy of his manner, and unwilling to commit himself by a hasty explanation, remained silent.

"I will not suppose," said Hugh Redgauntlet,
after a pause, "that you are either so dull as not
to comprehend the import of my words — or so das-
tardly as to be dismayed by my proposal — or so
utterly degenerate from the blood and sentiments
of your ancestors as not to feel my summons as
the horse hears the war-trumpet."

"I will not pretend to misunderstand you, sir,"
said Darsie; "but an enterprise directed against a
dynasty now established for three reigns requires
strong arguments, both in point of justice and of

expediency, to recommend it to men of conscience and prudence."

"I will not," said Redgauntlet, while his eyes sparkled with anger, — "I will not hear you speak a word against the justice of that enterprise, for which your oppressed country calls with the voice of a parent, entreating her children for aid — or against that noble revenge which your father's blood demands from his dishonoured grave. His skull is yet standing over the Rikargate, [1] and even its bleak and mouldered jaws command you to be a man. I ask you, in the name of God, and of your country, will you draw your sword, and go with me to Carlisle, were it but to lay your father's head, now the perch of the obscene owl and carrion crow, and the scoff of every ribald clown, in consecrated earth, as befits his long ancestry?"

Darsie, unprepared to answer an appeal urged with so much passion, and not doubting a direct refusal would cost him his liberty or life, was again silent.

"I see," said his uncle, in a more composed tone, "that it is not deficiency of spirit, but the grovelling habits of a confined education, among the poor-spirited class you were condemned to herd with, that keeps you silent. You scarce yet believe yourself a Redgauntlet; your pulse has not yet learned the genuine throb that answers to the summons of honour and of patriotism."

"I trust," replied Darsie, at last, "that I shall never be found indifferent to the call of either; but to answer them with effect — even were I con-vinced that they now sounded in my ear — I must

---

[1] The northern gate of Carlisle was long garnished with the heads of the Scottish rebels executed in 1746.

see some reasonable hope of success in the desperate enterprise in which you would involve me. I look around me, and I see a settled government — an established authority — a born Briton on the throne — the very Highland mountaineers, upon whom alone the trust of the exiled family reposed, assembled into regiments, which act under the orders of the existing dynasty.[1] France has been utterly dismayed by the tremendous lessons of the last war, and will hardly provoke another. All without and within the kingdom is adverse to encountering a hopeless struggle, and you alone, sir, seem willing to undertake a desperate enterprise."

"**And** would undertake it were it **ten** times more desperate; and have agitated it when **ten** times the obstacles were interposed. — Have I forgot my brother's blood? — Can I — dare I even now repeat the Pater Noster, since my enemies and the murderers remain unforgiven? — Is there an art I have not practised — a privation to which I have not submitted, to bring on the crisis which I now behold arrived? — Have I not been a vowed and a devoted man, foregoing every comfort of social life, renouncing even the exercise of devotion unless when I might name in prayer my prince and country, submitting to every thing to make converts to this noble cause? — Have I done all this, and shall I now stop short?" — Darsie was about to interrupt him, but he pressed his hand affectionately upon his shoulder, and enjoining, or rather imploring silence, —

[1] The Highland regiments were first employed by the celebrated Earl of Chatham, who assumed to himself no small degree of praise for having called forth to the support of the country and the government the valour which had been too often directed against both.

"Peace," he said, "heir of my ancestors' fame —
heir of all my hopes and wishes — Peace, son of my
slaughtered brother! I have sought for thee, and
mourned for thee, as a mother for an only child.
Do not let me again lose you in the moment when
you are restored to my hopes. Believe me, I distrust so much my own impatient temper, that I
entreat you, as the dearest boon, do nought to
awaken it at this crisis."

Darsie was not sorry to reply that his respect
for the person of his relation would induce him to
listen to all which he had to apprize him of, before
he formed any definite resolution upon the weighty
subjects of deliberation which he proposed to him.

"Deliberation!" repeated Redgauntlet, impatiently; "and yet it is not ill said. — I wish there
had been more warmth in thy reply, Arthur; but
I must recollect were an eagle bred in a falcon's
mew, and hooded like a reclaimed hawk, he could
not at first gaze steadily on the sun. Listen to
me, my dearest Arthur. The state of this nation
no more implies prosperity than the florid colour
of a feverish patient is a symptom of health. All
is false and hollow — the apparent success of Chatham's administration has plunged the country
deeper in debt than all the barren acres of Canada
are worth, were they as fertile as Yorkshire — the
dazzling lustre of the victories of Minden and Que-
bec have been dimmed by the disgrace of the hasty
peace — by the war, England, at immense expense,
gained nothing but honour, and that she has gratui-
tously resigned. Many eyes, formerly cold and
indifferent, are now looking towards the line of
our ancient and rightful monarchs, as the only
refuge in the approaching storm — the rich are

alarmed — the nobles are disgusted — the populace are inflamed — and a band of patriots, whose measures are more safe that their numbers are few, have resolved to set up King Charles's standard."

"But the military," said Darsie — "how can you, with a body of unarmed and disorderly insurgents, propose to encounter a regular army? The Highlanders are now totally disarmed."

"In a great measure, perhaps," answered Redgauntlet; "but the policy which raised the Highland regiments has provided for that. We have already friends in these corps; nor can we doubt for a moment what their conduct will be, when the white cockade is once more mounted. The rest of the standing army has been greatly reduced since the peace; and we reckon confidently on our standard being joined by thousands of the disbanded troops."

"Alas!" said Darsie, "and is it upon such vague hopes as these, the inconstant humour of a crowd, or of a disbanded soldiery, that men of honour are invited to risk their families, their property, their life?"

"Men of honour, boy," said Redgauntlet, his eyes glancing with impatience, "set life, property, family, and all at stake, when that honour commands it! We are not now weaker than when seven men, landing in the wilds of Moidart, shook the throne of the usurper till it tottered — won two pitched fields, besides overrunning one kingdom and the half of another, and, but for treachery, would have achieved what their venturous successors are now to attempt in their turn."

"And will such an attempt be made in serious earnest?" said Darsie. "Excuse me, my uncle, if

I can scarce believe a fact so extraordinary. Will there really be found men of rank and consequence sufficient to renew the adventure of 1745?"

"I will not give you my confidence by halves, Sir Arthur," replied his uncle — "Look at that scroll — what say you to these names? — Are they not the flower of the Western shires — of Wales — of Scotland?"

"The paper contains indeed the names of many that are great and noble," replied Darsie, after perusing it; "but "——

"But what?" asked his uncle, impatiently; "do you doubt the ability of those nobles and gentlemen to furnish the aid in men and money at which they are rated?"

"Not their ability, certainly," said Darsie, "for of that I am no competent judge; — but I see in this scroll the name of Sir Arthur Darsie Redgauntlet of that Ilk, rated at an hundred men and upwards — I certainly am ignorant how he is to redeem that pledge."

"I will be responsible for the men," - replied Hugh Redgauntlet.

"But, my dear uncle," added Darsie, "I hope, for your sake, that the other individuals whose names are here written have had more acquaintance with your plan than I have been indulged with."

"For thee and thine I can be myself responsible," said Redgauntlet; "for if thou hast not the courage to head the force of thy house, the leading shall pass to other hands, and thy inheritance shall depart from thee, like vigour and verdure from a rotten branch. For these honourable persons, a slight condition there is which they annex to their friendship — something so trifling that it is scarce worthy of mention. This boon granted to them by him who is most interested, there is no question they will take the field in the manner there stated."

Again Darsie perused the paper, and felt himself still less inclined to believe that so many men of family and fortune were likely to embark in an enterprise so fatal. It seemed as if some rash plotter had put down at a venture the names of all whom common report tainted with Jacobitism; or if it was really the act of the individuals named, he suspected they must be aware of some mode of excusing themselves from compliance with its purport. It was impossible, he thought, that Englishmen of large fortune (*f*), who had failed to join Charles when he broke into England at the head of a victorious army, should have the least thoughts of encouraging a descent when circumstances were so much less propitious. He therefore concluded the enterprise would fall to pieces of itself, and that his best way was, in the meantime, to remain silent, unless the actual approach of a crisis (which might, however, never arrive) should compel him to give a downright refusal to his uncle's proposition; and if, in the interim, some door for escape should be opened, he resolved within himself not to omit availing himself of it.

Hugh Redgauntlet watched his nephew's looks for some time, and then, as if arriving from some other process of reasoning at the same conclusion, he said, "I have told you, Sir Arthur, that I do not urge your immediate accession to my proposal; indeed the consequences of a refusal would be so dreadful to yourself, so destructive to all the hopes which I have nursed, that I would not risk, by a moment's impatience, the object of my whole life.

Yes, Arthur, I have been a self-denying hermit at one time — at another, the apparent associate of outlaws and desperadoes — at another, the subordinate agent of men whom I felt every way my inferiors — not for any selfish purpose of my own, no, not even to win for myself the renown of being the principal instrument in restoring my King and freeing my country. My first wish on earth is for that restoration and that freedom — my next, that my nephew, the representative of my house, and of the brother of my love, may have the advantage and the credit of all my efforts in the good cause. But," he added, darting on Darsie one of his withering frowns, "if Scotland and my father's House cannot stand and flourish together, then perish the very name of Redgauntlet! perish the son of my brother, with every recollection of the glories of my family, of the affections of my youth, rather than my country's cause should be injured in the tithing of a barleycorn! The spirit of Sir Alberick is alive within me at this moment," he continued, drawing up his stately form, and sitting erect in his saddle, while he pressed his finger against his forehead; "and if you yourself crossed my path in opposition, I swear, by the mark that darkens my brow, that a new deed should be done — a new doom should be deserved!"

He was silent, and his threats were uttered in a tone of voice so deeply resolute, that Darsie's heart sank within him when he reflected on the storm of passion which he must encounter, if he declined to join his uncle in a project to which prudence and principle made him equally adverse. He had scarce any hope left but in temporizing until he could make his escape, and resolved to avail himself for that purpose of the delay which his uncle seemed not unwilling to grant. The stern, gloomy look of his companion became relaxed by degrees, and presently afterwards he made a sign to Miss Redgauntlet to join the party, and began a forced conversation on ordinary topics; in the course of which Darsie observed that his sister seemed to speak under the most cautious restraint, weighing every word before she uttered it, and always permitting her uncle to give the tone to the conversation, though of the most trifling kind. This seemed to him (such an opinion had he already entertained of his sister's good sense and firmness) the strongest proof he had yet received of his uncle's peremptory character, since he saw it observed with so much deference by a young person whose sex might have given her privileges, and who seemed by no means deficient either in spirit or firmness.

The little cavalcade was now approaching the house of Father Crackenthorp, situated, as the reader knows, by the side of the Solway, and not far distant from a rude pier, near which lay several fishing-boats, which frequently acted in a different capacity. The house of the worthy publican was also adapted to the various occupations which he carried on, being a large scrambling assemblage of cottages attached to a house of two stories, roofed with flags of sandstone — the original mansion, to which the extension of Master Crackenthorp's trade had occasioned his making many additions. Instead of the single long watering-trough which usually distinguishes the front of the English public-house of the second class, there were three conveniences of that kind, for the use, as the landlord used to say, of the troop-horses, when the

soldiers came to search his house; while a knowing leer and a nod let you understand what species
of troops he was thinking of. A huge ash-tree
before the door, which had reared itself to a great
size and height, in spite of the blasts from the
neighbouring Solway, overshadowed, as usual, the
ale-bench, as our ancestors called it, where, though
it was still early in the day, several fellows, who
seemed to be gentlemen's servants, were drinking
beer and smoking. One or two of them wore
liveries, which seemed known to Mr. Redgauntlet,
for he muttered between his teeth, "Fools, fools!
were they on a march to hell, they must have their
rascals in livery with them, that the whole world
might know who were going to be damned."

As he thus muttered, he drew bridle before the
door of the place, from which several other lounging guests began to issue, to look with indolent
curiosity, as usual, upon an *arrival*.

Redgauntlet sprang from his horse, and assisted
his niece to dismount; but, forgetting, perhaps, his
nephew's disguise, he did not pay him the attention
which his female dress demanded.

The situation of Darsie was indeed something
awkward; for Cristal Nixon, out of caution perhaps to prevent escape, had muffled the extreme folds
of the riding-skirt with which he was accoutred
around his ankles and under his feet, and there
secured it with large corking-pins. We presume
that gentlemen-cavaliers may sometimes cast their
eyes to that part of the person of the fair eques-
trians whom they chance occasionally to escort;
and if they will conceive their own feet, like Darsie's,
muffled in such a labyrinth of folds and amplitude
of robe as modesty doubtless induces the fair crea-

tures to assume upon such occasions, they will allow that, on a first attempt, they might find some awkwardness in dismounting. Darsie, at least, was in such a predicament, for, not receiving adroit assistance from the attendant of Mr. Redgauntlet, he stumbled as he dismounted from the horse, and might have had a bad fall, had it not been broken by the gallant interposition of a gentleman, who probably was, on his part, a little surprised at the solid weight of the distressed fair one whom he had the honour to receive in his embrace. But what was his surprise to that of Darsie, when the hurry of the moment and of the accident permitted him to see that it was his friend Alan Fairford in whose arms he found himself! A thousand apprehensions rushed on him, mingled with the full career of hope and joy, inspired by the unexpected appearance of his beloved friend at the very crisis, it seemed, of his fate.

He was about to whisper in his ear, cautioning him at the same time to be silent; yet he hesitated for a second or two to effect his purpose, since, should Redgauntlet take the alarm from any sudden exclamation on the part of Alan, there was no saying what consequences might ensue.

Ere he could decide what was to be done, Redgauntlet, who had entered the house, returned hastily, followed by Cristal Nixon. "I'll release you of the charge of this young lady, sir," he said, haughtily, to Alan Fairford, whom he probably did not recognise.

"I had no desire to intrude, sir," replied Alan; "the lady's situation seemed to require assistance — and — but have I not the honour to speak to Mr. Herries of Birrenswork?"

"You are mistaken, sir," said Redgauntlet, turning short off, and making a sign with his hand to Cristal, who hurried Darsie, however unwillingly, into the house, whispering in his ear, "Come, miss, let us have no making of acquaintance from the windows. Ladies of fashion must be private. Show us a room, Father Crackenthorp."

So saying, he conducted Darsie into the house, interposing at the same time his person betwixt the supposed young lady and the stranger of whom he was suspicious, so as to make communication by signs impossible. As they entered, they heard the sound of a fiddle in the stone-floored and well-sanded kitchen, through which they were about to follow their corpulent host, and where several people seemed engaged in dancing to its strains.

"D—n thee," said Nixon to Crackenthorp, "would you have the lady go through all the mob of the parish? — Hast thou no more private way to our sitting-room?"

"None that is fit for my travelling," answered the landlord, laying his hand on his portly stomach. "I am not Tom Turnpenny, to creep like a lizard through keyholes."

So saying, he kept moving on through the revellers in the kitchen; and Nixon holding Darsie by his arm, as if to offer the lady support, but in all probability to frustrate any effort at escape, moved through the crowd, which presented a very motley appearance, consisting of domestic servants, country fellows, seamen, and other idlers, whom Wandering Willie was regaling with his music.

To pass another friend without intimation of his presence would have been actual pusillanimity; and just when they were passing the blind man's elevated seat, Darsie asked him, with some emphasis, whether he could not play a Scottish air?—The man's face had been the instant before devoid of all sort of expression, going through his perform- ance like a clown through a beautiful country, too much accustomed to consider it as a task to take any interest in the performance, and, in fact, scarce seeming to hear the noise that he was creating. In a word, he might at the time have made a compau- ion to my friend Wilkie's inimitable blind crowder. But with Wandering Willie this was only an occa- sional and a rare fit of dulness, such as will at times creep over all the professors of the fine arts, arising either from fatigue, or contempt of the pre- sent audience, or that caprice which so often tempts painters and musicians, and great actors, in the phrase of the latter, to *walk through* their part, instead of exerting themselves with the energy which acquired their fame. But when the per- former heard the voice of Darsie, his countenance became at once illuminated, and showed the com- plete mistake of those who suppose that the principal point of expression depends upon the eyes. With his face turned to the point from which the sound came, his upper lip a little curved and quivering with agitation, and with a colour which surprise and pleasure had brought at once into his faded cheek, he exchanged the humdrum hornpipe which he had been sawing out with reluctant and lazy bow for the fine Scottish air,

You're welcome, Charlie Stuart,

which flew from his strings as if by inspiration, and after a breathless pause of admiration among the audience, was received with a clamour of applause, which seemed to show that the name and tendency, as well as the execution of the tune, was in the highest degree acceptable to all the party assembled.

In the meantime, Cristal Nixon, still keeping hold of Darsie, and following the landlord, forced his way with some difficulty through the crowded kitchen, and entered a small apartment on the other side of it, where they found Lilias Redgauntlet already seated. Here Nixon gave way to his suppressed resentment, and turning sternly on Crackenthorp, threatened him with his master's severest displeasure, because things were in such bad order to receive his family, when he had given such special advice that he desired to be private. But Father Crackenthorp was not a man to be browbeaten.

"Why, brother Nixon, thou art angry this morning," he replied; "hast risen from thy wrong side, I think. You know, as well as I, that most of this mob is of the Squire's own making — gentlemen that come with their servants, and so forth, to meet him in the way of business, as old Tom Turnpenny says — the very last that came was sent down with Dick Gardener from Fairladies."

"But the blind scraping scoundrel yonder," said Nixon, "how dared you take such a rascal as that across your threshold at such a time as this? — If the Squire should dream you have a thought of peaching — I am only speaking for your good, Father Crackenthorp."

"Why, look ye, brother Nixon," said Crackenthorp, turning his quid with great composure, "the Squire is a very worthy gentleman, and I'll never deny it; but I am neither his servant nor his tenant, and so he need send me none of his orders till he hears I have put on his livery. As for turning away folk from my door, I might as well plug up the ale-tap and pull down the sign — and as for peaching and such like, the Squire will find the folk here are as honest to the full as those he brings with him."

"How, you impudent lump of tallow," said Nixon, "what do you mean by that?"

"Nothing," said Crackenthorp, "but that I can tour out as well as another — you understand me — keep good lights in my upper story — know a thing or two more than most folk in this country. If folk will come to my house on dangerous errands, egad they shall not find Joe Crackenthorp a cat's-paw. I'll keep myself clear, you may depend on it, and let every man answer for his own actions — that's my way — Any thing wanted, Master Nixon?"

"No — Yes — begone!" said Nixon, who seemed embarrassed with the landlord's contumacy, yet desirous to conceal the effect it produced on him.

The door was no sooner closed on Crackenthorp, than Miss Redgauntlet, addressing Nixon, commanded him to leave the room, and go to his proper place.

"How, madam?" said the fellow sullenly, yet with an air of respect. "Would you have your uncle pistol me for disobeying his orders?"

"He may perhaps pistol you for some other reason, if you do not obey mine," said Lilias, composedly.

"You abuse your advantage over me, madam — I really dare not go — I am on guard over this other Miss here; and if I should desert my post, my life were not worth five minutes' purchase."

" Then know your post, sir," said Lilias, " and watch on the outside of the door. You have no commission to listen to our private conversation, I suppose? Begone, sir, without further speech or remonstrance, or I will tell my uncle that which you would have reason to repent he should know."

The fellow looked at her with a singular expression of spite, mixed with deference. " You abuse your advantages, madam," he said, " and act as foolishly in doing so as I did in affording you such a hank over me. But you are a tyrant; and tyrants have commonly short reigns."

So saying, he left the apartment.

" The wretch's unparalleled insolence," said Lilias to her brother, " has given me one great advantage over him. For, knowing that my uncle would shoot him with as little remorse as a woodcock, if he but guessed at his brazen-faced assurance towards me, he dares not since that time assume, so far as I am concerned, the air of insolent domination which the possession of my uncle's secrets, and the knowledge of his most secret plans, have led him to exert over others of his family."

" In the meantime," said Darsie, " I am happy to see that the landlord of the house does not seem so devoted to him as I apprehended; and this aids the hope of escape which I am nourishing for you and for myself. O, Lilias! the truest of friends, Alan Fairford, is in pursuit of me, and is here at this moment. Another humble, but, I think, faithful friend, is also within these dangerous walls."

Lilias laid her finger on her lips, and pointed to

the door. Darsie took the hint, lowered his voice, and informed her in whispers of the arrival of Fairford, and that he believed he had opened a communication with Wandering Willie. She listened with the utmost interest, and had just begun to reply, when a loud noise was heard in the kitchen, caused by several contending voices, amongst which Darsie thought he could distinguish that of Alan Fairford.

Forgetting how little his own condition permitted him to become the assistant of another, Darsie flew to the door of the room, and finding it locked and bolted on the outside, rushed against it with all his force, and made the most desperate efforts to burst it open, notwithstanding the entreaties of his sister that he would compose himself, and recollect the condition in which he was placed. But the door, framed to withstand attacks from excisemen, constables, and other personages, considered as worthy to use what are called the King's keys, [1] " and therewith to make lockfast places open and patent," set his efforts at defiance. Meantime the noise continued without, and we are to give an account of its origin in our next chapter.

[1] In common parlance, a crowbar and hatchet.

# CHAPTER XIV.

## NARRATIVE OF DARSIE LATIMER, CONTINUED.

JOE CRACKENTHORP'S public-house had never, since it first reared its chimneys on the banks of the Solway, been frequented by such a miscellaneous group of visitors as had that morning become its guests. Several of them were persons whose quality seemed much superior to their dresses and modes of travelling. The servants who attended them contradicted the inferences to be drawn from the garb of their masters, and, according to the custom of the knights of the rainbow, gave many hints that they were not people to serve any but men of first-rate consequence. These gentlemen, who had come thither chiefly for the purpose of meeting with Mr. Redgauntlet, seemed moody and anxious, conversed and walked together, apparently in deep conversation, and avoided any communication with the chance travellers whom accident brought that morning to the same place of resort.

As if Fate had set herself to confound the plans of the Jacobite conspirators, the number of travellers was unusually great, their appearance respectable, and they filled the public tap-room of the inn, where the political guests had already occupied most of the private apartments.

Amongst others, honest Joshua Geddes had arrived, travelling, as he said, in the sorrow of the soul, and mourning for the fate of Darsie Latimer as he would for his first-born child. He had skirted the whole coast of the Solway, besides making various trips into the interior, not shunning, on such occasions, to expose himself to the laugh of the scorner, nay, even to serious personal risk, by frequenting the haunts of smugglers, horse-jockeys, and other irregular persons, who looked on his intrusion with jealous eyes, and were apt to consider him as an exciseman in the disguise of a Quaker. All this labour and peril, however, had been undergone in vain. No search he could make obtained the least intelligence of Latimer, so that he began to fear the poor lad had been spirited abroad; for the practice of kidnapping was then not infrequent, especially on the western coasts of Britain, if indeed he had escaped a briefer and more bloody fate.

With a heavy heart, he delivered his horse, even Solomon, into the hands of the hostler, and walking into the inn, demanded from the landlord breakfast and a private room. Quakers and such hosts as old Father Crackenthorp are no congenial spirits; the latter looked askew over his shoulder, and replied, "If you would have breakfast here, friend, you are like to eat it where other folk eat theirs."

"And wherefore can I not," said the Quaker, "have an apartment to myself, for my money?"

"Because, Master Jonathan, you must wait till your betters be served, or else eat with your equals."

Joshua Geddes argued the point no farther, but sitting quietly down on the seat which Crackenthorp indicated to him, and calling for a pint of ale, with some bread, butter, and Dutch cheese, began to satisfy the appetite which the morning air had rendered unusually alert.

While the honest Quaker was thus employed, another stranger entered the apartment, and sat down near to the table on which his victuals were placed. He looked repeatedly at Joshua, licked his parched and chopped lips as he saw the good Quaker masticate his bread and cheese, and sucked up his thin chops when Mr. Geddes applied the tankard to his mouth, as if the discharge of these bodily functions by another had awakened his sympathies in an uncontrollable degree. At last, being apparently unable to withstand his longings, he asked, in a faltering tone, the huge landlord, who was tramping through the room in all corpulent impatience, "whether he could have a plack-pie?"

"Never heard of such a thing, master," said the landlord, and was about to trudge onward; when the guest, detaining him, said, in a strong Scottish tone, "Ye will maybe have nae whey then, nor buttermilk, nor ye couldna exhibit a souter's clod?"

"Can't tell what ye are talking about, master," said Crackenthorp.

"Then ye will have nae breakfast that will come within the compass of a shilling Scots?"

"Which is a penny sterling," answered Crackenthorp, with a sneer. "Why, no, Sawney, I can't say as we have — we can't afford it; but you shall have a bellyful for love, as we say in the bull-ring."

"I shall never refuse a fair offer," said the poverty-stricken guest; "and I will say that for the English, if they were deils, that they are a ceeveleesed people to gentlemen that are under a cloud."

'Gentlemen! — humph!" said Crackenthorp — "not a bluecap among them but halts upon that foot." Then seizing on a dish which still contained a huge cantle of what had been once a princely mutton pasty, he placed it on the table before the stranger, saying, "There, master gentleman; there is what is worth all the black pies, as you call them, that were ever made of sheep's head."

"Sheep's head is a gude thing, for a' that," replied the guest; but not being spoken so loud as to offend his hospitable entertainer, the interjection might pass for a private protest against the scandal thrown out against the standing dish of Caledonia.

This premised, he immediately began to transfer the mutton and pie-crust from his plate to his lips, in such huge gobbets as if he was refreshing after a three days' fast, and laying in provisions against a whole Lent to come.

Joshua Geddes in his turn gazed on him with surprise, having never, he thought, beheld such a gaunt expression of hunger in the act of eating. "Friend," he said, after watching him for some minutes, "if thou gorgest thyself in this fashion, thou wilt assuredly choke. Wilt thou not take a draught out of my cup to help down all that dry meat?"

"Troth," said the stranger, stopping and looking at the friendly propounder, "that's nae bad overture, as they say in the General Assembly. I have heard waur motions than that frae wiser counsel."

Mr. Geddes ordered a quart of home-brewed to be placed before our friend Peter Peebles; for the reader must have already conceived that this unfortunate litigant was the wanderer in question.

The victim of Themis had no sooner seen the flagon than he seized it with the same energy which he had displayed in operating upon the pie — puffed off the froth with such emphasis that some of it

lighted on Mr. Geddes's head — and then said, as if
with a sudden recollection of what was due to civility, "Here's to ye, friend. — What! are ye ower
grand to give me an answer, or are ye dull o'
hearing?"

"I prithee drink thy liquor, friend," said the
good Quaker; "thou meanest it in civility, but we
care not for these idle fashions."

"What! ye are a Quaker, are ye?" said Peter;
and without further ceremony reared the flagon to
his head, from which he withdrew it not while a
single drop of "barley-broo" remained. — "That's
done you and me muckle gude," he said, sighing as
he set down his pot; "but twa mutchkins o' yill
between twa folk is a drappie ower little measure.
What say ye to anither pot? or shall we cry in a
blithe Scots pint at ance? — The yill is no amiss."

"Thou mayst call for what thou wilt on thine
own charges, friend," said Geddes; "for myself, I
willingly contribute to the quenching of thy natural thirst; but I fear it were no such easy matter
to relieve thy acquired and artificial drouth."

"That is to say, in plain terms, ye are for with-
drawing your caution with the folk of the house?
You Quaker folk are but fause comforters; but
since ye have garred me drink sae muckle cauld
yill — me that am no used to the like of it in the
forenoon — I think ye might as weel have offered
me a glass of brandy or usquabae — I'm nae nice
body — I can drink ony thing that's wet and
toothsome."

"Not a drop at my cost, friend," quoth Geddes.
"Thou art an old man, and hast, perchance, a
heavy and long journey before thee. Thou art,
moreover, my countryman, as I judge from thy

tongue; and I will not give thee the means of dis-
honouring thy grey hairs in a strange land."

" Grey hairs, neighbour ! " said Peter, with a wink
to the bystanders, — whom this dialogue began to
interest, and who were in hopes of seeing the
Quaker played off by the crazed beggar, for such
Peter Peebles appeared to be. — " Grey hairs !  The
Lord mend your eyesight, neighbour, that disna ken
grey hairs frae a tow wig ! "

This jest procured a shout of laughter, and, what
was still more acceptable than dry applause, a man
who stood beside called out, " Father Crackenthorp, bring a nipperkin of brandy.  I'll bestow
a dram on this fellow, were it but for that very
word."

The brandy was immediately brought by a wench
who acted as bar-maid ; and Peter, with a grin of
delight, filled a glass, quaffed it off, and then saying, " God bless me ! I was so unmannerly as not
to drink to ye — I think the Quaker has smitten
me wi' his ill-bred havings," — he was about to fill
another, when his hand was arrested by his new
friend ; who said at the same time, " No, no, friend
— fair play's a jewel — time about, if you please."
And filling a glass for himself, emptied it as gallantly as Peter could have done.  " What say you to
that, friend ? " he continued, addressing the Quaker.

" Nay, friend," answered Joshua, " it went down
thy throat, not mine ; and I have nothing to say
about what concerns me not ; but if thou art a man
of humanity, thou wilt not give this poor creature
the means of debauchery.  Bethink thee that they
will spurn him from the door, as they would do
a houseless and masterless dog, and that he may
die on the sands or on the common.  And if he

has through thy means been rendered incapable of helping himself, thou shalt not be innocent of his blood."

"Faith, Broadbrim, I believe thou art right, and the old gentleman in the flaxen jazy shall have no more of the comforter — Besides, we have business in hand to-day, and this fellow, for as mad as he looks, may have a nose on his face after all. — Hark ye, father, — what is your name, and what brings you into such an out-of-the-way corner?"

"I am not just free to condescend on my name," said Peter; "and as for my business — there is a wee dribble of brandy in the stoup — it would be wrang to leave it to the lass — it is learning her bad usages."

"Well, thou shalt have the brandy, and be d—d to thee, if thou wilt tell me what you are making here."

"Seeking a young advocate chap that they ca' Alan Fairford, that has played me a slippery trick, an ye maun ken a' about the cause," said Peter.

"An advocate, man!" answered the Captain of the Jumping Jenny — for it was he, and no other, who had taken compassion on Peter's drought; "why, Lord help thee, thou art on the wrong side of the Frith to seek advocates, whom I take to be Scottish lawyers, not English."

"English lawyers, man!" exclaimed Peter: "the deil a lawyer's in a' England."

"I wish from my soul it were true," said Ewart; "but what the devil put that in your head?"

"Lord, man, I got a grip of ane of their attorneys in Carlisle, and he tauld me that there wasna a lawyer in England, ony mair than himsell, that kend the nature of a multiplepoinding! And when I tauld

him how this loopy lad, Alan Fairford, had served
me, he said I might bring an action on the case —
just as if the case hadna as mony actions already
as one case can weel carry. By my word, it is a
gude case, and muckle has it borne, in its day, of
various procedure — but it's the barley-pickle breaks
the naig's back, and wi' my consent it shall not hae
ony mair burden laid upon it."

"But this Alan Fairford?" said Nanty — "come
— sip up the drop of brandy, man, and tell me some
more about him, and whether you are seeking him
for good or for harm."

"For my ain gude, and for his harm, to be sure,"
said Peter. "Think of his having left my cause
in the dead-thraw between the tyneing and the
winning, and capering off into Cumberland here,
after a wild loup-the-tether lad they ca' Darsie
Latimer."

"Darsie Latimer!" said Mr. Geddes, hastily;
"do you know any thing of Darsie Latimer?"

"Maybe I do, and maybe I do not," answered
Peter; "I am no free to answer every body's inter-
rogatory, unless it is put judicially, and by form of
law — specially where folk think so much of a caup
of sour yill, or a thimblefu' of brandy. But as for
this gentleman, that has shown himself a gentleman
at breakfast, and will show himself a gentleman at
the meridian, I am free to condescend upon any
points in the cause that may appear to bear upon
the question at issue."

"Why, all I want to know from you, my friend,
is, whether you are seeking to do this Mr. Alan
Fairford good or harm; because if you come to do
him good, I think you could maybe get speech of
him — and if to do him harm, I will take the liberty

to give you a cast across the Frith, with fair warning not to come back on such an errand, lest worse come of it."

The manner and language of Ewart were such, that Joshua Geddes resolved to keep cautious silence, till he could more plainly discover whether he was likely to aid or impede him in his researches after Darsie Latimer. He therefore determined to listen attentively to what should pass between Peter and the seaman, and to watch for an opportunity of questioning the former, so soon as he should be separated from his new acquaintance.

"I wad by no means," said Peter Peebles, "do any substantial harm to the poor lad Fairford, who has had mony a gowd guinea of mine, as weel as his father before him; but I wad hae him brought back to the minding of my business and his ain; and maybe I wadna insist farther in my action of damages against him than for refounding the fees, and for some annual rent on the principal sum, due frae the day on which he should have recovered it for me, plack and bawbee, at the great advising; for, ye are aware, that is the least that I can ask *nomine damni;* and I have nae thought to break down the lad bodily a' thegither — we maun live and let live — forgie and forget."

" The deuce take me, friend broadbrim," said Nanty Ewart, looking to the Quaker, "if I can make out what this old scarecrow means. If I thought it was fitting that Master Fairford should see him, why, perhaps it is a matter that could be managed. Do you know any thing about the old fellow ? — you seemed to take some charge of him just now."

" No more than I should have done by any one

in distress," said Geddes, not sorry to be appealed
to ; " but I will try what I can do to find out who
he is, and what he is about in this country — But
are we not a little too public in this open room ? "

" It 's well thought of," said Nanty ; and at his
command the bar-maid ushered the party into a
side-booth, Peter attending them, in the instinctive hope that there would be more liquor drunk
among them before parting.  They had scarce sat
down in their new apartment, when the sound of a
violin was heard in the room which they had just
left.

" I'll awa back yonder," said Peter, rising up
again ; " yon's the sound of a fiddle, and when there
is music there's aye something ganging to eat or
drink."

" I am just going to order something here," said
the Quaker ; " but, in the meantime, have you any
objection, my good friend, to tell us your name ? "

" None in the world, if you are wanting to
drink to me by name and surname," answered
Peebles ;  " but, otherwise, I would rather evite
your interrogatories."

" Friend," said the Quaker, " it is not for thine
own health, seeing thou hast drunk enough already
— however — Here, handmaiden — bring me a gill
of sherry."

" Sherry 's but shilpit drink, and a gill's a sma'
measure for twa gentlemen to crack ower at their
first acquaintance. — But let us see your sneaking
gill of sherry," said Poor Peter, thrusting forth his
huge hand to seize on the diminutive pewter
measure, which, according to the fashion of the
time, contained the generous liquor freshly drawn
from the butt.

"Nay, hold, friend," said Joshua, "thou hast not yet told me what name and surname I am to call thee by."

"D—d sly in the Quaker," said Nanty, apart, "to make him pay for his liquor before he gives it him. Now, I am such a fool, that I should have let him get too drunk to open his mouth, before I thought of asking him a question."

"My name is Peter Peebles, then," said the litigant, rather sulkily, as one who thought his liquor too sparingly meted out to him; "and what have you to say to that?"

"Peter Peebles?" repeated Nanty Ewart, and seemed to muse upon something which the words brought to his remembrance, while the Quaker pursued his examination.

"But I prithee, Peter Peebles, what is thy further designation? — Thou knowest, in our country, that some men are distinguished by their craft and calling, as cordwainers, fishers, weavers, or the like, and some by their titles as proprietors of land, (which savours of vanity) — Now, how may you be distinguished from others of the same name?"

"As Peter Peebles of the great plea of Poor Peter Peebles against Plainstanes, *et per contra* — if I am laird of naething else, I am aye a *dominus litis*."

"It's but a poor lairdship, I doubt," said Joshua.

"Pray, Mr. Peebles," said Nanty, interrupting the conversation abruptly, "were not you once a burgess of Edinburgh?"

"*Was* I a burgess!" said Peter indignantly, "and *am* I not a burgess even now? I have done nothing to forfeit my right, I trow — once provost and aye my lord."

"Well, Mr. Burgess, tell me farther, have you

not some property in the Gude Town?" continued
Ewart.

"Troth have I — that is, before my misfortunes,
I had twa or three bonny bits of mailings amang
the closes and wynds, forby the shop and the story
abune it. But Plainstanes has put me to the cause-
way now. Never mind, though, I will be upsides
with him yet."

"Had not you once a tenement in the Covenant
Close?" again demanded Nanty.

"You have hit it, lad, though ye look not like
a Covenanter," said Peter; "we'll drink to its
memory —(Hout! the heart's at the mouth o' that
ill-faur'd bit stoup already!) — it brought a rent,
reckoning from the crawstep to the groundsill, that
ye might ca' fourteen punds a-year, forby the laigh
cellar that was let to Lucky Littleworth."

"And do you not remember that you had a poor
old lady for your tenant, Mrs. Cantrips of Kittlebasket?" said Nanty, suppressing his emotion with
difficulty.

"Remember! G—d, I have gude cause to remember her," said Peter, "for she turned a dyvour on
my hands, the auld besom! and, after a' that the
law could do to make me satisfied and paid, in the
way of poinding and distrenzieing, and sae forth, as
the law will, she ran awa to the Charity Workhouse,
a matter of twenty punds Scots in my debt — it's a
great shame and oppression that Charity Workhouse,
taking in bankrupt dyvours that canna pay their
honest creditors."

"Methinks, friend," said the Quaker, "thine own
rags might teach thee compassion for other people's
nakedness."

"Rags!" said Peter, taking Joshua's words liter-

ally; "does ony wise body put on their best coat
when they are travelling, and keeping company
with Quakers, and such other cattle as the road
affords?"

"The old lady *died*, I have heard," said Nanty,
affecting a moderation which was belied by accents
that faltered with passion.

"She might live or die, for what I care," answered
Peter the Cruel; "what business have folk to do to
live that canna live as law will, and satisfy their
just and lawful creditors?"

"And you — you that are now yourself trodden
down in the very kennel, are you not sorry for what
you have done? Do you not repent having occasioned the poor widow woman's death?"

"What for should I repent?" said Peter; "the
law was on my side — a decreet of the Bailies, followed by poinding and an act of warding — a
suspension intented, and the letters found orderly
proceeded. — I followed the auld rudas through twa
Courts — she cost me mair money than her lugs
were worth."

"Now, by Heaven!" said Nanty, "I would give
a thousand guineas, if I had them, to have you
worth my beating! Had you said you repented, it
had been between God and your conscience; but to
hear you boast of your villainy — Do you think it
little to have reduced the aged to famine, and the
young to infamy — to have caused the death of one
woman, the ruin of another, and to have driven a
man to exile and despair? By Him that made me,
I can scarce keep hands off you!"

"Off me? — I defy ye!" said Peter. "I take
this honest man to witness, that if ye stir the neck
of my collar, I will have my action for stouthreif,

spulzie, oppression, assault and battery. Here's a bra' din, indeed, about an auld wife gaun to the grave, a young limmer to the close-heads and cause-way, and a sticket stibbler [1] to the sea instead of the gallows!"

"Now, by my soul," said Nanty, "this is too much! and since you can feel no otherwise, I will try if I cannot beat some humanity into your head and shoulders."

He drew his hanger as he spoke, and although Joshua, who had in vain endeavoured to interrupt the dialogue, to which he foresaw a violent termi-nation, now threw himself between Nanty and the old litigant, he could not prevent the latter from receiving two or three sound slaps over the shoulder with the flat side of the weapon.

Poor Peter Peebles, as inglorious in his extremity as he had been presumptuous in bringing it on, now ran and roared, and bolted out of the apartment and house itself, pursued by Nanty, whose passion became high in proportion to his giving way to its dictates, and by Joshua, who still interfered at every risk, calling upon Nanty to reflect on the age and miserable circumstances of the offender, and upon Poor Peter to stand and place himself under his protection. In front of the house, however, Peter Peebles found a more efficient protector than the worthy Quaker.

---

[1] A student of divinity who has not been able to complete his studies on theology.

# CHAPTER XV.

Our readers may recollect that Fairford had been conducted by Dick Gardener from the House of Fairladies to the inn of old Father Crackenthorp, in order, as he had been informed by the mysterious Father Buonaventure, that he might have the meeting which he desired with Mr. Redgauntlet, to treat with him for the liberty of his friend Darsie. His guide, by the special direction of Mr. Ambrose, had introduced him into the public-house by a back-door, and recommended to the landlord to accommodate him with a private apartment, and to treat him with all civility; but in other respects to keep his eye on him, and even to secure his person, if he saw any reason to suspect him to be a spy. He was not, however, subjected to any direct restraint, but was ushered into an apartment, where he was requested to await the arrival of the gentleman with whom he wished to have an interview, and who, as Crackenthorp assured him with a significant nod, would be certainly there in the course of an hour. In the meanwhile, he recommended to him, with another significant sign, to keep his apartment, "as there were people in the house who were apt to busy themselves about other folk's matters."

Alan Fairford complied with the recommendation, so long as he thought it reasonable; but when, among a large party riding up to the house, he discerned Redgauntlet, whom he had seen under the name of Mr. Herries of Birrenswork, and whom, by his height and strength, he easily distinguished from the rest, he thought it proper to go down to the front of the house, in hopes that, by more closely reconnoitring the party, he might discover if his friend Darsie was among them.

The reader is aware that, by doing so, he had an opportunity of breaking Darsie's fall from his side-saddle, although his disguise and mask prevented his recognising his friend. It may be also recollected, that while Nixon hurried Miss Redgauntlet and her brother into the house, their uncle, somewhat chafed at an unexpected and inconvenient interruption, remained himself in parley with Fairford, who had already successively addressed him by the names of Herries and Redgauntlet; neither of which, any more than the acquaintance of the young lawyer, he seemed at the moment willing to acknowledge, though an air of haughty indifference, which he assumed, could not conceal his vexation and embarrassment.

"If we must needs be acquainted, sir," he said at last — "for which I am unable to see any necessity, especially as I am now particularly disposed to be private — I must entreat you will tell me at once what you have to say, and permit me to attend to matters of more importance."

"My introduction," said Fairford, "is contained in this letter," — (delivering that of Maxwell.) — "I am convinced that, under whatever name it may be your pleasure for the present to be known, it is into your hands, and yours only, that it should be delivered."

Redgauntlet turned the letter in his hand — then read the contents — then again looked upon the letter, and sternly observed, "The seal of the letter has been broken. Was this the case, sir, when it was delivered into your hand ? "

Fairford despised a falsehood as much as any man, unless, perhaps, as Tom Turnpenny might have said, "in the way of business." He answered readily and firmly, "The seal was whole when the letter was delivered to me by Mr. Maxwell of Summertrees."

"And did you dare, sir, to break the seal of a letter addressed to me ? " said Redgauntlet, not sorry, perhaps, to pick a quarrel upon a point foreign to the tenor of the epistle.

" I have never broken the seal of any letter committed to my charge," said Alan ; "not from fear of those to whom such letter might be addressed, but from respect to myself."

"That is well worded," said Redgauntlet ; "and yet, young Mr. Counsellor, I doubt whether your delicacy prevented your reading my letter, or listening to the contents as read by some other person after it was opened."

" I certainly did hear the contents read over," said Fairford ; "and they were such as to surprise me a good deal. "

" Now that," said Redgauntlet, " I hold to be pretty much the same, *in foro conscientiæ*, as if you had broken the seal yourself. I shall hold myself excused from entering upon farther discourse with a messenger so faithless ; and you may thank yourself if your journey has been fruitless."

"Stay, sir," said Fairford ; "and know that I became acquainted with the contents of the paper

without my consent — I may even say against my
will; for Mr. Buonaventure "——

"Who?" demanded Redgauntlet, in a wild and
alarmed manner — " *Whom* was it you named?"

"Father Buonaventure," said Alan, — "a Catholic
priest, as I apprehend, whom I saw at the Miss
Arthurets' house, called Fairladies."

" Miss Arthurets ! — Fairladies ! — A Catholic
priest ! — Father Buonaventure !" said Redgauntlet,
repeating the words of Alan with astonishment. —
" Is it possible that human rashness can reach such
a point of infatuation ? — Tell me the truth, I conjure you, sir — I have the deepest interest to know
whether this is more than an idle legend, picked up
from hearsay about the country. You are a lawyer,
and know the risk incurred by the Catholic clergy,
whom the discharge of their duty sends to these
bloody shores."

"I am a lawyer, certainly," said Fairford; "but
my holding such a respectable condition in life
warrants that I am neither an informer nor a spy.
Here is sufficient evidence that I have seen Father
Buonaventure."

He put Buonaventure's letter into Redgauntlet's
hand, and watched his looks closely while he read
it. "Double-dyed infatuation !" he muttered, with
looks in which sorrow, displeasure, and anxiety
were mingled. " ' Save me from the indiscretion
of my friends,' says the Spaniard; ' I can save
myself from the hostility of my enemies.' "

He then read the letter attentively, and for two
or three minutes was lost in thought, while some
purpose of importance seemed to have gathered
and sat brooding upon his countenance. He held
up his finger towards his satellite, Cristal Nixon,

who replied to his signal with a prompt nod; and with one or two of the attendants approached Fairford in such a manner as to make him apprehensive they were about to lay hold of him.

At this moment a noise was heard from withinside of the house, and presently rushed forth Peter Peebles, pursued by Nanty Ewart with his drawn hanger, and the worthy Quaker, who was endeavouring to prevent mischief to others, at some risk of bringing it on himself.

A wilder and yet a more absurd figure can hardly be imagined than that of Poor Peter clattering along as fast as his huge boots would permit him, and resembling nothing so much as a flying scarecrow; while the thin emaciated form of Nanty Ewart, with the hue of death on his cheek and the fire of vengeance glancing from his eye, formed a ghastly contrast with the ridiculous object of his pursuit.

Redgauntlet threw himself between them. " What extravagant folly is this ? " he said. " Put up your weapon, Captain. Is this a time to indulge in drunken brawls, or is such a miserable object as that a fitting antagonist for a man of courage ? "

" I beg pardon," said the Captain, sheathing his weapon — " I was a little bit out of the way, to be sure; but to know the provocation a man must read my heart, and that I hardly dare to do myself. But the wretch is safe from me. Heaven has done its own vengeance on us both."

While he spoke in this manner, Peter Peebles, who had at first crept behind Redgauntlet in bodily fear, began now to reassume his spirits. Pulling his protector by the sleeve, " Mr. Herries — Mr. Herries," he whispered eagerly, " ye have done me

mair than ae gude turn, and if ye will but do me
anither at this dead pinch, I'll forgie the girded keg
of brandy that you and Captain Sir Harry Redgimlet
drank out yon time.   Ye sall hae an ample discharge
and renunciation, and, though I should see you walking at the Cross of Edinburgh, or standing at the bar
of the Court of Justiciary, no the very thumbikins
themselves should bring to my memory that ever I
saw you in arms yon day."

He accompanied this promise by pulling so hard
at Redgauntlet's cloak, that he at last turned round.
"Idiot! speak in a word what you want."

' Aweel, aweel.  In a word, then," said Peter
Peebles, "I have a warrant on me to apprehend
that man that stands there, Alan Fairford by name,
and advocate by calling.   I bought it from Maister
Justice Foxley's clerk, Maister Nicholas Faggot, wi'
the guinea that you gied me."

"Ha!" said Redgauntlet, "hast thou really such
a warrant? let me see it. — Look sharp that no one
escape, Cristal Nixon."

Peter produced a huge greasy leathern pocketbook, too dirty to permit its original colour to be
visible, filled with scrolls of notes, memorials to
counsel, and Heaven knows what besides.  From
amongst this precious mass he culled forth a paper,
and placed it in the hands of Redgauntlet, or Herries,
as he continued to call him, saying, at the same time,
"It's a formal and binding warrant, proceeding on
my affidavy made, that the said Alan Fairford,
being lawfully engaged in my service, had slipped
the tether and fled over the Border, and was
now lurking there and thereabouts, to elude and
evite the discharge of his bounden duty to me;
and therefore granting warrant to constables and

others, to seek for, take, and apprehend him, that he may be brought before the Honourable Justice Foxley for examination, and, if necessary, for commitment. Now, though a' this be fairly set down as I tell ye, yet where am I to get an officer to execute this warrant in sic a country as this, where swords and pistols flee out at a word's speaking, and folk care as little for the peace of King George as the peace of Auld King Coul? — There's that drunken skipper, and that wet Quaker, enticed me into the public this morning, and because I wadna gie them as much brandy as wad have made them blind drunk, they baith fell on me, and were in the way of guiding me very ill."

While Peter went on in this manner, Redgauntlet glanced his eye over the warrant, and immediately saw that it must be a trick passed by Nicholas Faggot to cheat the poor insane wretch out of his solitary guinea. But the Justice had actually subscribed it, as he did whatever his clerk presented to him, and Redgauntlet resolved to use it for his own purposes.

Without making any direct answer, therefore, to Peter Peebles, he walked up gravely to Fairford, who had waited quietly for the termination of a scene in which he was not a little surprised to find his client, Mr. Peebles, a conspicuous actor.

"Mr. Fairford," said Redgauntlet, "there are many reasons which might induce me to comply with the request, or rather the injunctions, of the excellent Father Buonaventure, that I should communicate with you upon the present condition of my ward, whom you know under the name of Darsie Latimer; but no man is better aware than you that the law must be obeyed, even in contradiction

to our own feelings; now, this poor man has
obtained a warrant for carrying you before a magistrate, and, I am afraid, there is a necessity of your
yielding to it, although to the postponement of the
business which you may have with me."

"A warrant against me!" said Alan, indignantly; "and at that poor miserable wretch's
instance?—why, this is a trick, a mere and most
palpable trick!"

"It may be so," replied Redgauntlet, with great
equanimity; "doubtless you know best; only the
writ appears regular, and with that respect for
the law which has been," he said, with hypocritical formality, "a leading feature of my character
through life, I cannot dispense with giving my
poor aid to the support of a legal warrant. Look
at it yourself, and be satisfied it is no trick of
mine."

Fairford ran over the affidavit and the warrant,
and then exclaimed once more that it was an impudent imposition, and that he would hold those who
acted upon such a warrant liable in the highest
damages. "I guess at your motive, Mr. Redgauntlet," he said, "for acquiescing in so ridiculous a
proceeding. But be assured you will find that, in
this country, one act of illegal violence will not be
covered or atoned for by practising another. You
cannot, as a man of sense and honour, pretend to
say you regard this as a legal warrant."

"I am no lawyer, sir," said Redgauntlet; "and
pretend not to know what is or is not law—the
warrant is quite formal, and that is enough for
me."

"Did ever any one hear," said Fairford, "of an
advocate being compelled to return to his task,

like a collier or a salter[1] who has deserted his master ? "

"I see no reason why he should not," said Redgauntlet, dryly, "unless on the ground that the services of the lawyer are the most expensive and least useful of the two."

"You cannot mean this in earnest," said Fairford; "you cannot really mean to avail yourself of so poor a contrivance to evade the word pledged by your friend, your ghostly father, in my behalf. I may have been a fool for trusting it too easily, but think what you must be if you can abuse my confidence in this manner. I entreat you to reflect that this usage releases me from all promises of secrecy or connivance at what I am apt to think are very dangerous practices, and that " ——

"Hark ye, Mr. Fairford," said Redgauntlet; "I must here interrupt you for your own sake. One word of betraying what you may have seen, or what you may have suspected, and your seclusion is like to have either a very distant or a very brief termination; in either case a most undesirable one. At present, you are sure of being at liberty in a very few days — perhaps much sooner."

"And my friend," said Alan Fairford, "for whose sake I have run myself into this danger, what is to become of him ? — Dark and dangerous man ! " he exclaimed, raising his voice, " I will not be again cajoled by deceitful promises " ——

"I give you my honour that your friend is well," interrupted Redgauntlet; "perhaps I may permit you to see him, if you will but submit with patience to a fate which is inevitable."

---

[1] Note V. — Collier and Salter.

But Alan Fairford, considering his confidence as having been abused, first by Maxwell, and next by the Priest, raised his voice, and appealed to all the King's lieges within hearing against the violence with which he was threatened. He was instantly seized on by Nixon and two assistants, who, holding down his arms and endeavouring to stop his mouth, were about to hurry him away.

The honest Quaker, who had kept out of Redgauntlet's presence, now came boldly forward.

"Friend," said he, "thou dost more than thou canst answer. Thou knowest me well, and thou art aware that in me thou hast a deeply injured neighbour, who was dwelling beside thee in the honesty and simplicity of his heart."

"Tush, Jonathan," said Redgauntlet; "talk not to me, man; it is neither the craft of a young lawyer nor the *simplicity* of an old hypocrite can drive me from my purpose."

"By my faith," said the Captain, coming forward in his turn, "this is hardly fair, General; and I doubt," he added, "whether the will of my owners can make me a party to such proceedings. — Nay, never fumble with your sword-hilt, but out with it like a man, if you are for a tilting." — He unsheathed his hanger, and continued. — "I will neither see my comrade Fairford nor the old Quaker abused. D—n all warrants, false or true — curse the justice — confound the constable! — and here stands little Nanty Ewart to make good what he says against gentle and simple, in spite of horse-shoe or horseradish either."

The cry of "Down with all warrants!" was popular in the ears of the militia of the inn, and Nanty Ewart was no less so. Fishers, ostlers, sea-

men, smugglers, began to crowd to the spot. Crackenthorp endeavoured in vain to mediate. The
attendants of Redgauntlet began to handle their
firearms; but their master shouted to them to
forbear, and, unsheathing his sword as quick as
lightning, he rushed on Ewart in the midst of his
bravado, and struck his weapon from his hand with
such address and force that it flew three yards from
him. Closing with him at the same moment, he gave
him a severe fall, and waved his sword over his head,
to show he was absolutely at his mercy.

"There, you drunken vagabond," he said, "I
give you your life — you are no bad fellow, if you
could keep from brawling among your friends. —
But we all know Nanty Ewart," he said to the
crowd around, with a forgiving laugh, which, joined
to the awe his prowess had inspired, entirely confirmed their wavering allegiance.

They shouted, "The Laird for ever!" while
poor Nanty, rising from the earth, on whose lap
he had been stretched so rudely, went in quest of
his hanger, lifted it, wiped it, and, as he returned
the weapon to the scabbard, muttered between his
teeth, "It is true they say of him, and the devil
will stand his friend till his hour come; I will cross
him no more."

So saying, he slunk from the crowd, cowed and
disheartened by his defeat.

"For you, Joshua Geddes," said Redgauntlet,
approaching the Quaker, who, with lifted hands and
eyes, had beheld the scene of violence, "I shall
take the liberty to arrest thee for a breach of the
peace, altogether unbecoming thy pretended principles; and I believe it will go hard with thee both
in a Court of Justice and among thine own Society

of Friends, as they call themselves, who will be but indifferently pleased to see the quiet tenor of their hypocrisy insulted by such violent proceedings."

"*I* violent!" said Joshua; "*I* do aught unbecoming the principles of the Friends! I defy thee, man, and I charge thee, as a Christian, to forbear vexing my soul with such charges: it is grievous enough to me to have seen violences which I was unable to prevent."

"Oh, Joshua, Joshua!" said Redgauntlet, with a sardonic smile; "thou light of the faithful in the town of Dumfries and the places adjacent, wilt thou thus fall away from the truth? Hast thou not, before us all, attempted to rescue a man from the warrant of law? Didst thou not encourage that drunken fellow to draw his weapon — and didst thou not thyself flourish thy cudgel in the cause? Think'st thou that the oaths of the injured Peter Peebles and the conscientious Cristal Nixon, besides those of such gentlemen as look on this strange scene, who not only put on swearing as a garment, but to whom, in Custom-House matters, oaths are literally meat and drink, — dost thou not think, I say, that these men's oaths will go farther than thy Yea and Nay in this matter?"

"I will swear to any thing," said Peter. "All is fair when it comes to an oath *ad litem*."

"You do me foul wrong," said the Quaker, undismayed by the general laugh. "I encouraged no drawing of weapons, though I attempted to move an unjust man by some use of argument — I brandished no cudgel, although it may be that the ancient Adam struggled within me, and caused my hand to grasp mine oaken staff firmer than usual, when I saw innocence borne down with violence. —

But why talk I what is true and just to thee, who hast been a man of violence from thy youth upwards? Let me rather speak to thee such language as thou canst comprehend. Deliver these young men up to me," he said, when he had led Redgauntlet a little apart from the crowd, "and I will not only free thee from the heavy charge of damages which thou hast incurred by thine outrage upon my property, but I will add ransom for them and for myself. What would it profit thee to do the youths wrong, by detaining them in captivity?"

"Mr. Geddes," said Redgauntlet, in a tone more respectful than he had hitherto used to the Quaker, "your language is disinterested, and I respect the fidelity of your friendship. Perhaps we have mistaken each other's principles and motives; but if so, we have not at present time for explanation. Make yourself easy. I hope to raise your friend Darsie Latimer to a pitch of eminence which you will witness with pleasure; — nay, do not attempt to answer me. The other young man shall suffer restraint a few days, probably only a few hours, — it is not more than due for his pragmatical interference in what concerned him not. Do you, Mr. Geddes, be so prudent as to take your horse and leave this place, which is growing every moment more unfit for the abode of a man of peace. You may wait the event in safety at Mount Sharon."

"Friend," replied Joshua, "I cannot comply with thy advice; I will remain here, even as thy prisoner, as thou didst but now threaten, rather than leave the youth, who hath suffered by and through me and my misfortunes, in his present state of doubtful safety. Wherefore I will not mount my steed Solomon: neither will I turn his head towards Mount Sharon, until I see an end of this matter."

" A prisoner, then, you must be," said Redgauntlet. " I have no time to dispute the matter farther with you.—But tell me for what you fix your eyes so attentively on yonder people of mine ? "

" To speak the truth," said the Quaker, " I admire to behold among them a little wretch of a boy called Benjie, to whom I think Satan has given the power of transporting himself wheresoever mischief is going forward ; so that it may be truly said, there is no evil in this land wherein he hath not a finger, if not a whole hand."

The boy, who saw their eyes fixed on him as they spoke, seemed embarrassed, and rather desirous of making his escape ; but at a signal from Redgauntlet he advanced, assuming the sheepish look and rustic manner with which the jackanapes covered much acuteness and roguery.

" How long have you been with the party, sirrah ? " said Redgauntlet.

" Since the raid on the stake-nets," said Benjie, with his finger in his mouth.

" And what made you follow us ? "

" I dauredna stay at hame for the constables," replied the boy.

" And what have you been doing all this time ? "

" Doing, sir ?—I dinna ken what ye ca' doing—I have been doing naething," said Benjie ; then seeing something in Redgauntlet's eye which was not to be trifled with, he added, " Naething but waiting on Maister Cristal Nixon."

" Hum !—ay—indeed ? " muttered Redgauntlet. " Must Master Nixon bring his own retinue into the field ?—This must be seen to."

NANTY EWART DISARMED.

Etched by F.S

He was about to pursue his enquiry, when Nixon himself came to him with looks of anxious haste. "The Father is come," he whispered, "and the gentlemen are getting together in the largest room of the house, and they desire to see you. Yonder is your nephew, too, making a noise like a man in Bedlam."

"I will look to it all instantly," said Redgauntlet. "Is the Father lodged as I directed?"

Cristal nodded.

"Now, then, for the final trial," said Redgauntlet. He folded his hands — looked upwards — crossed himself — and after this act of devotion, (almost the first which any one had observed him make use of,) he commanded Nixon to keep good watch — have his horses and men ready for every emergence — look after the safe custody of the prisoners — but treat them at the same time well and civilly. And, these orders given, he darted hastily into the house.

# CHAPTER XVI.

REDGAUNTLET'S first course was to the chamber of his nephew. He unlocked the door, entered the apartment, and asked what he wanted, that he made so much noise.

"I want my liberty," said Darsie, who had wrought himself up to a pitch of passion in which his uncle's wrath had lost its terrors. "I desire my liberty, and to be assured of the safety of my beloved friend, Alan Fairford, whose voice I heard but now."

"Your liberty shall be your own within half an hour from this period — your friend shall be also set at freedom in due time — and you yourself be permitted to have access to his place of confinement."

"This does not satisfy me," said Darsie; "I must see my friend instantly; he is here, and he is here endangered on my account only — I have heard violent exclamations — the clash of swords. You will gain no point with me unless I have ocular demonstration of his safety."

"Arthur — dearest nephew," answered Redgauntlet, "drive me not mad! Thine own fate — that of thy house — that of thousands — that of Britain herself, are at this moment in the scales; and you are only occupied about the safety of a poor insignificant pettifogger!"

"He has sustained injury at your hands, then?" said Darsie, fiercely. "I know he has; but if so, not even our relationship shall protect you."

"Peace, ungrateful and obstinate fool!" said Redgauntlet. "Yet stay — Will you be satisfied if you see this Alan Fairford, the bundle of bombazine — this precious friend of yours — well and sound? — Will you, I say, be satisfied with seeing him in perfect safety, without attempting to speak to or converse with him?" — Darsie signified his assent. "Take hold of my arm, then," said Redgauntlet; "and do you, niece Lilias, take the other; and beware, Sir Arthur, how you bear yourself."

Darsie was compelled to acquiesce, sufficiently aware that his uncle would permit him no interview with a friend whose influence would certainly be used against his present earnest wishes, and in some measure contented with the assurance of Fairford's personal safety.

Redgauntlet led them through one or two passages, (for the house, as we have before said, was very irregular, and built at different times,) until they entered an apartment, where a man with shouldered carabine kept watch at the door, but readily turned the key for their reception. In this room they found Alan Fairford and the Quaker, apparently in deep conversation with each other. They looked up as Redgauntlet and his party entered; and Alan pulled off his hat and made a profound reverence, which the young lady, who recognised him, — though, masked as she was, he could not know her, — returned with some embarrassment, arising probably from the recollection of the bold step she had taken in visiting him.

Darsie longed to speak, but dared not. His

uncle only said, "Gentlemen, I know you are as anxious on Mr. Darsie Latimer's account as he is upon yours. I am commissioned by him to inform you that he is as well as you are — I trust you will all meet soon. Meantime, although I cannot suffer you to be at large, you shall be as well treated as is possible under your temporary confinement."

He passed on, without pausing to hear the answers which the lawyer and the Quaker were hastening to prefer ; and, only waving his hand by way of adieu, made his exit, with the real and the seeming lady whom he had under his charge, through a door at the upper end of the apartment, which was fastened and guarded like that by which they entered.

Redgauntlet next led the way into a very small room ; adjoining which, but divided by a partition, was one of apparently larger dimensions ; for they heard the trampling of the heavy boots of the period, as if several persons were walking to and fro, and conversing in low and anxious whispers.

"Here," said Redgauntlet to his nephew, as he disencumbered him from the riding-skirt and the mask, "I restore you to yourself, and trust you will lay aside all effeminate thoughts with this feminine dress. Do not blush at having worn a disguise to which kings and heroes have been reduced. It is when female craft or female cowardice find their way into a manly bosom that he who entertains these sentiments should take eternal shame to himself for thus having resembled womankind. Follow me, while Lilias remains here. I will introduce you to those whom I hope to see associated with you in the most glorious cause that hand ever drew sword in."

Darsie paused. " Uncle," he said, " my person is in your hands; but remember, my will is my own. I will not be hurried into any resolution of importance. Remember what I have already said — what I now repeat — that I will take no step of importance but upon conviction."

" But canst thou be convinced, thou foolish boy, without hearing and understanding the grounds on which we act?"

So saying, he took Darsie by the arm, and walked with him to the next room — a large apartment, partly filled with miscellaneous articles of commerce, chiefly connected with contraband trade; where, among bales and barrels, sat, or walked to and fro, several gentlemen, whose manners and looks seemed superior to the plain riding-dresses which they wore.

There was a grave and stern anxiety upon their countenances, when, on Redgauntlet's entrance, they drew from their separate coteries into one group around him, and saluted him with a formality which had something in it of ominous melancholy. As Darsie looked around the circle, he thought he could discern in it few traces of that adventurous hope which urges men upon desperate enterprises; and began to believe that the conspiracy would dissolve of itself, without the necessity of his placing himself in direct opposition to so violent a character as his uncle, and incurring the hazard with which such opposition must needs be attended.

Mr. Redgauntlet, however, did not, or would not, see any such marks of depression of spirit amongst his coadjutors, but met them with cheerful countenance, and a warm greeting of welcome. " Happy to meet you here, my lord," he said, bowing low to a slender young man. "I trust you come with the pledges of your noble father, of B——, and all that loyal house.— Sir Richard, what news in the west? I am told you had two hundred men on foot to have joined when the fatal retreat from Derby was commenced. When the White Standard is again displayed, it shall not be turned back so easily, either by the force of its enemies or the falsehood of its friends. — Doctor Grumball, I bow to the representative of Oxford, the mother of learning and loyalty.— Pengwinion, you Cornish chough, has this good wind blown you north?— Ah, my brave Cambro-Britons, when was Wales last in the race of honour!"

Such and such-like compliments he dealt around, which were in general answered by silent bows; but when he saluted one of his own countrymen by the name of MacKellar, and greeted Maxwell of Summertrees by that of Pate-in-Peril, the latter replied, "that if Pate were not a fool, he would be Pate-in-Safety;" and the former, a thin old gentleman, in tarnished embroidery, said bluntly, "Ay, troth, Redgauntlet, I am here just like yourself; I have little to lose — they that took my land the last time may take my life this; and that is all I care about it."

The English gentlemen, who were still in possession of their paternal estates, looked doubtfully on each other, and there was something whispered among them of the fox which had lost his tail.

Redgauntlet hastened to address them. "I think, my lords and gentlemen," he said, "that I can account for something like sadness which has crept upon an assembly gathered together for so noble a purpose. Our numbers seem, when thus assembled, too small and inconsiderable to shake the firm-seated usurpation of a half-century. But do not count us by what we are in thew and muscle, but by what our summons can do among our countrymen. In this small party are those who have power to raise battalions, and those who have wealth to pay them. And do not believe our friends who are absent are cold or indifferent to the cause. Let us once light the signal, and it will be hailed by all who retain love for the Stuart, and by all—a more numerous body—who hate the Elector. Here I have letters from "——

Sir Richard Glendale interrupted the speaker. " We all confide, Redgauntlet, in your valour and skill — we admire your perseverance ; and probably nothing short of your strenuous exertions, and the emulation awakened by your noble and disinterested conduct, could have brought so many of us, the scattered remnant of a disheartened party, to meet together once again in solemn consultation ; — for I take it, gentlemen," he said, looking round, "this is only a consultation."

" Nothing more," said the young lord.

" Nothing more," said Doctor Grumball, shaking his large academical peruke.

And " Only a consultation " was echoed by the others.

Redgauntlet bit his lip. " I had hopes," he said, "that the discourses I have held with most of you, from time to time, had ripened into more maturity than your words imply, and that we were here to execute as well as to deliberate ; and for this we stand prepared. I can raise five hundred men with my whistle."

" Five hundred men ! " said one of the Welsh

squires. "Cot bless us! and, pray you, what eood could five hundred men do?"

"All that the priming does for the cannon, Mr. Meredith," answered Redgauntlet; "it will enable us to seize Carlisle, and you know what our friends have engaged for in that case."

"Yes — but," said the young nobleman, "you must not hurry us on too fast, Mr. Redgauntlet; we are all, I believe, as sincere and truehearted in this business as you are, but we will not be driven forward blindfold. We owe caution to ourselves and our families, as well as to those whom we are empowered to represent on this occasion."

· "Who hurries you, my lord? Who is it that would drive this meeting forward blindfold? I do not understand your lordship," said Redgauntlet.

"Nay," said Sir Richard Glendale, "at least do not let us fall under our old reproach of disagreeing among ourselves. What my lord means, Redgauntlet, is, that we have this morning heard it is uncertain whether you could even bring that body of men whom you count upon; your countryman, Mr. MacKellar, seemed, just before you came in, to doubt whether your people would rise in any force, unless you could produce the authority of your nephew."

"I might ask," said Redgauntlet, "what right MacKellar, or any one, has to doubt my being able to accomplish what I stand pledged for? — But our hopes consist in our unity. — Here stands my nephew.— Gentlemen, I present to you my kinsman, Sir Arthur Darsie Redgauntlet of that Ilk."

"Gentlemen," said Darsie, with a throbbing bosom, for he felt the crisis a very painful one, "allow me to say that I suspend expressing my sentiments on the important subject under discussion until I have heard those of the present meeting."

"Proceed in your deliberations, gentlemen," said Redgauntlet; "I will show my nephew such reasons for acquiescing in the result as will entirely remove any scruples which may hang around his mind."

Dr. Grumball now coughed, "shook his ambrosial curls," and addressed the assembly.

"The principles of Oxford," he said, "are well understood, since she was the last to resign herself to the Arch-Usurper — since she has condemned, by her sovereign authority, the blasphemous, atheistical, and anarchical tenets of Locke, and other deluders of the public mind. Oxford will give men, money, and countenance to the cause of the rightful monarch. But we have been often deluded by foreign powers, who have availed themselves of our zeal to stir up civil dissensions in Britain, not for the advantage of our blessed though banished monarch, but to engender disturbances by which they might profit, while we, their tools, are sure to be ruined. Oxford, therefore, will not rise, unless our Sovereign comes in person to claim our allegiance, in which case, God forbid we should refuse him our best obedience."

"It is a very cood advice," said Mr. Meredith.

"In troth," said Sir Richard Glendale, "it is the very keystone of our enterprise, and the only condition upon which I myself and others could ever have dreamt of taking up arms. No insurrection which has not Charles Edward himself at its head will ever last longer than till a single foot-company of redcoats march to disperse it."

"This is my own opinion, and that of all my family," said the young nobleman already mentioned; "and I own I am somewhat surprised at being summoned to attend a dangerous rendezvous such as this, before something certain could have been stated to us on this most important preliminary point."

"Pardon me, my lord," said Redgauntlet; "I have not been so unjust either to myself or my friends — I had no means of communicating to our distant confederates (without the greatest risk of discovery) what is known to some of my honourable friends. As courageous and as resolved as when, twenty years since, he threw himself into the wilds of Moidart, Charles Edward has instantly complied with the wishes of his faithful subjects. Charles Edward is in this country — Charles Edward is in this house! — Charles Edward waits but your present decision, to receive the homage of those who have ever called themselves his loyal liegemen. He that would now turn his coat and change his note must do so under the eye of his sovereign."

There was a deep pause. Those among the conspirators whom mere habit, or a desire of preserving consistency, had engaged in the affair, now saw with terror their retreat cut off; and others, who at a distance had regarded the proposed enterprise as hopeful, trembled when the moment of actually embarking in it was thus unexpectedly and almost inevitably precipitated.

"How now, my lords and gentlemen!" said Redgauntlet. "Is it delight and rapture that keep you thus silent? where are the eager welcomes that should be paid your rightful King, who a second time confides his person to the care of his subjects, undeterred by the hairbreadth escapes and severe privations of his former expedition? I hope there is no gentleman here that is not ready to redeem, in his prince's presence, the pledge of fidelity which he offered in his absence?"

"I, at least," said the young nobleman, resolutely, and laying his hand on his sword, "will not be that coward. If Charles is come to these shores, I will be the first to give him welcome, and to devote my life and fortune to his service."

"Before Cot," said Mr. Meredith, "I do not see that Mr. Redcantlet has left us any thing else to do."

"Stay," said Summertrees, "there is yet one other question. Has he brought any of those Irish rapparees (g) with him, who broke the neck of our last glorious affair?"

"Not a man of them," said Redgauntlet.

"I trust," said Dr. Grumball, "that there are no Catholic priests in his company? I would not intrude on the private conscience of my Sovereign, but, as an unworthy son of the Church of England, it is my duty to consider her security."

"Not a Popish dog or cat is there, to bark or mew about his Majesty," said Redgauntlet. "Old Shaftesbury himself could not wish a prince's person more secure from Popery — which may not be the worst religion in the world, notwithstanding. — Any more doubts, gentlemen? can no more plausible reasons be discovered for postponing the payment of our duty, and discharge of our oaths and engagements? Meantime your King waits your declaration — by my faith, he hath but a frozen reception!"

"Redgauntlet," said Sir Richard Glendale, calmly, "your reproaches shall not goad me into any thing of which my reason disapproves. That I respect my engagement as much as you do is evident, since I am here, ready to support it with the best blood in my veins. But has the King really come hither entirely unattended?"

"He has no man with him but young —— as aide-de-camp, and a single valet-de-chambre."

"No *man;* — but, Redgauntlet, as you are a gentleman, has he no *woman* with him?"

Redgauntlet cast his eyes on the ground, and replied, "I am sorry to say — he has."

The company looked at each other, and remained silent for a moment. At length Sir Richard proceeded. "I need not repeat to you, Mr. Redgauntlet, what is the well-grounded opinion of his Majesty's friends concerning that most unhappy connexion; there is but one sense and feeling amongst us upon the subject. I must conclude that our humble remonstrances were communicated by you, sir, to the King?"

"In the same strong terms in which they were couched," replied Redgauntlet. "I love his Majesty's cause more than I fear his displeasure."

"But, apparently, our humble expostulation has produced no effect. This lady who has crept into his bosom has a sister in the Elector of Hanover's Court, and yet we are well assured that every point of our most private communication is placed in her keeping."

"*Varium et mutabile semper femina,*" said Dr. Grumball.

"She puts his secrets into her work-bag," said Maxwell; "and out they fly whenever she opens it.

If I must hang, I would wish it to be in somewhat a better rope than the string of a lady's hussey."

"Are you too turning dastard, Maxwell?" said Redgauntlet, in a whisper.

"Not I," said Maxwell; "let us fight for it, and let them win and wear us; but to be betrayed by a brimstone like that"——

"Be temperate, gentlemen," said Redgauntlet; "the foible of which you complain so heavily has always been that of kings and heroes; which I feel strongly confident the King will surmount, upon the humble entreaty of his best servants, and when he sees them ready to peril their all in his cause, upon the slight condition of his resigning the society of a female favourite, of whom I have seen reason to think he hath been himself for some time wearied. But let us not press upon him rashly with our well-meant zeal. He has a princely will, as becomes his princely birth, and we, gentlemen, who are royalists, should be the last to take advantage of circumstances to limit its exercise. I am as much surprised and hurt as you can be to find that he has made her the companion of this journey, increasing every chance of treachery and detection. But do not let us insist upon a sacrifice so humiliating, while he has scarce placed a foot upon the beach of his kingdom. Let us act generously by our Sovereign; and when we have shown what we will do for him, we shall be able, with better face, to state what it is we expect him to concede."

"Indeed, I think it is but a pity," said Mac-Kellar, "when so many pretty gentlemen are got together, that they should part without the flash of a sword among them."

"I should be of that gentleman's opinion," said Lord ——, "had I nothing to lose but my life; but I frankly own that the conditions on which our family agreed to join having been, in this instance, left unfulfilled, I will not peril the whole fortunes of our house on the doubtful fidelity of an artful woman."

"I am sorry to see your lordship," said Redgauntlet, "take a course which is more likely to secure your house's wealth than to augment its honours."

"How am I to understand your language, sir?" said the young nobleman, haughtily.

"Nay, gentlemen," said Dr. Grumball, interposing, "do not let friends quarrel; we are all zealous for the cause — but truly, although I know the license claimed by the great in such matters, and can, I hope, make due allowance, there is, I may say, an indecorum in a prince who comes to claim the allegiance of the Church of England, arriving on such an errand with such a companion — *si non caste, caute tamen.*"

"I wonder how the Church of England came to be so heartily attached to his merry old namesake," said Redgauntlet.

Sir Richard Glendale then took up the question, as one whose authority and experience gave him right to speak with much weight.

"We have no leisure for hesitation," he said; "it is full time that we decide what course we are to hold. I feel as much as you, Mr. Redgauntlet, the delicacy of capitulating with our Sovereign in his present condition. But I must also think of the total ruin of the cause, the confiscation and bloodshed which will take place among his adherents, and all through the infatuation with which he adheres to a woman who is the pensionary of the present minister, as she was for years Sir Robert Walpole's. Let his Majesty send her back to the Continent, and the sword on which I now lay my hand shall instantly be unsheathed, and, I trust, many hundred others at the same moment."

The other persons present testified their unanimous acquiescence in what Sir Richard Glendale had said.

' I' see you have taken your resolutions, gentlemen," said Redgauntlet ; " unwisely, I think, because I believe that, by softer and more generous proceedings, you would have been more likely to carry a point which I think as desirable as you do. But what is to be done if Charles should refuse, with the inflexibility of his grandfather, to comply with this request of yours ? Do you mean to abandon him to his fate ? "

" God forbid ! " said Sir Richard, hastily ; " and God forgive you, Mr. Redgauntlet, for breathing such a thought. No ! I for one will, with all duty and humility, see him safe back to his vessel, and defend him with my life against whoever shall assail him. But when I have seen his sails spread, my next act will be to secure, if I can, my own safety, by retiring to my house ; or, if I find our engagement, as is too probable, has taken wind, by surrendering myself to the next Justice of Peace, and giving security that hereafter I shall live quiet, and submit to the ruling powers."

Again the rest of the persons present intimated their agreement in opinion with the speaker.

" Well, gentlemen," said Redgauntlet, " it is not for me to oppose the opinion of every one ; and

I must do you the justice to say, that the King has, in the present instance, neglected a condition of your agreement which was laid before him in very distinct terms. The question now is, who is to acquaint him with the result of this conference? for I presume you would not wait on him in a body to make the proposal that he should dismiss a person from his family as the price of your allegiance."

"I think Mr. Redgauntlet should make the explanation," said Lord ——. "As he has, doubtless, done justice to our remonstrances by communicating them to the King, no one can, with such propriety and force, state the natural and inevitable consequence of their being neglected."

"Now, I think," said Redgauntlet, "that those who make the objection should state it; for I am confident the King will hardly believe, on less authority than that of the heir of the loyal House of B——, that he is the first to seek an evasion of his pledge to join him."

"An evasion, sir!" repeated Lord ——, fiercely. "I have borne too much from you already, and this I will not endure. Favour me with your company to the downs yonder."

Redgauntlet laughed scornfully, and was about to follow the fiery young man, when Sir Richard again interposed. "Are we to exhibit," he said, "the last symptoms of the dissolution of our party, by turning our swords against each other?—Be patient, Lord ——; in such conferences as this, much must pass unquestioned which might brook challenge elsewhere. There is a privilege of party as of parliament — men cannot, in emergency, stand upon picking phrases. — Gentlemen, if you will extend your confidence in me so far, I will wait upon his Majesty, and I hope my Lord —— and Mr. Redgauntlet will accompany me. I trust the explanation of this unpleasant matter will prove entirely satisfactory, and that we shall find ourselves at liberty to render our homage to our Sovereign without reserve, when I for one will be the first to peril all in his just quarrel."

Redgauntlet at once stepped forward. "My lord," he said, "if my zeal made me say any thing in the slightest degree offensive, I wish it unsaid, and ask your pardon. A gentleman can do no more."

"I could not have asked Mr. Redgauntlet to do so much," said the young nobleman, willingly accepting the hand which Redgauntlet offered. "I know no man living from whom I could take so much reproof without a sense of degradation as from himself."

"Let me then hope, my lord, that you will go with Sir Richard and me to the presence. Your warm blood will heat our zeal — our colder resolves will temper yours."

The young lord smiled, and shook his head. "Alas! Mr. Redgauntlet," he said, "I am ashamed to say that in zeal you surpass us all. But I will not refuse this mission, provided you will permit Sir Arthur, your nephew, also to accompany us."

"My nephew?" said Redgauntlet, and seemed to hesitate, then added, "Most certainly. — I trust," he said, looking at Darsie, "he will bring to his Prince's presence such sentiments as fit the occasion."

It seemed, however, to Darsie that his uncle would rather have left him behind, had he not feared that he might in that case have been influenced by, or might perhaps himself influence, the unresolved confederates with whom he must have associated during his absence.

"I will go," said Redgauntlet, "and request admission."

In a moment after he returned, and without speaking motioned for the young nobleman to advance. He did so, followed by Sir Richard Glendale and Darsie, Redgauntlet himself bringing up the rear. A short passage and a few steps brought them to the door of the temporary presence-chamber, in which the Royal Wanderer was to receive their homage. It was the upper loft of one of those cottages which made additions to the Old Inn, poorly furnished, dusty, and in disorder; for rash as the enterprise might be considered, they had been still careful not to draw the attention of strangers by any particular attentions to the personal accommodation of the Prince. He was seated, when the deputies, as they might be termed, of his remaining adherents entered; and as he rose, and came forward and bowed in acceptance of their salutation, it was with a dignified courtesy which at once supplied whatever was deficient in external pomp, and converted the wretched garret into a saloon worthy of the occasion.

It is needless to add that he was the same personage already introduced in the character of Father Buonaventure, by which name he was distinguished at Fairladies. His dress was not different from what he then wore, excepting that he had a loose riding-coat of camlet, under which he carried an efficient cut-and-thrust sword, instead of his walking rapier, and also a pair of pistols.

Redgauntlet presented to him successively the young Lord ——, and his kinsman, Sir Arthur

Darsie Redgauntlet, who trembled as, bowing and kissing his hand, he found himself surprised into what might be construed an act of high treason, which yet he saw no safe means to avoid.

Sir Richard Glendale seemed personally known to Charles Edward, who received him with a mixture of dignity and affection, and seemed to sympathize with the tears which rushed into that gentleman's eyes as he bid his Majesty welcome to his native kingdom.

" Yes, my good Sir Richard," said the unfortunate Prince, in a tone melancholy yet resolved, " Charles Edward is with his faithful friends once more — not, perhaps, with his former gay hopes which undervalued danger, but with the same determined contempt of the worst which can befall him, in claiming his own rights and those of his country."

" I rejoice, sire — and yet, alas! I must also grieve, to see you once more on the British shores," said Sir Richard Glendale, and stopped short — a tumult of contradictory feelings preventing his farther utterance.

" It is the call of my faithful and suffering people which alone could have induced me to take once more the sword in my hand. For my own part, Sir Richard, when I have reflected how many of my loyal and devoted friends perished by the sword and by proscription, or died indigent and neglected in a foreign land, I have often sworn that no view to my personal aggrandizement should again induce me to agitate a title which has cost my followers so dear. But since so many men of worth and honour conceive the cause of England and Scotland to be linked with that of Charles Stuart, I must follow

their brave example, and, laying aside all other
considerations, once more stand forward as their
deliverer. I am, however, come hither upon your
invitation; and as you are so completely acquainted
with circumstances to which my absence must
necessarily have rendered me a stranger, I must be
a mere tool in the hands of my friends. I know
well I never can refer myself implicitly to more
loyal hearts or wiser heads than Herries Redgauntlet and Sir Richard Glendale. Give me your advice,
then, how we are to proceed, and decide upon the
fate of Charles Edward."

Redgauntlet looked at Sir Richard, as if to say,
"Can you press an additional or unpleasant condition at a moment like this?" And the other
shook his head and looked down, as if his resolution
was unaltered, and yet as feeling all the delicacy
of the situation.

There was a silence, which was broken by the
unfortunate representative of an unhappy dynasty
with some appearance of irritation. "This is
strange, gentlemen," he said; "you have sent for
me from the bosom of my family, to head an adventure of doubt and danger; and when I come, your
own minds seem to be still irresolute. I had not
expected this on the part of two such men."

"For me, sire," said Redgauntlet, "the steel of
my sword is not truer than the temper of my mind."

"My Lord——'s and mine are equally so,"
said Sir Richard; "but you had in charge, Mr.
Redgauntlet, to convey our request to his Majesty,
coupled with certain conditions."

"And I discharged my duty to his Majesty and
to you," said Redgauntlet.

"I looked at no condition, gentlemen," said their

King, with dignity, "save that which called me here to assert my rights in person. *That* I have fulfilled at no common risk. Here I stand to keep my word, and I expect of you to be true to yours."

"There was, or should have been, something more than that in our proposal, please your Majesty," said Sir Richard. "There was a condition annexed to it."

"I saw it not," said Charles, interrupting him. "Out of tenderness towards the noble hearts of whom I think so highly, I would neither see nor read any thing which could lessen them in my love and my esteem. Conditions can have no part betwixt Prince and subject."

"Sire," said Redgauntlet, kneeling on one knee, "I see from Sir Richard's countenance he deems it my fault that your Majesty seems ignorant of what your subjects desired that I should communicate to your Majesty. For Heaven's sake! for the sake of all my past services and sufferings, leave not such a stain upon my honour! The note, Number D., of which this is a copy, referred to the painful subject to which Sir Richard again directs your attention."

"You press upon me, gentlemen," said the Prince, colouring highly, "recollections which, as I hold them most alien to your character, I would willingly have banished from my memory. I did not suppose that my loyal subjects would think so poorly of me as to use my depressed circumstances as a reason for forcing themselves into my domestic privacies, and stipulating arrangements with their King regarding matters in which the meanest hinds claim the privilege of thinking for themselves. In

affairs of state and public policy, I will ever be
guided as becomes a prince, by the advice of my
wisest counsellors; in those which regard my private affections, and my domestic arrangements, I
claim the same freedom of will which I allow to all
my subjects, and without which a crown were less
worth wearing than a beggar's bonnet."

"May it please your Majesty," said Sir Richard
Glendale, "I see it must be my lot to speak unwilling truths; but believe me, I do so with as much
profound respect as deep regret. It is true, we
have called you to head a mighty undertaking, and
that your Majesty, preferring honour to safety, and
the love of your country to your own ease, has
condescended to become our leader. But we also
pointed out as a necessary and indispensable pre-
paratory step to the achievement of our purpose —
and, I must say, as a positive condition of our
engaging in it — that an individual, supposed, — I
presume not to guess how truly, — to have your
Majesty's more intimate confidence, and believed,
I will not say on absolute proof, but upon the most
pregnant suspicion, to be capable of betraying that
confidence to the Elector of Hanover, should be
removed from your royal household and society."

"This is too insolent, Sir Richard!" said Charles
Edward. "Have you inveigled me into your power
to bait me in this unseemly manner? — And you,
Redgauntlet, why did you suffer matters to come
to such a point as this, without making me more
distinctly aware what insults were to be practised
on me?"

"My gracious Prince," said Redgauntlet, "I am
so far to blame in this, that I did not think so
slight an impediment as that of a woman's society

could have really interrupted an undertaking of this magnitude. I am a plain man, sire, and speak but bluntly; I could not have dreamt but what, within the first five minutes of this interview, either Sir Richard and his friends would have ceased to insist upon a condition so ungrateful to your Majesty, or that your Majesty would have sacrificed this unhappy attachment to the sound advice, or even to the over-anxious suspicions, of so many faithful subjects. I saw no entanglement in such a difficulty which on either side might not have been broken through like a cobweb."

"You were mistaken, sir," said Charles Edward, "entirely mistaken — as much so as you are at this moment, when you think in your heart my refusal to comply with this insolent proposition is dictated by a childish and romantic passion for an individual. I tell you, sir, I could part with that person to-morrow without an instant's regret — that I have had thoughts of dismissing her from my court, for reasons known to myself; but that I will never betray my rights as a sovereign and a man by taking this step to secure the favour of any one, or to purchase that allegiance which, if you owe it to me at all, is due to me as my birthright."

"I am sorry for this," said Redgauntlet; "I hope both your Majesty and Sir Richard will reconsider your resolutions, or forbear this discussion in a conjuncture so pressing. I trust your Majesty will recollect that you are on hostile ground; that our preparations cannot have so far escaped notice as to permit us now with safety to retreat from our purpose; insomuch that it is with the deepest anxiety of heart I foresee even danger to your own royal person, unless you can generously give your subjects the satisfaction which Sir Richard seems to think they are obstinate in demanding."

"And deep indeed your anxiety ought to be," said the Prince. "Is it in these circumstances of personal danger in which you expect to overcome a resolution which is founded on a sense of what is due to me as a man or a prince? If the axe and scaffold were ready before the windows of White- hall, I would rather tread the same path with my great-grandfather than concede the slightest point in which my honour is concerned."

He spoke these words with a determined accent, and looked around him on the company, all of whom (excepting Darsie, who saw, he thought, a fair period to a most perilous enterprise) seemed in deep anxiety and confusion. At length Sir Richard spoke in a solemn and melancholy tone.

"If the safety," he said, "of poor Richard Glen- dale were alone concerned in this matter, I have never valued my life enough to weigh it against the slightest point of your Majesty's service. But I am only a messenger — a commissioner, who must execute my trust, and upon whom a thousand voices will cry Curse and woe, if I do it not with fidelity. All of your adherents, even Redgauntlet himself, see certain ruin to this enterprise — the greatest danger to your Majesty's person — the utter destruction of all your party and friends, if they insist not on the point which, unfortunately, your Majesty is so unwilling to concede. I speak it with a heart full of anguish — with a tongue unable to utter my emotions — but it must be spoken — the fatal truth — that if your royal goodness cannot yield to us a boon which we hold necessary to our security and your own, your Majesty with one word disarms ten thousand men, ready to draw their swords in your behalf; or, to speak yet more plainly, you annihilate even the semblance of a royal party in Great Britain."

"And why do you not add," said the Prince, scornfully, "that the men who have been ready to assume arms in my behalf will atone for their treason to the Elector by delivering me up to the fate for which so many proclamations have destined me? Carry my head to St. James's, gentlemen; you will do a more acceptable and a more honourable action than, having inveigled me into a situation which places me so completely in your power, to dishonour yourselves by propositions which dishonour me."

"My God, sire!" exclaimed Sir Richard, clasping his hands together, in impatience, "of what great and inexpiable crime can your Majesty's ancestors have been guilty, that they have been punished by the infliction of judicial blindness on their whole generation! — Come, my Lord ——, we must to our friends."

"By your leave, Sir Richard," said the young nobleman, "not till we have learned what measures can be taken for his Majesty's personal safety."

"Care not for me, young man," said Charles Edward; "when I was in the society of Highland robbers and cattle-drovers, I was safer than I now hold myself among the representatives of the best blood in England. — Farewell, gentlemen — I will shift for myself."

"This must never be," said Redgauntlet. "Let me that brought you to the point of danger at least provide for your safe retreat."

So saying, he hastily left the apartment, followed

by his nephew. The Wanderer, averting his eyes
from Lord —— and Sir Richard Glendale, threw
himself into a seat at the upper end ·of the apartment, while they, in much anxiety, stood together at
a distance from him, and· conversed in whispers.

# CHAPTER XVII.

## NARRATIVE CONTINUED.

WHEN Redgauntlet left the room, in haste and discomposure, the first person he met on the stair, and indeed so close by the door of the apartment that Darsie thought he must have been listening there, was his attendant Nixon.

"What the devil do you here?" he said, abruptly and sternly.

"I wait your orders," said Nixon. "I hope all's right?— excuse my zeal."

"All is wrong, sir — Where is the seafaring fellow — Ewart — what do you call him?"

"Nanty Ewart, sir—I will carry your commands," said Nixon.

"I will deliver them myself to him," said Redgauntlet: "call him hither."

"But should your honour leave the presence?" said Nixon, still lingering.

"'Sdeath, sir, do you prate to me?" said Redgauntlet, bending his brows. "I, sir, transact my own business; you, I am told, act by a ragged deputy."

Without farther answer, Nixon departed, rather disconcerted, as it seemed to Darsie.

"That dog turns insolent and lazy," said Redgauntlet; "but I must bear with him for a while."

A moment after, Nixon returned with Ewart.

"Is this the smuggling fellow?" demanded Redgauntlet.

Nixon nodded.

"Is he sober now? — he was brawling anon."

"Sober enough for business," said Nixon.

"Well then, hark ye, Ewart — man your boat with your best hands, and have her by the pier — get your other fellows on board the brig — if you have any cargo left, throw it overboard; it shall be all paid, five times over — and be ready for a start to Wales or the Hebrides, or perhaps for Sweden or Norway."

Ewart answered sullenly enough, "Ay, ay, sir."

"Go with him, Nixon," said Redgauntlet, forcing himself to speak with some appearance of cordiality to the servant with whom he was offended; "see he does his duty."

Ewart left the house sullenly, followed by Nixon. The sailor was just in that species of drunken humour which made him jealous, passionate, and troublesome, without showing any other disorder than that of irritability. As he walked towards the beach he kept muttering to himself, but in such a tone that his companion lost not a word, "Smuggling fellow — Ay, smuggler — and, start your cargo into the sea — and be ready to start for the Hebrides, or Sweden — or the devil, I suppose. — Well, and what if I said in answer — Rebel, Jacobite — traitor — I'll make you and your d—d confederates walk the plank — I have seen better men do it — half-a-score of a morning — when I was across the Line."

"D—d unhandsome terms those Redgauntlet used to you, brother," said Nixon.

"Which do you mean?" said Ewart, starting,

and recollecting himself. "I have been at my old trade of thinking aloud, have I?"

"No matter," answered Nixon, "none but a friend heard you. You cannot have forgotten how Redgauntlet disarmed you this morning?"

"Why, I would bear no malice about that— only he is so cursedly high and saucy," said Ewart.

"And then," said Nixon, "I know you for a truehearted Protestant."

"That I am, by G—," said Ewart. ' No, 'the Spaniards could never get my religion from me."

"And a friend to King George, and the Hanover line of succession," said Nixon, still walking and speaking very slow.

"You may swear I am, excepting in the way of business, as Turnpenny says. I like King George, but I can't afford to pay duties."

"You are outlawed, I believe?" said Nixon.

"Am I?—faith, I believe I am," said Ewart. "I wish I were *inlawed* again with all my heart —But come along, we must get all ready for our peremptory gentleman, I suppose."

"I will teach you a better trick," said Nixon. "There is a bloody pack of rebels yonder."

"Ay, we all know that," said the smuggler; "but the snowball's melting, I think."

"There is some one yonder whose head is worth — thirty — thousand — pounds — of sterling money," said Nixon, pausing between each word, as if to enforce the magnificence of the sum.

"And what of that?" said Ewart, quickly.

"Only that if, instead of lying by the pier with your men on their oars, if you will just carry your boat on board just now, and take no notice of any signal from the shore, by G—d, Nanty Ewart, I will make a man of you for life!"

"O ho! then the Jacobite gentry are not so safe as they think themselves?" said Nanty.

"In an hour or two," replied Nixon, "they will be made safer in Carlisle Castle."

·"The devil they will!" said Ewart; "and you have been the informer, I suppose?"

"Yes; I have been ill paid for my service among the Redgauntlets — have scarce got dog's wages — and been treated worse than ever dog was used. I have the old fox and his cubs in the same trap now, Nanty; and we'll see how a certain young lady will look then. You see I am frank with you, Nanty."

"And I will be as frank with you," said the smuggler. "You are a d—d old scoundrel — traitor to the man whose bread you eat! Me help to betray poor devils, that have been so often betrayed myself! — Not if they were a hundred Popes, Devils, and Pretenders. I will back and tell them their danger — they are part of cargo — regularly invoiced — put under my charge by the owners — I'll back"——

"You are not stark mad?" said Nixon, who now saw he had miscalculated in supposing Nanty's wild ideas of honour and fidelity could be shaken even by resentment, or by his Protestant partialities. "You shall not go back — it is all a joke."

"I'll back to Redgauntlet, and see whether it is a joke he will laugh at."

'My life is lost if you do," said Nixon — "hear reason."

They were in a clump or cluster of tall furze at the moment they were speaking, about half-way between the pier and the house, but not in a direct line, from which Nixon, whose object it was to gain time, had induced Ewart to diverge insensibly.

He now saw the necessity of taking a desperate resolution. "Hear reason," he said; and added, as Nanty still endeavoured to pass him, "Or else hear this!" discharging a pocket-pistol into the unfortunate man's body.

Nanty staggered, but kept his feet. "It has cut my back-bone asunder," he said; "you have done me the last good office, and I will not die ungrateful."

As he uttered the last words, he collected his remaining strength, stood firm for an instant, drew his hanger, and, fetching a stroke with both hands, cut Cristal Nixon down. The blow, struck with all the energy of a desperate and dying man, exhibited a force to which Ewart's exhausted frame might have seemed inadequate;—it cleft the hat which the wretch wore, though secured by a plate of iron within the lining, bit deep into his skull, and there left a fragment of the weapon, which was broke by the fury of the blow.

One of the seamen of the lugger, who strolled up, attracted by the firing of the pistol, though, being a small one, the report was very trifling, found both the unfortunate men stark dead. Alarmed at what he saw, which he conceived to have been the consequence of some unsuccessful engagement betwixt his late commander and a revenue officer, (for Nixon chanced not to be personally known to him,) the sailor hastened back to the boat, in order to apprize his comrades of Nanty's fate, and to advise them to take off themselves and the vessel.

Meantime Redgauntlet, having, as we have seen, dispatched Nixon for the purpose of securing a retreat for the unfortunate Charles in case of extremity, returned to the apartment where he had left the Wanderer. He now found him alone.

"Sir Richard Glendale," said the unfortunate Prince, "with his young friend, has gone to consult their adherents now in the house. Redgauntlet, my friend, I will not blame you for the circumstances in which I find myself, though I am at once placed in danger and rendered contemptible. But you ought to have stated to me more strongly the weight which these gentlemen attached to their insolent proposition. You should have told me that no compromise would have any effect — that they desired, not a Prince to govern them, but one, on the contrary, over whom they were to exercise restraint on all occasions, from the highest affairs of the state down to the most intimate and closest concerns of his own privacy, which the most ordinary men desire to keep secret and sacred from interference."

"God knows," said Redgauntlet, in much agitation, "I acted for the best when I pressed your Majesty to come hither — I never thought that your Majesty, at such a crisis, would have scrupled, when a kingdom was in view, to sacrifice an attachment which "——

"Peace, sir!" said Charles; "it is not for you to estimate my feelings upon such a subject."

Redgauntlet coloured high, and bowed profoundly. "At least," he resumed, "I hoped that some middle way might be found, and it shall — and must — Come with me, nephew. We will to these gentlemen, and I am confident I shall bring back heart-stirring tidings."

"I will do much to comply with them, Redgauntlet. I am loath, having again set my foot on British land, to quit it without a blow for my right. But this which they demand of me is a degradation, and compliance is impossible."

Redgauntlet, followed by his nephew, the unwilling spectator of this extraordinary scene, left once more the apartment of the adventurous Wanderer, and was met on the top of the stairs by Joe Crackenthorp. "Where are the other gentlemen?" he said.

"Yonder, in the west barrack," answered Joe; "but, Master Ingoldsby," — that was the name by which Redgauntlet was most generally known in Cumberland, — "I wished to say to you that I must put yonder folk together in one room."

"What folk?" said Redgauntlet, impatiently.

"Why, them prisoner stranger folk as you bid Cristal Nixon look after. Lord love you! this is a large house enow, but we cannot have separate lock-ups for folk, as they have in Newgate or in Bedlam. Yonder's a mad beggar, that is to be a great man when he wins a lawsuit, Lord help him! — Yonder's a Quaker and a lawyer charged with a riot; and, ecod, I must make one key and one lock keep them, for we are chokeful, and you have sent off old Nixon, that could have given one some help in this confusion. Besides, they take up every one a room, and call for noughts on earth, — excepting the old man, who calls lustily enough, — but he has not a penny to pay shot."

"Do as thou wilt with them," said Redgauntlet, who had listened impatiently to his statement; "so thou dost but keep them from getting out and making some alarm in the country, I care not."

"A Quaker and a lawyer!" said Darsie. "This

must be Fairford and Geddes. — Uncle, I must request of you" ——

"Nay, nephew," interrupted Redgauntlet, "this is no time for asking questions. You shall yourself decide upon their fate in the course of an hour — no harm whatever is designed them."

So saying, he hurried towards the place where the Jacobite gentlemen were holding their council, and Darsie followed him, in the hope that the obstacle which had arisen to the prosecution of their desperate adventure would prove insurmountable, and spare him the necessity of a dangerous and violent rupture with his uncle. The discussions among them were very eager; the more daring part of the conspirators, who had little but life to lose, being desirous to proceed at all hazards; while the others, whom a sense of honour and a hesitation to disavow long-cherished principles had brought forward, were perhaps not ill satisfied to have a fair apology for declining an adventure into which they had entered with more of reluctance than zeal.

Meanwhile Joe Crackenthorp, availing himself of the hasty permission attained from Redgauntlet, proceeded to assemble in one apartment those whose safe custody had been thought necessary; and without much considering the propriety of the matter, he selected for the common place of confinement the room which Lilias had since her brother's departure occupied alone. It had a strong lock, and was double-hinged, which probably led to the preference assigned to it as a place of security.

Into this, Joe, with little ceremony and a good deal of noise, introduced the Quaker and Fairford; the first descanting on the immorality, the other on the illegality, of his proceedings; and he turning a deaf ear both to the one and the other. Next he pushed in, almost in headlong fashion, the unfortunate litigant, who, having made some resistance at the threshold, had received a violent thrust in consequence, and came rushing forward, like a ram in the act of charging, with such impetus as must have carried him to the top of the room, and struck the cocked hat which sat perched on the top of his tow wig against Miss Redgauntlet's person, had not the honest Quaker interrupted his career by seizing him by the collar and bringing him to a stand. "Friend," said he, with the real good-breeding which so often subsists independently of ceremonial, "thou art no company for that young person; she is, thou seest, frightened at our being so suddenly thrust in hither; and although that be no fault of ours, yet it will become us to behave civilly towards her. Wherefore come thou with me to this window, and I will tell thee what it concerns thee to know."

"And what for should I no speak to the leddy, friend?" said Peter, who was now about half seas over. "I have spoke to leddies before now, man — What for should she be frightened at me? — I am nae bogle, I ween. — What are ye pooin' me that gate for? — Ye will rive my coat, and I will have a good action for having myself made *sartum atque tectum* at your expenses."

Notwithstanding this threat, Mr. Geddes, whose muscles were as strong as his judgment was sound and his temper sedate, led Poor Peter, under the sense of a control against which he could not struggle, to the farther corner of the apartment, where, placing him, whether he would or no, in a chair, he sat down beside him, and effectually prevented his annoying the young lady, upon whom he had seemed bent on conferring the delights of his society.

If Peter had immediately recognised his counsel learned in the law, it is probable that not even the benevolent efforts of the Quaker could have kept him in a state of restraint; but Fairford's back was turned towards his client, whose optics, besides being somewhat dazzled with ale and brandy, were speedily engaged in contemplating a half-crown which Joshua held between his finger and his thumb, saying, at the same time, " Friend, thou art indigent and improvident. This will, well employed, pro-cure thee sustentation of nature for more than a single day; and I will bestow it on thee if thou wilt sit here and keep me company; for neither thou nor I, friend, are fit company for ladies.".

" Speak for yourself, friend," said Peter, scorn-fully; " I was aye kend to be agreeable to the fair sex; and when I was in business I served the leddies wi' anither sort of decorum than Plainstanes, the d—d awkward scoundrel! It was one of the articles of dittay between us."

" Well, but, friend," said the Quaker, who observed that the young lady still seemed to fear Peter's intrusion, " I wish to hear thee speak about this great lawsuit of thine, which has been matter of such celebrity."

" Celebrity? — Ye may swear that," said Peter, for the string was touched to which his crazy ima-gination always vibrated. " And I dinna wonder that folk that judge things by their outward grandeur, should think me something worth their envying. It's very true that it is grandeur upon earth to hear ane's name thunnered out along the long-

arched roof of the Outer House, — ' *Poor* Peter
Peebles against Plainstanes, *et per contra ;* ' a' the
best lawyers in the house fleeing like eagles to the
prey ; some because they are in the cause, and some
because they want to be thought engaged (for there
are tricks in other trades by selling muslins) — to
see the reporters mending their pens to take down
the debate — the Lords themselves pooin' in their
chairs, like folk sitting down to a gude dinner, and
crying on the clerks for parts and pendicles of the
process, who, puir bodies, can do little mair than
cry on their closet-keepers to help them.   To see
a' this," continued Peter, in a tone of sustained
rapture, " and to ken that naething will be said or
dune amang a' thae grand folk for maybe the feck
of three hours, saving what concerns you and your
business — O, man, nae wonder that ye judge this
to be earthly glory ! — And yet, neighbour, as I was
saying, there be unco drawbacks — I whiles think of
my bit house, where dinner, and supper, and breakfast used to come without the crying for, just as if
fairies had brought it — and the gude bed at e'en —
and the needfu' penny in the pouch. — And then to
see a' ane's warldly substance capering in the air in
a pair of weigh-bauks, now up, now down, as the
breath of judge or counsel inclines it for pursuer or
defender, — troth, man, there are times I rue having
ever begun the plea wark, though maybe, when
ye consider the renown and credit I have by it, ye
will hardly believe what I am saying."

" Indeed, friend," said Joshua, with a sigh, " I
am glad thou hast found any thing in the legal
contention which compensates thee for poverty and
hunger ; but I believe, were other human objects of
ambition looked upon as closely, their advantages

would be found as chimerical as those attending thy protracted litigation."

"But never mind, friend," said Peter, "I'll tell you the exact state of the conjunct processes, and make you sensible that I can bring mysell round with a wet finger, now I have my finger and my thumb on this loup-the-dike loon, the lad Fairford."

Alan Fairford was in the act of speaking to the masked lady, (for Miss Redgauntlet had retained her riding vizard,) endeavouring to assure her, as he perceived her anxiety, of such protection as he could afford, when his own name, pronounced in a loud tone, attracted his attention. He looked round, and, seeing Peter Peebles, as hastily turned to avoid his notice, in which he succeeded, so earnest was Peter upon his colloquy with one of the most respectable auditors whose attention he had ever been able to engage. And by this little motion, momentary as it was, Alan gained an unexpected advantage; for while he looked round, Miss Lilias, I could never ascertain why, took the moment to adjust her mask, and did it so awkwardly, that when her companion again turned his head he recognised as much of her features as authorized him to address her as his fair client, and to press his offers of protection and assistance with the boldness of a former acquaintance.

Lilias Redgauntlet withdrew the mask from her crimsoned cheek. "Mr. Fairford," she said, in a voice almost inaudible, "you have the character of a young gentleman of sense and generosity; but we have already met in one situation which you must think singular; and I must be exposed to misconstruction, at least, for my forwardness, were

it not in a cause in which my dearest affections
were concerned."

"Any interest in my beloved friend Darsie
Latimer," said Fairford, stepping a little back,
and putting a marked restraint upon his former
advances, "gives me a double right to be useful
to "——. He stopped short.

"To his sister, your goodness would say," answered
Lilias.

"His sister, madam!" replied Alan, in the
extremity of astonishment — "Sister, I presume,
in affection only?"

"No, sir; my dear brother Darsie and I are
connected by the bonds of actual relationship; and
I am not sorry to be the first to tell this to the
friend he most values."

Fairford's first thought was on the violent passion which Darsie had expressed towards the fair
unknown. "Good God!" he exclaimed, "how did
he bear the discovery?"

"With resignation, I hope," said Lilias, smiling.
"A more accomplished sister he might easily have
come by, but scarcely could have found one who
could love him more than I do."

"I meant — I only meant to say," said the young
counsellor, his presence of mind failing him for an
instant — "that is, I meant to ask where Darsie
Latimer is at this moment."

"In this very house, and under the guardianship
of his uncle, whom I believe you knew as a visitor
of your father, under the name of Mr. Herries of
Birrenswork."

"Let me hasten to him," said Fairford; "I have
sought him through difficulties and dangers — I must
see him instantly."

" You forget you are a prisoner," said the young lady.

" True — true; but I cannot be long detained —· the cause alleged is too ridiculous."

" Alas!" said Lilias, " our fate — my brother's and mine, at least — must turn on the deliberations perhaps of less than an hour.— For you, sir, I believe and apprehend nothing but some restraint; my uncle is neither cruel nor unjust, though few will go farther in the cause which he has adopted."

" Which is that of the Pretend —"

" For God's sake speak lower!" said Lilias, approaching her hand as if to stop him. " The word may cost you your life. You do not know — indeed you do not — the terrors of the situation in which we at present stand, and in which I fear you also are involved by your friendship for my brother."

" I do not indeed know the particulars of our situation," said Fairford; " but be the danger what it may, I shall not grudge my share of it for the sake of my friend; or," he added, with more timidity, " of my friend's sister. Let me hope," he said, " my dear Miss Latimer, that my presence may be of some use to you; and that it may be so, let me entreat a share of your confidence, which I am conscious I have otherwise no right to ask."

He led her, as he spoke, towards the recess of the farther window of the room, and observing to her that, unhappily, he was particularly exposed to interruption from the mad old man whose entrance had alarmed her, he disposed of Darsie Latimer's riding-skirt, which had been left in the apartment, over the back of two chairs, forming thus a sort of screen, behind which he ensconced himself with the maiden of the green mantle; feeling at the moment, that the danger in which he was placed was almost compensated by the intelligence which permitted those feelings towards her to revive which justice to his friend had induced him to stifle in the birth.

The relative situation of adviser and advised, of protector and protected, is so peculiarly suited to the respective condition of man and woman, that great progress towards intimacy is often made in very short space; for the circumstances call for confidence on the part of the gentleman, and forbid coyness on that of the lady, so that the usual barriers against easy intercourse are at once thrown down.

Under these circumstances, securing themselves as far as possible from observation, conversing in whispers, and seated in a corner, where they were brought into so close contact that their faces nearly touched each other, Fairford heard from Lilias Redgauntlet the history of her family, particularly of her uncle; his views upon her brother, and the agony which she felt lest at that very moment he might succeed in engaging Darsie in some desperate scheme, fatal to his fortune, and perhaps to his life.

Alan Fairford's acute understanding instantly connected what he had heard with the circumstances he had witnessed at Fairladies. His first thought was, to attempt, at all risks, his instant escape, and procure assistance powerful enough to crush, in the very cradle, a conspiracy of such a determined character. This he did not consider as difficult; for, though the door was guarded on the outside, the window, which was not above ten feet from the ground, was open for escape, the common on which it looked was unenclosed, and profusely covered with furze. There would, he thought, be little difficulty in effecting his liberty, and in concealing his course after he had gained it.

But Lilias exclaimed against this scheme. Her uncle, she said, was a man who, in his moments of enthusiasm, knew neither remorse nor fear. He was capable of visiting upon Darsie any injury which he might conceive Fairford had rendered him — he was her near kinsman also, and not an unkind one, and she deprecated any effort, even in her brother's favour, by which his life must be exposed to danger. Fairford himself remembered Father Buonaventure, and made little question but that he was one of the sons of the old Chevalier de Saint George; and with feelings which, although contradictory of his public duty, can hardly be much censured, his heart recoiled from being the agent by whom the last scion of such a long line of Scottish Princes should be rooted up. He then thought of obtaining an audience, if possible, of this devoted person, and explaining to him the utter hopelessness of his undertaking, which he judged it likely that the ardour of his partisans might have concealed from him. But he relinquished this design as soon as formed. He had no doubt that any light which he could throw on the state of the country would come too late to be serviceable to one who was always reported to have his own full share of the hereditary obstinacy which had cost his ancestors so dear, and who, in drawing the sword, must have thrown from him the scabbard.

Lilias suggested the advice which, of all others, seemed most suited to the occasion, that yielding, namely, to the circumstances of their situation, they should watch carefully when Darsie should obtain any degree of freedom, and endeavour to open a communication with him, in which case their joint flight might be effected, and without endangering the safety of any one.

Their youthful deliberation had nearly fixed in this point, when Fairford, who was listening to the low sweet whispering tones of Lilias Redgauntlet, rendered yet more interesting by some slight touch of foreign accent, was startled by a heavy hand which descended with full weight on his shoulder, while the discordant voice of Peter Peebles, who had at length broken loose from the well-meaning Quaker, exclaimed in the ear of his truant counsel — "Aha, lad! I think ye are catched — An' so ye are turned chamber-counsel, are ye ? — And ye have drawn up wi' clients in scarfs and hoods ? But bide a wee, billie, and see if I dinna sort ye when my petition and complaint comes to be discussed, with or without answers, under certification."

Alan Fairford had never more difficulty in his life to subdue a first emotion than he had to refrain from knocking down the crazy blockhead who had broken in upon him at such a moment. But the length of Peter's address gave him time, fortunately perhaps for both parties, to reflect on the extreme irregularity of such a proceeding. He stood silent, however, with vexation, while Peter went on.

"Weel, my bonnie man, I see ye are thinking shame o' yoursell, and nae great wonder. Ye maun leave this quean — the like of her is ower light company for you. I have heard honest Mr. Pest say, that the gown grees ill wi' the petticoat. But come awa hame to your puir father, and I'll take care of

you the haill gate, and keep you company, and deil
a word we will speak about, but just the state of
the conjoined processes of the great cause of Poor
Peter Peebles against Plainstanes."

"If thou canst endure to hear as much of that
suit, friend," said the Quaker, "as I have heard out
of mere compassion for thee, I think verily thou wilt
soon be at the bottom of the matter, unless it be
altogether bottomless."

Fairford shook off, rather indignantly, the large
bony hand which Peter had imposed upon his shoulder, and was about to say something peevish upon
so unpleasant and insolent a mode of interruption,
when the door opened, a treble voice saying to the
sentinel, "I tell you I maun be in, to see if Mr.
Nixon's here;" and Little Benjie thrust in his mop-
head and keen black eyes. Ere he could withdraw
it, Peter Peebles sprang to the door, seized on the
boy by the collar, and dragged him forward into
the room.

"Let me see it," he said, "ye ne'er-do-weel limb
of Satan — I'll gar you satisfy the production, I trow
— I'll hae first and second diligence against you, ye
deevil's buckie!"

"What dost thou want?" said the Quaker, interfering; "why dost thou frighten the boy, friend
Peebles?"

"I gave the bastard a penny to buy me snuff,"
said the pauper, "and he has rendered no account of
his intromissions; but I'll gar him as gude."

So saying, he proceeded forcibly to rifle the pockets
of Benjie's ragged jacket of one or two snares for
game, marbles, a half-bitten apple, two stolen eggs,
(one of which Peter broke in the eagerness of his
research,) and various other unconsidered trifles,

which had not the air of being very honestly come
by. The little rascal, under this discipline, bit and
struggled like a fox-cub, but, like that vermin, uttered
neither cry nor complaint, till a note, which Peter
tore from his bosom, flew as far as Lilias Redgauntlet, and fell at her feet. It was addressed to C. N.

"It is for the villain Nixon," she said to Alan
Fairford; "open it without scruple; that boy is his
emissary; we shall now see what the miscreant is
driving at."

Little Benjie now gave up all farther struggle,
and suffered Peebles to take from him, without
resistance, a shilling, out of which Peter declared
he would pay himself principal and interest, and
account for the balance. The boy, whose attention
seemed fixed on something very different, only said,
"Maister Nixon will murder me!"

Alan Fairford did not hesitate to read the little
scrap of paper, on which was written, "All is prepared — keep them in play until I come up — You
may depend on your reward. — C. C."

"Alas, my uncle — my poor uncle!" said Lilias;
"this is the result of his confidence! Methinks, to
give him instant notice of his confidant's treachery
is now the best service we can render all concerned
— if they break up their undertaking, as they must
now do, Darsie will be at liberty."

In the same breath they were both at the half-
opened door of the room, Fairford entreating to
speak with the Father Buonaventure, and Lilias,
equally vehemently, requesting a moment's interview with her uncle. While the sentinel hesitated
what to do, his attention was called to a loud noise
at the door, where a crowd had been assembled in
consequence of the appalling cry that the enemy were

upon them, occasioned, as it afterwards proved, by
some stragglers having at length discovered the dead
bodies of Nanty Ewart and of Nixon.

Amid the confusion occasioned by this alarming
incident, the sentinel ceased to attend to his duty;
and, accepting Alan Fairford's arm, Lilias found no
opposition in penetrating even to the inner apartment, where the principal persons in the enterprise,
whose conclave had been disturbed by this alarming
incident, were now assembled in great confusion, and
had been joined by the Chevalier himself.

"Only a mutiny among these smuggling scoundrels," said Redgauntlet.

"*Only* a mutiny, do you say?" said Sir Richard
Glendale; "and the lugger, the last hope of escape
for," — he looked towards Charles, — 'stands out
to sea under a press of sail!'"

"Do not concern yourself about me," said the
unfortunate Prince; "this is not the worst emergency in which it has been my lot to stand; and if
it were, I fear it not. Shift for yourselves, my
lords and gentlemen."

"No, never!" said the young Lord ——. "Our
only hope now is in an honourable resistance."

"Most true," said Redgauntlet; "let despair
renew the union amongst us which accident disturbed. I give my voice for displaying the royal
banner instantly, and —— How now?" he concluded,
sternly, as Lilias, first soliciting his attention by
pulling his cloak, put into his hand the scroll, and
added, it was designed for that of Nixon.

Redgauntlet read — and, dropping it on the
ground, continued to stare upon the spot where it
fell, with raised hands and fixed eyes. Sir Richard
Glendale lifted the fatal paper, read it, and saying,

Painted by G. Hay, R.S.A.

PEEBLES. CATCHING ALAN.

Etched by F Huth

"Now all is indeed over," handed it to Maxwell, who said aloud, "Black Colin Campbell, by G—d! I heard he had come post from London last night."

As if in echo to his thoughts, the violin of the blind man was heard playing with spirit "The Campbells are coming," a celebrated clan march.

"The Campbells are coming in earnest," said MacKellar; "they are upon us with the whole battalion from Carlisle."

There was a silence of dismay, and two or three of the company began to drop out of the room.

Lord —— spoke with the generous spirit of a young English nobleman. "If we have been fools, do not let us be cowards. We have one here more precious than us all, and come hither on our warranty — let us save him at least."

"True, most true," answered Sir Richard Glendale. " Let the King be first cared for."

" That shall be my business," said Redgauntlet; "if we have but time to bring back the brig, all will be well — I will instantly dispatch a party in a fishing skiff to bring her to." — He gave his commands to two or three of the most active among his followers. — "Let him be once on board," he said, "and there are enough of us to stand to arms and cover his retreat."

"Right, right," said Sir Richard, "and I will look to points which can be made defensible; and the old powder-plot boys could not have made a more desperate resistance than we shall. — Redgauntlet," continued he, " I see some of our friends are looking pale; but methinks your nephew has more mettle in his eye now than when we were in cold deliberation, with danger at a distance."

" It is the way of our house," said Redgauntlet;

" our courage ever kindles highest on the losing side.
I, too, feel that the catastrophe I have brought
on must not be survived by its author.  Let me
first," he said, addressing Charles, " see your
Majesty's sacred person in such safety as can now
be provided for it, and then " ——

" You may spare all considerations concerning
me, gentlemen," again repeated Charles ; " yon
mountain of Criffel shall fly as soon as I will."

Most threw themselves at his feet with weeping
and entreaty ; some one or two slunk in confusion
from the apartment, and were heard riding off.
Unnoticed in such a scene, Darsie, his sister, and
Fairford drew together, and held each other by
the hands, as those who, when a vessel is about to
founder in the storm, determine to take their
chance of life and death together.

Amid this scene of confusion, a gentleman,
plainly dressed in a riding-habit, with a black
cockade in his hat, but without any arms except a
*couteau de chasse*, walked into the apartment without ceremony.  He was a tall, thin, gentlemanly
man, with a look and bearing decidedly military.
He had passed through their guards, if in the confusion they now maintained any, without stop or
question, and now stood, almost unarmed, among
armed men, who, nevertheless, gazed on him as on
the angel of destruction.

" You look coldly on me, gentlemen," he said.
" Sir Richard Glendale — my Lord ——, we were
not always such strangers.  Ha, Pate-in-Peril, how
is it with you ? and you, too, Ingoldsby — I must
not call you by any other name — why do you
receive an old friend so coldly ?  But you guess
my errand."

"And are prepared for it, General," said Red-gauntlet; "we are not men to be penned up like sheep for the slaughter."

"Pshaw! you take it too seriously — let me speak but one word with you."

"No words can shake· our purpose," said Red-gauntlet, "were your whole command, as I suppose is the case, drawn round the house."

"I am certainly not unsupported," said the General; "but if you would hear me" ——

"Hear *me*, sir," said the Wanderer, stepping forward; "I suppose I am the mark you aim at — I surrender myself willingly, to save these gentlemen's danger — let this at least avail in their favour."

An exclamation of "Never, never!" broke from the little body of partisans, who threw themselves round the unfortunate Prince, and would have seized or struck down Campbell, had it not been that he remained with his arms folded, and a look rather indicating impatience because they would not hear him than the least apprehension of violence at their hand.

At length he obtained a moment's silence. "I do not," he said, "know this gentleman" — (Making a profound bow to the unfortunate Prince) — "I do not wish to know him; it is a knowledge which would suit neither of us."

"Our ancestors, nevertheless, have been well acquainted," said Charles, unable to suppress, even in that hour of dread and danger, the painful recollections of fallen royalty.

"In one word, General Campbell," said Red-gauntlet, "is it to be peace or war? — You are a man of honour, and we can trust you."

"I thank you, sir," said the General; "and I reply that the answer to your question rests with yourself. Come, do not be fools, gentlemen; there was perhaps no great harm meant or intended by your gathering together in this obscure corner. for a bear-bait or a cock-fight, or whatever other amusement you may have intended; but it was a little imprudent, considering how you stand with government, and it has occasioned some anxiety. Exaggerated accounts of your purpose have been laid before government by the information of a traitor in your own counsels; and I was sent down post to take the command of a sufficient number of troops, in case these calumnies should be found to have any real foundation. I have come here, of course, sufficiently supported both with cavalry and infantry to do whatever might be necessary; but my commands are — and I am sure they agree with my inclination — to make no arrests, nay, to make no farther enquiries of any kind, if this good assembly will consider their own interest so far as to give up their immediate purpose, and return quietly home to their own houses."

"What! — all?" exclaimed Sir Richard Glendale — "all, without exception?"

"ALL, without one single exception," said the General; "such are my orders. If you accept my terms, say so, and make haste; for things may happen to interfere with his Majesty's kind purposes towards you all."

"His Majesty's kind purposes!" said the Wanderer. "Do I hear you aright, sir?"

"I speak the King's very words, from his very lips," replied the General. "'I will,' said his Majesty, 'deserve the confidence of my subjects by reposing my security in the fidelity of the millions who acknowledge my title — in the good sense and prudence of the few who continue, from the errors of education, to disown it.' — His Majesty will not even believe that the most zealous Jacobites who yet remain can nourish a thought of exciting a civil war, which must be fatal to their families and themselves, besides spreading bloodshed and ruin through a peaceful land. He cannot even believe of his kinsman, that he would engage brave and generous, though mistaken men, in an attempt which must ruin all who have escaped former calamities; and he is convinced that, did curiosity or any other motive lead that person to visit this country, he would soon see it was his wisest course to return to the Continent; and his Majesty compassionates his situation too much to offer any obstacle to his doing so."

"Is this real?" said Redgauntlet. "Can you mean this? — Am I — are all, are any of these gentlemen at liberty, without interruption, to embark in yonder brig, which, I see, is now again approaching the shore?"

"You, sir — all — any of the gentlemen present," said the General, — "all whom the vessel can contain, are at liberty to embark uninterrupted by me; but I advise none to go off who have not powerful reasons, unconnected with the present meeting, for this will be remembered against no one."

"Then, gentlemen," said Redgauntlet, clasping his hands together as the words burst from him, "the cause is lost for ever!"

General Campbell turned away to the window, as if to avoid hearing what they said. Their consultation was but momentary; for the door of escape which thus opened was as unexpected as the exigence was threatening.

"We have your word of honour for our protection," said Sir Richard Glendale, "if we dissolve our meeting in obedience to your summons?"

"You have, Sir Richard," answered the General.

"And I also have your promise," said Redgauntlet, "that I may go on board yonder vessel, with any friend whom I may choose to accompany me?"

"Not only that, Mr. Ingoldsby — or I *will* call you Redgauntlet once more — you may stay in the offing for a tide, until you are joined by any person who may remain at Fairladies. After that, there will be a sloop of war on the station, and I need not say your condition will then become perilous."

"Perilous it should not be, General Campbell," said Redgauntlet, "or more perilous to others than to us, if others thought as I do even in this extremity."

"You forget yourself, my friend," said the unhappy Adventurer; "you forget that the arrival of this gentleman only puts the cope-stone on our already adopted resolution to abandon our bull-fight, or by whatever other wild name this headlong enterprise may be termed. I bid you farewell, unfriendly friends — I bid *you* farewell," (bowing to the General,) "my friendly foe — I leave this strand as I landed upon it, alone, and to return no more!"

"Not alone," said Redgauntlet, "while there is blood in the veins of my father's son."

"Not alone," said the other gentlemen present, stung with feelings which almost overpowered the better reasons under which they had acted. "We will not disown our principles, or see your person endangered."

"If it be only your purpose to see the gentleman to the beach," said General Campbell, "I will myself go with you. My presence among you, unarmed, and in your power, will be a pledge of my friendly intentions, and will overawe, should such be offered, any interruption on the part of officious persons."

"Be it so," said the Adventurer, with the air of a Prince to a subject; not of one who complied with the request of an enemy too powerful to be resisted.

They left the apartment — they left the house — an unauthenticated and dubious, but appalling, sensation of terror had already spread itself among the inferior retainers, who had so short time before strutted, and bustled, and thronged the doorway and the passages. A report had arisen, of which the origin could not be traced, of troops advancing towards the spot in considerable numbers; and men who, for one reason or other, were most of them amenable to the arm of power, had either shrunk into stables or corners, or fled the place entirely. There was solitude on the landscape, excepting the small party which now moved towards the rude pier, where a boat lay manned, agreeably to Redgauntlet's orders previously given.

The last heir of the Stuarts leant on Redgauntlet's arm as they walked towards the beach; for the ground was rough, and he no longer possessed the elasticity of limb and of spirit which had, twenty years before, carried him over many a Highland hill, as light as one of their native deer. His adherents followed, looking on the ground, their feelings struggling against the dictates of their reason.

General Campbell accompanied them with an air of apparent ease and indifference, but watching, at the same time, and no doubt with some anxiety, the changing features of those who acted in this extraordinary scene.

Darsie and his sister naturally followed their uncle, whose violence they no longer feared, while his character attracted their respect; and Alan Fairford accompanied them from interest in their fate, unnoticed in a party where all were too much occupied with their own thoughts and feelings, as well as with the impending crisis, to attend to his presence.

Half-way betwixt the house and the beach they saw the bodies of Nanty Ewart and Cristal Nixon blackening in the sun.

"That was your informer?" said Redgauntlet, looking back to General Campbell, who only nodded his assent.

"Caitiff wretch!" exclaimed Redgauntlet;— "and yet the name were better bestowed on the fool who could be misled by thee."

"That sound broadsword cut," said the General, "has saved us the shame of rewarding a traitor."

They arrived at the place of embarkation. The Prince stood a moment with folded arms, and looked around him in deep silence. A paper was then slipped into his hands — he looked at it, and said, "I find the two friends I have left at Fairladies are apprized of my destination, and propose to embark from Bowness. I presume this will not be an infringement of the conditions under which you have acted?"

"Certainly not," answered General Campbell; "they shall have all facility to join you."

"I wish, then," said Charles, "only another companion. — Redgauntlet, the air of this country is as hostile to you as it is to me. These gentlemen have made their peace, or rather they have done nothing to break it. But you — come you, and share my home where chance shall cast it. We shall never see these shores again; but we will talk of them, and of our disconcerted bull-fight."

"I follow you, Sire, through life," said Redgauntlet, " as I would have followed you to death. Permit me one moment."

The Prince then looked round, and seeing the abashed countenances of his other adherents bent upon the ground, he hastened to say, " Do not think that you, gentlemen, have obliged me less because your zeal was mingled with prudence, entertained, I am sure, more on my own account, and on that of your country, than from selfish apprehensions."

He stepped from one to another, and, amid sobs and bursting tears, received the adieus of the last remnant which had hitherto supported his lofty pretensions, and addressed them individually with accents of tenderness and affection.

The General drew a little aloof, and signed to Redgauntlet to speak with him while this scene proceeded. "It is now all over," he said, " and Jacobite will be henceforward no longer a party name. When you tire of foreign parts, and wish to make your peace, let me know. Your restless zeal alone has impeded your pardon hitherto."

"And now I shall not need it," said Redgauntlet. " I leave England for ever; but I am not displeased that you should hear my family adieus. — Nephew, come hither. In presence of General Campbell, I tell you that, though to breed you up

in my own political opinions has been for many
years my anxious wish, I am now glad that it could
not be accomplished. You pass under the service
of the reigning Monarch without the necessity of
changing your allegiance — a change, however," he
added, looking around him, "which sits more easy
on honourable men than I could have anticipated;
but some wear the badge of their loyalty on the
sleeve, and others in the heart. — You will, from
henceforth, be uncontrolled master of all the property of which forfeiture could not deprive your
father — of all that belonged to him — excepting
this, his good sword," (laying his hand on the weapon
he wore,) "which shall never fight for the House
of Hanover; and as my hand will never draw weapon
more, I shall sink it forty fathoms deep in the wide
ocean. Bless you, young man! If I have dealt
harshly with you, forgive me. I had set my whole
desires on one point, — God knows, with no selfish
purpose; and I am justly punished by this final
termination of my views, for having been too little
scrupulous in the means by which I pursued them.
Niece, farewell, and may God bless you also!"

"No, sir," said Lilias, seizing his hand eagerly.
"You have been hitherto my protector, — you are
now in sorrow, let me be your attendant and your
comforter in exile!"

"I thank you, my girl, for your unmerited
affection; but it cannot and must not be. The
curtain here falls between us. I go to the house
of another — If I leave it before I quit the earth, it
shall be only for the House of God. Once more,
farewell both! — The fatal doom," he said, with a
melancholy smile, "will, I trust, now depart from
the House of Redgauntlet, since its present repre-

sentative has adhered to the winning side. I am convinced he will not change it, should it in turn become the losing one."

The unfortunate Charles Edward had now given his last adieus to his downcast adherents. He made a sign with his hand to Redgauntlet, who came to assist him into the skiff. General Campbell also offered his assistance ; the rest appearing too much affected by the scene which had taken place to prevent him.

"You are not sorry, General, to do me this last act of courtesy," said the Chevalier; "and, on my part, I thank you for it. You have taught me the principle on which men on the scaffold feel forgiveness and kindness even for their executioner. — Farewell ! "

They were seated in the boat, which presently pulled off from the land. The Oxford divine broke out into a loud benediction, in terms which General Campbell was too generous to criticise at the time, or to remember afterwards ; — nay, it is said that, Whig and Campbell as he was, he could not help joining in the universal Amen ! which resounded from the shore.

# CONCLUSION,

## By Dr. DRYASDUST,

### IN A LETTER TO THE AUTHOR OF WAVERLEY.

I AM truly sorry, my worthy and much-respected sir, that my anxious researches have neither, in the form of letters, nor of diaries, or other memoranda, been able to discover more than I have hitherto transmitted of the history of the Redgauntlet family. But I observe in an old newspaper called the Whitehall Gazette, of which I fortunately possess a file for several years, that Sir Arthur Darsie Redgauntlet was presented to his late Majesty at the drawingroom, by Lieut.-General Campbell — upon which the Editor observes, in the way of comment, that we were going, *remis atque velis*, into the interests of the Pretender, since a Scot had presented a Jacobite at Court. I am sorry I have not room (the frank being only uncial) for his farther observations, tending to show the apprehensions entertained by many well-instructed persons of the period, that the young King might himself be induced to become one of the Stuarts' faction,—a catastrophe from which it has pleased Heaven to preserve these kingdoms.

I perceive also, by a marriage contract in the family repositories, that Miss Lilias Redgauntlet of Redgauntlet, about eighteen months after the transactions you have commemorated, intermarried

with Alan Fairford, Esq., Advocate, of Clinkdollar,
who, I think, we may not unreasonably conclude
to be the same person whose name occurs so frequently in the pages of your narration. In my last
excursion to Edinburgh, I was fortunate enough
to discover an old cadie, from whom, at the expense
of a bottle of whisky and half a pound of tobacco,
I extracted the important information that he knew
Peter Peebles very well, and had drunk many a
mutchkin with him in Cadie Fraser's time. He
said that he lived ten years after King George's
accession, in the momentary expectation of winning his cause every day in the Session time, and
every hour in the day, and at last fell down dead,
in what my informer called a "Perplexity fit," upon
a proposal for a composition being made to him in
the Outer House. I have chosen to retain my
informer's phrase, not being able justly to determine
whether it is a corruption of the word apoplexy, as
my friend Mr. Oldbuck supposes, or the name of
some peculiar disorder incidental to those who have
concern in the Courts of Law, as many callings
and conditions of men have diseases appropriate
to themselves. The same cadie also remembered
Blind Willie Stevenson, who was called Wandering
Willie, and who ended his days "unco beinly, in
Sir Arthur Redgauntlet's ha' neuk." "He had
done the family some good turn," he said, "specially when ane of the Argyle gentlemen was coming
down on a wheen of them that had the 'auld leaven'
about them, and wad hae taen every man of them,
and nae less nor headed and hanged them. But
Willie, and a friend they had, called Robin the
Rambler, gae them warning, by playing tunes such
as 'The Campbells are coming' and the like, whereby

they got timeous warning to take the wing." I need not point out to your acuteness, my worthy sir, that this seems to refer to some inaccurate account of the transactions in which you seem so much interested.

Respecting Redgauntlet, about whose subsequent history you are more particularly inquisitive, I have learned from an excellent person who was a priest in the Scottish Monastery of Ratisbon, before its suppression, that he remained for two or three years in the family of the Chevalier, and only left it at last in consequence of some discords in that melancholy household. (*h*) As he had hinted to General Campbell, he exchanged his residence for the cloister, and displayed in the latter part of his life a strong sense of the duties of religion, which in his earlier days he had too much neglected, being altogether engaged in political speculations and intrigues. He rose to the situation of Prior in the house which he belonged to, and which was of a very strict order of religion. He sometimes received his countrymen, whom accident brought to Ratisbon, and curiosity induced to visit the Monastery of ——. But it was remarked that though he listened with interest and attention, when Britain, or particularly Scotland, became the subject of conversation, yet he never either introduced or prolonged the subject, never used the English language, never enquired about English affairs, and, above all, never mentioned his own family. His strict observation of the rules of his order gave him, at the time of his death, some pretensions to be chosen a saint, and the brethren of the Monastery of —— made great efforts for that effect, and brought forward some plausible proofs of miracles. But there was a circumstance which threw a doubt over the subject, and prevented the Consistory from acceding to the wishes of the worthy brethren. Under his habit, and secured in a small silver box, he had worn perpetually around his neck a lock of hair, which the fathers avouched to be a relic. But the Avocato del Diablo, in combating (as was his official duty) the pretensions of the candidate for sanctity, made it at least equally probable that the supposed relic was taken from the head of a brother of the deceased Prior, who had been executed for adherence to the Stuart family in 1745–6; and the motto, *Haud obliviscendum*, seemed to intimate a tone of mundane feeling and recollection of injuries which made it at least doubtful whether, even in the quiet and gloom of the cloister, Father Hugo had forgotten the sufferings and injuries of the House of Redgauntlet.

*June* 10, 1824.

# AUTHOR'S NOTES.

## Note I., p. 66.

Scotland, in its half-civilised state, exhibited too many examples of the exertion of arbitrary force and violence, rendered easy by the dominion which lairds exerted over their tenants, and chiefs over their clans. The captivity of Lady Grange, in the desolate cliffs of Saint Kilda, is in the recollection of every one. At the supposed date of the novel, also, a man of the name of Merrilees, a tanner in Leith, absconded from his country to escape his creditors; and after having slain his own mastiff dog, and put a bit of red cloth in its mouth, as if it had died in a contest with soldiers, and involved his own existence in as much mystery as possible, made his escape into Yorkshire. Here he was detected by persons sent in search of him, to whom he gave a portentous account of his having been carried off and concealed in various places. Mr. Merrilees was, in short, a kind of male Elizabeth Canning (i), but did not trespass on the public credulity quite so long.

## Note II., p. 80. — ESCAPE OF PATE-IN-PERIL.

The escape of a Jacobite gentleman while on the road to Carlisle to take his trial for his share in the affair of 1745 took place at Errickstane-brae, in the singular manner ascribed to the Laird of Summertrees in the text. The author has seen in his youth the gentleman to whom the adventure actually happened. The distance of time makes some indistinctness of recollection, but it is believed the real name was MacEwen, or MacMillan.

## Note III., p. 127. — CONCEALMENTS FOR THEFT AND SMUGGLING.

I am sorry to say that the modes of concealment described in the imaginary premises of Mr. Trumbull are of a kind which have been common on the frontiers of late years. The neigh-

'bourhood of two nations having different laws, though united
in government, still leads to a multitude of transgressions on
the Border, and extreme difficulty in apprehending delin-
quents. About twenty years since, as far as my recollection
serves, there was along the frontier an organized gang of coin-
ers, forgers, smugglers, and other malefactors, whose operations were conducted on a scale not inferior to what is here
described. The chief of the party was one Richard Mendham,
a carpenter, who rose to opulence, although ignorant even of
the arts of reading and writing. But he had found a short
road to wealth, and had taken singular measures for conducting his operations. Amongst these, he found means to build,
in a suburb of Berwick called Spittal, a street of small houses,
as if for the investment of property. He himself inhabited one
of these; another, a species of public-house, was open to his
confederates, who held secret and unsuspected communication
with him by crossing the roofs of the intervening houses, and
descending by a trap-stair, which admitted them into the
alcove of the diningroom of Dick Mendham's private mansion.
A vault, too, beneath Mendham's stable, was accessible in the
manner mentioned in the novel. The post of one of the stalls
turned round on a bolt being withdrawn, and gave admittance
to a subterranean place of concealment for contraband and
stolen goods to a great extent. Richard Mendham, the head
of this very formidable conspiracy, which involved malefactors
of every kind, was tried and executed at Jedburgh, where the
author was present as Sheriff of Selkirkshire. Mendham had
previously been tried, but escaped by want of proof and the
ingenuity of his counsel.

### Note IV., p. 221. — Coronation of George III.

The particulars here given are of course entirely imaginary;
that is, they have no other foundation than what might be supposed probable, had such a circumstance actually taken place.
Yet a report to such an effect was long and generally current,
though now having wholly lost its lingering credit; those who
gave it currency, if they did not originate it, being, with the
tradition itself, now mouldered in the dust. The attachment
to the unfortunate house of Stuart among its adherents continued to exist and to be fondly cherished, longer perhaps than
in any similar case in any other country; and when reason

was baffled, and all hope destroyed, by repeated frustration, the mere dreams of imagination were summoned in to fill up the dreary blank, left in so many' hearts. Of the many reports set on foot and circulated from this cause, the tradition in question, though amongst the least authenticated, is not the least striking ; and, in excuse of what may be considered as a violent infraction of probability in the tale told by Lilias, the author is under the necessity of quoting it. It was always said, though with very little appearance of truth, that upon the coronation of George III., when the Champion of England, Dymock, or his representative, appeared in Westminster Hall, and, in the language of chivalry, solemnly wagered his body to defend in single combat the right of the young King to the crown of these realms, at the moment when he flung down his gauntlet as the gage of battle, an unknown female stepped from the crowd and lifted the pledge, leaving another gage in room of it, with a paper expressing that if a fair field of combat should be allowed a champion of rank and birth would appear with equal arms to dispute the claim of King George to the British kingdoms. The story, as we have said, is probably one of the numerous fictions which were circulated to keep up the spirits of a sinking faction. The incident was, however, possible, if it could be supposed to be attended by any motive adequate to the risk, and might be imagined to occur to a person of Redgauntlet's enthusiastic character.

### Note V., p. 275. — COLLIER AND SALTER.

The persons engaged in these occupations were at this time bondsmen ; and in case they left the ground of the farm to which they belonged, and as pertaining to which their services were bought or sold, they were liable to be brought back by a summary process. The existence of this species of slavery being thought irreconcilable with the spirit of liberty, colliers and salters were declared free, and put upon the same footing with other servants, by the Act 15 Geo. III. chapter 28th. They were so far from desiring or prizing the blessing conferred on them, that they esteemed the interest taken in their freedom to be a mere decree on the part of the proprietors to get rid of what they called head and harigald money, payable to them when a female of their number, by bearing a child, made an addition to the live stock of their master's property.

# EDITOR'S NOTES.

(*a*) p. 8. "Fifish." Fife, and especially the East Nook, had a bad reputation for sanity: the county families, it was said, had intermarried too frequently. It is right to say that the reproach, if ever it had any foundation, has ceased to exist.

(*b*) p. 32. "Sir John Friend." It is impossible to clear this gentleman's character of participation in the plot for assassinating William III. A very minute account of the intrigues will be found in the Memoirs of Lord Ailesbury, who was imprisoned, though guiltless of this conspiracy.

(*c*) p. 75. "Skye and the Bush aboon Traquair." Sir Alexander McLeod of Skye did not join the Prince, and his clan's share in the Forty-five was limited to the loss of their piper in the Rout of Moy. Traquair was challenged by Murray of Broughton, the Judas of the party, in 1747. He declined, of course, to meet such a person, and Murray was arrested as he vapoured on the 'ground, behind Montague House, the site of the British Museum. (Stonor to Edgar, James's secretary, May 28, 1749.)

(*d*) p. 172. "*Literas Bellerophontis.*" See Iliad, vi. 169. The wife of Proetus accused Bellerophon, whom she had tried to seduce, of an attempt on her honour. "To slay him he forbare, but he sent him to Lycia, and gave him tokens of woe, graving in a folded tablet many deadly things, and bade him show those to the father of Anteia," the lady in the case, "that he might be slain." This is the one passage in Homer which refers to writing of any kind, and has much exercised commentators. Two things are clear: Bellerophon could have read the message, had the tablet been open; and, again, the Lycian king asked for the credentials of Bellerophon, on the tenth day after his arrival. This implies that such credentials were in common use.

(*e*) p. 221. "The champion's gauntlet." The authors of "Tales of the Century" were informed by a lady, who, again, had it from the Duke of Norfolk, that the gauntlet was not lifted, but that a white glove was thrown down in return. "But no person was seen, neither was it confirmed by the Duke that any billet was contained within the glove."

(*f*) p. 242. "Englishmen of large fortune." How far the English Jacobites were committed to a rising in 1745 is unknown. They certainly stipulated for "twenty thousand honest Frenchmen" to land on the south coast, like the Squire in "Tom Jones." In later years they still made similar stipulations, which are more to the credit of their prudence than of their patriotism.

(*g*) p. 291. "Those Irish rapparees." The Irish — Sheridan, Sullivan, and others — probably urged Charles on his desperate project. They formed an inner circle about the Prince, and thwarted Lord George Murray, who had the brains of the party. Unhappily, Lord George advocated the retreats from Derby and Stirling ; he abandoned, doubtless with reason, the surprise at Nairn ; and, when he wrote from Ruthven to Charles, after Culloden, he was still inveighing against the Irish. All this made Charles regard his loyal and worthy adherent with suspicion, and, instead of joining the force at Ruthven, he fled to the Islands with some of his Irish companions.

(*h*) p. 340. "That melancholy household." The discords in Charles's household were a source of deep sorrow to loyalists like Bishop Forbes, and may be studied in his manuscript, "The Lyon in Mourning," among the last accents of those who hoped against hope, and toasted Louisa of Stolberg as "the Fairest Fair." Perhaps the old Laird of Gask, who would not let his chaplain pray for King George even after the death of Charles, and hoped that the Pope would give the Cardinal a dispensation to marry, was the last of the staunch old friends of the fallen house.

(*i*) p. 343. "Elizabeth Canning." See Mr. Paget's "Paradoxes and Puzzles." It is even now impossible to discover the truth about Elizabeth Canning, and her story of detention and ill-usage.

ANDREW LANG.

*January* 1894.

# GLOSSARY.

**A'**, all.

**Aboon, abune**, above.

**Advising**, the deliberation of a cause or process so as to give judgment upon it.

**Ae**, one.

**Ainsell**, own self.

**Airt**, to direct.

**An**, if.

**Ane**, one.

**Anes**, once,

**Arles**, earnest-money.

**Attour**, above or over.

**Aught**, to own, to possess.

**Auld-warld**, ancient.

**Awa**, away.

**Back-spauld**, the back part of the shoulder.

**Bairn**, a child.

**Baith**, both.

**Bannock**, a kind of cake.

**Bawbee**, a halfpenny.

**Bearmeal**, barley meal.

**Bein**, snug, comfortable.

**Belike**, probably.

**Ben**, within.

**Besom**, a contemptuous designation for a low woman; a prostitute.

**Bide**, to stay, to remain, to endure.

**Billie**, a term of affection and familiarity, applied to a comrade.

**Bleezing**, making an ostentatious show.

**"Bona roba,"** a courtesan or mistress.

**Brae**, a hill.

**Braw**, brave, fine.

**"Brent broo,"** a high brow.

**Brock**, a badger.

**Brose**, oatmeal over which boiling water has been poured.

**Browst**, a brewing; as much as is brewed at one time.

**Buckie**, an imp.

**"Buff nor stye,"** neither one thing nor another.

**Bumbazed**, stupefied.

**"Bye and attour,"** over and above.

**Ca'**, call.

**Cadie**, a messenger or errand boy.

**Callant**, a lad.

**Canna**, cannot.

**Canny**, quiet, cautious.

**Cantle**, a fragment.

**Caterans**, freebooters, robbers.

**Caup**, a cup or wooden bowl.

**Chap**, a fellow.

**Cheat-the-woodie**, cheating the gallows.

**Chiel**, a fellow.

**Chucky**, a barn-door fowl.

**Clavers**, idle talk.

**Cleek**, to lay hold upon.

**Cleugh**, a narrow glen.

**"Closes and wynds,"** passages and turnings from off the streets.

**Clour**, to strike heavily.

**Cockernony**, the top-knot caused by a young woman's hair.

**Cogie**, a small wooden bowl.

**Coup**, fall.

**Crack**, gossip.

**Craig**, the neck.

Crawstep, the step-like edges of a gable seen in some old houses.

Creenfu', a basketful.

Crowder, a fiddler.

Curn, a very little.

Daft, crazy, mad.

Dauredna, dared not.

Daurg, darg, a day's work.

Dead-thraw, the death-agony.

Deil, the devil.

"Deil's buckie," imp of Satan.

Delict, misdemeanour.

Den, a dell or hollow.

Ding, to knock.

Dittay, an indictment.

"Drappit egg," a fried egg.

Drouth, thirst.

Dyvour, bankrupt.

Ee, the eye.

Een, eyes.

Enow, enough.

Evite, to avoid.

Fashious, troublesome.

Faur'd, favoured.

Fause, false.

Feck, space.

Fifish, eccentric.

Forby, besides.

Forgie, to forgive.

Forpit, the fourth part of a peck.

Frae, from.

Frist, to postpone, give credit.

Gae, go.

Galloway, a stout cob, originally bred in the old Scottish county of Galloway.

Gane, gone.

Ganging, going.

Gar, to force, to make.

Gate, way, road.

Gauger, an exciseman.

Giff-gaff, give and take, mutual obligation.

Girded, hooped with twigs, like a barrel.

Gliff, an instant.

Goud, gold.

Gree, to agree.

Gude, good.

Gudeman, the husband and head of the family.

Gumple-foisted, sulky, sullen.

Gumption, common-sense.

Gyte, a contemptuous name for a young child, a brat.

Ha', hall.

Hae, have.

"Haill gate," the whole way, all the way.

Hairst, harvest.

Hallan, the partition in a cottage.

Harum-scarum, rash and rattling, harebrained.

Haud, hold.

Havings, behaviour.

Hempy, a rogue.

Heritor, a landholder.

Heuck, a sickle.

Hoddin-grey, cloth manufactured from undyed wool.

Hout! tut!

Hussey, a lady's needlecase.

Ilk, ilka, each, every.

Ilk, of the same name.

Ill-deedie, ill-deedy, mischievous.

Ill-faur'd, ugly, ill-favoured.

Jazy, a wig.

"John Barleycorn," beer or ale.

Jorum, a drinking-vessel, or the liquor in it.

Jow, to toll.

Keek, look.

Ken, to know.

Kittle, ticklish, difficult.

Laigh, low.

Landward, belonging to the country, as opposed to the town.

Lave, the remainder.

Lee, to lie, to tell an untruth.

Limmer, a loose woman, a jade.

Loon, a fellow, a rogue (in a humorous sense).

Loopy, crafty.

Louis d'or, a French gold coin worth from 16s. 6d. to 18s. 9d.

Loup-the-dyke, giddy, unsettled, runaway.

Loup-the-tether, breaking loose from restraint.

Lug, the ear.

Mailing, a small farm or rented property.

Mair, more.

Maun, must.

"Maut abune the meal," half-seas over.

Menyie, retinue.

Messan, a lapdog, a small dog.

Mickle, much, great.

Mischanter, mischief.

"Mounted lobsters," a name given to mounted soldiers because of their red coats.

Muckle, much, great, big.

Mull, a snuff-box.

Multiplepoinding (legal), the method of settling rival claims to the same fund.

Nalg, a nag.

Neuk, a corner.

Nipperkin, a liquid measure.

"Ower far ben," too intimate or familiar.

"Pike out," to pick out.

Plack, a small copper coin.

Ploy, a harmless frolic, a fête.

"Poinding and distrenzieing," Scots legal terms for distraining.

Pooin', pu'in, pulling.

Prie, taste.

Pund, a pound.

Rampauging, roaring.

Rant, to speak noisily.

Rapparee, an Irish plunderer; a worthless fellow.

Rax, to stretch.

Reiver, a robber.

Rigging, the back.

Row, to roll.

Rudas, a jade or scold.

Sae, so.

Sall, shall.

Saut, salt.

Sculduddery, loose, immoral; looseness, immorality.

Sealch, sealgh, a seal.

Sea-maw, a sea-gull.

Semple, a common or ordinary man.

Shakle-bone, the wrist.

Shilpit, poor or shabby.

Shoon, shoes.

Sib, related (by blood).

Sin, since. Sinsyne, since then.

Skivie, harebrained.

Sleekit, smooth.

Sloken, to quench.

Sneeshin, snuff.

Snell, sharp, terrible.

Sonsy, good-humoured.

Sort, to chastise.

Souple, supple.

"Souter's clod," a kind of coarse black bread.

Sowp, a spoonful.

Splore, a spree, a frolic.

Sprattle, a struggle, a scramble.

Sprush, spruce.

Spulzie, spoil.

"Spunk out," break out.

Stibbler, a ludicrous name for a probationer or Scots divinity student.

"Stoup and bicker," a liquid measure and a wooden bowl.

Stouthrief, theft with violence.

Suld, should.

"Suspension intented," a Scots legal term.

Syne, ago, since.

"Tace is Latin for a candle" is a proverbial expression enjoining silence and caution.

Tack, a lease.

Tae, the one.

"Take the rue," to repent of a proposal or undertaking.

Tass, a glass.

Tauld, told.
Tent, notice, care.
Thae, these or those.
Thegither, together.
Thumbikins, thumbscrew, an instrument of torture.
Tither, the other.
Trance, a passage within a house.
Trow, to guess, to believe.
Tuptowing: conjugating the Greek verb τύπτω, I strike; hence he was beating the boys instead of teaching them.
Tyne, loss or forfeit.

Unchancy, unlucky.
Unco, very, uncommon, particularly.
Usquabae, usquebaugh, whisky.

Wad, would.
Warding, awarding (legal).
Warrandice, security.
Waur, worse.
Weel, well. " Weel to pass," in easy circumstances, in comparative affluence.
Weigh-bauk, scales.
Wha, who.
" What for," why.
Wheen, a few, a small number.
Whilly-whaw, to wheedle.
Withershins, backwards in their courses, in the contrary way.
Wowf, deranged.
Wud, mad.
Wunna, will not.

Yill, ale.

END OF VOL. II.

*Printed by* BALLANTYNE, HANSON & CO.
*Edinburgh and London*

Lightning Source UK Ltd.
Milton Keynes UK
UKHW021159180219
337529UK00010B/636/P